THE MAN GAME

ALSO BY LEE HENDERSON

The Broken Record Technique

THE MAN GAME

Lee Henderson

VIKING
CANADA

VIKING CANADA

Published by the Penguin Group

Penguin Group (Canada), 90 Eglinton Avenue East, Suite 700, Toronto, Ontario, Canada M4P 2Y3 (a division of Pearson Canada Inc.)

Penguin Group (USA) Inc., 375 Hudson Street, New York, New York 10014, U.S.A.
Penguin Books Ltd, 80 Strand, London WC2R 0RL, England
Penguin Ireland, 25 St Stephen's Green, Dublin 2, Ireland (a division of Penguin Books Ltd)
Penguin Group (Australia), 250 Camberwell Road, Camberwell, Victoria 3124, Australia (a division of Pearson Australia Group Pty Ltd)
Penguin Books India Pvt Ltd, 11 Community Centre, Panchsheel Park, New Delhi – 110 017, India
Penguin Group (NZ), 67 Apollo Drive, Rosedale, North Shore 0632, Auckland, New Zealand (a division of Pearson New Zealand Ltd)
Penguin Books (South Africa) (Pty) Ltd, 24 Sturdee Avenue, Rosebank, Johannesburg 2196, South Africa

Penguin Books Ltd, Registered Offices:
80 Strand, London WC2R 0RL, England

First published 2008

1 2 3 4 5 6 7 8 9 10 (RRD)

The author acknowledges the pioneering work of historian J.S. Matthews.

We acknowledge the support of the Canada Council for the Arts which last year invested $20.1 million in writing and publishing throughout Canada.
Nous remercions de son soutien le Conseil des Arts du Canada, qui a investi 20,1 millions de dollars l'an dernier dans les lettres et l'édition à travers le Canada.

Canada Council for the Arts Conseil des Arts du Canada

Manufactured in the U.S.A.

Library and Archives Canada Cataloguing in Publication

Henderson, Lee, 1974–
The man game / Lee Henderson.

ISBN-13: 978-0-670-91147-9

1. Title.

PS8565.E56165M35 2008 C813'.6 C2008-902751-5

Visit the Penguin Group (Canada) website at **www.penguin.ca**

Special and corporate bulk purchase rates available; please see **www.penguin.ca/corporatesales** or call 1-800-810-3104, ext. 477 or 474

www.themangame.org
www.leehenderson.com

FOR JP SAWATSKY

THE CAST

Kat, *our narrator*
Minna, *a close friend*
Cedric, *a threat*
Ken, *a new homeowner*
Silas, *a freeloader*
Molly Erwagen, *the mind*
Sammy Erwagen, *the Hastings Mill bookkeeper*
Toronto, *a ward*
Pisk, *first man*
Litz, *a loyal ally*

~

Furry & Daggett's Logging Concern, *a crew of lumberjacks including:*
Furry
Daggett
Campbell, at five foot even, *early witness to the man game*
Meier, *seven-and-a-half foot*
Boyd, *with monobrow*
Smith, *a silent Thor*

~

John Clough, *a one-armed rummy, prison guard, lamplighter, & poundkeeper*
RH Alexander, *manager of Hastings Mill*
Mrs. Alexander, *a wife*
Mrs. Litz, *a young bride*
Constable Miller, *the po-lice*

(continued)

Peggy, *a whorehouse madam*
Bud Hoss, *a contrarian & bookie*
Moe Dee, *a loudmouth woodsman*
The snakehead from San Francisco, *a business associate*
RD Pitt, *a cowboy shit disturber*
The Knights of Labour, *a pro-union activist group*
Calabi and Yau, *bakers*
The Whore Without A Face
Miguel Calderón, *proprietor of the portable Bar Rústico*
Joe Fortes, *a bartender & swimming coach*

He that wrestles with us strengthens our nerves, and sharpens our skill. Our antagonist is our helper.

– **EDMUND BURKE,** *REFLECTIONS ON THE REVOLUTION IN FRANCE*

ONE

> The basis of ethics is man's right to play the games of his choice.
>
> — ISAAC BASHEVIS SINGER

We weren't meant for each other but for a long time we were never apart. That's how it was for Minna and me, even if it can't be the same ever again. If you called her on the phone and suggested you pick her up in your car, a Chrysler Dynasty in my case, she wasn't the kind of girl who asked: Where are we going? She was the kind who asked: *When* are we going? No, I don't think she much cared where. There was a flippancy to her that was partly confidence, partly generosity, and nested inside that was her flawless inhibition.

It felt to me like we were leaving the city, but according to the unfolded map we were headed only for the far east, where I'd heard about something called a man game that was about to take place. I heard about the man game at a provincial wrestling tournament my cousin was competing in. These two teenage guys sitting behind me in the bleachers talked about it like it was going to be the most amazing thing ever. Purely word of mouth. No flyers, no ads. According to the teenager the sport was very hush-hush on the downlow.

Worth the effort, the kid said, to go so far east in the city. And this kid then says how the man game was going to be way better than what we were watching, which happened to be my cousin getting the shit kicked out of him.

This was back in January. The trees were barebones along the road where we parked. We were so far east that nothing was recognizable. Not the streets, which sloped and undulated. Not the shapes of the houses, which all looked like miniature churches set up one beside the other. They're called Vancouver Specials because there's so many of them, charmingly ubiquitous split-levels, red and orange brick on the bottom, white stucco or panelling on the top floor, and a peaked A-frame roof. Each house was like an arrowhead or a mountain peak garnished with electric bulbs strung along the rooftop gutters, around the windows, and above the motorized garage door. I was unfamiliar with the style of the yards, which were two concrete slabs with a beach table and some chairs, surrounded by a white-painted iron-wrought fence with more arrowheads at the top of each post and bulbous avocado sculptures at each corner facing the street. The picture windows on the top floors reflected the image of their neighbours opposite. I no longer felt we were in the Vancouver I identified with. Even just stepping out of my Dynasty it felt as though the area was governed by a quite different set of habits. The sun shone weakly behind its white curtain. No rain today, but still, you could never tell. In Vancouver, rain could happen all at once.

I was hungry and nervous, always the case when I was with Minna. She never stopped thinking about food and I permanently worried about life.

I saw people head down a mulched alley between two blue houses with lawns stewing with fertilizer. Presumably these folks were aimed in the same direction we wanted, so we followed. To me the neighbourhood felt downcast and quiet; the houses seemed to sulk, the landscape was neutered.

A long-nosed boy sat in a corner of the yard beside a tree, one hand inside a black silk top hat, no pants on. That kind of neighbourhood. Poor magic. I watched a man at work on the pickets of his half-crushed fence, and he didn't look too amused, nor did his wife, leaning out the window, pulling at the ropes of her crowded laundry line.

Our footfalls matching, heads lowered, we concentrated on the two slips of dry tread along the alleyway that led towards a puckered cul-de-sac—more post-war bungalows and Vancouver Specials—where individuals from all rotten walks of life gathered to await a spectacle.

A thick crowd of people milled between a fence and a house with pink vinyl siding as they gradually squeezed their way into the backyard. We assumed this was where we wanted to be too. The thing about the house, which was otherwise pleasant and well-maintained, was how it had caved into its own foundation. Along the front corner opposite the garage the house sank a good two or three feet below the lawn. There was a basement window diagonally halved by ground-level topsoil and sod, looked clogged on the inside, too. Somehow Minna and I, and this troubled and hesitant love we shared, had ended up here at this weird beat-up house with the sag of a broken jaw.

I think we're going to enjoy this, I said.

This is the kind a thing you only ever hear aboot, said Minna, but you never actually get to see it or witness it.

Whatever it is we're aboot to see or witness, I said.

Exactly, she said.

We walked a little on. The cold Canadian sun shone on us.

I can't remember, Minna said. Does your guy's apartment have an elevator?

No, I said. After this we'd scheduled a trip to buy me a bed through Minna's quote unquote *Chinese connection,* a paranoid couple living on Knight Street who sold mattresses, frames, bedsprings, the whole bit out of a corrugated aluminum shanty in their backyard. Two days ago I'd moved into an apartment with a new roommate and I needed a bed, and though it's true I prefer to dress ready for business, I don't actually make much money, so this is how a man like me gets a boxspring.

Lopsided house on an obscure cul-de-sac. Indivisible from the throng, we proceeded into the grassy canyon between the fence and the house, flowing as a mob into the backyard. The vinyl siding quivered from the muffled noise of a living room stereo at full volume busting out a glitchy woof of something violent.

I heard a guy say: They make it hard to be over there for longer than three months unless you're a citizen, so you can't get a job, unless, you know, you work under the table, you don't have the right to proper health care, can't go to the dentist, you can't even rent an apartment—it's ridiculous. I hadda work under the table, get another guy in my squat to pull out my fucking rotted tooth 'cause I didn't have health care.

Like Minna and me, people seemed to arrive in pairs or groups. But we were the only ones who looked unacquainted with the day's event. A lot of people were screaming for the sheer hell of it. Over by the remnant of a tree, four overweight and juvenile men wearing deranged ballcaps leaned against their girlfriends. Petite little wet T-shirted chorus girls. Their boyfriends were teeth, hair, groins, in that order.

I considered the possibility that we should definitely leave, but I didn't want to look timid in front of Minna. I despise crowds, and she knows.

Man, lots a people here, I said.

Just enjoy this, she said. Can't you just enjoy us being together?

We could be anywhere, I said.

Uh-huh. And we're here because a something you overheard a teenager say at a wrestling match?

I have my own connections, yes.

The cheers and whoops from the audience around us only made me feel *less* enthusiastic. People kept putting their hands in the air and waving them like they didn't care if they looked like imbeciles. We were all young, but I was the only one wearing a tie, never mind leather shoes. The rest had shirts that might as well have been branded garbage bags. I wanted to scream if not for the fact that it would only make me fit in more.

Relax a bit, said Minna, rubbing my lower back. Her hand rubbed up my shoulder blades, then across my stiff spine. I smiled carefully for her. I was enjoying the attention on the inside. She appeared, as always, patient. I'm not. But Minna didn't call for me to amuse her, much as I endeavoured. Daily life was all the amusement necessary; she didn't need me, at least not the way I needed her. She was hot and serene. Nothing fazed her, not even me.

At last the music began to die away, and after a brief round of spastic hollering the crowd succumbed to silence, prepared for the true event drawing ever closer to go-time. We waited for it.

Upon this cue of quiet, those with a porch view nudged to squish on either side to make a path to the door. I tried to get a look into the window, but shadow blacked out everything.

A figure emerged, followed by another. They passed without incident through the canal of spectators and totally ignored the extended palms demanding high and down-low fives. Two young men walked onto the killed grass of the backyard.

The players stood on the pitch side by side, then split up to find a dry corner opposite each other, where the taller, hairier of the two proceeded to undress completely. Off came The Bay's tricoloured boxer briefs. Minna and I shot each other hesitant but inquisitive glances, and although I watched her lips part and one black eyebrow cock up, she chose to say nothing.

A spectator's gleeful whoop soared into the air and a baritone voice called out, All right. There was sustained applause.

You going to get down to it? said the naked man to his still boxered opponent.

The guy shook his head while he looked to the ground, a *No* gesture, and all at once the audience erupted in hisses and catcalling. They stamped up and down and swatted insults at him. Get outta the yard; Go home; Go back to wherever you came from; Take your sorry self back to that shameful place.

After all this stress from the mob, the player finally agreed to take off the boxers. The crowd loved this. The crowd noise was embarrassing as he pulled the folding holes down over his ankles and left the elasticized underwear in the dirt of his corner. He stood, gently rocking on the balls of his feet, under the steaming gaze of some hundred or so people.

They're naked, said Minna. Kat, you didn't say anything aboot buck.

I had no idea. I wouldn't have brought you if I'd known.

They got great bodies, said Minna.

I had no comment. A little younger than me, but they still looked as physically fresh as if they'd come straight from the high school gymnasium. All those endurance runs and flexed arm-hangs, push-ups, and basketball had left a good imprint.

I'm a little confused what's happening, she said.

This definitely isn't what I pictured.

We watched as the two men warmed up. The stocky guy with the long curly hair greased back did a one-armed handstand. He made it look like the kind of thing a person just does. I checked my wrist for a watch, for something else to do instead of gaping at the naked men while they limbered from the necks on down. It was a big show of loosening various flat-toned street muscles along their arms, backs, chests, legs, and necks. I ignored it. Not to be outdone, the taller, more heavily built and unshaven one did a backflip, landed on a single foot. Deep breaths and neck cracks led to flippering wrists and more heaving breaths. They danced on their toes and dodged left and right. I wasn't paying attention. After both guys relaxed to a neutral position and shared a moment of staring stillness, they walked to the centre of the yard and shook hands.

I'm Silas, said the tall one.

Hi there, I'm Ken.

They backed away and hunched down, arms held out at the ready, same as Olympic wrestlers. I had a good idea of what was about to happen and I thought of my poor cousin, relieved he wasn't out in front of me.

By the rise in idiot cheering throughout the yard, and without a referee or any coaches watching, I assumed this was probably going to end much worse than it began.

It's a wrestling match, I told Minna. It's naked wrestling.

I'm ready to go whenever you are, she said.

Yeah, I said.

We arranged ourselves for a delicate exit.

Silas was the big one, and cromagnonically hairy. It was impossible to ignore the hair all over him. Not to mention that his arms were frightening—slablike muscle carpeted straight to the fuzzy knuckles. And his knees were scabbed in long stretches.

Ken was the one with less bulk and height but more sinew. He was square and scribbled; he looked like a car battery, capable of great shocks and acid attacks. He did agile footwork I thought looked sketchy. Even with less hair he looked more animal than Silas. Perhaps his size could account for that, or his winter tan, or his thick, crusty hands.

He was the first to move. In a spider-fast sprint Ken was across the yard, nothing but pure tendon and rippled muscle and a delicate layer of pale bluish skin. A person had to be more alert than me to know he was coming. He seemed to glide through my blind spots until he was on top of the game, locking and freezing Silas in his arms. The headlock made it look like a holdup at a nude beach *{see fig. 1.1}*. Ken started to run backwards and Silas kept

---

FIGURE 1.1

The Cherry Tree Clutch

Calabi's commentary: Requires the steadiness of a pillar and the flexibility of the longest branch to take the force of the opponent, coming as fast as a boulder down a mountain, and to bend him through twists and turns as if the clod was instead a cat in the clutches of a cherry tree.

apace as they ran faster and faster. It was the kind of prank that ended in skull fractures. To get out of Ken's grip, Silas swung him over his shoulder, cranking his own neck and hips almost three hundred degrees as Ken flailed and landed on his heels, gambolling furiously to his side of the yard to regain his composure while we, vitalized audience, freaked holus-bolus.

Minna took my arm in her hands and pressed herself against me and I said: What's behind all this?

Bad upbringing? Garbage society?

I'm inclined to agree, but?

I don't know, she said. It's a clown show.

A decent part of me hadn't yet accepted what I'd seen. I was simply confused. Was Minna spinning the same bafflement through her head, and if so, why was she smiling so indecently? A new violence, or something invented long ago. I wanted to know.

//

A woman named Molly Erwagen. She arrived in Vancouver on June 13, 1886. Travelling in a donkey-drawn carriage underneath a deerhide cabriolet and huddled up together beside a hay-spiked Hudson's Bay wool blanket. She lay half-asleep next to her husband. She thought she heard pellets of rain. It was so hot and dry today, though. It was in fact ash flicking against the deerhide above them. She and her husband Samuel Erwagen rode towards Vancouver towed by an Indian and his donkey down the New Westminster road. Their heads toggled back and forth as the wagon staggered over rutted and dried mud. They lay together, husband and wife, Samuel wanting nothing more than to sleep, a virtually impossible task.

The air smelled of salmon. The wind that day gusted over a hundred miles per hour. As they approached Vancouver the gargantuan trees on either side of the road made an uncommon sound as they twisted in the gales. Sammy and Molly and the Indian were shielded from the wind's full force by the enormity of this forest of spruces, firs, cypresses, innumerable blues and greens, a massively dense coastal forest tolerating immense winds, creaking and cracking for tortuous stretches, groaning, bellyaching as wind passed through their uppermost canopy.

She faced him so that her lips were right beside his cheek. He lay there on his back, immobilized, feeling her breathe.

The fire was many miles away but even so ash dropped on occasion to the forest floor nearby. The vibration of the wagon wheels over the road was like a riddle, and Sammy let it rattle around in his head. He tried to ignore all the bumps and stalls. This was a logging road (they all were at the time) and meant hell on the radials. Luckily the Indian carried a fifth cedar wheel on the back; they'd probably have to use it.

The two had been travelling for so long and were exhausted beyond belief. Molly made clucking sounds. Something she did when she was near a dream. It would wake Sammy, this palatal clucking—it often did—but he wouldn't do anything about it. Little brief oneiric utterances, he called them.

How are you? she asked in a yawn. She petted his face and kindly wiped the sleep from the corners of his eyes. Are you doing okay, are you hurting, in pain?

He awoke. I'm wonderful, he said with a dry smile.

Oh shush, you liar. She laid her head on his lap. Damn you, she said, and he looked up at the tarp and he didn't raise a hand to her head to run his fingers through her hair.

You'd never leave me would you? he asked. He'd asked her the same thing before, probably too many times; one of these times she was going to give the wrong answer.

I'll never leave you, she said and flipped her head over on his unfeeling lap to look him in the eyes. You sweet fool, she said.

New friend, may I ask what's your name? Molly called out to the Indian astride the feeble ass. This sorry pair was supposed to take them on a three-hour trip due north, though Sammy doubted greatly the mule's strength to live out the next four steps.

Toronto, was the Indian's answer.

How peculiar, Sammy said, that's our old home.

Whitemans name me Toronto.

What an awful tag, thought Sammy.

No good in Vancouver come from Toronto, so say Salish peoples, said Toronto.

I see, said Sammy unhappily. His wife sopped his sweaty hair with a kerchief.

//

They stood about three feet apart, taking and blocking with only the hands' heels, palms flat and the heel of each hand used to bat and thwart. Ken kept advancing. Silas was constantly on the back up. Their elbows swung out and down, over and in. Silas had to manoeuvre such that he didn't get trapped into a corner.

Rook Takes Pawn *{see fig. 1.2}*, a spectator shouted out, and I assumed correctly that it was the name of a move. The cry sparked a moment of applause. The force of their attacks, so stern and unsympathetic, was too quick to fake. Ken, with the stronger arms, connected, and Silas's head whiplashed back. Was it a point for Ken? Was it even a game of points?

FIGURE 1.2

Rook Takes Pawn

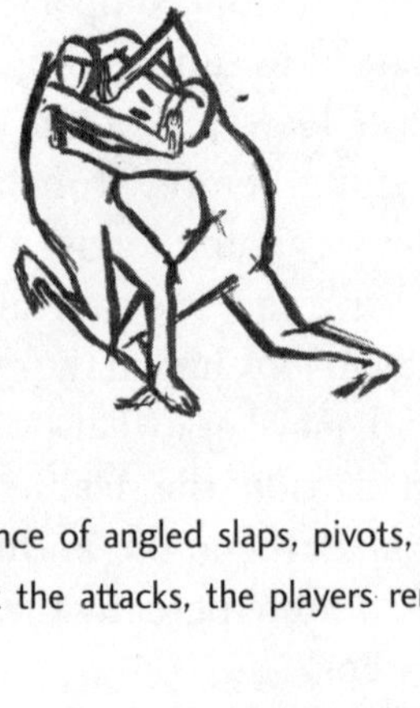

Calabi's commentary: A great dance of angled slaps, pivots, slaps, twists, and slaps, and no matter how violent the attacks, the players remain in step to a common rhythm.

I couldn't tell. The audience went silent. Someone was going to get tripped or hit on the head or both at once. The players were mustardy smelling in sweat. The furious beat and rhythm of their hands had them in a lather.

Sun glowered off their bodies.

In the background I noticed for the first time something not unlike music, sound but without true music in it. A rev. A revving noise going on underneath the sounds of the guys' palms and wrists colliding in swift, jabbing thrusts, parries, and psychs. Now and then Ken's left palm would connect: swivel up and clap.

//

What Sammy Erwagen needed was a safe home and an end to this miserable journey.

Should we have stayed where we were? he said to his wife. Have I made a grave mistake bringing you out west? Look at me. I'm a wretch, a burden, a cripple.

Shh, said Molly. Don't worry, it'll be so wonderful once we're settled.

Their Indian guide Toronto made a sound, an atonal sound, a mutter under his breath while the donkey clopped unsteadily and made his own defeated noises, sad snorfling equine noises. And the air made its own moan through the forest in such a chorus—a tenor for every tree.

To no one in particular Toronto said: Pretty loud for wind.

Douglas firs towered on all sides, some of them seventy feet around at the base, their enormous roots knuckling out of the topsoil, gripped to the earth, their trunks extending into the white vapour of space, swaying in the breeze. The trees cracked and wheezed without end, tossing back and forth at their peaks while down below the air merely fanned by to keep the heat from feeling unbearable.

Curly bits of char floated through the heat, carrying a few embers towards them, not enough to startle Molly and Sammy, but enough to make them curious. At first they thought it was rain—it *sounded* like rain—until one peck landed on their cover and didn't seem moist. It didn't dissolve. What it did was singe straight through the deerskin and land on Sammy's hand.

He didn't notice *where* it fell, but Molly leaned over. She too had seen it fall, and bent forward to identify. There it was on his hand, this little red ember making a welt in his palm. He felt nothing, no sensation of it cooking there. Before she had a chance to flick it off, the welt in his hand engorged and blistered open and finally she said: Oh, dear, your hand, something ash burned it. He saw the leaking furuncle pooled with blood and the modest rag of coal there to the side where she'd knocked it away, cooling to a delicate white. Sammy suggested she find something to staunch the blood. She proceeded to remove finger by finger one of her kid gloves.

That's a perfectly good glove, said Sammy.

That's a perfectly good hand, said she.

No, said Sammy, unable to conceal the despair in his voice, no, it's not.

Please shush up, said she. Then another piece of hot cinder burned a cigar cherry hole in the hide and landed on her dress and ignited a middling fire there on the frilly edge. She swatted it out with an envelope found next to her. What's this? Molly said. Another two or three pellets bounced off the tarp and left behind smoke.

You worried? he asked.

Yes, but only for you.

That didn't make him feel better. The wagon stopped. They heard Toronto drop from the donkey's back and crunch his way down the path to meet them.

There's a fire, he said.

Where?

Up ahead.

Where up ahead?

Everywhere up ahead.

I'll be nary a moment, she told Sammy and hopped out of the wagon.

I'm worried, he said.

Okay, just give me a moment, she said. He waited there flat on his back while she looked at the fire. She came back and confirmed there was a tremendous fire ahead of them. She hopped back into the wagon after she saw his pant leg asmoke and a bitty flame there.

Hold on, she said and smacked his thigh. There. She pushed a cooled ash off a singed hole in his slacks. You'll be fine, she said and kissed the little bit of newly exposed skin. He didn't feel it but he saw her do it. She smiled at him. Despite all the danger she seemed oddly pleased, flushed and glistening from the heat. Maybe for her the adventure had begun. For him the adventure was over before it even had time to start. Sammy, she said, it's not good out there.

What then? he said.

How strange he thought it was to see how much she glowed against the fire behind her, flickering in the black milk of her eyes. It seemed as though this scorched terror was a wondrous thing to her and, Sammy felt, that it touched some deep nostalgia within her, a sentiment she found disagreeable normally. He knew she'd seen many tragedies and dangers in her short lifetime. Her childhood had been spent in music halls, following her parents as they performed in Yiddish and in vaudeville, her extended family a motley rotation of nomads, midgets, clowns, and acrobats. Her mother and father, who sang, danced, told jokes, played tragedies, barked at carnivals and who could tell wild tales and do magic tricks. Her parents would perform on the shiny bartop at a saloon if it meant getting out from between the middle of two desperate situations. Admittedly, there were things about her he would never fully know. To know Molly was as much a calling to a certain kind of man as reaching the horizon of the earth is to the wanderer, and was why Sammy felt so light-headed about her. Her life before they married was a thousand novels and his was brutally uneventful doggerel.

The younger of two brothers, Sammy was from a long line of accountants and managers. His father was a respected bookkeeper living out his final days in Toronto with his ailing wife Esme, Sammy's mother, who was sick from having too much substance, who'd treated Sammy like an infant his entire life, and who'd been deeply perplexed and distraught when he announced he planned to marry Molly. A loony decision, she said. To Mother Esme, this girl was no better than a gypsy beggar, and she treated the union as if her son, in a delirium, had wedded a passing cloud. Sammy's older brother, Dunbar, did not even attend his wedding, out of devotion to his sturdily dying mother, and also because he'd already moved to Wyoming where he ruled over a community of other anti-social farmers. Dunbar spent his nights writing angry letters home still demanding things of his younger brother even after all these years. Sammy did his best to ignore the letters, and began a lifelong tradition of burning all correspondence immediately after reading.

Now married and far from Toronto, Sammy considered himself free of his family once and for all. He had decided long before his accident in the train tunnel that caused his paralysis that he would cut off all ties with his family as soon as he arrived in Vancouver. Ever since the accident his resolve had wavered but, no, he was still sure he wouldn't speak to them again no matter what happened next. He was free, he must remember that. He was no longer the prisoner in a family of tyrants. He knew he was afraid, but could she tell, did she know how much and in how many ways he needed her? This was the woman he loved, seventeen years old, yet for one instant she looked all of nine and the next she could've been his mother.

I'm not safe here, he said.

I know. We'll get us to safety.

Before he could reply she was gone. He had time to think but could not decide what to think about.

She came back. Trees are falling, she said.

The fire is moving east?

It's *spreading* east.

Go, he said. Leave me here.

He could tell she was thinking about his situation. When she passed her eyes over his benumbed body it made her features go from tense and riled to flat, blank, neutral, completely undisturbed, until she had to vigorously swallow to regain a sense of time.

You don't feel a thing? she said in an unfamiliar voice.

No, he responded.

There's fire everywhere out there.

I can feel it on my face, Chinook.

To help cool him down she undid the buttons of his shirt, fanned him with an envelope addressed to Sammy on the Hastings Mill letterhead, to give his chest air. He felt his head chill off a bit. She loosened her own collar by two buttons to reveal the damp overlay on the skin of her breastbone. The heat was unbearable.

She lit a cigarette and tipped her head to one side to look out one of the six burn-holes in the hide. She said: The air is trembling with heat.

Why are you smiling at me like that?

Smoking at a time like this. I love you.

Ah, she returned her eye to the hole. What's the difference?

A girl your age. You're not scared are you?

She shook her head while taking a big drag. I've seen things like this, she said. She pointed the coal of her cigarette against the freckled dermal tarp and another sizzling aperture appeared just big enough for her to see through towards the scorched and claustrophobic skyscape.

Don't stop loving me just because a this or that, she said. We'll survive this strange miracle just as we did your accident.

The northern cup of the sky lay all black and reamed with

fire at the horizon. Sammy could see the giant flakes before they slipped up his nostril and exploded into choking carbon nets. Already in the east the smoke was sometimes as low as two feet from the ground. The fire raged in oven blasts across the stumped slash. They passed by streams that ran with currents of blood clogged by burnt and disgorged carcasses of domesticated animals that floated down the bubbling current.

A dot-by-dot bombardment of little fires landed on the carriage and everything started to light up. A tree some hundred yards away had burst into flames without warning. There wasn't even any fire near the tree; just the heat of the air itself was enough. Bits of the tree exploded into the air straight at them like ammunition, cindering skyward. They just barely got Sammy out of the carriage before the thing was in flames. Left with no choice, they tied Sammy to the donkey's back and continued to trudge on foot. The creature was covered in a sweat like scrubbed dentifrice. Occasionally Toronto patted his mule and wiped the sweat away from its deadpan lonely pony eyes. The heat was devastating. Molly complained of loss of breath. They were scared and unprepared to discover what lay ahead.

Have you seen fires like this, Toronto? Sammy asked assback, forced to stare up into five-storey flames.

There's lot a forest, Toronto said. Lot a fires. This one, I believe, made by Whitemans.

Sammy saw something dance from a copse of trees and disappear down a smoke-cleaned valley. What was that? he asked.

A deer go hide in river.

Poor frightened thing.

Then three more deer darted out of the bush and followed the first one towards the creek.

Those are the first animals I've seen since I believe Manitoba.

Many more where them from.

I understand there's a lot a salmon.

Ha ha, said the Indian.

It was so hot, it hurt to see. The donkey breathed hard. It

made these monophthongal pleas: *Uuu-u-u;* vowelly desperate sounds.

I'm too heavy, Sammy said. I'm going to kill the old chap.

No, no, said Toronto, who fed his donkey from a withered canteen and delivered handfuls of dried and salted corn. The long equine tongue curled up to meet the stream of water and also pull back the nuggets.

//

Continuing west they saw up ahead two lumberjacks with raised fists. Around them most everything was black and smoking. One had a beard and the other had a moustache. The bearded man took off his hat. It appeared they were getting ready to fight. They didn't take notice as the travellers approached. The men squared off.

You don't spit at me, said the bald bearded man. What I ever do to *you* except make us money?

In a boxer's stance, fists raised, they started making a tight semicircle along the ground, heads bobbing, expecting a fist to come out. The flint in their eyes and the methodical way they semicircled in preparation to box and the fact that they were down to their calico underclothes made for a troubling sight. With flames lashing out in every direction.

Whatever's the matter? whispered Sammy.

Shhh, let's watch, replied his wife.

The lumberjacks were in that silent prelude of sussing out and buying time before coming to blows, neither man quite yet ready to get punched in the face. No one really wants to get punched in the face. Fists raised and kind of dancing, but no punches had yet been swung. Inevitably they would punch each other in the face.

The Indian, donkey, and Erwagens continued to approach. The men continued to bob and weave, still no punches thrown. Smoke clouds accumulated around them, turbulent plumes of black ash. Lips stretched into strange snarling curls, errant canine tooth showing. Huge varieties of swear words were exchanged. They were so close to all-out battle and they knew it. This was how they'd settle the argument, toe to toe. Swearing and flinching and tense and sweaty. Bohunk. Poltroon. Mewler. The swearing was all about building up steam, goading and picking at the other. Piebutt. Minkhole. Then all of a sudden the two men were at it. There were fists and elbows and knees and the clack of jaws and the snapple of gutpunches, shinkicks, and broken noses.

Oof, said the moustached one, and there was dirt in his mouth. He was on the ground now. The bearded one watched him get up. Gathering to form a whole man. Legs first and then after a shudder his spine carried his arms and head up and he was standing. They could see the bruises appearing on his face after he wiped off the dirt and blood. The lumberjacks were beating each other senseless, not holding back at all. They were hunched over with fists in front of their faces. Wallop by wallop, the punches increased in force. After two merciless blows the other man went sailing to the ground like a snipped marionette and then with insane tenacity dredged himself back up again and proceeded to push the other man to the ground.

Sammy could feel his wife's fingers gripped to his cheeks. Extraordinary, she said. Who *are* these men? she asked their Indian guide Toronto. Do you know them?

Yup, said Toronto. Logging partners, woodsmen. Names Litz and Pisk.

Litz and Pisk, said Molly. We should try to stop them.

Fighting is everyday thing here, said Toronto.

//

A violent January, or that was how I would come to remember the month that Minna and I first discovered the man game. These two guys in this backyard performing mad versions of old familiar dances and other steps that weren't so familiar, and never without a particularly sporting twist to it. A polonaise, a shamming mongrel version of that Polish dance involving chin attacks—chin pushing chin, while stepping in time despite all the kicks and skipping to dodge kicks and shin parries. At one point the men reared up like mountain goats, forehead to forehead *{see fig. 1.3}*. They were on their toes, foreheads aimed, bodies ready for a violent plunge. They took a couple quick paces each, and I heard Minna gasp into her upheld hands right at the moment of collision. As she covered her eyes, I saw the pain ripple down their faces when their two hairlines met with an audible crack. Ken's neck tendons were stretched out. Silas gritted his teeth and let loose a wild shofaric sound, deep and loud, that seemed to rush straight up from his bowels and out his mouth. It was unreal. The men staggered but remained locked at the forehead. Silas and Ken pushed so hard forehead to forehead that their feet were digging back into the dirt. The strain was visible over their entire bodies. Perspiration ran down their faces and fell from their elbows. Time elapsed.

One of them might crack open, Minna said, holding her forehead. Her hair was up, scooped inside a paisley bandana. Her forehead was smooth. I'd have liked to put my hand there.

//

A swatch of mossy earth collapsed into a burnt-out hollow in the ground and all that fresh oxygen ignited, shooting

FIGURE 1.3
Banger

Calabi's commentary: A cocksure move on the part a both players, who unwisely confuse the hardness a the brainpan with the durability a the flesh.

antheridia into the sky as an array of squirming sparks.

Molly, Sammy, and their guide Toronto trod cautiously towards the centre of town. They looked into the flame ahead knowing they must stop. It was incredibly hot, too hot. They were fools. What drew them so close? Moth ecstasy? To the east, black smoke rose in gargantuan plumes, to the west, the fires still raged. They stood there wondering what not to do next when the windows of a three-storey manse exploded and the walls fell inward against a shivering tumult of fire. A man came running towards them, maybe fifty or sixty feet away when he threw off his hat. No sooner did they see him than the man vanished inside a huge lick of orange flame. Sammy saw him take one last step before he went off into the air as separate black flakes inside a vast cremator.

Molly threw her Stars & Stripes to the ground and stubbed it out in anger. Dry pine needles crackled under her leather boot. I can hardly breathe, she said.

They passed a smoking body, a man or woman no one could tell for sure, a headless figure twisted like black driftwood. The legs were twisted underneath the body. When a cyclone blew across the earth, an arm crumbled off and black blood dribbled out. All the while the neck whistled like a kettle, still boiling up the blood inside the chest.

Birds continued to fall from the sky, cooked and or suffocated.

The burning roofbeam of a stable crumbled and fell on hay with a gush of sparks, a stableful of horses screamed like mothers. The owner of these ponies was nowhere to be seen. The dry bale in the corner that fed the horses now fed the fire. The hay was soaked in flame in seconds and the heat pushed the roof straight off into the air. The sound of those horses perishing was enough to put Sammy to the brink.

A dark horse came rearing down the street towards them with its whole body alight, white teeth exposed as she screamed, looking devilish, shaking a mane of fire. Suddenly the mare stopped, took a step to the side, burning ferocious flames off her back and neck, and then toppled to the ground dead.

We should turn back, said Molly.

Toronto stopped the donkey.

We must go to Hastings Mill and see if my boss is alive, said Sammy, expressing the last of his courage.

Yes, sir, said Toronto.

At the corner of Dupont Street, Sammy and the others encountered a couple scathed and destitute young women mostly naked, wearing oddments of burnt clothing, picking along the hot smoking ground for whatever was left untorched.

Hello, said Molly.

Don't know how I'm alive, said one of the women.

I don't know neither, said the other.

They had sticks, these two women, which they used to upturn the ground. Now and again this tilling alighted small pockets of fire which they stomped out using their bare feet. Only a short distance away was a huddle of more young girls in similarly bad shape who appeared out of a thick, coarse smog. About ten of them in all, really nothing more than children but for the looks in their faces. Their soft bodies were exposed to the fire. Then the eldest appeared, a woman whose mane of sopping wet, curly hair dashed side to side flinging ashen sweat as she commanded her flock. She stepped forward and called ahead: Come back here, girls, don't go getting lost out here now. That's all we need.

At the sound of the woman's voice, the two girls awoke from the daze of this terrible trauma. Looking for the first time at the three travellers, the girls mistook Sammy for a corpse tied to a half-dead mule, and squealed a little when he startled them by saying hello.

Who are you? one of the girls said to Molly.

I'm Mrs. Erwagen, she said, and pointing to Sammy, This is my husband.

Such a pretty face for a day like today, the girl said to Molly, weeping.

Do you need help? Molly asked.

Do *you*?

Come back here, girls. Tell your friends to follow if they wish.

The girls looked at Molly. She asked them: Should we follow you?

The woman in the middle distance continued to beckon them back to the flock, and one girl said to Molly: We never go nowhere safe.

Is that your mother? Molly asked.

Her? Hell, no, not our mother, ha ha, that's Peggy.

Once they returned to their ragged band of sisters, it quickly became impossible to tell them from the others. The girls were kept in a tight formation and slowly faded from view as layers upon layers of dank smoke blew across the path.

The Indian coughed into his sleeve, and Sammy's view of the world changed when the mule was turned around and began to walk again.

It's Sunday, Molly said. We should go see if the church is safe. People will be there.

Oh, no.

But not everyone had been in church that day, as the threesome soon learned. Among the fire's victims was an atheist's family who'd sought refuge down a well and died there when the fire passed overhead and sucked all oxygen out of the air around them and from inside their lungs. They saw the family, from the smallest child to the tall, thin father, when they passed beside a group of weary survivors hoisting the family one at a time back over the edge of the well to lay them out in a flat row, dead and grey, melted and dried with a final look of fright across each of their faces.

Do something, said a man.

Do what? said his partner.

They looked at the family for what seemed like eternity.

//

Amid the mounds of glowing ash where an entire block of buildings once stood, a single set of brick walls remained, roofless and smoking. Groups of people unable to control their weeping examined the wreckage of tailor shops, soy factories, opium dens, and sushi parlours, all of which had once crowded together to share this small area of town. Now everything was flattened across the razed black earth, with only charred bonelike sticks of wood poking out here and there from the hissing ground. But when Toronto saw the one brick building that still stood, he raised his arms and, sounding as if he'd just remembered the plight of his own kinfolk, cried: Wa, wa, Calabi and Yau.

He ran towards the rubble, where Sammy and Molly could see a fair crowd already forming around this single fireproof edifice. On the ground in front of the building was a puddle of glass, the window of a burnt shop. Molly asked a soot-covered man beside her what the place once was, and he pointed to two Asian men being consoled by everyone and explained it was their bakery. People took turns embracing the bakers. Toronto took his turn. The men were both much older than he but still robust. They were bald, wrinkled and dark, with sunken eyes, but their arms were thick and strong and their bellies stuck out under their aprons. The Calabi & Yau Bakeshoppe was known for its Dutch oven and the remarkable pastry they made in it. The pastry was the result of a secret recipe. The crowd in front of the bakery all exclaimed that without Calabi and Yau no one would be capable of imitating this pastry.

Yeast is safe, said Calabi in his English. Dutch oven is safe.

The crowd applauded. Toronto stood slump-shouldered with a look of sorrow and relief across his face. Molly was curious to learn more. She took a place in line and finally introduced herself to the bakers. Unable to approach the Rubicon of her eyes, the bakers greeted her with bowed heads and humble noises, hardly speaking. Yau was the older of the two, a hunchback from years stoking the stoves. He wore his short hair inside a black Mandarin toque. Calabi, in a wide jacket and wider pants, was more contemporary in his style, and wore his sleek black hair in pigtails. His features were more symmetrical; he was a tall, intelligent-eyed, wide-shouldered and outspoken fellow, fluent in English, who told Molly that Toronto was one of many many residents in town whose main source of nourishment was Calabi&Yaus, popular pastries. The extraordinary and renowned pastries made by Calabi and Yau were considered by Vancouverites as almost the highest achievement in foodstuff anyone could ever have created, and most of the population lived off them. Blackberry Calabi&Yaus with cream cheese icing formed the majority of Toronto's daily food intake. He often ate a dozen a day. The pastry itself had a sweetness that was a perfect molten combination of honey and maple, a sweetness that burbled and popped below the instant tang of orange zest that hit you the moment the Calabi&Yau met your tongue, and that finished with the savouriness of a fried chicken crust, plus the various fillings that changed with the seasons as certain fruits became available. While they always served a loyal dozen flavours that ranged from blackberries to chocolate, salmon to bacon, wasabi to red devil chili, the seasonal variety was what made so many residents of Vancouver addicted.

As they talked, Sammy noted how the two bakers seemed to be awed by his wife's unmistakable beauty, so much so that by the end of their conversation, both men were finally in tears. As she separated from their embrace, the heavy realization of how close they had come to total annihilation struck the bakers suddenly and with great force. They fell on each other sobbing while the Dutch oven behind them stood as immutable as a stone pillar from antiquity.

We should look for my boss now, said Sammy.

Yes, said Toronto with visible anguish, we go see Whitemans RH Alexander now.

//

We watched Ken and Silas avoid the possibility of broken bones, dancing or wrestling or both, back to back, hand in hand, traipsing side by side in a struggle to upend the other or start something. While they pulled and fought they still managed to be nimble, keeping up a one-two step, slap and thwack, twist and dodge *{see fig. 1.4}*. The crowd was hyper. Frothed by the action of this vile entertainment, laughing with fat teeth, they all knew this one-two step. Thump-thump, pompom ... This jock's dance was side to side, a gutless masquerade of barbarity that passed for suburban joy. I was pale and logical compared to its lumbering rhythm. My tie was pale blue with an elegant design, the atomic shape of the silk molecule. I didn't know how to be here.

Can we leave now?

What's wrong? Minna asked.

Nothing, I said.

You don't want to stay a little longer, please?

FIGURE 1.4
Dip the Schnitzel

Calabi's commentary: It is like seeing a waltz performed by starlings, fast as light on water, a delicate pattern visible even as the men strike, dodge, and pummel.

I guess I can wait a little longer. It's just that—

What?

Oh, nothing.

Whatevs, Minna said, hugging my arm. Why would you think aboot something like that right now? Don't dwell.

I thought to myself: How could we talk of *love* in this context? Wasn't that obviously what we were talking about when we talked about rejection? My intentions weren't coming across.

The yard's grass was doomed. These guys were ruining it. What did I care? I wanted to have an out-of-consciousness experience. Instead I was over-intellectualizing everything. I tried to figure out what else I was thinking just then. If I was fated to think, what was the most intelligent thing I was thinking? Finally I said to her: You remind me a someone I've yet to meet.

Who's that? she asked.

Oh, I said, you know, the love a my life, perhaps.

That's not fair. I'm a real person.

Hm, you're right. I suppose it isn't. I'm sorry. Fairness doesn't come naturally to me. It's because I'm introverted.

I'm a real person, not some half fantasy.

I'm still sorry.

Yes, yes. But aboot what?

I felt a little sad. It was the sadness of being exposed as the dumber one. Of course she was right. She wasn't on earth for my purposes. There was nothing more or less real than Minna on a day like today, as we spectated this weird sport.

I thought one of them might not just cramp or dislocate a shoulder but lose an entire arm. What they were doing to each other was carelessly dangerous, somewhat like watching elementary school children re-enacting cartoon pratfalls that would shatter the hips of your average adult.

I said: Ouch.

She said: No kidding.

They started doing something else that was like mutual, competitive Indian burns, like attempting to wring blood out of each other's elbows at the same time. Ken was flushed and sapped, copiously sweating down his back in forking streams, and looked ready to call uncle, even while turning up the heat with his own twisting grip on a wretchedly screaming Silas. The pain showed in Ken's mouth and eyes, but Silas was screaming at the top of his lungs *{see fig. 1.5}*. A lot of people in the crowd were involuntarily clenching their jaws.

FIGURE 1.5
The Mary Shelley; aka the Great Fire

Calabi's commentary: Torture by the burning grip; a dance greatly unbalanced in favour a the cruel flames that lick at the leader's conscience.

TWO

> Mr. Plod: "I wish I knew how you reach your results."
> Sherlock Holmes: "I reached this one by sitting upon five pillows and consuming an ounce of shag."
> — ARTHUR CONAN DOYLE

Evil is brought from the north over all the inhabitants a the Earth. Thus spake prophet Jeremiah, said Dr. Langis to the manager of Hastings Mill, RH Alexander.

Is this a prescription or a counselling? said RH, pointing to his doctor's leather case, which sat at his feet.

Y-yes, said the doctor. He bent over and opened the case and fished through it while continuing to speak. Y-yes, what I mean is, firstly, that the Lord does deliver us signs, forewarnings, and we are wise to heed them.

Vancouver's doctor should have no truck with the Bible, said Alexander. Reason and science and observation should be his Trinity.

Now in his sixties, RH was a strong, long-legged capitalist with a spider's patience. He sat patiently in his chair like that, waiting to snap. His bloodshot eyes were stuffed inside loose bags of purple flesh and covered by tangled eyebrows. His white moustache was stained a coppery colour at the ends from the pipes he smoked or, less likely, the blood he sucked: the doctor could not be certain without examining his patient more closely. The veins in his neck pumped, and these cords curled their way to the paperthin skin on the backs of his hands, which were spread into a startlingly wide radius over the wide armrests of his leather chair. But it was RH's bloodshot eyes that Dr. Langis studied carefully, and that offered the best view of what kind of rotten state he was in. RH's irises were foggy, dark pools of turpentine.

The two men were seated in RH's study. The room was an immaculate tomb with blood-red curtains and steep bookshelves. There was a globe on a brass axis and other trinkets of power. The doctor recognized the heavy scent of vanilla and coca evaporated into one another. The source of this smell was a telltale smoke. It was produced by a substance that happened to come into Alexander's possession via the medical case sitting between the doctor's feet. Langis freed the buckle and opened the top of the leather case to remove a glass phial full of a dark liquid—the substance—and handed it to RH, who bowed his head in thanks and passed back his payment.

I regret to say so, Langis stammered, but, w-well, you see, RH, lately my research suggests that continued intake a the laudanum might adversely affect one's health. After time, the body becomes addic—

—The world is full a such nonsense, said RH. I know better than to take orders from a country doctor. You see that I need it. Just as some men need the stimulation in tobacco. When I'm without, I get the worst vomitous headaches, unsafe drowsiness. Stupidity. Dysentery. I'm prone to influenzas. The laudanum is the antidote, as you can attest to from your very own observations a my health. I am suited to it. And so is my wife.

You see, the—, back east, it's the medical establishment, they declared it ...

Are we living all the way in Vancouver on the edge a the known world in order to follow the directions a the establishment? Pardon my manners, Langis, but I respect *you*. Don't listen to the east. I respect your opinion on matters a health. Why should I follow the command a this establishment when I have you?

Th-thank you, RH. You know the feeling's mutual. But you see, I was compelled to make an oath.

Are all your dealings so readily visible to this false establishment?

There's paperwork I must fill out on all occasions.

Such a shame. You and I, we must forge ahead, even if it means leaving behind what we're told to believe. I'd like to write a letter, Langis, to tell the establishment what a disservice he's doing to his fellow man, how a gentleman struggles under such fool and foul conditions to build the new world. Ah, it's such a shame. And there's nothing we can do together as gentlemen to sort this out between us? No, eh? RH slumped into his chair. He took to staring gravely at Langis's left shoe and, obviously deep in thought, scratched the top of his head like an ape.

Very little was left standing after the Great Fire a month ago, but RH Alexander's grandiose and unwelcoming house was perfectly spared. That day the servants, under RH's close watch, covered the whole roof in wet blankets. Not that soaking wet blankets would have changed the fates of most other homes and shops in the area, all of which were completely incinerated, some in a matter of hot seconds. The flames licked RH Alexander's house but didn't come nearer, as if by his glare alone Alexander could halt nature's course.

Now, let me see if I have this straight, said Dr. Langis, picking up the lost thread of a conversation that was ostensibly the reason he was asked to come visit RH. You tell me you hired a bookkeeper paralyzed from the *neck down* and you want me to visit him? To evaluate his condition?

Startled from his thoughts, RH blinked and sucked his teeth, then said: Hm, yes, hm, yes, yes, that's why I've asked you here today, in fact. To see for yourself. When I met Erwagen the day a the Great Fire, he described his predicament to me. He said he was *petrified*. RH chuckled a little. Imagine my heart, Langis. There's nothing to see for miles but blackened earth, smoking with the most noxious stink like from the vents a Hell. Souls walking to and fro in complete shock, dressed in rags. And here comes a man towards me, ha ha, across this maniacal landscape, tied to a donkey, accompanied by the Indian Toronto, and the most beautiful young girl you've ever set your eyes upon. I mean it. And the man says, from the back a this donkey, tied there to him, he claims to be my new bookkeeper.

His wife is …

Langis, believe me now or never, Erwagen's young bride is … talk aboot your se*raph*. If I could a cupped that face in my hands, felt that skin, and for just one minute stared into that perfect face, this whole nightmare would a ended. When you meet her, you can imagine the contrast. Her face, this black burning world behind her … my god. You almost have to look at her from out the corner a your eye to really see her.

Like the sun.

The sun is a mediocre star in comparison.

My, I'm sure curious to meet this couple. Scientifically speaking, I'm curious. But I stand by my belief. Like the prophet Jeremiah, you should be wary a signs like this, RH.

Calling attention to the words a God, Langis.

I don't recommend a cripple in charge a your finances.

You should see this man, Langis. I want you to. Samuel Erwagen. He's more than made up for his frozen limbs with the fire in his skull. I see a terror in his eyes, as from a vision. A vision a my future finances. Ha ha. He's a mystic just like you and I, Langis. As you are a mystic a medicine and I, capitalism, I believe contrary to your, what shall we call it—*medical prophecy*—that Samuel Erwagen is going to have an excellent effect on my finances.

As your doctor, may I suggest a cure for Mammon?

No.

Now tell me, RH, said Langis, gracelessly apropos of nothing, do you know who started this fire? There is a rumour some a your lumberjacks with a donkey engine …

Indeed, after hearing the same, I immediately conducted an internal investigation, and you're welcome to tell the man on the street I did so. I can't reveal the details, but I made sure the persons responsible won't be seen again in this city.

So it *was* your own employ.

Let's not excuse Mother Nature for the contribution a her wrath. The fierce winds were a factor that day, too, undoubtedly. Still, I remain disappointed that such stalwart fellows as my own good hires could allow a burn to get so out a hand.

Who were they? Litz and Pisk?

Cannot say.

They let loose Hell that day and haven't been seen since. Good then. I hope you meted out some a your own hell on them.

Yes, and whoever they be, they deserved their punishment.

Lately, I see nothing good in this place, said Langis, looking at his hands' fingers as he locked and unlocked them. I don't know how long I can last out here in this jungle.

There's worse things than being a doctor in the land a evil, I should think. After all, business is brisk. This is prime real estate. The Gates, my friend, are nearby.

North and South.

For a few more minutes they argued like gentlemen about money, God, and women until RH had had enough.

No chance you give me laudanum next time I see you, eh?

I'm sorry, Mr. Alexander, said the doctor as obsequiously as he could muster, pushing his pince-nez spectacles up the bridge of his moist noise.

RH nodded his head.

Very well then, said Langis, seeing that his time with this wealthy man was up. He stood and smoothed his pants and scratched his beard. The two men shook hands.

//

Langis went to see the Erwagens immediately, flushed from the conversation and the heat of curiosity. And if fear of the unknown was the reason he held steady to the banister as he reached the front porch, then seeing Molly, and in particular Molly's venerable beauty, was what caused the real loosening in his step. The wobbles. She deboned his legs just by looking at him so intently. He rashly accused her of having muddy steps, then immediately apologized for his impoliteness and blamed his own clumsiness for stumbling down three steps and bruising a shin.

I'm very sorry, he said. Since I got my licence in '75, I've been a farm doctor in Saskatchewan—coldest winters imaginable—, Montreal the same but with city problems, Swift Current—a mudhole—, and now Vancouver. Never once in all that ice do I slip on a house call.

It's quite all right. Here, please, let me help.

No, no, all I need to do is adjust the kneecap here and … voilà, tip-top shape again.

She helped him gather his doctor's tools and put them back in his leather case, and he thanked her after three attempts to say the simple words. The fresh sweat on his nose meant he had to continually push his pince-nez spectacles back up his bridge.

Please have a look at my husband and tell me if there's anything you can do. It is terrible for a wife to ever be in a position to pity her husband. Wouldn't you agree? He deserves so much more. Will you be honest with me?

Abso-certainly, said Dr. Langis, limping along as he followed her into the house, watching her hips swing and the slow motion of her smooth round haunches under her skirts. I'm an h-h-honest man, he said and his face blushed deeper red, constricting towards purple.

But, listen to me, Molly said, trembling, and promise you'll do as I say. If you judge his condition, and it looks to you that he won't *live,* don't tell me. I don't want to know.

I understand.

Promise me?

Y-yes.

First he studied Sammy's pipestem legs for signs. The toes were as responsive as dried apricots. The knees did not react to repeated raps of the hammer. Langis massaged his pituitary glands. He hammered on Sammy's ribcage and listened to his heartbeat stethoscopically in his ear. The heart, the stomach, the organs continued their chores. He laid Sammy on his stomach, pressed the steel amplifier to Sammy's back (nothing so much as an involuntary twitch at the touch of cold metal), and heard the collapsing flesh muffle his shortened breath. He rolled the peak of each vertebrae in his fingers, examining the contours for fractures.

The wedge of skull at the top of the neck was the first place Sammy's sensation returned, but in the fibres and tissue below that point there was a total, ghastly absence.

Molly finished the sip of her tea. She looked at the doctor with a hopeful smile. He clinkily replaced the spoon to the porcelain saucer beside his cup after stirring the cream that he momentarily watched fulminate in the orange pekoe like incense.

The intellectual faculties are entirely intact, he told Mrs. Erwagen.

She said: I'm aware a that.

Y-yes, well.

Toronto stood in the hallway looking at the ray of light passing through the living room.

What are the chances?

The chances? the doctor said. Why, I thought we weren't …

The chances he might recover some …

My dear, he said, awkwardly, intimately condescending to her feminine ignorance, ah, the, well you see, the vicissitudes a the human anatomy … it's a system a veins …

He was briefly taken aback by the arresting image of her sitting there across the kitchen table from him. Her eyes shone. He would remember them as green, flecked by a saffron cascade of falling flames. His breath globbed in his throat like an undigested foam called ardour.

… There is always hope, my dear.

She clasped his hands in hers. The slender reed of her ring finger scratched his knuckle with the gold bands. The diamond was the size of a tear.

Sammy and I came to Vancouver to start a life for ourselves that we couldn't imagine anywhere else. In Toronto, Sammy was a back-row seat, Dr. Langis. Civilized society already saw him as a cripple. In Toronto, I was a Little Miss Muffett. Everybody wanted to scare me away. Toronto never wanted me, never wanted Sammy. Every genteel bourgeois burgher in Toronto thinks he was born with blue blood in his veins. Is it so much the same in Vancouver, are there as many masks, as much pretense?

A little, my dear. We have our share a burghers.

Burghers everywhere. If a man is born poor, helpless, with peasant blood burning his heart, he should not be so ashamed that when he makes his fortune he tries to buy himself a new lineage.

I agree.

I would rather live with a true cripple than a liar hiding stilts under his slacks. Sammy's mind and spirit is strong.

Dear, sweet Mrs. Erwagen, I shall pray for your husband.

Thank you.

He bowed his hat to her as he walked backwards down the steps of their verandah and bid the angelic Mrs. Erwagen a formal adieu, turning to the street with her visage in his mind's eye.

//

VOWS HASTINGS MILL BOSS RH ALEXANDER: BRICKS REBUILD CITY THIS TIME ROUND; AGREES TO SELL PLOT TO CPR, RECOUP LOSSES

Illiterate bastards, he complimented. There wasn't a thing in the *Daily Advertiser* RH Alexander didn't already know. In fact, there was little news in Vancouver that didn't directly pertain to him. The headline amused him, for he knew that by the time the CPR got to their land, the best of the forest would already be lumber in his mill. Just because his men weren't allowed to log on that land didn't mean he wouldn't get the timber in any case. If this so-called journalist and some Toronto railway magnate both figured Alexander had been made a sucker in the deal, all the better. The ignorance of the news calmed him. He didn't let go of the newspaper because there was a certain quality to the paper in his fingers that he appreciated. He sat in his high-ceilinged library with what Langis had left with him, therefore not alone, but haunted by the opiate. Listening to the music in his head, his thoughts returned to the doctor, then Samuel Erwagen and his stunning wife Molly, turning again to thoughts of the Great Fire and God's mercy on his home, and finally unravelling his memory to the day a few weeks ago when he met with the woodsmen Litz and Pisk. Based on his bookkeeper Samuel Erwagen's description of the two men he saw fighting the morning of the Fire, RH Alexander paid a secret visit to these men's camp in Mount Pleasant south of False Creek. He staked out in the morning and portaged south from Coal Harbour into bear country, past the beaver dam to the cranberry swamp where he knew their shack was located. The land around there was swampy and sulphuric. It was a messy camp and Litz and Pisk were the only ones left sitting over the heat of the embers of a tiny campfire. The two lumberjacks were all alone among the dregs of forest, waiting for what next.

RH sat down on an empty stool. He brought out a wad of opium and they brought out a wad of hashish and they combined these and smoked a bowl together.

Upon exhale, RH said: Boys, you're young, healthy. I've been here since '69. I've seen things you couldn't imagine. I'll tell you what I told the men at my mill recently. I said to them, When I first moved here the Indians presumed we were white ghosts from across the ether. Can you imagine their fear seeing our great ships rise over the edge a the ocean with the wind in the sails? What a shock to see us riding our islands from the edge a the water to their land and our white faces coming ashore. That's what they thought our ships were, islands. Indeed. The bloodless white faces coming ashore, from their point a view, from over the edge a the earth. When my son HO was born, they'd never seen a white baby before. Indians crowded around outside the house waiting for us to show him. The horror and awe in their eyes was—we didn't show him in public for a while after that. When our son TK was born a year later, it was the same thing. They brought gifts. Our house smelled a that fish grease for days after. Oh, I know, we *all* know they're a filthy breed, these Indians. I've seen them spit in their own food while it cooks. Nevertheless. What I came to realize, and you think aboot this, both a you: We're all Chinamen here in Canada, except for the Indians. We all came from under the ocean to get here. So long as you're a Chinaman in this country, you'll work for a Chinaman's wage or you'll get out.

Hm, said Litz, picking his fingernails with a shiv.

They smoked another bowl.

Pisk said: We didn't start the fire.

RH laughed and said: I don't want to see the two a you ever again. Go home. Back across the ether whence you came.

I'm not leaving Vancouver, said Pisk. We didn't start no fires. That was not us. I can tell you who it was.

Don't want to hear your conspiracies.

You *know* who started this, Mr. Alexander.

Regardless a who *you* suspect, RH said, the city believes it was you two.

This is my home as much as anyone's. We won't leave.

You will, said RH. Your names aren't worth spoiled milk around here.

Litz remained silent. Pisk did all the talking.

If we're John Chinamen, said Pisk, who are you?

RH smiled. Behind the mask of his face and the holes of his eyes, a little scared rabbit was looking out. He said: Who am I? I'm the father a this town, that's who.

Listen, I got a better idea, said Pisk. How aboot me and Litz stay out a sight and log all that CPR land you sold and sell it you for ...

RH Alexander's eyes brightened. Yes, go on, I'm listening, you were aboot to say you'd sell it for half, so go on.

Half-price timbers ..., said Pisk.

Litz brought out his own supply of opium. RH's eyes brightened yet further.

Litz lit the next bowl and passed it to RH. Litz was the son of a wild man from Regina, Saskatchewan, who believed in the crucible. That is to say, Litz's education came in whippings. His father told him that for every blow Litz received, he should deliver one back. And when Litz could defend himself properly, then he'd see an end to beatings. Litz grew up, like this father, to be a stout, unapologetic young man. But before he ever had a chance to take his pa down a notch, the old man died in a dock fire. Like his father, Litz wore mutton-chop sideburns connected to a moustache.

Pisk was bearded. At twenty-seven, his beard was thick as nettle and already salted. The top of his head was bald. He was raised by his mother in the fog of Penticton, a burgeoning mill town in south-central British Columbia, dangling off the bottom of Okanagan Lake. Pisk grew up around livery barns, blacksmiths, big game hunters, and hemp farms. He started working in the mill when he was eight, tossing ends. Every day he was surrounded by the same iron machinery that ground down his father's life. Black from piston grease, the mills screamed and smoked against the wood, fleshing lumber from forest. Penticton's first wood buildings were on skids so that a team of horses could be hitched and drag them to a new location, to suit the needs of the community.

When he thought of that meeting again, RH was as amused as ever by his woodsmen. What foolish tenacity. What did they hope to achieve by staying here? RH prided himself on his successes. Despite his many shortcomings and luckless, dismal childhood, the usual stack of debts from early business ventures, he'd found a place to prosper here in Vancouver. Therefore he loathed to see men with familiar sensitivities become such obvious failures. But, if these woodsmen were stubborn enough to sell him black-market lumber off land he'd sold his claim to, without any way for the CPR to know where the forest all went, then so be it. What RH planned to do with this lumber was sell the logs, bark and all, straight to the Chinese Emperor, who wanted to build a great fortress, and who paid RH monthly with large sums of cash and chartered a specific boat for the distinguished purpose. RH had to say that it was a successful arrangement on both sides. Savouring that fine reverie, daydream, recollection, call it what you will, he returned his misty eyes to the newspaper in his lap:

MRS. RED'S SOOTHING SYRUP - WILL ALLAY ALL PAIN AND SPASMODIC ACTION; SURE TO REGULATE THE BOWELS; DEPEND ON IT,

MOTHERS! IT WILL GIVE REST TO YOURSELVES AND RELIEF AND HEALTH TO YOUR INFANTS. SOLD BY ALL CHEMISTS, AT 1/2D PER BOTTLE.

RH was old enough to know Canadian men who'd fought alongside the British and Hindoos against China in the Opium War of 1839. He paid gratitude to their sacrifice every day. In fact, in the reverie of his gratitude, he forgot the newspaper in front of his eyes. He was no more paying attention to it than he was to the voice in the back of his head. He lowered the newsprint in a bird's flutter to his lap, where it folded down to rest.

He heard the sound of feet softly treading, the lash of silk, and then, as if a hallucination or spell of déjà vu, there was the lady herself. He saw a puff of white hair. She was in an evening gown that concealed her round figure like the cover over a stagecoach, and the whiteness of her skin and the light amber of her teeth confused her husband's vision for a moment. As he rose to greet her he realized he was still in his chair, the paper still on his lap, the same ray of light still passing through the room.

Darling, she said. I'm talking to you.

To me, he said.

Yes, darling. Where have our *clothes* all gone, eh?

All our clothes. I'm sure they're perfectly safe.

Safe. Safe has nothing to do with it. Where are they?

... I had a boy take them to Chinatown.

Boy. What, when? When did you do this? Darling, I asked you a question. Darling?

Yes, he said.

What's the matter? I said to you, I said, look at me when I—, darling, I said, when did you have our laundry taken to Chinatown?

It must have been this morning.

Outrageous. What inspired this? When have you ever taken an interest in our *lau*ndry?

Didn't seem clean.

Yes, our laundry—

What I saw on the clothes looked as if it should be taken to be laundered.

Yes, well—, but darling. We have a *day* when laundry is taken. There's a day in the week we reserve for this chore. The men down at the laundry have many customers.

It couldn't wait.

What's this? she said. Darling ...

Hm?

Please pass me the tin on the sidetable next to you, dear. Thank you.

LONG-LIFE MUD, said the tin. There was a smudge of black in one corner. She swung her hands before him with the tin in her palms, the lid wide open under his nose. This is my—did you—this is *my* reserve, she said.

Yes, I apologized already.

No, you didn't.

I remember I apologized many times.

She sat down on the piano chair and leaned in to him. You're in no more pain than I am, she said. Have I ever taken from your reserve?

No, he said.

We're not in pain at all, she said and pet his long moustache. I wouldn't blink an eye if I thought you *were*.

No, yes, he said.

Darling, did you *just* take this?

I did ... ago, he said.

This morning then—, she said.

Hm, he said. I should a taken it right in the morning, but.

And you're out?

Yes, obviously I am, RH said, lying. He'd hidden his final stash of laudanum that Dr. Langis gave him this morning, his last reserve unless he found new means.

What will we do? Did you speak with Langis?

Hm.

What did he—

Said it was very expensive. Short supply as it is, men come in who need it more than we—

Yes, the injured.

Yes, he snapped, yes, the *in*jured. A lot a them *my* men.

Well, she kissed him once on the cheek. This can't end here, she said, and dabbed her finger in the gummy crud in the corners of the tin to get any extra that she could into her mouth. It can't end here, she said.

//

RED & ROSY'S GENERAL STORE IS OPEN FOR BUSINESS AGAIN SINCE GREAT FIRE. In the months after the Fire, Vancouver subsisted almost entirely on the generosity of Women's Temperance Leagues in New Westminster, Victoria, and Nanaimo for the necessities of life, food, water, clothes, and carpenters. Only recently were the stores beginning to reopen.

It was September, and Molly, a young bride with plenty of energy, ideas, and necessities, had already begun to show signs of impatience. She wanted to go in to town and visit the stores. Sammy made her promise to be careful, and she said she would, so there was no other choice but to let her go. After all, it was only Red & Rosy's, what trouble could she come across there? Sammy preferred to stay at home. The incapacitant was not prepared for an outing. He preferred to focus on his work for the mill.

There was no accounting for the surds of love, thought Sammy Erwagen. How could any man tally a woman? There was no counting—if she wanted, a woman might have a dozen fingers on each hand, and all of them proactively nimble. And if he wanted, a man might have the presence of two minds when the time comes to love.

But the moment she left, a sudden wave of horror hit him, in which the stony surface of his thoughts fell away to reveal the raw, terrible murk below. The day of the accident appeared before his eyes as though it was happening all over again. En route through Alberta again, train-travelling through fields of wheat, eager to see their new home, darting off in the afternoon for lovemaking sessions in their private cabin. Yes, lovemaking. And with boundless joy in each other's limbs, in the smell and taste of each other. In the explosions of each other. This newly married couple, primal numbers ajar of each other, on a train for two more days before they'd arrive in Vancouver. What a luxury to spend so long locomotively, pushing into the future. Yes, thought Sammy, a train was indeed a love machine.

Later, while she sponged, he sat in the half-full restaurant cabin milking a cup of tea, watched scenery squiggle by at the pace of a rabbit run, and behaved as best he could like a gentleman who wasn't elated. He stirred the teabag around in his single-serving pot.

Less than two days to go before Vancouver. He was too impatient to stay in his seat. He passed from car to car until he was back with his wife: I'm madly in love with you, he reiterated.

And here we are on a train, she responded curiously.

Yes, he said, here we are on a train.

Another quaint pause. A kiss. They glanced out the window of their berth and marvelled together at late-afternoon Alberta. The mountains painted pink. Molly and Sammy looked at this light and these Albertan fields spread under it and refell in love. He kissed her on the forehead and then twice on her neck. That feels like warm ice, she said, and you smell so wonderful. Keep doing that, she said. He kissed her twice more on her neck and once on her cheek.

Sammy said: I really would like to meet the conductor. I'm so curious as to what kind of man he is.

Well, why don't we? she said.

And yes, he thought, why don't we? It was as easy as that.

The engine car was a steel belly full of nocks and plugs and pegs and pedals the conductor occasionally luxated or uncorked or tightened. The conductor was grease-stained, thick-skinned, and wiry, and his eyes were as white as chalk.

Sometimes I do imagine I'm inside some kind a big ugly demon, said the conductor. I like to think aboot myself as a tiny angel cleaning the grit from inside a devil, sticking my fingers in his tubes, eh. But my job's never done. The devil keeps on making grit.

What eloquence, Sammy said, nodding to his wife.

She scolded him in coded gestures for his condescension.

I got a lot a time to read, said the conductor.

Is that so? Molly asked. What do you read?

What? said the conductor, wincing over the engine's screams and hisses as the train rounded a corner. Oh, well, *screed* mostly, he said in answer to her question.

Hm, said Molly.

You know, I can stop the train any time I want, he said. I'm ahead a schedule. They made them times up back when nobody knowed how to ride the Rockies.

Look how close the trees come to the rails, said Sammy.

Heck, he said. See how close the trees come? You want to ride the cowcatcher? *Then* you'll see how close they darn well do. Don't worry, it's safe. It's a big enough apron there for you to stand on. The Queen a England rode on it, why shouldn't you? It won't fit two, actually, safely I mean, but you could ride it one at a time.

How delightful, said Molly.

Steady now, said the conductor as he manoeuvred the train to a halt.

When Molly was seated properly atop the cowcatcher the train urged forward again with her there in front as its beacon. Molly, the sharp point of this megaton conveyance.

Wee, she cried.

Inside the engine, the conductor faced Sammy with one eye raised irretrievably, and said: Your wife?

Yes? said Sammy.

Finest lady I seen.

Sammy paused to think. He scratched his Adam's apple (oh, to have itches again). Another pause. Separated by blinks. Is that right? Sammy finally decided was the thing to say.

A magnificent woman.

I'll make sure to tell her you said so.

No, no, said the conductor. You mustn't. A lady goes too vain when she hears a man's compliments. Keep it a secret between yourself and I.

Indeed I will then.

Two miles on it was Sammy's turn. Oh, Sammy, she said as she hopped off the cowcatcher and pet flat her hairstyle, now dishevelled from the wind, it's the most wonderful feeling ever. They embraced on the gravel embankment overlooking the Rockies. I'm so excited for you to try it.

I am too, he said.

Take off your hat, she said, and lifted his bowler from his head. The wind might blow it away.

He leaned in for a kiss and whispered: Mind the conductor, will you? He seems to have a bit a interest in you.

She grinned: Ah-ha, a gentleman admirer?

Indeed, he said, smiling. But maybe do that collar button up.

She rolled her eyes, pecked him on the chin, and danced away back to the conductor, leaving him there on the cowcatcher.

Sammy was more uneasy with the situation than he preferred to admit. But as the engine hissed to a start and the train rolled forward with the ground only inches from Sammy's shoes, every other thought simply left his mind. He forgot all about the conductor. The silly thrill of riding like this swept away his concerns. Watching the ground scroll along below his feet and vanish ever faster under the train behind him. He held fast to the bars in a fairly cowardly grip, but who would criticize him for that? The train jostled onward in its wiggle of segments. Sammy's feet were wedged between the iron bars extending up behind his back. He was excited by the approach of a turn in the rails, shrouded by an arboreal hood of deciduous leaves almost dark green enough to feel blue. Beyond the graceful bend, the trees on either side of the tracks gave way to immense hacked walls of granite.

Are you having fun oot there? he heard his wife say.

It's fantastic, he replied. It's so fantastic.

Quartz and black crisps of mica tinselled in his eyes as the sun beamed against the rockface. How pretty were the ingredients of a mountain, he thought, the likes of which we never really knew before dynamite. These profound beginnings of earth were now available to the naked eye after so many eons of silence and invisibility and more silence. If he could lean out and touch the rock he'd be touching time itself, the igneous shadow of God.

You want to get off? called out the conductor.

Oh, cried out Sammy, I want to go through the tunnel up ahead. Can I go through the tunnel?

I suppose you can, said the conductor. After that then, I'll stop the train.

This will really be something, he told himself, thrilled by the oncoming blackness of the tunnel. Holy smoke, he said.

The mountain the train was about to slip through extended beyond view, its peak somewhere high and inside clouds. The many slopes were all thick with trees. It was a mountain made of other mountains. He wished he saw however briefly the movement of wildlife, but couldn't.

He was an inch off the ground with vertigo. He swooned. The soles of his feet tingled fiercely.

He was being pushed by the powerful force of the locomotive through a door into darkness.

The wind scooped across his face. The lamp atop the engine car shone against the rockwall and along the silvered lips of the track in front of him. He would go around the dark bend. The exit was only suggested by blueless sunlight on the wall around a curve.

He was really in love, finally, and for the rest of his life.

Arms outraised, like a winged man, he cried out for his love, Molly: I love you, I love you, I love you.

And she returned the call with one of her own. You fool, she said. I love you, too.

He lost his balance. With frantic agility he avoided plunging straight forward onto the tracks where the train would have instantly crushed him. Instead he reeled sideways and managed to bounce off the cowcatcher and into the narrow gutter between the train and the wall. The floor was all rock, big and small, sharp and blunt—dynamite debris.

He came to in the arms of his wife, looking up at her wet face. The train was well on its way again. Sammy had lost six hours unconscious; the conductor had lost one and a half to the emergency, and was behind schedule now and furious at himself.

He was completely paralyzed below the neck. Not only paralyzed, he'd lost all feeling. The flesh below his chin was nothing more than a sack his head was tied to. For many hours he lay there under the close supervision of his wife, who, despite her youth, remained calm and optimistic. He tried to make the most out of his last hours on earth. If he couldn't move, if not even a muscle would respond, then at least he would taste what he could, listen with all his strength, and try not to weep. One can't waste one's last precious hours blinded by tears. He looked out the window at whatever useless acre of nature the train passed through, and honestly figured he might as well die now. Why wait. What was that that passed by the window? He was still jarred whenever he thought to raise an arm or bend a knee, to get up or change his view, and nothing happened, nothing moved. He thought he was fated to die in Alberta.

Among the cabin and crew and the good Christian travellers aboard the train, everyone prayed anxiously for Sammy to recover. They sat on their stained maple benches, wobbling in unison as the country rolled under them on the tracks hammered in by Chinamen, praying into their hats for the speedy recovery of their dear crippled son, *poor* thing.

//

FURRY & DAGGETT'S LOGGING CONCERN REQUIRES ABLE MEN; BUCKERS, SWAMPERS, AXEMEN ~ $1 P/D ...

Daggett read his own sign, tore it off the maple tree, and chucked it aside. Positions filled. Now that Litz and Pisk were gone, Furry & Daggett remained the only major company of lumberjacks in town. Together they might employ fifty men at a stretch. All year round they employed four of the strongest men in the area. These folks were probably drinking, and that's where Furry & Daggett wanted to be.

Furry stood on the shaded street corner in the same clothes he'd stood in for the last five months. His dungarees were tattered and personally patched and mended to a point where perhaps nothing of the original denims remained. Same went for his shirts and plaid jacket. He stank like spoiled meat. He was dirty, covered in biting lice, and tired. Every muscle was stiff and nothing but drinking and whoring was going to ease his temper. And that was a goddamn fucking fact. He stared down passersby while Daggett leaned against the alley wall and pissed into a greasy crumple of yesterday's *Daily Advertiser* used a second time as sausage wrap and discarded, where it now dissolved under the moonshine pressure of Daggett's noon-time stream. He raised his head to the sky for the inspiration to clinch another jetting sprinkle on the news.

Furry saw a sooty rat scale the clapboard building and engage in battle with a stubborn crow on the precipice.

Are you done yet? he said. He tugged down the sleeve of his monkeyjacket and brought his wrist to his mouth to bite off some sinewy stitching unravelled at the cuff. Yikes. He caught a whiff of his own armpit. He'd bathe soon enough or he'd see no mink tonight. He wasn't the kind of man, and neither was Daggett, who got mink if he wasn't clean as a pony. They had a long ways to go. They were dressed in work clothes and two seasons' worth of dirt.

I said are you fucking done yet?

Keep your fucking panties on, Jesus fucking—I'm pissing here …

When a Chinaman coming from Carrall Street with a cart of vegetables passed the intersection, Furry gave him a look that turned him right around, trying to look natural doing so. And Furry, in his twelve-inch brimmed felt hat, leaned down, chose a cobble, and threw it down the street a hundred yards and hit the Chinaman upside the head. Shocked, the Chinaman touched his face, then pulled the carriage quickly out of sight before Furry had a chance to throw the second rock he'd fisted.

They dingled open the doors of Red & Rosy's General Store and brought their dirt and stink and thudding boots inside, looking around, pawing things, asking each other what the fuck is that, and will you take a fucking look at this, handling the wares like they were testing everything for durability.

The other customers all said quick goodbyes to the man behind the counter, nodded deferentially to Furry & Daggett, and tripped out the door to safety. All the customers escaped save one. Molly Erwagen lingered at the back of the store, examining garden shears and cans of lard and the price of different compasses. Her hair was up inside a large bonnet, and her neck—equestrian in its supple form—was there for all to see. She stepped lightly here to there without quite paying attention to Furry and Daggett, who did *not* pay her the same respect. Daggett whistled for six counts, rocking his head. Furry just lost his hearing from seeing so much.

Oo-wee, said Daggett, I sure'd like to see—

What can I do you for? said the salesman. He walked along his side of the counter to meet the men near the front of the store. He'd been standing at the back near Molly and his face was flushed pink. He walked with a pronounced limp, a controlled, sluggish lope. He flattened his white apron with his hands and addressed them politely as sirs, inquiring again if they needed any help.

Daggett leaned over and barked into the salesman's ear: How much is that?

The salesman didn't answer immediately.

We're gyppo loggers, said Furry, touching the brim of his hat. This is my partner Mr. Daggett and my name's Furry.

They shook strong hands with the clerk.

I heard your names before, the clerk said, pinching his moustache, drawing their attention to the mangled state of his ear and the evil scar on his cheekbone.

That right? said Daggett, unintimidated. Price a doing business, eh. Every bohunk's got a story to tell and not one a them you can trust. You're Rosy's new employ.

I am, said the clerk. Name's Stan, his brother.

Good to meet you, Rosy, said Daggett. Listen, what's it worth you to tell me if you seen those handloggers Pisk and Litz pass through your doors?

Rosy shrugged. Nothing. I seen nobody called that.

Furry picked up the handle to a big iron roller. What's this thing? he asked.

That's for your lawn.

My lawn.

You press your sod flat with it.

You do, huh? Well, that's not what we're here for.

No, sir; I dare say I can tell you aren't.

Need to outfit thirty men, said Furry. Clothes all the way on up. The works, cookstove, camp cots, you name it. Dishes, matches. Everything you can think a, we need it.

Okay, Rosy said and clapped his hands together. Still in that position of prayer, he turned to Molly for a moment and asked her if she needed anything or if he should go ahead and help these gentlemen. As she turned to face them, opening her mouth to answer, Furry and Daggett saw her face for the first time, and without warning both their bellies started to growl. And with their teeth showing, they tipped their hats to her. She agreed that the clerk should go ahead and help the men while she browsed. She was in no hurry, after all; it was such a fine day for an outing.

Okay, all righty, said Rosy. Let's look-see what we got.

Rosy walked them through the store. There were cans of beans shelved all the way to the ceiling, iron shovels in all sizes hanging off coat racks, and bullets of all casings; they bought in bulk. They bought new hogskin gloves and denim trousers with copper riveting. Ten pounds of chewing tobacco. They bought fifty pounds of bacon in oilcloth sacks, another three sacks of flour waist-high, and cans of cream, syrup, and salt. Enough butter to last a season. Excited by the biggest sale since reopening after the Fire, Stan Rosy set out to prove his crockery was sturdy enough to be thrown on the floor and not break. Molly was in the midst of replacing a compass on its glass pedestal when the dish landed; she never even startled. They took Rosy's advice when it came to jackscrews and ratchet screws, and he convinced them to buy an extra spool of iron chain. When he showed them the saws and axes, Daggett said to Rosy: You're going to bust the bank.

Oh, but look at these sweethearts. Rosy petted the sleek face of an axeblade. It gleamed with silver veins. It was easy to convince them to upgrade the whole kit. They debated different swamper's axes and chose an eight-foot double-handed saw that looked like a killer whale's jaw.

Feel the heft, eh, said Rosy, giving them each a new pinewood long-handled axe to caress and admire. The perfect silken finish made the wood glow like skin. The handle curved like a slender body in repose. The blade was made of the strongest Gallic metal. At five feet long, only a man of Furry or Daggett's height could wield such a blade. They bought two each and received free of charge the companion handaxes. Slip her right in your belt loop, Rosy said.

They came again to the kitchen supplies and Molly tipped her head down demurely, eyes like candles burning below the shadow of her hatbrim as she flitted by.

She's a beauty, said Rosy, buffing the white enamel door of the Acorn cast-iron cookstove. Wood burning, he said.

Yeah, said Daggett, giving the stove a once-over. He opened the enamelled door of the oven and waved his hand around inside. We'll take a couple a these.

Furry turned over a pair of thick leather logging boots and studied the frizz of spikes all over the sole.

Those're guaranteed, said Rosy.

How much for all this? said Furry.

Including the cost to ship the goods to your plot a land, Rosy said, your at a grand total a sixty and five.

Sixty and five, Daggett said. No, no, sixty and five, Rosy, that's too high, it's never more than fifty when we buy.

Well you got the chains for your logs and the two cookstoves ..., Rosy said unperturbed.

Are we fucking bartering here or no? Daggett said, and stuck out his jaw. His eyes hesitated, and then he looked at

Molly to see what kind of impression his foul language had made on her smooth innocent body. Seemed to be none. Relaxing again, he looked back to Rosy. Are we … or what? he said. I don't see it's very busy in here, Rosy. You should be thankful for our business. You don't sell many a them cookstoves, I bet.

We sell enough.

'The fuck you think you are? said Daggett, losing his temper completely. This time Rosy tipped away from the counter and stood upright, out of range of their threats and fists. He looked over at Molly with an apologetic smile.

I'm sorry, ma'am, I'll only be a minute longer.

She nodded her sweet head. They saw her tongue's tip when she said: That's fine. She walked towards the men and they all watched her as she did, no one saying a word, not even Daggett, who could always be relied on to insult a lady. She put her elbows on the counter and stretched out her gloved hands and proceeded to wait for Furry and Daggett to finish up right there beside her at the counter.

//

Walking out the doors of Red & Rosy's General Store, Daggett beat his fist against the rail and said: What a mink. That Rosy made us pay sixty and one for that.

What could we do? Wouldn't budge.

We should wait here for that lady to get, then go back in there and straighten the nose on that bohunk.

If she weren't there, said Furry, I'd a meted out some punishment on that gimp. Making us pay that much.

Was she a beau*ty*, said Daggett.

Hotter than a mouthful a moonshine.

What a set a *totooshes*.

Oh my god, her totooshes, said Furry, making lewd gestures. Mmm, her *totooshes*.

I'd go blind overnight just from thinking a her, Daggett said.

One look at her ee-na and I'm good for a season chopping trees, said Furry.

They pushed their hats down against the sun and walked a few paces, still cursing at Rosy for greasing them. Back in the street they appreciated the sunlight for how it shone on their new long-handled axes. For having it cost them nearly full price to suit up the fall season, the two loggers felt a little sick and light-headed. These axes would fell a lot of trees, and hard, or Rosy was going to hear about it. They wondered aloud whether or not to spend the night at Wood's or save some chickamin and stay at a Methodist rooming house.

There were other men on the street asking themselves the same question. There were many men like them in need of a good shave. Men in dire need of a steady job. The coolies were taking over. The navvies seemed more frustrated now than they were last winter. The sailors were all drunker than they were this same time last year. As they walked along the street, they approached a young man with a face shaved to its pink cheeks and a wet chin who stepped on and off the logs and swerved past them, twirling on one foot, and said: Damn, I be too drunk.

Where'd you get? Daggett asked the drunkard.

He spun around and pointed a finger at the sky and said: Sunnyside Hotel.

That's aboot right, Daggett said to his partner. Let's hit her.

Yeah, said Furry, any more a that burial grounds moonshine I'm liable a going berzerk. I'm higher'n a motherfucker.

A gaunt old miner with a shirt open to his bare ribcage lugged a canvas sack over his shoulder. Jammed full of a wrinkled old suit, shaving gear and toolkit, and all his other belongings in the entire world, he was being turned away from the better hotels and was resigned, like most poor folk, to share a Methodist's room with four other men. Just so long as he could get off these corns.

It was sunny out. In a pallid, omnipresent way, the September sun shone on the muddy streets and the clapboard buildings. When Daggett and Furry got within a couple blocks of the Sunnyside Hotel & Saloon, they confronted a sight. They stopped to watch a taut, slow-speaking Chinaman at the corner, a swaggering young man in leather, silk, and gold. Hands on his hips, he was shouting commands at an organized mob of two dozen starved coolies who waited at a corner for some work to do.

Boys more like, the coolies were all as soft as babybottoms. Daggett could tell by their soft faces that these were not men, they were shrimps afraid to be seafood. Nevertheless, hard labour was their fate, and Daggett understood well enough from experience how much a man can adapt when he must. By the same token, he knew, at least instinctually, how stubbornly a person can be in sticking to his beliefs, no matter where he went in the world. And at the first opportunity, a man will remake his surroundings to his liking. When Daggett compared Chinatown to the rest of Vancouver he didn't like what he saw. So if anyone was going to assimilate it was the Chinamen, because no way was Daggett let alone Furry going to assimilate in their direction.

The snakehead aimed to rent these farmers' sons from Sze-Yap cut-rate. What Daggett wanted to know was how this young snakehead could afford such a glistening pair of leather Shanghai boots. Silk Western bowtie. Gold-handled opium pin dangling from his neck on a silver chain.

What kind a clothes do we wear, Furry? Do we deport ourselves wrongly?

Even the brand-new duds we bought at Red & Rosy's don't compare, said Furry, obviously brooding on much the same thoughts. He leaned against a strut under the boardwalk with his hands in his pockets. He wore his new handaxe looped on his belt, with the eight-foot long-handled falling axe resting next to him. Daggett stood beside him, expectorated in one direction and then another, sleeved off any spittle trapped in his beard, and began punking stones out of the hardpacked dirt road. He too wore his new handaxe in a belt loop. He yawned for something to do. Furry yawned as well, stretched his arms, and cursed to make a noise.

Fuck is right, said Daggett. Fuck is right.

Who are all these coolies? said Furry.

Fucked if I know.

When the snakehead stepped across the street towards them in his Shanghai boots, Daggett flicked his partner a look and then his trap opened: 'The fuck you think you're doing?

The Chinaman broke pace, remonstrated a pearl button on his jacket, and otherwise unfazed by the provocation (he didn't know English, just a little Chinook), continued towards them with a smile, almost a laughing smile, open enough to see down his throat to its pasty back wall. His mouth was a tunnel railroaded with silver fillings.

They started to conversate. Daggett rose to his true height, six foot and nine. Furry, shoulders outstretched, was six foot and two. The Chinaman was five and a bit. In a laxatived voice, smooth and unexpectedly fast, the Chinaman spoke a long list of ill-memorized syllables. He expected them to understand Chinook. They did understand Chinook. The problem was he hardly knew what he was saying and didn't know a word to hear it.

'The hell are you on aboot? said Daggett.

Velly tenas chickamin, said the Chinaman smiling as gingerly as his teeth allowed. One dallah, he said, then pointed to the Chinamen across the street, klone mans. Ikt chickamin, klone mans.

We ain't interested, Daggett said.

Ikt chickamin? Velly good deal. Klone mans, ikt chickamin.

I said, no. Daggett felt the little snakehead was not taking his anger seriously enough, and this got him even madder. When he said: Not interested, this meant nothing to the Chinaman, who stood his ground and implored them with hook-fingered motions to look over his employables across the street.

Klone mans …

What? said Daggett.

Ikt chickamin.

Yeah, yeah, he said. I heard you the first time you—.

Furry raised himself off the wood beam where he'd been leaning and swung a hand to grab the handle of his axe, lifted it off the ground in a cutting pendulous upswing, let it fly, and caught it in his fist right below the axeblade. He put an arm around the Chinaman and said: Why don't we go somewhere more private if we're gonna talk business? All right with you?

Daggett made a motion with his hand near his mouth, and the Chinaman seemed to understand that they were taking him where they'd talk privately over a drink. What they did instead was take him down past the shacks to a spot just up from the ocean and tie him upright to a tree.

The Chinaman didn't understand what was happening until the rope started to come out, and by then Daggett had him in his grip. He shook his head no, begging like that.

Me and Daggett, said Furry, swinging the axe, we're on another level. No one's coming around here. Me and Daggett, we're on a level old-timers show respect. Old-timers ask permission to talk to us. Follow me? We walk the streets, Chinaman, people don't look us in the eyes. Who sent you? San Francisco?

The Chinaman nodded yes, slobbered his words.

Even when you don't see me smile, Furry said, in fact I am smiling. He took out a handkerchief from his shirt pocket and wiped the tearstreams and mucus off the Chinaman's face, then stuffed the kerchief deep into the man's mouth.

And believe me, eh, said Furry, I took some bohunks off the shelf. God forgive me, I got a graveyard under my belt. You don't know what I been through to get to where I'm at.

Furry axed off the leg and the Chinaman tried to scream through the handkerchief when he saw his leg and boot fall to the ground, tip over. The blood immediately started to gush from the wound just above the knee. Then he fainted. They untied him and he fell to the ground beside his boot, and just laid there shaking, bleeding like a motherfucker.

Furry tugged the kerchief out of the snakehead's mouth and used it to wipe the blood from his axeblade.

The newsmen wrote: CHINAMAN MURDER! MYSTERY BOOT FOUND; FOOT, LEG INSIDE; CULPRITS UNKNOWN; CHINATOWN UNDER CLOSER SURVEILLANCE SAYS CONST. MILLER.

The police took charge of the damning evidence, a Shanghai boot found in broad daylight on a rocky north-facing beach with a leg still inside it, bleeding from the perfectly clean cut below the kneecap. Constable Miller hung the boot by its buckles to the branch of a maple tree outside the mews, having first rid it of the amputated limb (incinerated). They knew who killed the Chinaman. Everyone did. Even Ed Shermang who laid the type and inked the rollers and distributed the news knew the real story. This wasn't a message to a murderer on the loose. That boot hanging there was a message to all snakeheads.

//

A murder never stopped the bars from opening at ten A.M., when there'd be men waiting on the step already. By around eleven, the bar at the Sunnyside Hotel had fifteen or twenty men lined up at the counter and every round came with a song and a dance and everyone had facial hair. They'd drink all day, pacing out their chickamin to last until bed, perhaps ordering a pot pie if the stomach started to act up, but otherwise just drinking. By mid-afternoon the Sunnyside was packed and would stay packed until closing time. One thing the bartender liked to say was that the Sunnyside never left a man wanting more. More booze, more fights, more women, more hash, more opium. There were plenty of bootleggers to compete with. Plenty of bootleggers and some of the ripest soil for potatoes. The potato moonshine that was going around these days, it was liable to burn the backs off your eyes, right in that place where the cords connected to the sphere. There was no other place like Vancouver anywhere in the world. It was slop, and here a man was swine. Times when you found a pile of them, three or four bohunks passed out in an alley, so drunk on bootleg they looked stone dead.

In between the rains, Vancouver cherished a sunny day among the quickly tapering afternoons. A murder did not stop the trout from idling in the creek. The creek wended its way unperturbed by man's violent soul, meandering through the handsomely primitive garden behind the Erwagen house. When the Erwagens had moved in they didn't touch a thing on the property, just put in some fenceposts and looked at its wildness with great, frightened admiration. Sammy was terribly fond of wildness. The creek jagged through their yard, flowing around the cedar shake fenceposts, solid beams shaved to a point at the top and covered in a soft algae at the bottom, where the fish pushed one another through this gateway to the sweet untouched pond beneath the boughs of a pine where insects hatched year-round. He liked it, like the writhing chaos of it.

Hidden in the reflection of the small hemlocks and fruit trees that marked the way to and from the pond, the trout gathered to eat, safely out of reach from bear claws, wolf jaws, and pollution from sawmills, fish canneries, smelting operations that dumped into nearby streams like this one or from the thousands of smokestacks and woodstoves that gave the air over Vancouver a sometimes greasy aftertaste like a burnt egg stuck in the back of your throat.

The Erwagens' verandah was partially covered against the western sun, sturdily built by local men shortly after their arrival in June on the day of the Fire. A simple, split-level A-frame is all the Erwagens asked for. On two floors were three main bedrooms including the master, one for their ward Toronto, another for guests or, perhaps, under other circumstances, a child. A den, study, and living room, as well as kitchen and servants' quarters—smaller rooms to the east, facing the garden—and that was all. Clapboard walls covered in shiplap and papered over in a subdued blue with a gold filigreed pattern of blushing crystalloids. They hung a landscape painting on one wall.

What are you reading? she asked her husband with a sigh.

A dictionary a Chinook Jargon, said Sammy, turning his eyes from the pamphlet propped in front of his face on a music stand. And, like music sheets, Sammy's ward Toronto assisted his reading by turning the pages at his cue.

Chinooky, it's our language, Molly exclaimed. Tell me more aboot Chinook. How does one say *come hither*?

Hm, well, *mamook chahko.*

Mamook chahko.

Don't tease, Chinooky. But I might also, in keeping with the tone a the conversation, compliment your gorgeous *totoosh.*

What, my … she raised her hips.

No, my dear, I'm afraid the closest I can find for that is *ee-na.* I want ee-na. Ha ha. I shall have to write the author a thank you for his fine work in compiling this educational pamphlet. It seems he's also using it to publicize his business as an importer and repairer a firearms. Clever man indeed. Shall I purchase a firearm, dear?

Oh, Sammy, she said, turning onto her back and kicking her legs in the air above her head. I'm more bored than ever. Let's go tip our hats for no decent reason at all. Decency be damned. Let's drink.

He considered the idea and said: I could wet my lips.

Would you? said Molly, sitting up and beaming at him.

Yes, it's been months now. Aboot time, he said and shrugged with his mouth, his eyes, nothing else.

You're ready to go out?

I might as well admit I'm alive. I expected to be dead by now.

We'll go then. I'm sure we'll have a splendid time.

How could we not on such a splendid autumn day?

I do feel impatient today, she said and flapped her hands, I don't know why. Let's go right now.

She pulled at the lap of her dress and made static. Otherwise the house was silent. The sun shone straight in the window and captured the smallest motes of dust as they followed the current of air. A half hour later they were ready. She opened the door and with Toronto's help wheeled her husband out into the solitude of the day. Even on good days, Sammy was willing to admit at least to himself that he felt imprisoned in the worst way imaginable.

THREE

> There is nothing like a feud to make life seem full and interesting.
>
> – ERIC HOFFER

Count the faces. Impossible for Sammy to tell apart the faces on all these bachelors, all these transient dirtbags, homeless peons, and outcast poltroons. Anyone who was anyone in logging was in the bar that day.

Along the far wall of the saloon, two filthy sconces burned their wicks' end while another sconce was blackened and unlit. The funnel shapes of soot on the wall marked a thousand cheap paraffin candles burned in their scalloped glass. The Sunnyside had survived the Great Fire with that one wall intact. Instead of tearing it down, it stood as a gross, charred memento for the disrepair the place was in before that fateful day in June. In rebuilding the Sunnyside attention had been paid to such modern details as finely crafted mouldings, a varnished mahogany bartop, exotic floral ribbons on the banister knobs, even a player piano. The place had an air of quality and propriety far and above the general countenance of its daily visitors, who were halfwits, in no better shape than the old wall.

No one in the room had ever seen a paraplegic before 1886. A cripple was a mythic creature, an ember in the fire of God's eye sent to Earth to inspire religious worry. Raving cripple, Jesus was not far from the raving cripple. A man with an unclean spirit who had his dwelling among the tombs, as St. Mark would have it. Gives a healthy man shivers down his back. Sammy was evidence that *He'd* discovered his wayward men, His West Coast flock, whispering: Beware the eye a the Almighty, eh.

Making things worse, also among the Sunnyside's clientele were two other worrisome men, Furry and Daggett, wearing the same clothes as on the day they killed the Chinaman, and every day since.

Serving drinks was the big Negro Joe Fortes. He tapped two drafts for Molly. She paid him with two bits and sought a table for herself and her husband where they could drink and stare at each other without talking or needing to talk.

Deal, said a man with his hands flat on a table to a man shuffling and reshuffling a deck of cards.

Tell you what, said one, a young drunk cowboy bachelor with a dirty wool mitt for a face, a cowboy straight from Alberta with the name RD Pitt. I'm sick a seeing them Celestials on my streets. Don't even need no explanation. Look aroond. They're ever-where like fleas, you know, sucking, sucking the blood out a me. Asiatic spectacle. If I see pigtails today …

His buddy laughed and nodded, looking into his beer for the words he'd lost.

I'll take those pigtails and twist them around.

Furry and Daggett sat in the corner where they always sat, looking brutal.

One thing I like since that damn Fire, said Daggett, is that I don't have to put up with looking across the Sunnyside at them ugly faces, Litz and Pisk.

I'll toast to that, said Furry. Furry rarely needed to say much more. His partner did the talking. Furry simply stood his ground, immutable minotaur at the centre of this forest labyrinth.

Furry & Daggett's Logging Concern toasted along with their bosses. Meier, Boyd, Smith, and Campbell, heavy drinkers, each a stumbling god, each with a unique beard and hairstyle.

Near the entrance, a logger named Moe Dee was being interviewed by a green boss over tall shots of whisky, and Dee finally came out and said: You want to drive that schooner, well, that's your business, mister. You couldn't pay me enough to take that wasp's nest on open waters. I knowed that boat before you did. I knowed the owner who had it way before you. I worked for him, eh? This is way before you even went and bought it. Back *then* it was a no good boat. Thing is made a spit, man. Are you crazy? Forget it. Your mistake, not mine.

The wee boss fell silent. He tapped his fingers on the table. It's a generous contract, Dee, he said.

Generous like shit. Should a spent your chickamin on a better boat. Nice to meet you.

Hey, now, what the?—aargh …

I got better business requiring my attention. Moe Dee bottomed up, rubbed his chin, took to his feet, stomach out, prattling to himself with gastronomic satisfaction, directing himself through the tablesful of muddy faces on his way to the commode. The door bounced on its hinges when he shut it, and though he wasn't drunk he rested his left arm on the facing wall as he stared down the hole in the floor to the sloshing waves below while his arcing piss-stream flew off unevenly in the wind, reaching the ocean in single drops.

He spat down the hole. Straightened up and went back to the bar.

Now tell me, Mr. Erwagen, bellowed Fortes from behind the bar. Towelling off wet tureens he asked, How is Mister *Alexander?*

Why did he ask? Sammy wondered. Drawing all the attention to him. A bar full of men waited to hear his answer, say something anything from that mouth. He was dumbstruck. Sammy's face and ears burned. At full height he was six foot even, a shy and modest man, a cityman, a bookkeeper. Finally, gathering his wits, he called out to Fortes: Robust as ever.

Fortes shook his head, and, absently wiping the shining counter, said: Well, I see your boss Mister Alexander, hoo-ee, him and his wife be decked out head to toe in ee-na. That's right. Man, that's a stunny fur. We never seen fur so fine as Canada be having, not down in my islands. Put that against your skin. Canada is famous for een-a. Hats, long coats, shoe-tops. Look good on them both, I tell you. I like to get *me* some ee-na.

As would I, said Sammy amicably.

Mr. Alexander sure work *hard,* don't he?

Naturally. But then, who doesn't?

Ha ha. That's the truth. Who don't. So how in the Lord good graces he get so rich while I'm so broke-ass?

The men in the room started to repay attention to their own business now that they heard Sammy talk with a kind of banality they recognized. There were fewer and fewer sidelong glances at the spectacular oddity of the Erwagens. And guys pretty much gave up on catching a smile from the wife, or, barring that, a glimpse of her bosom. Molly was not seen to smile, and her stiff collar was fashionably high. In public she was not a smiler, yet with nothing of her skin to see but her face, a smile was a man's only chance at seeing her intimate side. Demure. Seraphic. Men spoke of her smile on their own terms inside the solitude of their hearts.

She lifted his glass of beer to just below her bottom lip and like a kiss blew the froth off, then brought the mug to Sammy's face and let him take a sip of his pale ale.

The one-armed fellow in the corner booth with four glasses of beer in front of him in various states of undress rose from his bench and courageously made his way over to where the Erwagens sat. He smoothed down his nicotine-stained beard with a hand, and smiled a gold incisor.

He offered his hat over his buttons, and said with dusty grace: Pardon me. I just thought, why, I hope I'm not bothering no*doby,* but, I wanted to—why, I'd like to introdush myself. Clough's the name. I helped build your house you're living in.

How interesting to meet you, said Molly, not serving him the back of her hand to peck, though she tilted her head down so the brim of her straw hat covered the tender blued lids of her eyes as they shut respectfully.

Oh, you're welcome, stammered Clough, looking around to see who was looking at him. Why, once you get to know me, he said, I'm always glad to lend a hand.

Molly nodded.

Sammy gave him an expression.

Anyways, said Clough, who was used to being the worst cripple in a room and stood in front of his rival as stump-still as an old bollard. Clough wavered there in growing unease, a blink or two more of puttering indecision, speechless as Sammy gaped, and then, like clouds parting, Molly opened her buoyant lips to show the glinting tip of her pink tongue and the suggestion of the hollow of her throat. She said: Clough, would you mind terribly moving to the side?

Pardon?

It's only that—, she said, and pointed to the scene behind Clough's back.

Mr. Erwagen's jaw was still dropped.

What's this? said Clough, swinging around to see two figures partly silhouetted by the papery light through the door to the saloon, boots clomping across the hardwood, a waft of old sap off their clothes, hard to tell who it was. Clough put his hand to his eyes to shade the backlight.

The first man was Pisk. Acknowledging no one and keeping his eyes below his hatbrim, he found an empty table while the other—and it was Litz—stood in the doorway and scanned the faces around the bar, friends or foes. Namely, Daggett and Furry at the far end of the bar, whose jaws ground down tight.

They got an empty table underneath the cobwebby moose head that had eightballs in its eye sockets.

After collecting his first pints from Fortes at the bar, Pisk sat down at the table with Litz, swept an indelicate litter of breadcrumbs and beer driblets off the surface with his jacket sleeve, leaned back in the canewood chair, and took a deep breath.

First to shake their hands was Moe Dee.

Well I'll be damned if a bolt a lighting didn't just strike twice in the same place, said Clough. Where the hell you boys been hiding?

Pisk called out: Fortes, let's say a round for the house.

Fortes said: Good to set eyes on you, boys.

Same here.

Clough nudged his way through the busy bar, sat down on an empty stool at a poker game one table over and, facing the two exiles, said: Tell me one good reason not to torch you both.

Pisk said: I'd keep my eyes on the future if I was you, Clough.

What's that supposed to mean?

Means, who the fuck cares what you think?

Can't believe you all even got the sand to step in here, said Daggett, rubbing his thick beard, eyeing Pisk.

Why wouldn't we? said Pisk.

Litz raised his boots onto an empty chair, decidedly unworried, a man with a basic moustache and slow, philosophizing eyes, silently twitching his muttonchops. Litz was the kind of man who liked to take up two or three chairs.

After alls you done, you shouldn't be allowed to drink in New Westminster let alone Vancouver, said Daggett.

After all *we* done? Pisk looked to his partner. We didn't do nothing.

That so?

Pisk said: Damn right it's so. You got some fucking nerve. What you been up to this summer? I seen how clumsy you two old navvies are with a slash and burn. Might a been *you*.

You burned this city down, Pisk, you. And you know it.

Come over here and say that again, you mink.

I come over there and you going to tell me different? Now Daggett smiled without pleasure, but didn't stand up yet. Nevertheless, conversation in the Sunnyside had levelled off. The argument between these rival woodsmen occupied everyone's attention. And even with no one else's talking to contend with, neither man had lowered his voice.

Daggett said: I could snap your arm in ten seconds.

How? With your halitosis? Pisk said calmly, leaning back to sit again but not yet sitting.

Ten seconds. I break your arm in ten seconds.

You can't break nobody's arm in ten seconds.

Ten seconds.

What you want me to do? said Pisk, Just stick it out and let you crack it across your whore-mother's knee?

A good round of laughter from the halfwits paying attention assured Pisk he had at least a couple of friends among the foes.

Joe Fortes leaned across the bar to demonstrate he was aware of what was escalating.

Sammy noted how far he was from the door, and how many tables now seemed to completely block any clear path to safety. It seemed undeniable that all these dirty slouching giants were moments from jumping to their feet to start a real brawl.

I'm sorry, dear, we should never have come—

She had her eyes on the men by the door. Remember those two? she asked her husband.

Who?

The ones getting all the attention, this Litz and Pisk.

Remember them from when?

We saw them fighting the day a the Fire, remember?

Oh, said Sammy.

You don't remember, do you?

No. It was quite a day.

When he looked at his wife, she seemed as delicate as a vase on the edge of a table. But he knew just how durable she was. A childhood in vaudeville and the Yiddish theatre had acquainted her with more than he cared to imagine, a mind and memory able to heal quickly after the sight of violence, a body that needed to stay limber and totally conscious in order to leap the fence or worm through a tunnel, all these frightful European burlesques, one look into her eyes and it was obvious to Sammy. Just from her unfazed reaction to the escalating hostility. She was more familiar with the signs than Sammy, who was raised on crème de menthe and saw the world through curtains and pane-glass windows. He knew nothing of how to survive. He knew only numbers. Even in her calmness, which no one but Sammy would mistake for anything but innocence, he could see that her fastidious movements, preparing her gloves, his necktie, their belongings, signalled danger, she wanted them to leave, she didn't like what she was seeing.

I'll fucking cut you down, said Daggett. I'll shiver your arm down, five pieces in ten blinks.

Enough already, said Pisk, and returned to his mug of beer, quarrel over.

Who here thinks I can break his arm in ten seconds?

Furry spoke up. Pisk, he said, arm wrestle my man Daggett here. We win, you go. We never see you again. That's the deal.

Who do you figure you are, eh? You're not my boss. I'm not giving my arm to this poltroon for nothing, said Pisk. We don't got to win back our right to live here.

Yeah, you do, said Furry.

Alls he wants to do is break it anyway.

No, said Daggett. No, okay. Let's arm wrestle.

You fat moose, I don't want to arm wrestle you. I don't even want to touch you.

From a seat along the wall beneath a framed Ontario plantation diorama, complete with hunched Negroes, a lowly chinless navvy perked up and said: A dollar on Pisk.

A fucking *do*llar on *Pisk?* roared Daggett. You call out a fucking dollar? I'm going to shove that silver so far up your rear you'll use it for a cap on your buck tooth, you rabbit-shit.

I say Pisk takes you, the navvy said.

Why do you pipe up? said Pisk. Who asked you?

Silence in a bar full of men—fifty-seven men, by Sammy's count—meant only trouble. Sweat trickled down Sammy's sideburns. It purled along the waxed maze of his ear, trickling towards the centre of his brain where it puddled and cooled. He looked at his wife. His amazed expression went unnoticed. Sammy had been trying for a while now to impart to his wife a sense of his anxiety. Watery eyes and a forced smile. But she didn't seem to notice. Finally he broke down and whispered: Dear, isn't it aboot time we be off?

She leaned over and gave him a faint peck on the cheek, whispered: Mustn't make a scene. I'm concerned if we move you … what if we interrupt them … it will break their concentration.

You prefer to stay, he said.

If you don't mind.

Live through everything only to die here, god.

Shhh, put your pity aside for the moment. Let us watch and learn.

Daggett came over to Pisk's side of the bar and sat down across from him, put his elbow on the table, his arm up. Wrestle, he said. Arm wrestle me. Do it.

Get out a my face.

Daggett faced the bar. Who's taking bets? I'll beat this mink fair and square.

You can trust me to hold the money, said a fat axeman named Bud Hoss.

I'll bet a dollar you take him, said local cowboy RD Pitt, holding his betting money in his hand. He was a plastered bachelor, a member of the Knights of Labour. Pitt liked to think of himself as their leader.

Here we go, said Daggett, waving a hand at Pitt. A good man stands among us.

Pisk spat on the floor. You got your own employee Bud Hoss holding the chickamin. I don't like that.

You can trust me, said Hoss again.

I agree to this only so long as Fortes holds our elbows on the table.

I can do that, said Fortes, slapping his towel down on the counter.

The two sat down. Daggett composed himself, rotated his head, cracked his spine, loosened the wingspan of his shoulders. He put his arm out. Pisk wedged his hand inside Daggett's.

Watch his arm, said Daggett. Watch his fucking arm. Let's have a go. He's moving his arm. I saw him move his fucking arm. And straighten your wrist. I'm not going to wrestle you like that with your wrist bent forward on mine like that. I'm not going to wrestle this asshole if he keeps moving and shifting his fucking arm.

Daggett, look, he not moving no arm, said Fortes. I got you both steady. We not even started yet, man.

All right. I'm ready. I'm fucking ready.

An' … *Go,* said Fortes.

The crowd erupted. Men at the back of the bar were standing on the tabletops, shouting. The old-timers came in close and shook their fists right in their faces, yowling advice as spittle foamed and flicked off their mouths. The pressure was on for Pisk to upend this giant, or for Daggett to smother this prodigal. Smother him like the Fire he caused. Lay him out before he can do any more damage.

Arm wrestle, said Daggett.

'The fuck you think I'm doing?

Arm wrestle. Straighten your wrist. Straighten your wrist. Fucking straighten your wrist. Don't use your body. Watch him, Fortes. Make sure he don't use his body. Watch his ass is on the seat. You see that? Did you see him stand up? Are you blind, Fortes? You can't stand up, Pisk. *Arm* wrestle, Pisk, you bohunk. Arm wrestle. Stop standing up.

I'm not standing up.

Tell him to stop standing up.

He's not standing up, said Fortes, so quit your screaming. His butt's on the chair.

Then straighten your wrists. Fucking arm wrestle. What did I say?

Daggett was straining way back, hand rattling under the pressure but holding on a little longer, the tendons in his forearm pronged out.

Arm wrestle, he screamed from his spongy red face, squirting sweat. Arm wrestle. Arm wrestle … Aw, fuck.

Daggett's knuckles were flat on the table under Pisk's grip.

Jesus Christ, well I'm not going to beat him if he keeps standing up. No one says a fucking thing. You were all looking at him.

He's got arms like a goblin, Moe Dee said, he's all fucking leverage.

Shut the fuck up, how aboot that?

Nice work, said Litz, counting their earnings.

You fucking cheats, said Daggett.

He took a swing at Pisk that Pisk ducked without effort and everyone's fury and greed boiled over, some crying out for their money and others trying to protect their losings and still others just plain excited for a brawl. Fists rolled through the air. The player piano kept going *a-rinky-dink-dink* underneath the melee.

Okay, okay, said Fortes in his voice, hoisting Daggett by the collar off Pisk. He told them: Take it out*side,* boys. Nobody fights in a establishment under my fob. I be the only one breaking some arms if you all don't get the *hell* out a here.

A chicken, for whatever reason, a single reddish chicken wobbled and pecked at the road in front of the Sunnyside Hotel where the men began to pour out the doors, boots chugging down the steps, a rusty baritone choir of questions and speculations as the men began to form a semicircle on the road, startling the chicken from the mindless concentration of its nature, clucking its way to safety beneath the boardwalk.

I said I'm not going to fight you, said Pisk at a safe distance from Daggett, his arms raised in a defiant or imploring gesture. With both men now on the street, the crowd formed a Y-shape with Daggett in the bowl of it as they waited for Pisk to come away from the rim so they could wrap around and shut the men in.

Think I'm just going to let you walk away, you fucking arsonist?

It was you and Furry who burned us all down. Don't pin this on us.

Get the preacher, said Daggett to his audience. Make the man confess. Your guys' territory. Everyone here knows we never log that area. We always been logging south past the Snauq reserve and you know it. You boys always log those soft spars north a us, burning all your dead stumps.

All your lies don't stack up to no truth.

I got friends who saw you up there with your goddamn donkey engine dragging them logs up to be burned.

Friends. Don't feed me that, said Pisk, spitting. When was the last time you kept to your area? You're a liar, a thief—.

The verbal battle raged for a few more spittled minutes.

The audience sought to shape itself moblike in the street, surrounding the fighters. The smoke haze blended indelicately with the sea air off Coal Harbour. Joe Fortes came out, threw a towel over his shoulder, leaned against a glossily painted balustrade along the boardwalk, and saw Molly wheel her husband to the edge of the walk.

Ah, I should a guessed the men here love to gamble, said Molly.

Sammy studied her face, looking for a sign of her thoughts. Her complexion, normally so silken, looked sapped, and her eyes were fixed in a tighter jaded mien as she gazed down on the street brawl. He turned his attention to the scene on the road. The men below had forgotten all about him and Molly.

Using his thumbs, Fortes untwisted his pair of old greying black suspenders hooked to the cedar buttons on his trousers, patted his moist bald head, and gave Sammy a kind of bemused but charitable eyeballing, which was, all told, a better expression than people usually mustered in his presence.

Be better you folks stay up here for safety, said Fortes. Mrs. Erwagen, he added.

Yes?

Please stand back, won't you, ma'am.

Sounds wise, Molly, said Sammy.

Molly demurred with a bow of her head to Fortes and stepped back from the rail, her eyes a rare green flash against the white banister. Her expression dropped below Fortes's sightline. In return, Fortes gave her the radiant grin he used on children, whose hearts unavoidably melted, like biscuits on the ocean, for one of his smiles. She didn't see it though, a minor disappointment to him, as if he'd extended his hand to shake hers and she hadn't responded. So to save face, he morphed the smile into a grimace, then used it on the crowd of idiots below.

He might be able to win an arm wrestle, but there's no

way he's winning this, eh, said Clough, one-arming his way through the crowd to get a better view.

Tell you what, Daggett's got the worst slowest left I ever seen, said Bud Hoss, the young fat sprout who worked for Daggett and Furry as handlogger, rigger, and driver.

Pisk is fast, he's all fast, said Moe Dee, an older, hairier, leaner man who was loyal to his pursestring and none other. He don't look so fast, but Pisk's fast. And it's aboot his fastness, that's what will help him here, eh.

Pisk can't take a punch, said Clough.

Sure as fuck he can.

Daggett is drunk. I don't know what that means. What a you think?

Aboot him being drunk?

Yeah.

Pisk is a fucking China doll compared, said Clough. One good ka-nocking he's down.

Daggett is slow, said Hoss. It's his slowness he's got to think aboot now.

He's huge, eh.

He is a mammoth, eh.

Only bohunk around here bigger than Pisk has got to be Daggett.

Someone whispered: I tell you it don't matter if you're slow or fast, if you killed somebody, then you know what it takes to do it again. It's high on his mind.

Daggett?

Shhh.

That's the truth?

Alls I'm saying is I lay my fucking chickamin on the murderer.

Clough, said the cowboy RD Pitt. You always got them strays following you ever-where … that one nearly bit my—.

My fucking god, said Moe Dee, but isn't Daggett one big slab a meat on a bone.

He's a fatty, for sure, said Bud Hoss.

Who's the one talking, you fat fuck, said Campbell, another man working alongside Hoss on Furry & Daggett's logging crew.

I don't think they're gonna fight at all, said Hoss, ignoring his bunkmate. Look at them, not even angry no more by the looks on their faces.

Get rid a the canine before I kills it, said RD Pitt.

He's under my jurisdiction, cowboy Pitt, Clough said, and grabbed the spotted dog by the ears and made him sit by his feet. Get yourself back, dog, this is no time for grandstanding. Why, I'd just as soon put you back in the pound with the rest a the strays, my friend. You won't get your ovation here.

I can see the fleas popping off him, drawled cowboy Pitt, swatting his hands around him.

With all your complaining, cowboy, I'd just as likely bet you're from Montreal, eh. Ha ha. Now never mind the dog, Pitt. Daggett's had more than a skinful, by the looks. And sure as hellfire I know that look in his eyes. Daggett's my man, but he's pickled to the bone. He's wobbling like he drank the whole bar.

He can hollow a bottle and we all know it, said Campbell.

Ah, but he fights dirty, said Hoss.

Campbell said: You got another way to fight? Now listen here, Hoss. This is *our boss* you're talking aboot, eh. If you're speaking against Daggett, then—.

Alls I know is truth.

Pinching his knees together, Clough said: Man, I *got* to leak …

Despite forecasts it was a bright September day, translucent yellow leaves turning to red near the treetops, surrounded by purple berries. The faces of the men were camouflaged by the leafy shadows of autumn trees hanging over the assembly.

Pisk was so used to the outdoors that his skin didn't even tingle to the breeze. He threw his clothes to Litz one dusty item at a time, monkeyjacket and shirt and denims and then his patterned calico drawers, until all that remained was his bowler, which he tipped off his head and let roll down his leg to hook on his big toe, a perfect vaudeville trick, naked. He genuflected theatrically to the hollering audience, then cupped his nutsack in his hand.

What in the hell are you up to? said Daggett.

You want a fight? said Pisk. Come on then. Strip down and fight me.

I don't want to come *near* you, said Daggett, I just want to beat the living shit out a you.

You afraid to fight?

Bare knuckle is one thing. Come on.

You coward, you poltroon. Let's see who can *rea*lly fight. I know you, Daggett. I know you, guttersnipe. I seen how you scrap. I saw you used a knuckleduster on an unsuspecting man's smile. I know you use your belt, you use your fucking *boots,* you use your fucking whatever you have hidden in your pockets. I even seen you use axes, Pisk said, and paused for effect. And I saw you use your tobacco pipe. I bet you'd beat a man with your silver tooth if you had to. I saw you. So strip down and let's see what you can do without all that currency. Let's see who you are under all that dirt you got on. I suspect all you are is another fucking whore.

This is outrageous, said Sammy. These men are absolute barbarians. I'm very sorry you have to hear this, Molly. We shouldn't—

It's true, said Fortes. But they got no one to look up to, you know. These boys got no daddies, they got no mamas. A course they don't got no children. All they got is working and drinking.

Her open lips appeared a deeper red, seen against the moonsliver white of her upper teeth. And was it really true he'd never noticed before how really long her neck was? Perhaps she was craning it more than ever? But really it was the most luscious neck, pale like that, heaving like that. Was the white hazy air around him infused with incoming rain or her intoxicating perfume?

Next to her on the banister a grey squirrel appeared, ejaculated a vowelful squeak, and ramped the post on a spiralling path towards the awning above, giving a last, hostile snap of its tail before bidding farewell. She didn't seem to notice. He could look at his wife—never mind the stout, utterly naked man in the middle of the street surrounded by homicidal men in all directions—and reject everything else about his life. Sammy shut his eyes. Drowning would be the way to go, he figured, a blissful bottomless end to an abject life.

What are you afraid a? said Pisk.

Nothing.

If you're a scared motherfucker go to church.

You better pray I don't geld you, said Daggett.

Take off the dungarees, Daggett, you fat cow.

Fuck my—, you … you pissant, said Daggett, wiping his greasy mouth. I had aboot enough a you.

He was dressed head to toe in scum. In a boxer's pose, one fist hovering in front of and a bit higher than the other, Daggett shuffled quickly across the dirt to mark this fight officially launched, hoping to get in a good clean clocking on Pisk's face. If he got Pisk upside the ear he could have him on the ground without further notice. These fists on Daggett were as good as mallets. He kept in time with his own pulse, gaining momentum as his fist recoiled. Daggett's approach made everybody hustle in, angling for a better view and pinching off any gap where Pisk might make an escape. Pisk watched Daggett come closer and maybe you could interpret that squint as a reaction, because otherwise Pisk didn't budge. He was in position. There it was, Daggett's left fist (just as it had been predictably hoisted in the bar). Pisk dodged it by turning his face only a bit.

As Daggett swung by, Pisk reached out and took Daggett's outstretched fist in his hand and lay his other hand on Daggett's waist and, making jolly of momentum, stepped Daggett gaily around the road as if it were a ballroom. When

Daggett nearly recovered his balance, Pisk spun him free and landed him on his ass *{see fig. 3.1}*.

For this wild act Pisk received shocked applause and coarse, spontaneous laughter. Spontaneous clapping, too, for something never before seen. All the ingrates, including Clough, an otherwise loyal friend of Furry and Daggett, applauded the move. Including any performance ever invited to the Pantages, this impromptu dance inspired more caterwauling, jabbering, and extended bouts of *hee-haw* than the town had yet heard.

I liked that, said Moe Dee.

Daggett sat murderously still on the dirt and waited for everyone to simmer down. He spat on the ground, nearly on his own hand. Then, pulling up his shoulders, Daggett almost stood, to fight some more, but—. Hesitation. He slumped again. His indecision wasn't lost on anyone.

With tears in his blond eyes, Fortes called out from his perch on the sidewalk: Daggett, my pal, ha ha, you ain't never going to be free a this.

Molly didn't twit a smile. She just stood there, stilled, as if only a framed photograph of herself remained beside him, her green stare reaching beyond the image into what can only be called the future.

FIGURE 3.1
The Pisk

Calabi's commentary: The lunging right hook transformed into a fey waltz and a tossing finish; the original move, as eloquent as a continuous stroke a the sword across the torso.

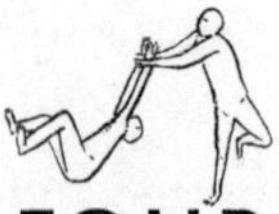

FOUR

> There are three types of the genus vagrant, the hobo, the tramp and the bum. The hobo works and wanders, the tramp dreams and wanders, and the bum drinks and wanders.
>
> — BEN REITMAN

A few days after the fight, Molly learned in her naturally assiduous and charming way that Toronto knew how to get in contact with these notorious exile lumberjacks she'd seen in the Sunnyside, Litz and Pisk. It was the crack of dawn. He was on his way out the door to harvest chanterelles for their morning eggs. Oh, yes, I know their names, she said. She stood close enough for him to smell her bedsheets. Toronto confessed that he often received letters from Pisk to secretly add to the mail delivery when he rode in to the main post office in New Westminster. Molly needed Toronto to do her this, as she put it, *very unique favour*. This stays between us, she told him. I want to meet with those two loggers. A location, anywhere, their preference, somewhere private, concealed, not easily accessible. There I shall make them a gainful business proposition.

That evening, when the sun was gone and the mice awoke and Toronto retired to his chores, Sammy, unaware of his wife's request, made his own confession: he was deeply, terribly frightened by what he'd seen that afternoon at the Sunnyside. I'm no longer sure we're safe out here, he said.

Could happen anywhere. We're safe as kittens.

You always know exactly how to ease my mind.

We could provide Toronto with a rifle …

Yes, I thought a that, too, said Sammy.

Hm, I see, she said, reading his expression. You're worried he'll use it to end his life.

Mmm, said Sammy. Yes, no, see ... I ...

You mustn't worry yourself, she said. I saw towns in this condition all across Europe. My parents, they had a strategy for places like Vancouver. Keep moving. Never stop in a place like Vancouver. Keep moving. Make Vancouver laugh and cry then go. Never stay. Never stay in a town long enough to get caught against a wall, in a valley, or on a busy street. My choice is different. I can't follow them. I choose to stay. Molly paused, straightened up. She'd been doing hamstring stretches on the floor the whole time they'd been talking. My imagination, she continued, all I can think aboot is that afternoon at the Sunnyside. Sammy, I love the Canadian spirit. I want to be a Canadian, Sammy. I want to look Canadian, I want the philosophy, the suspicions, the credibility, the voice. I want the Canadian life. I don't want to be a minstrel, a travelling amusement, a heathen performer tattooed with Europe's borders. I want to be Canadian.

One a those men could be dead today if things had gone conventionally, said Sammy.

But it ends up not to be so in Canada. In Europe, a slanderous argument always ended in death. I was *most* interested in how that one man Pisk handled his opponent, very Canadian.

The one who undressed.

Yes.

The one who showed it all.

Not for the sake a lewdity, jealous man. For the sake a civilization. Come now, she said, standing up and suppressing a hiccup by pressing the palm of her hand to her chest, let's call Toronto to help us up to bed.

Change the subject, said Sammy. Well, speaking a bed, I plead with you for a night without waking me up for your midnight snack.

I'm seventeen, a growing girl. I can't help it, I get hungry.

Why that means *I* must eat, I can't figure.

Come now. It seems everyone else wants to be dressed in ee-na around here. I'll start a fire in our room while Toronto gets you ready.

I think I'll stay up tonight instead and read from the journals a Sancho Panza.

Chi*nook*, Molly cried, and tugged on Sammy's whiskers. If you don't come to bed I can't fall asleep. I don't want to be alone after all we talked aboot just now.

That bald bearded logger really did get under your skin, I see.

Foolish husband. I meant *Eu*rope. I meant that I can't think aboot Europe anymore, not without such *sor*row. If I'm to be a good wife, I can't stew in my sorrows. Not running away, instead going to bed. Please, come.

They went to bed together, as they did every night; Toronto, once the couple were settled, listening to them from his room on the main floor as he said his evening prayers with not even a candle lit to flicker against the walls. Molly, like a wick that burned inside a man, kept the Erwagen house awake when the rest of Vancouver was dreaming hard.

In the following days she seemed patient enough to spend her afternoons tending to her husband, shopping for perishables and winter supplies, and practising ballet in the living room. On her walks in the morning with Toronto to buy a box of Calabi&Yaus she never said a word, spoke only of the striking, mortal beauty of autumn in Vancouver. Look around us, our world is in a cold sweat, she said.

Then came the day when Toronto had news from the woodsmen Litz and Pisk. He and Molly spent that morning at Calabi & Yau's in conversation with the bakers. Toronto liked to make his choice for the morning and be gone. Unless he had extra silver and planned to stay for coffee, he was usually in and out the door in less than a half minute. Molly was different. When they went together they stayed for an hour.

She liked to discuss things with the bakers, and her questions were motivated by such a naturally curious intuition that the bakers felt they had no choice but to answer her as candidly as possible. Like everyone who first encountered the pastry, Molly wanted to know how they made it.

Can't tell you that, said Calabi, shaking his head. Calabi was a middle-aged man with thinning black hair, two moustaches, one at each corner of his mouth, and broad shoulders.

Yau was a thin leathery man like the tongue of a boot, with his skin cracked and creased from working for so long in front of the scorching heat of the Dutch oven.

Molly smelled of pomegranates, wet aloe, and her skin was as fragile and perfect as a fresh eggshell.

They talked around the subject of the pastries, already breaking Molly's own rule and talking about Europe a little, the countries and cities they were all familiar with. The bakers recognized the streets she named in Constantinople, Berlin, and Paris, mapping her memories out in the white flour on the table. She seemed overjoyed to learn they had once visited a music hall in the Jewish district of Bingen am Rhein where her parents performed. This amused them. Something sad about the memory of those years, too, made them all grow quiet for a moment.

They assumed she would use this contemplative pause to persist in asking about the pastries. The bakers maintained looks of cautious expectation. She never asked.

Of the two bakers, Calabi was the first to realize that Molly cultivated an aura around a secret of her own. He looked at the table where Molly had used her finger to make a street map of Bingen am Rhein in the flour. Suddenly Calabi scooped another handful of flour from a sack and tossed it across the table. Then another. The streets all vanished. In the flour Calabi began to draw out his own picture, a rough diagram of intersecting ellipsoids and snake shapes in wrapped helices.

Imagine here is dough sweet pastry, Calabi said, drawing, and here is flaky somewhat savoury pastry, yes. Two are entwined like coiling smoke, see?

Mmm, yes, lovely, said Molly.

On an average day the bakers could sell twenty dozen. Cross a doughnut with a light Danish, in thin layers of immaculately folded phyllo and various doughs and pastries. Able to fit in the palm of one's hand and as light as a tennis ball, the obvious mystery was how they got it to stay together—it looked as if the helix or loops never quite touched, and the pastry stuck together by some force beyond perception.

Two farmers' children came in the doors and interrupted their conversation. Calabi wiped his hands on his apron and went to the front of the store to serve the children, who left their vegetable wagon at the door.

I start with cheese parts and eat all them and save sweet and blackberry for last, the little boy told Calabi.

Is that you plan? he asked the child, while he tonged their regular order onto wax paper.

Me, too, said his sister. I like to put a whole one in and feel the cream splode out my mouth.

Me, too, said the boy.

Sure, said Calabi, and slid four across the counter to the kids. That'll be fifteen cents.

You must be so happy to know how much the town appreciates your work, said Molly.

I am so lonely, said Calabi.

Hm, said Molly. And you, Yau? Is work enough, or do you feel lonely, too?

Yau took a wad of dough off a tray and punched it around and slapped it down on the table. Me, not so much, no. Do it, he said to Calabi with contempt in his voice. Marry and have child we can teach to make Calabi&Yaus.

After saying their goodbyes, Molly walked happily out the door of the bakery and onto Powell Street. Toronto followed along. That was the first time he'd seen either of the bakers say anything about how their pastries were made. As to how Molly was able to coax out such precious information, Toronto could only assume from his own feelings that the bakers wanted to share with her some level of intimacy; they wanted her approval, but they also wanted to be understood. Molly, if no one else, could understand. And as long as Molly was around, the bakers were a little less alone in the new world.

She and Toronto walked a little farther, then stopped at a log by the side of the road next to an open stable full of restless, steaming geldings, children lined up nearby for the chilly morning chore of filling up at the water pump. Sitting on a cushion of vermilion moss draped over the log, Molly stared at her pastry.

You think you understand how they make one, she said, and then you turn the Calabi&Yau even a bit and suddenly everything looks different. What a delicious puzzle.

He smiled and laughed nervously, and with a sticky mouth, said: Oh, I meet Pisk and Litz in Chinatown last night.

Yes, and?

Molly listened intently as he explained the directions in great detail. He gradually outlined a careful path for her to take through some of the denser, more chaotic forests to the south of Vancouver. The more he explained the more he began to smile again, as only now was he becoming aware of how totally absurd the directions were. Litz and Pisk wanted her going sideways, north, south, and backwards, and he told her so. Nevertheless, she asked him to carry on. She needed no explanation for why the directions were so circuitous. She wanted only to know when.

//

MUGGER ON THE LOOSE On streets of Vancouver; TWO BATHERS ROBBED Under a tree; CITY OFFERS PLENTY REWARD To the man who restores justice. POLICE OUTRAGED At implication.

After returning from the bakery, Molly gave her husband a manicure and pedicure while he read the headlines and advertisements in the *Daily Advertiser,* which he preferred to the other rag. He couldn't feel her push back his cuticles, but he appreciated her diligence all the same. She could be doing any kind of work. She could be playing a calimba. All he loved was her proximity. The tart pomegranate scent of her hair, the dunes of her desert skin, the spark off her fingers. She clipped his white moons and filed him smooth. Sometimes her tongue poked out the window of her mouth as she worked, lollygagging over the proceedings. He adored the way she lost herself in this small yet meaningful task.

You must have had dolls growing up, he said. Combed their hair and dressed them. Didn't you?

She laughed and pushed her hair back off her shoulders. Come now, you're not my doll. This, my dear sweet Chinook, this I would do for you even if you could lift this house. I don't know why but I like trimming your nails. I much prefer it to scrubbing the floor. And no, she added, I never did have dolls. If anything, this reminds me a how I used to care for the horses. I didn't think about dolls at all, to know they existed or what for. That I should desire one. This was not my life. Instead I was surrounded by clowns and acrobats and confidence men, you know. What did I need with the inanimate. Night after night, I saw every fantasy come alive. My parents were unhappy people. We never had a penny. I remember them. Remembering my parents singing, rehearsals at all hours a the day, laughing hysterical one hour and sobbing the next. No matter the situation, we always found a way to laugh or cry aboot it. And one day that is all supposed to be gone? This did not occur to me? Am I making sense?

Yes, a course, Sammy said, hoping she would make herself clearer and more detailed as she continued. If you'd like to speak with me aboot your family, your mother, father … I shall not interrupt.

When you ask me to think a my mother, my father, Molly said, you ask a terrible thing. Will it satisfy your curiosity to know that when I try to remember my mother and my father all I can see is that day I went for bread, and when I came back from the bakery, it was to see the whole theatre gone? Razed. A blackened pile. Imagine my grief. My parents were in there, I was sure. And so I ran. Where does a young girl go? Canada.

She wouldn't say more. He felt like a rock skipping across a lake, covered in tears but never sinking, amazed but missing the point. Maybe he would never know her. This sinking he desired maybe was not necessary. Maybe he didn't need to know. Maybe he knew her already. Whatever the case, when Toronto arrived home again later in the afternoon from his daily trip to the post office, he had in his hand a telegram that had arrived at Hastings Mill for Sammy. It was from Father Erwagen back east in Toronto.

It read: SEPT IF YOU DIDNT KNOW STOP HAPPY BIRTHDAY SAM STOP.

Sammy asked Toronto to burn the well wishes in the fireplace. His wife raised an eyebrow.

The more I learn aboot you, the more there is to know, he said. Every time I inquire into your past, I feel as though I have changed completely after hearing you. To hear you speak is like reading a book where most a the print falls off the pages as soon as you open it.

Indeed, she said. Who was the telegram from?

A business associate, nothing, a trival … a message from the Orient, said Sammy, deceiving his wife so as not to trouble her with his contempt for his family. Hm, yes, and speaking a high society, he said, the Emperor a China has promised to buy a great deal a lumber from the mill to build his fortress. I shall arrange for the sale. This is boring you. Let's talk aboot you again.

I must be on my way, she said.

Without hesitation, Sammy said: Please do go. A young lady needs the stimulation a fresh air. Such a safe place Vancouver is for a merry young lady to walk alone. According to the news headlines I read, there is proof the po-lice are vigilant. They've hung a man's boot from a gallows, with half the victim's leg still in it, attracting flies. Delightful. And now didn't I hear there's a mugger on the loose?

You think I could be mugged?

I know you're unmuggable.

I'll probably catch him.

Will you still love me while you're gone?

Inevitably.

That's what I like to hear.

//

When the canoe was ready, she kissed her husband one final time and went to meet Toronto by the boat where it was beached close to a nearby stream. With Toronto guiding her—she still hadn't quite made her mental map of the hundreds of creeks and rivers that flowed through the forest—she toured slowly around the coastline, southeast through creeks and flooded valleys, through channels in the muskeg and swamp-grass, before setting down on the banks of the North Fraser River. From there she travelled due north through a dense maze of blackberry bush to where Litz and Pisk met her, introduced themselves, blindfolded her, and took her to a secret glen where they sat and ate sunflower seeds and talked.

I didn't want to fight him, Pisk told her. It wouldn't a been a simple scrap, eh. He'd put me out in broad daylight. That's Daggett's style. Seeing him move in like that. What a bull. What else could I do to save my life? That's me spur-a-the-moment.

Litz felt compelled to add: There's a difference between a temper and being a killer. Pisk's got a temper.

Daggett's a killer, said Pisk. It wasn't my day to die, not in disgrace. Sorry if I offended you, me showing you all I'm packing. But you probably don't kumtuks how …

Thank you, she said, but no, I wasn't offended. I trust that once we're better acquainted you'll see I do understand.

Y-yes, said Pisk, looking at his fingers. He thought to himself, What use is a suitjacket if you don't even remember to clean your nails?

I heard stories, the Shanghai boot …, she said.

I'm no coward, eh? Daggett's born for murder. Other than fight him, what was I supposed to do? Took a screwing a my courage to do what I did. Still got my skin.

Why have you chosen to stay here? Molly asked.

This is our home as much as anybody's. I never left somewhere in disgrace and I don't plan to start today, said Pisk.

This is your camp, where are we?

You ask a lot a questions, said Pisk.

We got safe cover, said Litz. No one will ever find us.

I heard that man Clough is an excellent trapper.

You heard that, eh? said Pisk. Who told you that, Clough himself? Clough couldn't sniff out a bird dropping if it landed on his fingers.

Litz cracked a sunflower seed between his molars. Shells lay pell-mell at his feet. He looked above them and saw the polestar, then, eyes dilated, asterisms began taking shape in the darkening skyscape. He saw the winged horse Pegasus. It was time to start a fire. The thought of her skin, the sight of her features cast in the dancing light of a fire, set Litz's hands to work in search of kindling. Under cover of darkness from a view no one knew possible, they whispered like kids, surrounded by seaweed and tiny white crabs.

This town lacks for good entertainment, said Molly. For this outpost, entertainment must blend with life. I watched how quickly men worked to rebuild the town after the Fire. It was an activity, a direction. The men in Vancouver come to participate, not to watch from the bleachers. The pews are empty. The pulpit is in the street. Every man can speak his mind.

Hmm, eh, said Litz, not totally following her logic.

As Molly continued to talk, gesturing to the sky, the earth, and each of their bodies, Pisk's hands remained in his pockets. He needed a bath and he knew it. As clouds went by a friendship was beginning to take root among the three that was different from a friendship that existed between two men. Pisk was impressed by her graceful movements. The more at ease he felt with her presence, the less at ease he felt with his own, an unexpected slip down the learning curve. Litz spat the sunflower shells into the fire now, and watched them burn on the logs until they were nothing but black junk slowly frittering away to nothing. He listened as Molly talked. It didn't seem as if anything she said was out of the ordinary. Her observations seemed logical but he just couldn't make sense of them, any more than he could explain how the millipede avoids tripping himself. He couldn't have put her observations into words himself, but he trusted she knew where she was going.

... I thought tomorrow? she said, finishing a thought Pisk didn't hear, having lost his concentration.

Tomorrow, he said.

I have an idea for a ... *sport* I'd like to share with you, if you'd be so patient.

Sport, he said.

If it works, you could stand to make some money from bettors. What do they call money around here, in Chinook?

Chickamin, said Pisk.

Yes, chickamin. A lovely jargon, Chinook.

It's not really meant for uh, *ladies* to use, said Pisk. Chinook's for business between us and Indians and Chinamen.

I do love this part a the world.

Hm, said Pisk, suddenly perturbed by the thick calluses on the palms of his hands, which he scratched at as they hid inside his pockets.

So, are you interested?

Might as well give it a try, Litz said.

Again here?

No, said Pisk. I know a better place. I'll draw you a map. But don't show it to nobody.

I'll memorize and destroy it.

With a grin, Pisk set down to mapmaking. She looked over his shoulder and he could smell pomegranate as the breeze passed through her hair. Yes, I see, she said. She took the map and looked at it one final time before pushing the page into her mouth and chewing it. The two men watched her with almost concave absorption as she swallowed.

Breaking free the spell, Pisk said: We'll meet you in the afternoon how's aboot?

Perfect.

How old are you? asked Pisk.

How old are you? she asked.

Well, I'm twenty-one, said Litz.

Twenty-seven, said Pisk. I'm the old man, I suppose. How old are you?

I'm seventeen, said Molly.

Seven-*teen* is still young, said Pisk, rolling his eyes. Where'd you grow up to get such ideas, eh?

Tangiers, my birthplace, is a great sandcastle populated by maniacs and mystics selling rugs and baskets. I never lived there. Mine is such a thin bloodline, a bloodline a one, that I might thread a needle with it. The theatre society, my true adopted family, they are all interlopers. Not regular, calm people. The theatre lives by dusklight.

Litz nodded.

Pisk likewise felt at a loss for how to contribute. He took off his hat and polished his slightly fuzzy bald pate with his coatsleeve.

Where is your family from? she asked.

Oh, Germany, a course. My mother, she lives in Penticton now, a little lumber town a few hundred miles east a here.

And yourself, Litz?

Poland, but all that's left a my family is me, too.

Yes, said Molly.

This is personal, said Litz.

This is *business*, said Pisk. Furry and Daggett force us to hide so as they can take over more land. That's what this is really aboot. This isn't aboot the fucking Fire. This isn't aboot that.

I know that, said Litz.

It's *not* personal.

Yeah, said Litz. You know what I mean.

I'm talking to *her*, said Pisk.

I know that, said Litz, looking at him with a blush of anger for being admonished, corrected, in front of a brilliant lady. When they were done talking, the tide looked so far out it might have actually drained back under the American mountains and left her canoe stranded in gravel.

We're exiles, said Pisk. In more ways than you know. We shouldn't be out here like this.

We're exiles, said Molly. Count me among your outcasts then. Men will gravitate to the game, she told them. Men gravitate to performances with strength, agility, endurance, and violence. Men want to watch the exiles battle for a position in society.

Litz nodded his head graciously and scratched his moustache. He was on the tip of saying something, if he could only think of something to say.

I saw you the day a the Fire, Molly said.

Y-you did? said Litz, scratching his collar.

Yes, you were fighting. Very nasty. Fists and bullocks out. You fought that day the way you did in front a the Sunnyside versus Daggett.

I'll tell you one thing aboot fighting in the buck, miss, said Pisk. Keeps you honest.

Hm, yes, I see. Whatever caused you two partners to *brawl* on such a dangerous day?

So, uh, you're from Morocco? said Pisk, abruptly changing the subject. He was not much quicker with words, but no matter how much he tried to keep the attention on her, the small talk lasted only a moment before she was on the water anyhow. Miffed perhaps. In a matter of a blink and a stammer, the canoe was on its way. She did reply but her words were lost in the waves. Pisk felt only the beginnings, the murmur of consolation in the tone of her voice, which was beautiful and intent, even canoeing away into the dark distance.

With Toronto in the back, she canoed home to Sammy, who was waiting in the living room in a chair he'd soiled. She ran to him with desperate apologies. Sammy was calm and graceful. It was one of those things.

//

They made their way back through the woods to their hideout, to the dwindling stack of firewood, the leak in the roof, the faulty cookstove, and to the woeful Mrs. Litz, who was cloistered there for her own safety on this tiny nook of land caged in on all sides by acres of gnarled blackberry thistle, with nothing to do with her time but go absolutely skookum. On their way back to this grim nest, they discussed Mrs. Erwagen's proposition.

I never did go in for music halls, said Pisk at a whisper. So maybe I get her idea. Damn, Litz, what are we thinking here? Are you sure we should go with this lady?

What a we got to lose?

Try making our living off something doesn't exist except in her mind? The more I think aboot it, the more I don't know, eh …

Don't split hairs, said Litz at low volume.

Split hairs? Well, I—

And before Pisk could interrupt further, Litz added: You know this is our answer.

How do I know that?

Because, don't you want to be good at something for once?

We're good loggers.

No, I mean something people care aboot. No one cares when a logger's gone. We're no more important to businessmen than a piece a blotting paper.

They crawled through the long narrow passageway under the blackberry bramble and finally arrived at what had become their home. It looked like a pile of sticks, a giant beaver dam hugging the titanic pillar that was an old dead cedar tree in the middle of harsh forest. Mrs. Litz was outside, waiting for them, hands on her little hips, her sloe-eyed expression one of deep despair, almost madness. For such a small pretty creature, she had a great set of lungs. After they swallowed their pride and listened to every last one of Mrs. Litz's complaints and demands, they ate dinner. Litz tried to make it up to her with gentle, obsequious noises by which he meant to compliment her cooking. They ate mutton and potato stew using the wooden spoons she'd carved. After they were done, he tried to touch her smooth soft cheek but she recoiled as if frightened that his thick fingers might cut her. It won't be much longer, Litz promised her, pretty soon we'll have it all taken care a, and we can go back to living normal. But she didn't want to wait any longer. She was all alone out here.

For a while the married couple argued while Pisk sat on his chair and smoked tobacco. By the end of the conversation Mrs. Litz was drunk and crying, and then she fell asleep. Litz looked at Pisk and without a word the two of them went back outside to chop firewood and wash up in the creek.

What choices do men got around here for some entertainment? Litz said as he cleaved the firewood in half and threw all the shivers aside. If a man wants to watch a fight, and we know he's up for that, then he's just as soon to watch this. That's all we need around here, Pisk.

I'm listening, said Pisk, rubbing the garments up and down a soapy washboard next to the creek.

In Chinatown it's checkers or dominoes and those lotteries. Them Chinee, they spend a lot a money on that. Men are so bored they play cards all day. You seen men around here bet on fist fights. Stand a good chance they bet on this idea. Everybody around here is bored to death. They gamble and drink and fight. What else is there to do when work is scarce?

Pisk hung their clothes on the line to dry and went over to help Litz stack the firewood. There's nothing out here for us anymore, Litz said. What I suppose I learned because a our exile is there never *was* nothing for us here. The only thing anyone ever goes and does in Vancouver is drink and fuck away their fortunes. None a these men have futures. Pisk, man, I want a future. I was raised to be nobody. But I don't want to end up some bohunk like ol' Clough, drinking himself to death. We're all killing ourselves out here, for what?

Pisk stopped before throwing a log and considered what Litz said.

I don't want to die a boredom. Already we smoke too much a the opium, hashish, and drink our faces off. I don't want to lose my soul to that neither. I don't want to die in this forest worth less than what I came into the world with, said Litz. There's got to be more to life than being a handlogger.

Who do you think you are, Litz? You're nothing special. You and me both, we're just bohunks.

Not me.

Ah, said Pisk. You're just in love again.

Who, with Molly?

That's right, Molly. Exactly Molly. Good guess, partner. But listen, you don't have to love every ee-na just because you want to get some of it.

Look, said Litz. If you want to horse around, fine. Me, I'm ready for a better—more good from life. I'm not interested in anyone but my wife. You can see that Molly's got plans. We need something. We're prisoners right now. We need to do something, not just the same thing, eh? Or we'll never get ourselves out a this situation. You and me are different from the rest. We always set apace ahead. Let's do this.

Pisk heard what he was saying. They went back inside, stoked the fire, and lay in bed with Mrs. Litz. As they quarrelled over the blanket, she, between them, angrily, did not stir. They lay there on the mattress, with a myth on the brink of conception floating around in the men's heads, keeping them awake while Mrs. Litz dreamed. Without knowing what Molly intended, what she had planned, how could they know anything except their instincts?

//

Angry to be alive. Minna and I saw how the game was played. We saw the crowd it generated. The whole ordeal, event, continued to make me feel uncomfortable. It seemed that the least dangerous people in the yard that day were the sportsmen. The rest were good for fuck-all. All their money went to rims. All their dreams went to coastlines. All their time went straight to the streets. Angry to be alive, angry enough to kill.

Every time something awesome happened on the lawn, a perfectly executed Medical Breakthrough for example *{see fig. 4.1}*, badly postured, spotty-eyed, omnivorous young men in the audience whelped and fisted the air with increasing hostility. Yeah, they announced from the lowest pits of their voices. Yeah, yeah, boo-yeah. Just standing next to one of them was too much for me. It was like standing next to the speakers at a rock show. From beneath their jerseys and slack belts and the silver crosses of no meaning that dangled there on long silver thread across their chests, an amplified bear howl escaped from every one of their hearts.

Motherfuck your dada, said one, handrolled grass pinched in his fingers. I'll fuckin' show your dada how to act, I'll stub him in the face with my stooge rocket.

FIGURE 4.1
The Medical Breakthrough

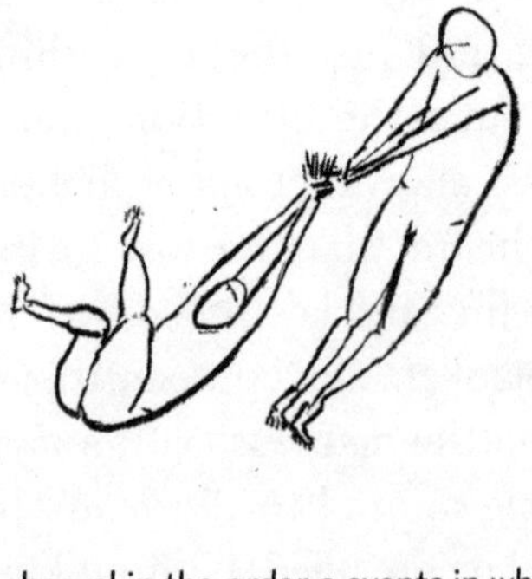

Calabi's commentary: A complete upheaval in the order a events in which any move is redirected using momentum to swing his opponent one complete rotation before releasing him.

Who are they talking to? I asked.

Apparently the men there, said Minna, nodding to our sportsmen.

I'll fucking tie your dada in a purple knot and Jack trip him, said a bleach-blond neckface.

I'll fuckin', I'll fuckin', I'll fuckin—, said another, searching through his grey matter for a wizened slur. Nothing appeared.

Across their shaved heads lurched a series of fast shadows, ear to ear, as eastbound crows lured themselves to power stations for another night of anger. That pitiless catechism of crowsong, it echoed in the altitude, it kept the neighbours up. All crows are men.

Minna wasn't really my *girl*friend, but I loved her nonetheless for who she was and I accepted the awkward halted romance we had because it was better than nothing at all. I did feel frustrated and vulnerable. Mostly it was the fact of the nudity, the lack of it in our relationship and the proximity to it at this very moment.

Ken wormed his way into a handstanding bourée. Silas uprocked it. Now the game was more and less interesting *{see fig. 4.2}*. I was preoccupied with not becoming entangled in the moshing thrusts of the troublemakers and their allies.

FIGURE 4.2
The Boxing Chinee

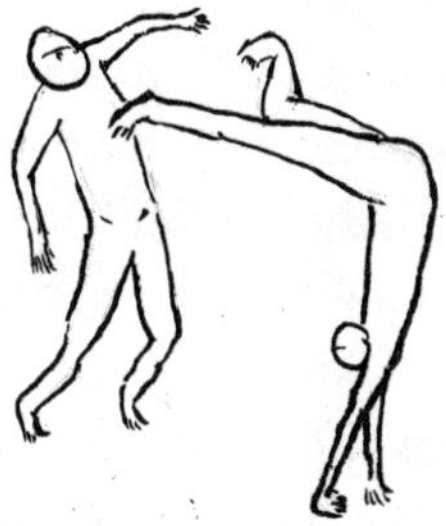

Calabi's commentary: The skilled player uses his feet and knees as accurately as a lion tamer his whip and chair.

FIVE

> Come, then, soldiers, be our guests. My life was one of hardship and forced wandering like your own, till in this land at length fortune would have me rest. Through pain I've learned to comfort suffering men.
>
> — DIDO, VIRGIL, TRANS. R. FITZGERALD

Bud Hoss had gotten the job on the donkey engine by answering Furry & Daggett's note on the blackboard at the Sunnyside Hotel. There'd been all sorts of tough jobs chalked up. Doyle wanted a bucker for $1 a day; Rowling needed ten axemen for a slope in Langley; Furry & Daggett were hiring rigging slingers for $1 to help clear a giant job and were looking for a guy who knew how to do a controlled burn. That was a specialty of Hoss's—fires, that is. He'd never lost control of one. A man who worked the donkey engine gathered up debris and set it ablaze, a means of getting rid. Easy enough work on a rainy day, and there were lots of those, but rather more dangerous business on a dry hot windy summer afternoon, as Vancouver well knows.

Over bottles of whisky Daggett laid it out for Hoss, as he said, in plain English: You walk off my job it's mutiny. I bury rats and mutineers. Every coward costs me chickamin. You quit when I say it's quitting time. Walk off a job, consider me and Furry your enemies. Run, hide if you see us. I will cut both your ears off.

Cheers, said Hoss, who summoned the courage to survive the job from the hair tonic bottle he raised in a toast, then drank from the potato moonshine inside.

After a few months working hard and losing some of his baby fat—he was still only eighteen—Hoss had grown to sympathize with Daggett, much as the mutt will obey his owner even if that owner is a penniless lunatic. Furry scared Hoss same as always. After the Shanghai boot was found, he feared them both again even more. Bud Hoss was the middle man on a shared mattress with six others, Furry and Daggett at either side. He hardly slept. When he did he had nightmares where he was falling to his death from atop a tall tall spar, the tallest whitest fir in the woods.

Few were as eager as Furry & Daggett to shave this coastline. Their ambition helped them net boastworthy contracts with government and private business. Men determined to work as hard as they usually came with prized recommendations, and Furry & Daggett awarded these men decent salaries and some respect. Hoss had gotten little to no respect thus far, never mind his impressive coordination, perfectly choreographed slash and burns, and noticeably dramatic fire control. The older men, Campbell, Meier, Boyd, and Smith—their reputations were well established. Older meaning they ranged from twenty-one to thirty-one. Each was known for his strength, his beard, his foul breath, and his violent temper. Other facets of their physique, disposition, and height better highlighted their differences, and yet for all they argued and disagreed with one another, to a stranger they would seem as one. Furry & Daggett's Logging Concern. The fact that they were all older than Hoss was an issue, and he supposed they each had histories, along with more scars and more problems. He was a natural. They didn't like that.

Boyd you would recognize a block away just from that thick black caterpillar of a monobrow wiggling above his tiny brown eyeballs. Smith was a balding blonde with a flat face like a red brick. Meier was close to seven-and-a-half feet tall. Campbell was five foot even, the goat. You couldn't knock Campbell off his balance with a mallet, but it was said that Furry could take him down with a slap. It was also said that Furry could knock out a charging ox with a single blow. Hoss hadn't seen either feat with his own eyes yet. He could testify to the fact that what took the average man six chops took Daggett no more than three.

Daggett had a saying that he shared over lunch with new day-labourers like Hoss: This is war. Trees want to kill us. We're here to kill every one a them. Are you with me? Do I hear your Yep?

Yep, said all.

Yep, said Hoss.

The bigger the tree, the more I hate it. More I want to kill it. Slaughter all his family. Whether it's sap or syrup or sawdust, I want to see some *blood* on the floor a the forest at the end a the day, eh? You seen me do it, men, I spit on their stumps when work's done for the day.

Hoss learned fairly quickly how the day went: you woke before dawn in the bed you shared with the other men, five-six men in a bed. Every last one of you in a set of stinking, sweaty calico drawers, and you got up one by one, scratching your nuts, expectorating and flatulating, dressed right on top over your calicos in your filthy monkeyjackets and dungarees, aimed your kerosene lamp out of your lean-to, and went out to the steaming cold dark to meet the other men from the camp at the mess tent.

Hoss sat down on a bench and didn't say a word, lest he annoy another man's hangover. He ate a breakfast of fried eggs, cornbread and butter, side bacon and coffee, and then took a long pull of opium before going to work. Unlike when he smoked it in the basements in Chinatown and felt the quick sinkage of self, like a stone into a swamp, out in the open and with an axe over his shoulder the drug left Hoss feeling painlessly alert and courageous. There was something in the clean fresh air and in the mental and physical concentration it took to strip a timber of its limbs. Taking each branch down one at a time as he slowly climbed its trunk, tossing limbs spinning and crashing to the ground as he hung there in mid-air. Busy birds' nests, eggs and all, squirrels' acorn stashes—it all fell along with the branches. He climbed higher into the sky along the thinning tree. It got so that Hoss could arrive at the top of a tree having no memory of how he'd cleaned the whole trunk to get there. Looking at the ground a hundred seventy feet below, he saw nothing but the carrion of torn leaves and splintered wood he'd created. And Hoss would look out over the feathery haze, over the untouched glory of the northern forests, the mountains' crests and furrows, the bluing islands in the ocean, the marble grey ocean ... It made him want to stay this high forever, perfectly unaware of his own solitude and wanting for nothing.

Noontime was the same, only more opium and more meat in the food. Evenings came when the sun went down and then it was always more opium, and devouring food, itching for sweet things of every variety—Calabi&Yaus by the dozen daily—to the point of intestinal lockdown. Huge shanks of lamb, mashed potatoes and corncobs, chicken livers, raw salmon, beef burgers and hot cross buns, and butter. So much butter. And inevitably, when it felt to Hoss like he couldn't stand upright a minute longer, he was simply going to pass out from exhaustion, that's when all the others took to sitting around the campfire smoking the mud and listening to Daggett.

Anyone who valued their job was at the campfire. Boyd looked walrus-like in the flickering dark with his black monobrow ruling the top half of his head and the moustache taking the lower half. And like an animal he could neither read nor write nor brush his teeth. Whereas beside him, Meier had the same demeanour as an axeblade. He liked to cut people down to size. He spent his days slaughtering trees and spelling *tough* aloud as many ways as possible: tuff toff tough taughf tawf tuf touf ... in his loudest voice, every letter, as many combinations as you doubt possible, on and on for hours, so you knew what he expected from you.

While he talked, Furry, the silent partner, paid attention to the men, watching for rats and treason.

Hoss sat down on a log and tried to make himself comfortable enough to fall asleep there.

... And speaking a competition, said Daggett, I'm only going to say this once. Fucking don't want to hear any a you say Litz or Pisk's name unless it's to curse their beings to

Hell's lowest level. Got that? Anyone so much as hears rumour where they are and don't come straight to me … serious flogging. Fucking *swear* on my mother's untimely grave that if I ever see them again I'll kill them *both* with my bare hands. Anyone got objections they can fuck off this job. Otherwise, those're willing to help me get revenge, say Yep.

Yep, said all, campfire rippling, plumes of woodsmoke in their faces.

Yep, said Hoss, eyes shut to Furry's gaze.

Fucking I came here same as alls you guys, started doing some clearing work, Daggett said, rousing up a choir of sparks with a black-tipped log, ascendant and vanishing among the stars. That's all I was good for in my early days. Maybe I was eleven-twelve. You get older, you single out a couple a people you can work with and label yourself so you can separate yourself from the rest. With Furry, and myself, we worked with a crew called BLO. In the seventies. Stood for Best Loggers Out. He took his turn on the pipe going around, then continued his story. But on BLO, he said, this was when I introduced myself to Furry. I didn't know him from paint. And he was just another nut like me looking for work clearing. Long time ago. Way before your time. This was more than fifteen years ago, eh. Back then there weren't so many Chinamen. Now, you can't get these jobs because they hire the Chinamen. They cut off these jobs from boys like yourself and *then* how does a Canadian get a start, eh? Fucking used to be you got your experience that way, now I don't know what you do. All them Indians and Chinamen take these jobs. I know some poor folk and I know'd some real Whitemen who're tycoons at the same time, that's for fucking sure. I know'd some gents got beaver fur-coats, come up here from Toronto, speculating. Some days it'd be like a man come into town, take everything around you and the ground you're standing on, put it in his pocket, eh, and take it back with him to Toronto, sell little bits here and there to littler tycoons, and then these goddamn littler tycoons would all come out here and try and sell it back to you. And there's always enough bohunks around here interested in real estate with no fucking idea in their heads. None a them to figure they were turning more little tycoons into big tycoons, and all a them living in Toronto. Railroad goes west and drives every cent back east.

Bud Hoss sucked the last of the dried beanbroth from dinner off his thumb and index, and swirled his tin cup (now spotless clean) around it, and said: Well, 'night everybody, I'm off to bed.

No one else said a word. Hoss nodded his hat to his bosses and stood to leave.

We're having a conversation here, said Daggett. Why don't you sit down and take another puff and listen for a change?

Hoss swept off his pants. That's all right, Mr. Daggett, you continue on withoot me, I'm tuckered.

Still no one else spoke, but Hoss could tell he shouldn't just turn and leave for the cabin. Furry stood up from his log on the other side of the bloody glow of the campfire and all the men watched him but Daggett, who continued to stare at Hoss. Hoss shifted his weight, lowered his shoulders. Furry put his hands on his belt and said to Hoss: Why don't you sit the fuck back down?

Hoss pointed at the cabin and said politely, weakly to Furry: It's just that I'm beat, and want to get some sleep and—

Furry leaped straight over the fire, his belt freed of the loops on his dungarees and swinging through the air. The buckle whipped Hoss right across the face and he quailed and took another whipping across the hands, and then he fell to the ground. Furry held him down with one hand and belt-whipped him mercilessly while the whole camp watched.

That's for mutiny, screamed Furry, whipping him hard. That's for insubordination. That's for disrespect. That's for contempt. This one's for insolence. That's for your own good. This one's for your fucking mother-dog for birthing you. And the curses went on and on in his roaring voice as he whipped Hoss. This one's telling you go pack your shit. This one's telling you you're officially fired. And *that's* to get the fuck out a here.

Hoss howled and staggered off immediately, tripping dazedly as he made his way through the nightwoods towards civilization. Swollen from the savage belt-whipping, he limped off to Wood's, the salubrious bordello on Dupont Street, where he took a hot bath and a woman of great expertise. She nursed his head gashes, the burst lip, the broken flesh on his back where blood drenched his clothes. And no one would know if he cried into the bosom of that girl, sobbed and sobbed, and she might not even hear him if he whispered for help, and love, and more. She might only feel his wet breath on her warm chest. She might even confuse his tears for kisses.

//

Sammy lay in bed watching her sleep like a pool of cream in bed beside him, rippling in the breeze. He wanted to lap her up. He could feel her warmth and hear her heartbeat.

Earlier that night over dinner Molly had explained her plans. He calmly accepted what she had to say. After their meal he chose to sit by the fire and feign reading while she practised acrobatics on the staircase. Then they proceeded to bed.

He wasn't tired. He thought she was very cunning when she wanted to be. But now under the warm covers, looking at her face in profile, he began to agonize. She had told him over beets that she wanted to create a sport. She hoped to enlist two exiled lumberjacks to begin with. Was he losing her already? He hated himself for this injury. He hated himself for loving her so much, for needing her so badly. Now what? Was it her eyes or her mouth that he loved more? He thought about it in bed. He thought about Molly's eyes and mouth.

She woke with no warning, quickly blinking away the sticky dust of sleep, and was unperturbed to see him looking back at her, wide and awake.

What are you doing? she asked.

He fought back his tears. Why do you want to spend time with these fools, these imbeciles? I don't understand it.

She touched his hair as if removing the worry itself from his follicles. And then she mussed it again by saying: There was a time when I wanted to feel completely overwhelmed by a man. I love how a man can make the rest a the world shrink to his feet.

You're being insensitive.

Don't you see that you still have that influence over me, more than ever?

I'd like to agree.

So much a life for me is grist for a vaudeville folly.

Oh, Molly, he said, tearily and with an attempt to stay confident. You want that feeling again, refreshed, anew, overwhelmed by a man, and I can't provide it, can I?

She tapped the ash off the nighttime cigarette she'd lit, then came back to pet his hair more, knowing that his lonesomeness was undone by her touch. She said: I shan't ever betray.

Nevertheless, he said.

It's what I do. Theatre, lights, tra la la. I know I can do it here, too. Differently.

No, you mustn't, Sammy said. This town frightens, appalls me. They inspire you.

I love these men.

Don't say that.

As performers. When you see them, you'll love them, too, as you did the vaudevillians.

I don't believe you. Alas, I … what if I forbid …?

You don't want to forbid me. I'll make you proud. I shan't betray. Oh, it's going to be lovely. You remember those early days when we courted in the empty seats at the back a the theatre, watching the program … the strongman skits? You remember how you laughed?

These men are boors, out come curses like sputum with every breath. I can kiss your cheek every day now if I like, not just in the backs a theatres. I don't need …

She leaned her face in to him with a grin so he could kiss her rosy button-cheeks, and said: Yes, you can kiss me. And no one else. Now I will simply do what comes natural, provide us with some entertainment that befits this wild-mouths land.

What aboot theatre? The Pantages? What aboot the—, but he didn't finish his defence when he saw her puckered face, as if he'd squeezed a lemon into her mouth.

Oh, she said, it's so provincial. So puritanical. For this town at least. These men treat vaudeville as a London factory boy would treat the opera, a fancy irrelevant treat, almost oppressive in its irrelevance.

Vancouver *is* vaudeville you're saying.

Hm, no, it is something new, better, more physical—no boundaries between natural and supernatural.

He watched as his wife became more animated in her speech, until she had to use her elbow to fully prop her head on her hand so she could concentrate on delivering her words, even as he found himself growing more tired.

The moon was thinner than a smile.

What are you really thinking? he asked her.

Oh, stop asking, she said. I can't think two things at once like you. Tell me what were *you* thinking.

Smell a your stockings.

Tease, she said, already drifting into her plans for tomorrow. Or into sleep. Contented sleep. Her lips were contentedly posed, like two fragments of Greek pottery. How quickly she was on the brink of sleep again, quiet as clay. Sammy could see there were literally sparkles on his wife's skin. He could see them on her cheeks, her neck, on her shoulders, as if embedded in her skin were the tiniest granules.

Good night, sweet Chinook, he said.

She smiled, pressed shut her eyes, and drifted back happily to sleep.

He stayed on the precipice between sleep and stress, trying to sort out good thoughts from bad, hoping to avoid a nightmare. He recollected some events and tried to connect them to his present-day conundrum. His childhood in particular, which he so often denied having any relationship to the man he'd become, suddenly impressed upon him its formative traumas. His father fleeced a major accounting contract for a coke factory. The old man looked down on his child, and his child looked up at his eyes bulging from the wet sockets below the million white legs of his perversely spider eyebrows. Father raised his cane, and said: Don't enjoy this too much. He tapped the silver tip of his cane against Sammy's shoe, once, then a second time with a little more pressure. As usual his father made a comment for which Sammy had no good response. Those chalky grey, practically glass eyeballs crammed inside his father's face, staring at him. Sammy's bowels cursed his gutlessness. Yes? said his father. Yes, said Sammy with a squeak instead of a vowel.

Light as a wafer under the tongue, his consciousness dissolving beneath a frenulum of blankets, Sammy fell asleep. Molly snoozed along beside him, his warm, inert body next to hers.

//

Mrs. Litz woke before her men to prepare them for the day ahead. She was up pre-dawn to beat the dirt off their checked lumberjackets and copper-riveted pantaloons. Woodchips got in everything. Dust was inevitable. She dug out the little splinters in the wool of their jackets and the big chips in their pant pockets, even inside their boots. Then she lit the stove wood with some punk, put on the skillet, two cuts of butter, and cracked in seven eggs. The butter melted and bubbled.

Insisting on pretending he was still asleep, Litz groaned and rolled into her space in the middle of the bed, sniffed.

Pisk's eyes were shut, but his grip on the blankets wasn't going to allow Litz to pull the covers off his body at the far end of the mattress. Pisk slept next to the cedar log wall that whistled in his ear. He wrung out every last drip of sleep.

The men loved to sleep.

Of all methods, the smell of coffee was the best alarm clock to rouse her men. Invented by wives, coffee's exotic scent and intravascular kick had inspired men through the centuries to grunt off to hard labour, support the seeds of love, with time for little else. It is said that history is written on the backs of such men.

As soon as they sat to eat their breakfast, she was on them: I am sick living oot here, eh? Wa, she cried.

Quit yapping, said Litz. Can't you see I'm trying to eat?

They hadn't started the day and already she was on them about things. Pisk was not in the mood. She cried: Wa. She said: What a I do when you leave for work, eh? What a I do? Can't visit Vancouver. Prisoner here. I fear bandits. Find me, kill me or worse, eh. I bead and bead, make me go crazy. You see? … I *must* visit my sister.

Not yet, said Litz between fried eggs. I'll tell you when.

Why. Every day, Not yet. Not yet, not yet, all you say. Yes, the stars move more faster than you. What? Look at *me* in anger? You never talk. You bringem food and, and I see no one but you for so many days. I must see my sister.

If anyone followed you …, said Litz as he picked up his mug and swallowed a second cup of coffee. We'd all be dead.

She gripped the table with her fingernails, making the utensils and plates tremble. Pisk chewed up his food with unconcerned impatience. I am Whoi-Whoi, she said. No one follow me, no Whiteman. Whoi-Whoi live here before Whiteman on earth, eh. Eldest Whoi-Whoi are stones to-day. No one follow me. Promise. I am alone all day, eh.

Listen—

Wa, she said. You work. Me, no, no work, my beads. No one to *talk* with. Wa, she cried. She said: I pluck, I clean, I wash, I dry, I smoke, I am still alone, I—. You, no family. I—please let me see my sister. Please. I must see my sister.

Alls I got is my Ma, said Pisk, a dribble of milk on his chin from the oatmeal.

Your ma live Penticton. Many days. *My* sister live here. By canoe. It is me, Litz, his wife implored, squeezing a chunk of his arm in her hands. I love you. Please. At least I see my sister.

Pisk put on his jacket and spiked boots. He pat the pockets in his dungarees to ensure he remembered to collect the hashish. Not reluctantly, he stepped out the leather door and took a whiff of the new day. Inside the hut the argument continued.

No excuse, she said.

Baby, he said.

You burn down Vancouver? she asked.

... No, he said. You know that.

Well ...

The clouds washed away any signs of atmosphere, its replacement a white immateriality. The temperature was of a dead body. With a pipe and plug of warm black tobacco, Pisk waited over on the mossy knoll for his partner to finish conversations with his wife. It was a grain of privacy for them as much as for himself.

Pisk snacked. Blackberries were abundant and ripened late, thanks to the slope's westerly pitch. The thick, thistly briar of the blackberry patch was excellent cover for their home, but it was penetrable. He could not argue with Mrs. Litz's anxiety, alert as she was to a real insecurity in their fortress. No matter how often her husband reassured her that a plan was in the works to rebuild alliances, she was the one unprotected from invasion.

The leather door flapped open and Litz paused for a last goodbye, then approached foot over foot in a stumble.

What you tell her?

I told her I'd let her see her sister.

Will you?

No, said Litz glumly. It's been what, near to four months out here like this. Can't blame her for going a tad stir-crazy. She knows winter's around the corner. Gets colder. There's no light. It's going to be tough. What's a man to do? I got to protect her.

Get a hold a yourself. Forget your woes, said Pisk.

Litz shrugged.

They looked both ways and then slipped down into the secret tunnel and away from their exiled hideaway. Mrs Litz knew nothing about any tunnel, she had no idea how they escaped every day, and perhaps she understood the dangers well enough not to search. Litz didn't take her situation lightly, but as he often explained to her, it was only temporary. Soon they'd find a way to improve their lot. He promised her so.

He was two paces behind Pisk on the invisible trail, a series of exact footsteps through the undergrowth that left no print. They climbed the side of a rockface, where the wet moss dripped off the edge. The ferns were so abundant they seemed omniscient, a carpet burdened with the consciousness of the entire forest. Their rainsparkled green blades and dark interior folds went on forever up and down the cliffs and hills. They poured over the earth like follicles of hair.

A wild rabbit saw them, stopped, and with its belly low to the ground and its ears straight up, hopped once over a rotted log, escaped to safety.

Watch for mud, said Pisk.

I see it.

The fir trees lay in rhythmic sequence, a pattern that seemed graphed. The cedars wore their moss like robes. Nothing died here. Dead trees, white as stone sentinels, grew new trees out of their empty souls. Broom bristles could sprout a bouquet of greenery and draw bees year round. There was great abundance of fungi.

When will you take her to town, then? Pisk asked as they walked.

Ah, said Litz shaking his head, I didn't say *when*, eh. You know, I told her if she goes to town, it's her risk. I don't know if someone wants to kill her, right? I mean, they want to kill us.

Yeah.

Groundwater was seeping from bright green moss. The air was full of cinammon and mint and fresh soil. They caught whiffs of smoke and red berries. The ground was dark, patched with vermilion moss and scattered with bright golden chanterelle mushrooms tucked like hankies into pockets in the earth.

Careful, don't step on the chanty town here.

I see it, said Litz, stepping gingerly on his boot toes around the chanterelles. It's for her safety, is what I told her.

You got to settle your wife down, Pisk said. She talks too much.

Fourteen after all.

Alls I'm saying is I want some silence from her tongue-wagging.

Mind your business.

They trekked on wordlessly through the rainforest, pressing back the wet doors of giant swordferns and emerging into tiny green glades of sunlight. They were careful to leave no trail. They stepped lightly around chanterelle mushroom patches and over Indian sandpaper. In single file, they avoided mud under the rubbery duff off a Sitka spruce that Indians had stripped of bark fifty feet up, its bare flesh seeming more violated than if they'd simply cut it down. Jumping across a puddling creek without breaking a single bulrush, they rested on the erratic boulder nudged all the way from the Arctic Circle to this isolated fork on the riverbank by the declension of the Ice Age.

In 1886, it was Doyle's boulder. Doyle logged here, but really it was the muskrats that owned the land. Their purpose was to appear from unknown crevices to eat shoots and leaves, fuck and fight—burly little monsters with wet hair. Pisk counted twenty of them as he sat back and contemplated. It was a reliable rock with a dramatic perspective on life for a man who didn't know his own needs. The earth seemed to lean over just so Pisk would have a grand view. They heard a tree felled by Doyle's hand in the echoed distance. Life, for the moment, was harmless. They smoked the hashish until the jungle was a bubble and they were a mote of dust swirling downward along the contour of its oily surface.

Hey, Litz, said Pisk.

What? said Litz.

Pisk reached into the pocket of his sweater and unfolded the piece of paper from inside, laid it on the rock between them, and gave Litz a short pencil.

What you want me to write? asked Litz.

Dear Ma … Life's treating me well out here in Vancouver, and I hope …

//

At the time, without any knowledge of the history of the game and how it was played, there was no way for Minna and I to guess how long the fight would last or how it was segmented. Not that it mattered. I was intrigued. Minna looked far from bored. She was getting giddy. I was trying to make sense of it all. In the time since we arrived in the backyard the house had caved even deeper into its foundations. The yard was looking much worse also. The audience had ruined the perimeters and the players were gouging and trampling the rest. The unmown grass now lay irregularly flattened, similar to morning hair, from all the footsteps and wrestling marks. I wondered if not far underneath the sod there was a layer of wet mud, swamp gum, or some other liquid that the house was sinking into. The grass was like a tarp laid over top. Maybe not a tarp, a trap. The lawn was whorled crop circle–like, and was balding at the centre where Ken and Silas were at the moment completely hammerlocked. The situation passed for wrestling motions before it stepped up to aggressive moves—I overheard names like the Wheelbarrow, Spanish Layover, the Pisk. Every time I prepared to wince back from an ugly scene the struggle transformed into something calmer. So I wasn't convinced it was a fight, but I couldn't see how it was staged, either. For one thing, if it was some kind of sort of performance piece, Ken's shins looked too gruesome. He really chewed them up on a fall after being trapped knee over knee. He fell hard, and looked angrily at himself, and the one named Silas apologized. But the audience seemed to think Silas had scored big.

I watched this game unfold with an increasing sense of the strange. Even the long intermittences when the players just stood bent over and caught their breath seemed unusual. I felt more and more irrelevant.

I liked that move where it was kind a jazzy, a dance routine like you see in old movies, said Minna.

You mean the one where he dragged him around by the neck *{see fig. 5.1}*?

Yeah.

Even though just after that he swung around and tried to hit him in the face?

Funny, yeah.

They don't ever seem to actually hurt each other on purpose, I said. So I'm puzzled.

I think they want to make it look like they want to hurt each other, but really they actually don't.

Then she went down on her knees. Struggling, she pushed her hands through the side pockets of her high-altitude camping bookbag, looking for the good shit. Finally there it was. She stood up with the paraphernalia in hand. Made from cedar and much the same size as a tin for lozenges, the paraphernalia looked solid but was in fact hollow. Indians on the West Coast used to make clothes from cedar; that's how light it was. She flipped the object over in her hands, levered the top open along a joint, and shook out a cigarette-sized brass straw from where it was kept inside a smooth pipeline bored into the wood. She fiercely tapped one end of the brass straw into the larger

---

FIGURE 5.1
The Spanish Layover;
an early study

Calabi's commentary: A sympathetic opponent will retreat with you as quick as a hound, but if you've hooked a feisty player he will treat you like a Sunday fisherman who's caught a live one.

hollow where the pot was stowed, plugging a hoot of grass into the end of it. She'd bought the whole package on Vancouver Island in Nanaimo from an Indian kid who carved them on a street corner beside a fast food restaurant and sold them for fifteen dollars each, including the brass pipe made from plumbing parts. He'd carve an orca on it for you, but that cost twenty dollars extra. She had the thirty-five-dollar version. I called it her one-hit wonder. True that Minna gave me a hard time, or it felt like it, and I didn't have to take it, but it's true that I did. I was going through an experience. I was, like many, in search of a girl.

//

Toronto was on his way down Hastings Street towards his destiny: The Calabi & Yau Bakeshoppe. With him travelled not only hunger but also secrets, some his own, some he'd been given, including another message from Molly Erwagen to the exiles he foresaw bumping into any day now.

He weighed his options. He glanced in the general vicinity of some other Indians, who paid him explicitly no attention. Would they kill him if he said hello? He motioned. They huddled more closely under hat rims and their Hudson's Bay blankets. A pipe's fume rose from their mass, like a wandering-away ghost. He shrugged, supposed that yes, they would kill him.

A murmur turned into a yowl upside his stomach. A Calabi&Yau pastry would soothe his lonely spirit, or at the very least his hunger.

He hardly followed the planks down Columbia Street, for the seasonal dry spell left him mud-free options.

A horse clopped by, covered to the stiffles and withers in the muck from New Westminster road, followed by the dusty brougham of an eastern tycoon, seen better days than this. He waved his hat to Toronto and Toronto nodded back.

Coming from the side street, the black hat and pink face was unmistakably Vicars, and beside him his friend

AE Terry Berry, a spirited man. Vicars was a bit poltroonish himself, as Daggett might say. They walked with a tree climber's gait, for sure, all bowed, knock-kneed, and rolled ankles. Toronto wondered if his impressions of others in any way reflected how they thought of him. Was his face as obvious, revealing all his weak intentions, and did he walk with that much fear of the earth?

It was a conversation without Toronto having to say a word. Vicars talked enough for everybody. Terry Berry was good at agreeing. Eventually little caches of white spittle caught at the sides of Vicars's mouth, lowering his air of respectability another notch. He was tired of the woods, and he and Terry Berry were going to open a dry goods warehouse to compete against the Oppenheimer brothers. Quit all this backbreaking work with no security and the Chinese fifty-centing them at every step. Throw the axes and saws aside and forget that life and settle down to something safe and presentable that you can count on into your old age. No man can log his entire life unless he dies early because of it. Besides, the city could use another food distributor, and if there's one thing Vicars knows it's business.

Toronto wished them well and carried on his way, hoping to lose no more time. From behind the wide stump of a giant red cedar, he saw an exhale of smoke.

Klahowya, Toronto, called out a neighbour on the opposite side of the street, hand up, armpit exposed. Couldn't remember his name at the moment, but he was a Greek with thick, bright-white front teeth and an even temper. He set his ice cream cart down the block from Red & Rosy's General Store where bananas hung in green-yellowing bunches alongside grey and brown grouse and the bodies of fresh deer, antlers aimed to the sidewalk, twisting in the breeze ever so slightly on their knotted hind legs.

Toronto, it is you, said the Greek, shaking his friend's hand. Ah, it's almost nearly winter, so what a I do? The Greek looked at his ice cream cart, watching a drizzle of melted ice fall from a bottom corner of the sweating casket. In my home, he told Toronto, I writer for newsprint, yes? I write many news, many news. Then I must leave. English, ah, not so much, not for me. English is skookum, yes? Ha ha. Nobody pay me chickamin to write English, ha ha. Hm. I still get chickamin with my hands, he said, holding out their calluses, you kumtuks, Toronto? My hands.

Yes, Toronto understood him.

Any way to get chickamin, the Greek added. Yesterday I get mugged. You believe me? I who got so few chickamin. No chickamin to spare. Mugger mug me. You believe me, Toronto? Ah, such a pity.

Seen the mugger's face?

No, only black garment. Little man. Small, thin, like insect. Great big knife in hand. Sharp thing. What he said do, I do. For me, what other choice? Life it is misery, you agree? Sure you no want ice cream?

Okay.

Okay now, ha ha, that more like it. He opened the lid of his casket and rolled a nice big scoop of spumoni for the Indian and dropped it into a waffle cone.

Klahowya, Toronto, the Greek said as Toronto walked away, ice cream in hand. Raising the nickel in his fingers, the Greek called out to him: Don't forget you-me: billiards.

Klahowya, said Toronto and waved goodbye. He nodded his head and left the Greek to his day. He walked for a while trying to figure out the size of the world.

From a Chinese breezeway leading to a handmade noodle shop in the alley, a hand yoinked Toronto into the shadows.

Whaa-a? cried Toronto, happy at least to have spilled the cone.

Shh, don't say nothing. Shit, brother, you got spumoni all over me.

The shadowy surprise came with a ripe smell of long-term uncleanliness, an odour and voice he easily recognized; once able to retrieve his composure and his hat, he saw none other than Pisk.

A stranger limped by without noticing them stowed in the slippery, smelly, bowelly dark breezeway between one Chinese cookout and another, right in the noodle hole. Farther into the darkness, Toronto made out a second figure, doubtless it was Litz. Who else? Pisk dug into his pocket and brought out an unsealed envelope. He handed it to Toronto, said: Can you mail this?

Toronto looked it over. The letter inside almost fell out when he flipped the envelope to see if there was a stamp or address anywhere on it. All it said was: For Ma Pisk.

He nodded. I can mail it for you, he said. This was the same kind of meeting he'd had with the men when he passed on Molly Erwagen's message.

Any news from your side? said Pisk. From Mrs., ah, Molly . . .?

Says she can meet this afternoon, said Toronto.

This aftern—, ok*ay*. Pisk smiled and chucked Toronto on the shoulder the way a man thanks another man whom he owes more than words could ever express.

Toronto smiled at Pisk, flapped the letter in the air to let him know it was in safekeeping, and humbly fled the noodle hole, back onto the street, where he pocketed the envelope, attention once again aimed at the Calabi & Yau Bakeshoppe, within sight, and more importantly, within smelling distance.

There were no boardwalks in Little Tokyo, as Powell Street was often called, not like there were on some of the other streets. Here there were only a few scattered boards to jump to one by one over the mud, and muddy doorways no matter how tidy you were. Nevertheless, fronting the Calabi & Yau Bakeshoppe was a fine bit of boardwalk, not to mention three solid stone steps leading to the glass door framed in gorgeous maple scallops.

The brass doorbell ding-dingled as it always did when the door swung open, and Toronto fully whiffed the exalted aroma of Calabi & Yau's freshly baked pastries. Calabi was behind the counter as usual, and raised his eyes to acknowledge Toronto before he returned to his present customer, a shoeless kid counting out filthy pennies.

Ah, son, you are one penny short, said Calabi. Nine cents. What shall we do?

The boy looked up at the baker with uncomprehending anxiety.

Yau walked over to the glass trays where the Calabi&Yaus were kept and the boy followed him. Calabi tonged a chocolate and banana Calabi&Yau into a little foldable pastry box. The little boy was wordless, soundless, afraid of his own hunger. Calabi held the tongs aloft in his crossed arms and looked at the kid, but the kid didn't know about jokes like this, and Calabi squinted. He tonged in a blackberry Calabi&Yau with cream cheese icing then swiftly tied the box shut with twine and handed it to the boy. Last penny on me, said Calabi and winked. Ding-dingle.

Klahowya, Toronto, best wishes, welcome welcome. How is your day?

Klahowya, Toronto, called out Yau from the back where he was soaked in sweat from sliding pallets of pastry into the Dutch oven.

Hi, hi, klahowya. Good.

Calabi took out his kerchief and started to polish off the kiddie fingersmudges from the glass sides of the pastry counter. Clever child, yes? he said. *Al*ways one penny short. Ah, now, sir, how is Mrs. Erwagen?

Toronto nodded. Busy, he said. Mr. Erwagen is o-kay. Wife o-kay, too. Keep busy.

Ah, busy, said Calabi, winking. He was crouched beside Toronto and had to stop polishing the glass and look almost straight up at him to make his point: Many lady I see—busy. So busy. I do not see Mrs. Erwagen busy like other lady.

That was true, thought Toronto.

Coffee?

Toronto decided he would have a cup. He sat down on a swivel stool. When Calabi was satisfied with his work polishing the glass he returned to his station behind the counter, where he automatically served Toronto a plate of three blackberry Calabi&Yaus and poured him a cup of coffee from a brass thermos the size of an outhouse.

Toronto hunkered down to his pastries, ate one very fast, and tested his coffee, which was rich and thick and oily. He saw Yau sweating in the back room as he hoisted plates of dough into the astonishing Dutch oven. God was merciful in saving this pastry kiln, this blazing womb of pure goodness. He waved goodbye to the bakers and was back on the street avoiding the huge puddles and mudholes. Everywhere around him the world looked a little greyed out, a little paler since September had rolled around, more anemic, or undead. In fall when it rained it was as thin as pins, and when the sun shone it always felt like it was for the last time.

When Molly learned that he'd relayed her message to Pisk and Litz, she immediately set about preparing to leave the house for the afternoon. She would leave her husband alone in the study while the Chinaman in the kitchen finished preparing that night's ham quiche and Toronto transcribed more of Sammy's diary for him. Normally a man in his position, neutered to the limit, would be wary of letting his young beautiful wife explore the streets unaccompanied. The muddy, rapacious streets of Vancouver least of all. He'd no more stop her if he wasn't paralyzed.

You take care and watch yourself. I love you.

I will, she said daintily, halfway out the door, a toe in the air. I love you, too.

There's the mugger, remember.

I remember.

//

The sun chopped a cloud in half and fanned itself through the space, pushing the cumulonimbus farther and farther apart until Vancouver was rewarded with a brief show of blue sky, so blue, so unlike clouds that the blue didn't look real. September was the last month for a chance to see clear skies in 1886.

Business on the street was brisk. Say you were a Chinaman, you could sit on a stump, put a fish on a piece of newsprint in front of you, and sell it within the hour. Gambling too was claiming a tenacious hold on lives. The fan tans in Chinatown were all doing hourly lotteries. The boardwalks teemed with men on errands.

She travelled in balletic steps among the men as if they were no more than phantasms and she the only person on the road. In a sense this was true, and in a sense so was the opposite. They were the nameless men who toiled to make Vancouver a home for more ladies like herself. She was a vision of the future these men had yet to grasp. They wanted that life, the life they believed she represented. They yearned hard for that life especially on those nights when the cold and rain got right into your bones, seeping in through the joints and freezing you from the inside, nights when the only bed in town was at a Methodist rooming house on a mattress with three other jobbers like yourself. She was a stark contrast to the day-to-day agony of making a decent wage.

//

Seated atop his horse, holding the reins in his one hand while the other arm sleeve was folded up flat and pinned to his shoulder, there was Clough, leader of the chain gang, prison guard for the ditch-diggers, cheroot smoker. A beard in need of a trim starting to take on a life of its own, a greasy, wide-pored nose the colour of your thumb after you hit it with the hammer. The tobacco smoke poured out both his wide hairy nostrils and eventually dissipated into the late September day.

When Clough saw Molly coming down the path, he shifted his rifle from his lap back to its holster on his carriage then wiped his face cleanish. Instinct drove him to feel around for his flask, make sure it wasn't in view. He coughed and cleaned his throat of debris in hopes of sounding somewhat presentable. No matter the tumour that was his nose and the sulphuric reek of halitosis, let alone the cloacal whiff of his twopenny cigar, his bloodshot eyes, and his earlobes hanging halfway down his jaw.

Moe Dee was in the trench with the rest of them—for starting something at the Sunnyside as usual. Dee was a talker. He never stopped. Even while he shovelled he gassed on like that.

Know who you remind me a? Clough said to Dee. You remind me a prisoner I once knowed who served twenty-five years for mouthing off to the wrong bohunk. You in that gulch for fighting or yakking? Now I want to see this whole block done by sundown or I'll keep you guys another day.

You're not the law, said Moe Dee.

I'm your keeper. I let you out when I see fit.

See fit. Put in the drunk tank so many times they make you warden. Whoever heard a that?

Now listen close, Dee, because I mean what I'm aboot to say. For every word that comes out a your mouth starting now you get another day. If I make myself clear nod your damn stupid head.

Dee nodded his head, and having not yet seen Molly coming down the road, set to work on the ditch like it was Clough's own face.

And that goes for the lot a you. Clough was seated on the metal spoon on the front of the carriage that had brought the chain gang to the ditch. To dig like animals, like badgers tunnelling to make a sewer system. The earth seemed to gasp and suck with every shovelling, like a swimmer up from a long dive in icy grey water. He listened to them dig and watched her swaying towards him.

She, in complete contrast, walked as if on stilts, long steep steps down the lane faster than Clough thought a lady should walk, and yet her poise was musical and persuasive, her skin a translucent white. As sights go in Vancouver, she was as brief as blue sky. With his voice cracking on his introductory syllables, Clough raised his hat, said to her: Why, ha-ll*o*, how do you do, Mrs. Erwagen? Lovely day all a sudden, wouldn't you say?

You think?

I don't need the sun to feel warm, said Clough.

Moe Dee laughed to himself, but Clough heard him well enough.

I hardly care for the sun, either, she answered gaily. One of the spotted mutts that followed Clough everywhere got up from the ground where he'd been asleep next to the carriage and walked over to Molly to sniff her dress. Hello, dog, she said and refrained from touching him, seeing that fleas bounced and popped off him like little cannons in all directions.

You want to know how a man such as myself makes do around here? said Clough in a conscious effort to sound authoritatively sober. Ma'am, you see me up here in charge a the ditch-diggers, well, that's one occupation I can claim. Po-lice put a lot a trust in me, why, so much so that they gave me the standard-issue rifle and let me … well, trust. See, Mrs. Erwagen, let's just say it could be *me* down in the muck with these gents, eh. But I got the trust a the community, Mrs. Erwagen. For instance, when your home was being built I was one a the men on the job.

Thank you again, yes, I recall you saying so that day in the Sunnyside Hotel.

Eh? What day was that? said Clough, who thumbed his shirtsleeve, fidgeting with a black hole in his memory.

The day that great brawl took place outside on the street when the man Pisk stripped down.

Oh, oh, ma'am, don't tell me you saw all *that*. I got to apologize for this town sometimes, most a the times.

Not at all.

Well, anyways, as I was saying, the other things I do around here is I light the street lamps, you may a seen me do that past your home. And poundkeeper. I'm an expert at trapping. If ever you see a stray horse, cow, goat, anything, or a dog, like this one here, you notify me and I'll come collect him. Sound good?

She shooed the dog away.

I won't make too much a my crippledness on account a your own husband's situation … the extra I got to do simply to get by. One arm or two, though, I'm still a great trapper. Ever any a these guys try to escape, they can rest assured that freedom won't last long. You hear that, boys?

The chain gang groaned, took this moment to lean on their shovels, stand at rest in what was becoming a mass grave of their own making, and stare at her and mouth-breathe.

Get back to work, Clough shouted, then laughed privately to Molly, to show her that being the disciplinarian was a mask he could put on and take off at his choosing. If there's anything I can do for you …

Another time, perhaps, she said, waving goodbye.

Say klahowya to your husband for me.

She floated away. He watched her recede into the landscape, become a shadow shaped by fog and haze. He wanted to do something for her, like catch the mugger, but he also felt a great anxiety over the presence of such a fine lady in his vicinity. The safer the town got, the more ladies like her would come to live in Vancouver, and the harder his life was going to get.

//

Not an hour later, the chain gang was once again interrupted from their task by Furry and Daggett, who came running at full keel down the road with broadaxes crossed over their plaided backs and beards still drizzling with beerslosh, hollering: You seen Litz and Pisk?

Hell, no, I haven't seen em, Clough called back, taking off his hat for the second time and mopping his brow. Remembering to unholster his rifle again, he shouted down to the chain gang: Any a you boys know where're Litz and Pisk at? Nah, not a snitch among em.

Daggett said: We heard from the Greek they're around.

Pindar, eh? Where'd he see them two?

Hiding out in Chinatown, he says.

Well, what are they doing around there?

How the fuck am I supposed to know that? said Daggett.

How the fuck am I supposed to know what you know and don't know? said Clough.

Well, I don't know what the fuck they were doing in Chinatown.

Why didn't you just say so?

Jesus, Clough. You're goddamn aggravating.

You're the one who's aggravating, said Clough.

Well, if you see them, said Daggett, you tell them we're looking for them.

Sure will, said Clough.

The two beastly handloggers took off at a sprint in no particular direction, scaring strangers on the street with their questions. To the men on the chain gang, Clough said: Get back to work, you flea-bitten minks.

//

She walked alone under the shade of the forest. Molly in the breeze. The cool sun was above the clouds and beyond reckoning. It was the sun from a northern perspective, bright but not warm, concluded by chilly shadows. Two hundred feet in the air a peregrine falcon circled the airstream, its vision fierce enough to spot mice on the forest floor. The falcon saw Molly as she kept looking at her hand-drawn map and changing directions. Hearing the bird's high-pitched cry, she looked up and saw the falcon on a fleet-winged course, his swift pinions carrying him over earth's darkness and bringing him in contact with the infinite, gliding along the airstream in a descent from Heaven.

The falcon spotted Litz and Pisk, too, and no less than thirty yards in front of them, Furry and Daggett—then suddenly the swift bird was taken upon by two crows whose wings and talons nicked at its feathers, turning and wrestling in mid-air, the falcon using its greater strength to keep the crows at bay. Yet their trickster strategies prevailed, the crows forcing the falcon to sweep low across the sky and nest for a minute in the parched limbs of an old fir tree dozing in the wind, poised between the two packs of men walking towards each other on the forest floor.

Litz and Pisk were careful around the dry needles of a shedding fir. Besides the tricky path itself, the men stopped at even the smallest sound. If a single stick broke it was cause for alarm. The rule was to stop, stand still, then make a fast duck behind safe cover. Now having done that, they lay hiding in the roots of a monolithic cedar, watching the forest, expecting to see a deer's head turn in the shadows, or worse, a Vancouverite.

Ah, hell, it was nothing, said Furry, and stood up from a blend of foliage. It was them birds, he added, seeing the crows swooping above them trying to dive in at the peregrine.

Holy fuck, thought Litz and Pisk simultaneously. A hideous smile pulled across Litz's face, and Pisk's teeth were heard to grit.

Both men thought of the survivor's credo: Silence, stillness, stealth, and sightlines.

Daggett hoisted himself up from the ground and looked around. His axeblade flashed in Pisk's eyes. He was ten paces from where Litz and Pisk hid in the tree's muddy, tangled roots. This was what they were up against. The trees were speckled with yellow and white lichen, the floor was waves of fern blades. For the moment, Daggett and Furry didn't see Litz or Pisk in the overload of greenery and penumbra.

We're out a time, said Furry, pinching the bridge of his nose.

This is supposed to be the place, eh. Gave me good details. Said near them fucking old chutes on ol' Fraser's camp down by Bell's Island.

Furry coughed. They'd spent the last hour circling Doyle's land, hunting for the hideout.

Daggett took a deep breath, spat, and said: Oh, I can smell them sweating. They're so close I can feel it. I can feel their beings here. This is the place, I fucking feel it, eh.

Daggett's spittle was practically on their faces. It was humiliating. Pisk looked at Litz with overboiling irritation, irrationally blaming him, and Litz looked back at him as if to say,

What a you expect us to do? Neither was known to hide from rivals. It was *not* ordinary for a lumberjack to avoid a fist fight. It was downright yellow. Snaking into an inguinal cranny between the kneecapped talons of an ancient tree did not feel right. It felt to Pisk that he'd reached the lowest a man agreed to stoop to collaborate with a woman. Silence. Stillness. They were cowards for her love. Litz didn't look much more impressed with their predicament. Still, he made it clear by his expression that he'd never forgive Pisk if he stood up. The time would come, patience, patience, the time will come.

Stealth. Sightlines. Oh, Pisk was grinning with mischief, barely able to suppress his desire to leap to his feet and break Daggett in two.

Litz mouthed the four S's … and Pisk winced in anger, for he knew better than to need a reminder. It was hard to contain himself and follow his own good advice. Litz did not take an eye off his partner, ready to pull him back if he so much as flinched.

Fuck it, said Furry. Fuck these woods. We won't find nothing in here. It's dark as a bronze eye.

Can't find any tracks for all the fucking ferns, neither, said Daggett. If my nose weren't plugged I bet you I'd smell those dick-biters from here. I bet you I would. Came oot all this ways just for nothing. Really chaps my ass. Those dudes are getting my wrath when the time comes, eh.

Sure, said Furry.

They finally gave up, walked off northwest, Daggett yakking to Furry the whole time, cursing everything that ever lived, axehandles at rest over their shoulders. For a few minutes more, Litz and Pisk lay in hiding as their rivals muttered and crashed into the great overwhelming cave of the wilderness, quieter and quieter until gone, good riddance. If it weren't for Molly they might have left town altogether and not been hiding here like crickets against the earth. When the coast was clear Litz and Pisk got up from the tree roots, brushed the wet crud from their dungarees, and checked both ways.

A sound, nothing more than an embittered eagle taking flight from a dry hemlock, gave them pause, listening for what smacked of human among the forest's whispers, just in case. Once the coast was well and truly clear, they proceeded on without discussion. It was a sorry day for their partnership and they knew it.

I don't like hiding from, Pisk said. It's a fucking splinter in my sock.

What a you think a Furry?

The brains.

Definitely the brains. But how much?

I want to bludgeon them both.

I want to beat them with their own bones.

We'll mulch them bohunks, said Pisk.

Damn straight, said Litz.

This lady better know what she's doing.

She does. I can smell it.

Oh, man, said Pisk. You greedy.

What aboot you, eh? Come on. She can bend you with her pinky finger.

At least I don't got marriage shackled on me.

Walking through intermittent rain, Litz felt it like a cold frost on his bare neck. It was a falling freezing mist. The rust-coloured bark of the cedars was spaced at chaotic intervals across a slanted floor of dried coniferous needles, spongy black mulch, and a brilliant array of green and yellow lichen. All of it was soaked through by rainfall. Giant splashes fell to the ground or exploded on Pisk's bald scalp. They were on Horne's land now, a secluded, bear-infested stake in the coniferous forests.

//

She sat on a Hudson's Bay blanket as if on a picnic. She even had a wicker basket stocked with *not quite* picnic items. No one in history ever brought, for instance, a bag of flour, two quarts of milk, a dozen beef sausages, and three dozen raw eggs on a picnic. Still, it was food. She smoked a cigarette. They waited in the shadows, peeping her like Toms. No denying her inner beauty. She had what in these parts of the world they called nice *totoosh lackles.* That was Chinook for holy bosoms. Her fashionable smock was made of imported cotton. She was spotless.

A wild rabbit peaked its brown-white ears above the long grass, then leaped to hide again.

She don't look frightened to be here all alone, whispered Litz.

Pisk regarded her. I don't think she'd care if we never showed up, he said.

They gazed at her. There was a certain infinite placidity to her smile. She never got a bored look. She sat with her knees bent to one side, her ten toes stacked single file up her bare feet. The bare feet was her one show of intimacy.

Man, said Pisk under his breath.

What? said Litz.

Her back was to them, but as she turned her neck they saw her face in profile. She tucked the cigarette between her lips and sucked with plush inhalation, then let the burly cloud exhale once it had seen what it was like inside her. Her brand of tobacco smelled like the best tobacco. By some miracle it had stopped raining, and where she sat the grass seemed to be as dry as a cat's tongue; even the sun was willing to make an appearance. There was no easy way for Pisk to express how golden her skin looked in the sunlight without sounding weak. He wasn't like Litz, all syrup the minute he laid eyes on a beauty. Her complexion looked as if a thin protection of glass was set over European paint. She caressed her blanket as she waited. Absently, she unfurled the balding wool, mashed it into a spongy wad of Hudson's Bay colours—red, yellow, and green on a cream background—, and then, noticing what she'd done, tried to press the wool back into the weave to no avail. She was looking in the opposite direction. All they saw was her back, her black hair, and a thin horn of the moon that was her face. Not even one corner of her lip was in view. Her hair was pinned up in two swooping chignons. Her ears were as white as marble pedestals in contrast to her hair's stormy voluptuousness. Her white nape was shadowcrested. Ah, she said, there you are.

Klahowya, said Pisk, instantly climbing up out of the foliage to greet her, followed closely behind by Litz, who was blushing and kept his eyes lowered, not wanting her to see by the look on his face that they'd been watching her for some time now, enough time to long for more.

She greeted her men with handshakes, her wrist bent ever so slightly. She smelled like the spray off a northern waterfall. They forgot all about their brush with Furry and Daggett in the forest a moment ago and found themselves concentrating on her green eyes. Molly stood up gaily without bending her knees, skipped over to her woodsmen and asked: Tell me how you balance on the logs out on the water like that. She mimicked a logroll, laughing, and jumped away with a balletic jeté.

Litz said: It's balance. Plus we got steel spikes on our boots. Takes practice.

I'd like to try something today, she said. Might not work. Are you ready? She craned her neck and flicked away the dragonfly hovering next to her. We'll start with clothes on, she said.

Fuck it, said Pisk. Let's go.

No, no, she said. Stay clothed. Put on your dungarees, Pisk. Please. For the time being you'll practise with me.

All the more reason, Pisk said. I'm not going to shame myself for nothing. He stood there with a shirt on and his hands on his bare hips, waiting for a better reason to put his pants back on.

Molly grunted. It was a girl's grunt, adorable. Fine, you keep your pants off, but only if you slap me.

Slap you?

Tell your partner to try to slap me, Molly said to Litz.

In reply, Litz licked all around his mouth, a weird loner's expression of embarrassment and confusion, and then he looked at the ground where something knuckle-hard needed to be bunted away.

Don't be afraid a me, said Pisk, just 'cause I got no pants on. Come on.

Put your pants on if you don't have the guts to slap me. Or let this be your first test. Molly threw her Stars & Stripes on a gravel patch, and Litz, moving a step closer, politely pressed it out with the toe of his leather boot. Call it a dare, she said. I bet if you tried, you'd miss.

I'd miss, how would I miss?

A course you'll miss. If you slap me, I show you how to pavane with your clothes off. If you miss, we do things my way.

He swung his palm out half-heartedly and she shifted her weight and swatted his arm out of the air so forcefully that he had to laugh when he stumbled.

Try again.

He swung his hand out a bit more forcefully and this time she stepped aside. Okay, I get it, he said.

You hardly tried at all. You want to put your pants back on, is that it?

What a you mean?

Is that how you slap a *man*? No wonder you wouldn't fight Daggett.

You want me to slap you?

Hard as you can.

He shook his head. I don't find this funny.

That's your problem, she said. I'm a very funny girl.

This time he really let her have it. He came down on her with the back of his hand fast enough to split a fence-board. When he connected it was with his face to the earth. How she did it he wasn't sure. She dodged him by a hair's breadth. He could feel the air off his swing buff her cheek. How she was able to lunge and kick him off his balance while knocking his hand out of the sky with her arm, he didn't know. In a fell swoop she levelled him and he was down on the ground with his legs splayed awkwardly and a mouthful of grass. She was still standing.

He spat out dirt. How the fuck—?

Put your pants on so we can get started.

He rethought his hopes. Molly was too extraordinary for his domestic visions. Pisk had trouble doing up his fly buttons. He said: What was that supposed to be, a lesson? How'd you pull that?

I can teach you how to do that, too. For now, get your pants on and let's pavane.

//

Every morning they ate breakfast with the groceries Molly supplied them, getting ready for the day like they were going off to log, leaving Mrs. Litz back at their hideout. They would sneak through the forests, occasionally embarking on a clandestine trip into town for Chinese opium, or maybe to give Toronto a letter for Pisk's mother in Penticton. Then, careful to avoid alerting Furry and Daggett, they'd portage south to the clearing on Doyle's land where they practised the man game with Molly. Starting with basic ballroom holds, Pisk and Litz took turns learning new steps. From that foundation she taught them how to do the volta, how to shika, crip walk, and do a faster version of the Boston waltz. There was groundwork, too, including an adaptation of the classic Corker. These and other combinations of European dance, the martial arts she'd learned while touring the Orient, and acrobatics formed the basic grammar of the man game, which included a repertoire of moves. But in those early days it was not at all clear to either of them what she intended. A day that began with traditional sparring and ended with two-man naked barrel rolls was not the most comprehensible. She continued to refer to it as theatre, and then rephrase it as a sport.

Nor was she a relaxed coach. Rather she was forceful and exact, strict and impossible to ignore (*Again,* she demanded;

Please, she squeaked). And unlike other ladies of her stature, Pisk didn't get the sense when he talked to her that she thought he was a slug. Where is the problem? was a frequent question of hers. He'd met circus girls before but none of them were ever like Molly either. None of those girls carried themselves with such sophistication, good humour, and steady spirit. None were so fetching. Molly didn't fit properly into any type of society, not any kind Pisk had ever known. For Pisk the only character similar to Molly was alcohol. That cruel beautiful prohibited drink could traverse the whole world unscathed.

There were days when Pisk held her in a dance move and had to resist the urge to crush her. He knew better. She could put him flat on his back. But whenever he felt his desires eddy down his intestines and his body erupt in sweat, the only thing left for him to do (he thought) was crush her. They danced chest to chest. It was unavoidable, the pleasure of it, and the pleasure was awful. Pisk had never held a woman so delicately. His throat was a wedge of nerves like he'd swallowed a shoehorn. He knew that if he were a gentleman he could dance with a lady and not feel the way he did. What was the difference between him and Sammy? Nothing in his years had prepared him to dance with Molly Erwagen, let alone in a secluded field on the edge of the world. Her right hand lay in his left hand like a baby bird. Her left hand on his right arm, experiencing the bicep there under his shirt, which she insisted he relax. Your arm is too stiff for dancing, she said, you're not trying to hit me, you're trying to dance with me; could she read minds, too? She counted aloud in a sweetened whisper knowing he still needed the cues not the rhythm. Her black hair fell around her shoulders in the intermittent sunlight, his concentration never far from crushing her. His right hand on the small of her back, feeling the meridian of her spine shift and revolve through the steps, whisking her skirts against his legs terribly, made his heart leap to conclusions, and rather than voice them, he was determined to crush her. But when he took the breath she caught the tension in his fingers and it took only one unexpected step from her to make him lose his balance, and in recovering it, lose his will.

Don't think I'll ever learn it right, Pisk said while they relaxed with some weed after one long day feeling he'd accomplished nothing.

Once you see yourself as a performer and not my suitor, she said, it will come easily.

Not the answer he'd expected. He sat on a log and caught his breath, staring disconsolately at his fuzzy gut heaving, the bleeding scab on his knee, and wondered what he thought he was doing with this lady who threw matches at his temper. He stamped out his cheroot under his bare foot.

While Pisk aimed to loosen up in the early days (she called them rehearsals), Litz was already so weakened and wobbly on his feet. He couldn't make a proper fist when he tried. She would say: Make a fist, show me a fist. And he'd make one, and she'd come over and peel open his fingers like the petals of a wilted tulip. None of the lessons or plans for the man game disturbed him. Fighting with his best friend without a stitch on was not a problem. Lumberjacks were used to seeing each other in the buck. It was Molly herself that perverted him. To Litz's eyes, her beauty seemed forever moonlit. When he danced with her, she had to keep reminding him not to watch his feet. He was too shy to admit that her shining ankles were what held his attention, clad in the fairest fashion of embroidered leather from the realms of the unreal. From out of these boots came the goddess who smiled in his ear. He accepted that when dancing she would lead because after all it was her, his love. It was because of her that his knees demobilized out and he tripped, frequently. She spoke with dramatic concision. Every word required only its neighbours. To Litz, even her most unreasonable demands—Strangle Pisk upside down while he's running, she once said *{see fig. 5.2}*—were far sweeter than the throbbing lyre. Her voice was more golden than gold. Litz had heard enough about poetry to think so. He wondered if he could remember the poet who wrote, If you do not change direction, you may end up where you are heading. That anonymous line was stuck in his mind. Trying to perform an applejacks for her was all he wanted from life. It surprised him how easily he could do a one-handed spinning handstand, and her delight in that early success was food for a week. They practised until they were raw and not a tendon would stretch and their lungs might shred and they finally gave up. She loved every minute of it. They could tell from her applause.

By day's end, the sun was rarely more than a perforation in a sheet of clouds laid across the sky's desk. It was under this hooded eventide that Litz and Pisk returned home back through the woods to their hideout, more exhausted than after a day of logging. Every muscle burned. Stubbed toes. High above them it was pouring cold rain. Beneath the trees it was only icy cold and as humid as the inside of a lung. They made their way over and across the many chattering creeks, stepping from stone to stone over waters swollen with salmon. At first glance the glittering water seemed uninhabited until your eye

FIGURE 5.2
Sausage Links

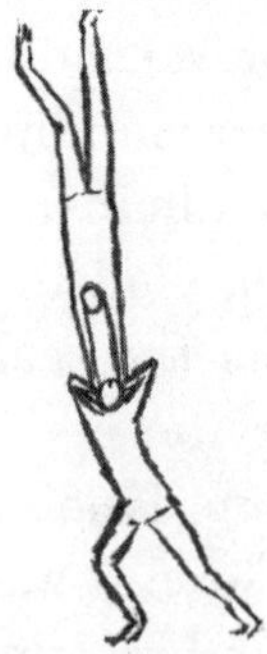

Calabi's commentary: The giant timber made of two men, head to head, the branches trying to strangle the trunk, which, out a fear, has uprooted itself, and desperately looks for help among the other trees in the forest.

caught sight of one, a huge fish sheathed in a silvery chainmail coat, then another and another, all camouflaged, rippling like the water and the sunlight and coloured to match the wet stones beneath. There were dozens of them within only a small pool of water, resting in the calmer eddies or keeping pace with the speed of the current, waiting for the strength to lunge ahead a foot or two over and around the boulders to their next available resting spot. Many were already half-dead, exhausted, their torn and shredded scales exposing the pink flesh underneath, with just enough energy left in them for one last attempt to make it to their destination. Here and there the men could see bright glistening roe draped like strange clusters of orange pearls over thin branches and hanging off rocks just under the surface of the water. More out of frustration than hunger, Pisk chose one heavily laden stick, pulled it out of the river, and swallowed all the little bubbles, every egg that was on it, then threw the stick aside. Good stuff, said Pisk, nice and salty. Litz was amused by him at first and tried to smile but found he couldn't. He knew Pisk's appetite, the greedy side of him that wanted to grind his teeth into everything.

The men carried on past all the riverways. It was a difficult walk and they took it slowly, cautious for sounds—Furry-and-Daggett–like sounds. When they arrived back at the hideout Mrs. Litz would be entitled to deliver her profanest summary of the nine-ten hours' worth of solitude, cursing her husband and his partner with every word she knew in her language, Sto:lo, and every word she knew in English—; and subsequently they'd be obliged to do something about the dwindling stack of firewood, the leak in the roof, and all the other deprivations she endured while they spent the day free as birds, out in the forests cutting down spars (so she believed), her languishing here in this tiny expanse of a hideout walled on all sides by acres of gnarled and thorny blackberry bush, with nothing to do with her time but go absolutely skookum and talk to the sky.

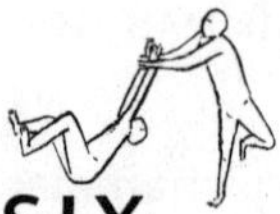

SIX

My mother always said, Democracy is the best revenge.
— BILAWAL BHUTTO ZARDARI

The early-morning streets of old Vancouver were littered with slimy old logs, ravaged by lichens and moss and rotted to the core. Shadows played in the fog. The zombie lope of a raccoon family crossed in a nose-to-tail line down the rutted mud. Snowy rain fell. The steely boom from a foundry startled the raccoons, who stopped, listened, blinked their dead diamond eyes, then prowled some more, passing unafraid right beside the man asleep—but waking up—under a tree.

Upon being awakened, Clough went immediately on a search of his person for his suede bag to fix himself a wad of tobacco. The crust sealed around his eyelids made opening them a second priority. Reclining on his grass bed he finessed a nice pinch of fresh tobacco into a paper rolled up one-handed, smoked it. When he finally opened his eyes to look around for who was attached to those whiskers that had sniffed his face, he saw only his spotted dog curled up with his chin on the ground, looking at him from a fair distance away with his ears perked.

What's all that aboot, eh? Who's supposed to be guarding me, eh? said Clough, and the dog wagged his tail and came right over. What's the use even having you around, you old bone-bag. Come here.

He stuck the rollie back in his mouth and ruffled the dog's ears, fished around in his jacket again and dropped the dog a linty sausage treat that it snapped up before it hit the ground. Clough coughed glue-ily. He still had the empty hair tonic bottle, once full of potato liquor, between his feet. How long had he been out? Where was he? Clough turned his head and saw the fresh ditch behind him. The horses had pulled the chain gang's carriage about two feet as they grazed on the long white-tipped grass. He was supposed to have brought the carriage back to the mews last night after the men were finished digging. Seems he forgot. The chain gang must have straggled off single-rowedly.

Constable Miller and the po-lice came down the road and saw Clough sitting woozily against a cherry tree not far from the GL Boot Store. He appeared to the po-lice to be in a moonshine stupor. It was serious moonshine on the streets these days. Rumour had it the potatoes were being grown in Indian burial grounds. That's what you heard in Vancouver. The po-lice did their job, came up, slapped Clough out of it, and took him to the pen to sober up.

What time is it? Clough asked. Behind him and his escorts, another man was taking charge of the horses and readying to bring them and the carriage back to their stable.

Eight, said the constable. After our chain gang appeared on our doorstep, naturally we came looking for our warden, our guard, and our horses and carriage.

Good men, Clough said as they dragged him down the street, you po-lice are good men. You found us all safe and sound.

Well, buddy, said the po-lice, just doing our jobs. Lucky we made you warden or you'd be late for work.

And I admire you for your good sense, said Clough, who managed to walk without any influence over his knees, and was halfway down the block before he realized they were carrying him under his arms to the jail.

Let's make one more stop before we take Clough home, said Constable Miller.

So they wandered down Pender Street swinging batons with their free hands all the way through Chinatown. Clough stumbled along between them. Besides him and the po-lice, the only people awake were vagrants and coolies and worse. Clough shook his head, cast an eye to and fro through the pale muddy streets under a pale muddy sky. Ten feet behind them Clough's skinny dog rubbed his muzzle along the sidewalk, following.

That dog ever *not* follow you? asked the po-lice.

What dog? said Clough. I'm the poundkeeper, too, you know. If there's a stray, that's my business. I can catch stray dogs, stray men, and stray muggers.

Yeah, right, eh. How you ever expect to catch that mugger when you're always on the anti-fogmatic?

Clough waved his finger in the air. Call me a sap, but I swear I'll catch that mugger. Why, did I ever tell you how I chased a man across five islands?

Yeah, you did.

Five islands, eh.

They paused at Westminster Street and watched a horse and buggy roll by, nearly tip over a dodgy hillock, and continue wobbling down the mudpacked road. The new clapboard buildings on the south side of Dupont Street were all part of Chinatown's most recent expansion. They were raised on stilts over the mudflats of False Creek, and at high tide the water would rise to the height of the sidewalk, lapping at your pantcuffs, spitting up along the boardwalks, sloshing in the gutter. Each building had its own plank bridge that connected it to land. If a man were to come stumbling out drunk and worried he couldn't walk a straight line over that gangplank, he might prefer the tide be in so that he'd splash into water instead of falling ten feet onto mud.

If the po-lice met any Chinaman coming out of an establishment and choosing to walk to the mainland, they asked questions. Where you been? Where you going? What's your name? What's *your* name? Where do you live? What're you doing, eh? Speak English?

A snakehead down in San Francisco had hired them, bringing them over from Sze-Yap and other rural provinces whose farmers were exposed to the worst natural elements. He'd sold ten thousand of them to the Canadian government, which in turn sent them to mountain passes up in the Rockies where they hammered CPR spikes day in day out. After they were laid off and denied the return ticket to China promised in their contract, they came to Vancouver and took any job offered. Since they were only allowed to live in one part of town, that part of town had become rather overcrowded. They lived for pennies saved and in the meantime they endured. The situation on Pender was neither safe nor sanitary, not for those who lived on the street or for anyone else in nearby bordellos.

He'll stay, warned the constable. He'll *stay* and he'll *breed* and soon enough we'll all be Chinamen.

Me, I'm not unwilling to accept a bit a pessimism. But I'm not so easily polished neither, Clough said. You read aboot the Yellow Peril in the *Daily Advertiser* every day and just flat-out believe it, eh? Myself, I'm not so sure. You can't trust all you read in the papers, eh. Once they get paid for space to sell hair cream and tonics and rolling pins, well. In fact I read one a them Yellow Peril stories the other day, it was written by the tailor, has a shop way over on Beatty and Robson, see? And everyone still goes to Wah On Tailors, eh, down in Chinatown, because he's the better tailor.

Don't need papers, said the constable. See it for myself with my own eyes, every day.

They stopped in front of a two-storey fan tan making too much noise for the po-lice's taste.

Might as well be Shanghai not Vancouver, eh? said Constable Miller.

I'm out here doing my part so that don't happen, said the po-lice.

We need to do *more,* boys, more, said Miller.

What can you do? said Clough.

One a these times when we bust a fan tan you should come along.

I'd like that, said Clough. I never seen inside one.

Turn the beetle over and see all his crawly legs, eh, said Miller.

They circled back, this time paying attention to the north side of the street and the whorehouses; busiest among them Wood's, hosted by Madam Peggy. Her house was set back from the street with a simple boardwalk to the front door where a kerosene lantern in the shape of a pomegranate swung in the evening breeze. In Peggy's yard the po-lice saw that a couple young Sitka girls were daintily soliciting a Whiteman. Lots of laughter, ugly laughter, conspicuous tongue-wagging. They told old John to get lost.

It's not yet nine in the morning, said the po-lice to the whores.

It's a living, cried a skinny half-breed, half-laughing, half-weeping.

Innocent virgins, said Constable Miller in a low monastic voice, alas, ye perish hither Wood's.

What? Oh, forget it, said one of the girls, sticking out her arms for the ropeknot. Just get it over with.

Tying her slender wrists, Miller said: Children grow up so much faster to-day and it so seldom does them any good.

Pay the fine or it's off to jail with you all, said the po-lice.

Put your finger in my cunny and call it even, eh.

Don't give me that language, girlie, said Miller. We'll have no flouncing on our front porches, you hear? Schoolchildren will one day have to pass by your seething hell a immorality, you ever think a that?

//

The first clue Clough learned about the man game was there in the prison mews; having slept off his hangover, he woke up in the afternoon to hear it as gossip from the lips of a young prostitute in the pen next to his. His left ear was flat against a wood bench that smelled of another man's hair grease. His right ear was listening to the prettiest squaw voice.

Peggy say they fight tomorrow.

Wha'? Who fight? Who're you talking aboot, squaw? said Clough.

Litz and Pisk.

Litz and Pisk? Well, don't clam up now, girlie. Spit.

Show fight, alls I know.

Show fight, said Clough. What the hell's a show fight?

Litz and Pisk, said the young Whoi-Whoi.

Fighting each other.

Behind Calabi & Yau.

Back a the bakeshoppe, eh? Litz and Pisk, eh? Hmm, said Clough.

After sobering up and paying his fine, and the fines of the Indian girls who'd given him the clue, Clough was back on the street. The stars were out. An old raggedy spotted Lab was right there on the road outside the station waiting for him. Together they walked through the neighbourhood, looking for more gossip, more news, more clues. The dog's nose sniffled down the walls looking for chicken bones and eggshells. His muzzle was shaggy and sticky. Don't waste your time with that crap in the alleys, for God's sake, boy, Clough said and reached into his pocket, retrieved another sausage treat. The dog's eyes lit up. Yeah, buddy? Yeah? When the sausage left his fingers and not a moment too soon the dog's jaws were on it. Before the dog had time to slam Clough against the wall and demand more, Clough was completely dominating the creature, blinding him with one hand as he put a knee on his ribs and said: Good, buddy, you're just lucky I was here, eh? A treat like that? Now, hey, no biting, or

I'll—that's right, good, buddy, good, calm down. The two of them sat for a half an hour or so like that, Clough razzing the dog and dominating him until the dog grew tired and they sat down, Clough on a wood step and the dog beside him. I'm either catching guys like you, Clough said to the dog, or I'm watching over you, or I'm one a you. Look at me, fresh out a jail and I catch my first stray. How do you like that, eh? The dog finally curled up for a short, fitful rest. Clough adjusted his cap to the breeze, a light westerly hush against his cheek tiring him with its softness and grating his nerves with its unceasing breath. Booze, booze was all he needed. When he couldn't afford the bodega, local moonshine hit all the spots. Every single spot got hit. Each swig of the potato killed him awake a little more. He quickly spotted an old haunt, an unhinged door in Chinatown between two tofu huts. Here you could knock three times and a Chinaman with no front teeth top or bottom would give you a bottle of hair tonic for two bits.

The hair tonic was close to one hundred percent alcohol. The hair tonic obviously worked best on a man's self-confidence if taken orally. Root-based ingredients, essentially. The amber bottle showed the face of a Klondike man whose beard had overtaken his entire body—and the rest of bottle. This particular potato crop was like a bootlegger's dream, a gorgeous, totally hidden, undulating acreage of ravenous topsoil. Underneath the taters, so the rumour went, was a thousand-year-old midden. Generations' worth of human cremains, a massive Squamish burial ground of sorts. The debate was whether it was Indian burial cremains or an ancient Indian garbage dump. Why, Clough knew where it was, and he was sure it was cremains. It was just a few days north of the city, in one of many cold isolated forests along the coastline. A bountiful midden of spongy black earth growing miracle-cure potatoes. Upon his first swig Clough had a distinct flash of remembrance: he'd once stumbled upon this Squamish midden where the bootlegger harvested. It was the second and third skull that convinced him all the other little bones were human, too, and that this was a burial mound, zitted by big purple potatoes. That's a good type a earth to grow potatoes in, he said to the lip of his bottle.

The dog awoke and snouted for more treats from Clough, who explained the rules: No more treats until you come back to the yard. The dog stood awhile longer, scratched his ear, bit his tail, then ever so slowly scented his way out of Clough's reach, and clicking his nails on the leaves, vanished into fugitive smog.

Three dollars a week was good extra money for Clough to round up strays, feed them and treat them properly, and still a little left over for a drink at the end of it. With that in mind, he found a spot of relative comfort in the alley behind the Calabi & Yau Bakeshoppe to wait for the *show fight,* and slipped into a deep, ulcerous sleep.

//

And sure enough, at the first blue shadows across the peaked roofs the next morning, the alley started to fill with shifty bachelors, rubbing their snotty nosepieces, feeling the cantankerous excitement of being awake for the sake of mystery.

From his hiding spot, Litz snickered to his partner: Doesn't look like Clough expected to see a crowd.

I didn't expect so either, said Pisk.

Next, Litz pointed out Moe Dee over there picking his teeth, and Bud Hoss in a corner against a black wall, hard to miss, he was a big guy. As Hoss walked towards Clough the two men muttered some morning greetings. Hoss asked something Litz didn't hear, though he could easily guess, and Clough croaked back: What's it *look* like I'm here for, I was getting some sleep, what are *you* here for? Clough got up and walked away, eyeing Hoss suspiciously for a while until he set himself up a spot beside a crumbling fence, looking wary of everyone, and waited.

Litz watched Bud Hoss go over to shake Campbell's hand next. It might look like a friendship, but Litz knew better. He knew as well as anyone how Hoss had been fired from Furry & Daggett's logging camp where Campbell still worked. Hoss's insubordination, the strap-whipping and all. Everyone knew the story. So what did it mean that Campbell was here this night? Litz and Pisk were on guard for signs of Campbell's owners, Furry & Daggett.

Just because Campbell's here doesn't mean we can't do this, Pisk said. Money's money. I'd rather take *his* chickamin than anyone's. If he's going to place a bet on you or me, all the better.

Don't like it, said Litz.

Clough came over and asked Hoss: What're you writing in that small notepad?

Taking bets, said Hoss in a whisper.

Taking bets, is that so? On this show fight?

Hoss nodded.

Since when?

First time.

Clough looked at the crowd, some dozen Chinamen and six or seven Whitemen, and there in the corner the Erwagens' ward, the Snauq Indian exile Toronto. Why was he here? Then again, maybe no one looked certain why he was here. Clough put his hand on Hoss's shoulder and said: What's to say this here doesn't get shut down by the po-lice?

Po-lice don't know, said Hoss firmly.

How many a these have I missed so far?

Listen, you going to bet or shove over?

Clough turned to face a queue of Chinamen standing one behind the other like a pack of cards. They wore pigtails and tanned cotton smocks. Jesus, he cried, where you coolies all get enough chickamin to go gamble with?

It was also the first time Clough ever remembered seeing Calabi outside his bakery. Even though it was only the alley behind the bakery, it was still jarring just to see him lean against the back door and watch. So he walked over to the baker and said: I'm a suspicious man by nature but this show fight seems to me more like a confidence game. Am I wrong here?

Wha'? said Calabi.

Getting nothing from that, Clough next went up and spoke with Campbell.

Klahowya? the logger asked Clough and they shook hands.

I'm here, answered Clough. Don't know why I'm here, but I'm here. Why aren't you with Furry & Daggett?

Campbell sniffed, horked, and spat. Yeah, I got the day off.

Day off. Clough passed Campbell the potato moonshine. Having never in his life heard of a man on their crew get a day off, he hoped the drink would loosen Campbell's lips.

So tell me, where's Daggett?

I told you already.

Who you bet on?

I bet you're drunk.

Ha ha, said Clough, well, odds are …

It was early in the morning. The air retained its arctic edge. It was pre-dawn, post-stars, cobalt blue ozone and deep, catatonic silence. The moonshine was unbearably good. And then, showing no remorse, the sun seared up the eastern lowlands and skipped off the bricks and ashbins, pushing shadows low and long, and began the day.

In the light, two figures appeared and caught everyone off-guard. The crowd quickly shaped themselves into something concentric with a space in the middle for the two men to insert themselves. In haste and with no warning, Litz and Pisk undressed and no one spoke. A few frowns but not a word. Clough was shocked. He kept rattling his head and squinting his eyes to see better. Were they really stripping down?

The man game began when Litz and Pisk shook hands.

Shut up and watch the game, said Litz nervously to the noisome crowd.

Using the diversion, Pisk snuck up behind Litz and locked his arm around his neck. But Litz twisted out of it, got himself through a complicated hip-and-leg turnstile, spun Pisk through the air, and caught his hands again while doing a risky undersweep. Having dipped Pisk between his legs, he let him loose to draggle and buck and crash into the skidboards behind Calabi & Yau's Bakeshoppe, scraping his shins as he came to a stop and angering a rat banquet in a dough bag *{see fig. 6.1}*. The rats scattered in all directions.

Pisk wiped off his face. Motherfuck you, he said.

That's a point for me, said Litz.

Clough marvelled at what he saw. It was indecent and awesome, better than a fist fight or the music hall. It's one thing to see children slap each other incessantly in the face, but entirely another to see grown men do it naked in an alley. And it wasn't quite that they were just slapping each other in the face either, because now that he noticed they were doing three steps back and two steps forward in a gentle swirl, not obviously though, as if the slapping was actually a kind of

---

FIGURE 6.1
The Spanish Layover, alternative study

See Calabi's commentary on p. 109.

distraction for the real trick of the move, which was … what? Clough was about to speculate when Pisk said: That's my point *{see fig. 6.2}*.

Pisk gave him one last slap across the cheek, then repositioned himself near the edge of a ruddy fence behind a laundry house.

That's one-one, Litz said.

I know what it is, said Pisk.

Let's fucking showtime, screamed one of the gambling guys standing near Clough. You go at it, Litz. I gots to make some chickamin this morning, or I'm more fucked than a five-cent whoore.

What kind a man game is this? How was that a point? Clough asked the seaman once he settled back down.

Reeking of gull shit, the sailor said: Man game? Hell, I didn't see what happened. I just know it's Pisk's point.

Campbell took the opportunity to flip his lid, and ran for Pisk with his fists uncuffed and vengeance on his breath. He said: Get the fuck out a Vancouver, and cracked Pisk hard across the shoulder before six or seven men swarmed in to break it up.

While some of the mob tried to quell the violence, others joined in, and Clough for one tried to catch some of the action, single fist roundhousing as he went. But as men backed away from the melee, Litz and Pisk were nowhere to be seen.

FIGURE 6.2
Rook Takes Pawn, alternative sketch

Calabi's commentary: An early derivation of the Litz, where without so much attention paid to footwork the slaps become far more musical and percussive.

'The fuck—?

Campbell stormed off on his pony to alert Furry and Daggett.

Hoss calmly lapped his thumb and flipped over dollar bills, paying out to three stevedores who'd bet on Pisk. He stashed the rest of the money in his pocket, turned a knob, and sank behind a black door.

Itchy from the moonshine, tired, and broke, Clough was the last man in the alley. He decided to go back to his shack in the woods and sleep it off. Sleep it all off.

//

Ken darted across the backyard in imitation of a stiff-armed cyborg, then at the push of a button fell into a perfect roll. Silas jumped aboard and ran over Ken's body as it rolled beneath him twice over before he fell off, landing unsteadily on his feet. Ken unfurled to a handstand behind Silas, then sprang and kicked him in the shoulders with his feet. They collapsed in a pile with Ken on top *{see fig. 6.3}*. That, according to the crowd, was worth applauding. I couldn't help following suit. A beer spritzed open. There was beer? Someone with two fingers in his mouth whistled. Clapping was the norm.

Minna said: I was already thinking aboot what we'll eat next. Are you coming over for dinner after?

FIGURE 6.3
The Boxing Chinee, study 2

Now Ken and Silas were waving their arms, almost fencing, kind of striking each other with elbows, hands, and fingers, and I was liking the texture of the technique, this combat of arms. I loved the cinematic effect of the arms flickering back and forth between one another so quickly it was impossible to truly appreciate the high level of skill. And yet, at the same time, I realized it was a naked mockery of talent. I enjoyed the martially artistic swordplay of blocking and batting, but it was uncomfortable to watch the arm movements change to pattycake *{see fig. 6.4}*. I felt joked upon.

Did you hear me?

I said: I was listening. Sorry. Dinner, yes. After we drop off the bed at my place?

Oh, right. Yeah. Well, if they're home. Then dinner if I'm not too tired after. I forgot aboot the bed. Pass me the lighter.

They might not be? What a you mean?

I don't know. It's not like I can call in advance.

Right. I guess it's just that I really need a bed.

I know I know.

FIGURE 6.4
The Litz

Calabi's commentary: A dance a labour, a lumberjack's dance, wherein the first player to fall to the ground either from fatigue, loss a balance, or concussion can at least remain proud to have given his opponent such a tiring, hard-won point.

Silas's commentary: The original variant of the Rook Takes Pawn, where if you choose to attack with your legs, your opponent can attack only with his arms, and vice versa, all while moving in a sixteen-bar rhythm.

What am I going to do if they aren't home? Stay at your place?

With a feminine shrug, she said: You can if you want to. She packed the pipe again, assessed the quantity she'd bunted into the tube, and decided to light up. She took a fast drag: King size is more bed than I need. King size is so much bed. It gets lonely. She coughed, turned her head and spat. Just don't get ideas, she said.

No ideas? Forget it then.

Oh, right, I forgot it's impossible for you not to get ideas.

I like ideas. I'm very fond a ideas. I always was.

She shook her head with a calm and flattered grin there on the middle of her.

I'm fucking tired, said Ken. Let's take a break.

The two men all sweaty and naked and ripped with seriously taut muscles walked back into the house.

Some applause.

That was it. I expected more.

Maybe more by the time it's over, Minna said.

I said: You want to stay?

She shrugged happily.

A red plastic cooler full of ice and beer had a cardboard sign above it marked five dollars.

I want beer, I said.

Minna said sure.

We walked over to the cooler to stand in line. On the way I overheard a guy in an overly tight jacket say to his friend: Essentially I teach yoga to get laid, but you know. I also like to stay in shape.

His friend said: Yeah.

I let my eyes wander. A guy walked up behind us and my eyes casually studied him. He was brutal-looking, from his fat white sneakers and muddy blue jeans right on up to his wheaty-blond hair. All his facial features seemed to be swollen as though he'd just swallowed something he was allergic to, and the skin itself was completely covered in pockmarks. Every pore seemed to be a pock. His eyes were a waxy grey, like a blind dog's. His mouth was open and I could see a little bubble hanging off the end of his tongue. He said: 'The fuck do you think you're looking at?

He pushed me, with his eyes. He was ugly all over. At first I thought he had a misaligned jaw because of the way his mouth moved when he talked, or that it was a distended neck; something was causing his mouth to move side to side when he talked and not up and down like anyone else's. It could have just been some gristle caught between molars that he was using his tongue to pry out. Whatever it was about his jaw, the effect was undeniable. His hair was so thin that by the strength of the winter sun I was able to see right through every follicle, and underneath this pile of transparent noodles I could easily see that his skull was terribly malformed. Dented. So I wondered to myself: What *was* I looking at?

Now where to put my eyes, I thought.

'The fuck you looking at? he said, paraphrasing himself. This time he aimed a knobby-ended finger at me and stabbed me in the chest with it. That's when I saw there weren't any fingernails on any of his fingers.

Meanwhile, Minna was bent over, returning the one-hit wonder to a zippered compartment of a side pocket on her mountaineering bag, bent over and subliminally wriggling.

I savoured her accidentally bared skin, as I always did, when suddenly I felt something, must have been as painful as a long steel thorn, prick its way through my heart. It hurt, and I wondered how I could go another day with Minna. I held my breath through the sting. And to tell the truth, I *did* turn to look at him again, right in the damn demonic eyes on his speckled face.

I said to him: No, no nothing, ha, I wasn't looking at anything.

I scratched the top of my hand with my teeth. I was suddenly keenly aware of the fact that I was the only person in the yard wearing a tie. In contrast, I was now convinced that this guy was the tallest ugly man I'd ever seen. He must've been seven feet tall.

He laughed, or gagged, at me: *Haw*. Throat adaquately cleared, he said: Bro-*ther*, who is *that*? Leaning on me like I was a kitchen counter, the guy proceeded to full-on leer at Minna as she rose from her tree planter's saddlebag and straightened her shirt out, covering her navel, to my relief, and then smiling at me. Oh, those sloe eyes. I gazed at her same as him.

What? she asked me. What's wrong?

Nothing, I said.

He gave Minna a look, as if intrigued to see that she and I were here together, then patted me on the shoulder and said with a smile: Nah, ha ha, I was just fucking around, man.

Why, what happened? Minna said.

We were conversating, he said. Me and this guy here. I was fucking with him. You were scared, right? Shit, brother, I'm sorry. But ha ha, that was a funny scene, right?

I said: That's not how I'd paint the picture, no.

Ha, ha, okay. Nice work, Picasso. He leaned over to place a hand on Minna's back as if to help her stand up straight, but she was already fully erect. See, he told Minna, it was funny, what you missed was me pretending to be all tough and shit. I was acting all threatening, you know? I'm such an asshole, I know. That's my picture. That's my status. That's my sense a humour. My name's Cedric.

Minna laughed giddily as they shook hands. She really was too giddy, laughing way too generously for my taste. I drooped my head. I might as well have drooped right to hell. These unforgettable episodes. That's all life is, isn't it? Nothing but a series of quiet humiliations, defeats, and intangible shavings-off of promise.

The guy laughed again, put one of his mangled hands on my shoulder again. I'm sorry, buddy. I'm just fucking with you.

Minna laughed with him again and we all shook hands (with those fingers) and introduced ourselves and I realized he was telling the truth. He had been joking with me. I put on the mannerisms of someone who was cool, with the vague chance he'd think I'd been playing along the whole time.

I re-entered the conversation with a harsh, dry swallow.

I was thirsty. A marijuana-induced panic chuckled down my neck, arms, and fingers. I said: That's funny.

What's wrong? Minna said. She petted my arm delicately.

Oh, nothing, I said, quietly. Nothing now, only now the only thing left intact is my lack a dignity.

Huh?

He's trying to impress you with his wit, the guy said to Minna, leaning completely over me to say it.

She laughed again. He doesn't have to worry. I've been impressed by his wit for ages.

Oh, man, he said to her chest. I can tell he's a real wit. It's all in the timing, isn't it? No, no. I'm just fucking with you again. Seriously, I'm a sweet guy underneath all the layers, the layers, the many layers. What's your names again?

Minna.

What are you doing here anyway?

We came to see the show, she said.

What show?

The men, the wrestlers.

What *wrestlers*?

She gave him an easy push: Don't be a prick. You know what I'm talking aboot.

Seriously, I don't know how you heard aboot this, but it's not a show. It's not wrestling. I don't mean to insult you.

Whatever.

Those are my friends out there. Ken and Silas, for them it's annoying to hear it called that, is all. They don't see it like a show, and they aren't perceiving themselves as wrestlers. When you've been hanging with these guys as long as I have, watching them totally improve, with no one paying any attention, it's frustrating to see them get an audience a people who *still* don't seem to get what they're watching.

Okay, fine, so ..., Minna said, shifting her weight from hip to hip. She seemed eagerly unimpressed.

Well, no, I should—I mean, I didn't—. He gave Minna a sort of bashful smile meant to remind her of other, more sensitive, less indecent smiles. It's no big deal, really, he said, that you didn't know.

Tell us aboot it, if you're such an expert.

I liked nothing about the jollity or aggravated intimacy of their conversation. I interrupted: All I want is beer, actually.

What? As if. A course you want to know, Kat. My god, you dragged me here. You better want to know. We might as well figure out what we're watching, right?

I raised my eyebrows. Then, when nothing changed, I lowered them.

Right?

I shook my head and sighed and rolled my eyes and said: I didn't *drag* you here.

Minna, this girl who owned my love on a shoestring budget. I should have dreamed of others: one-scene starlets, women with smiles they saved for the internet, the chesty baker who crossed the *t* on my birthday cake, every woman in a commercial for hair and makeup, my sister's boyfriend's brother's ex-girlfriend's best friend, the one with the legs. I can dream of Molly *now,* not that it does me any good. But I know that men loved Molly. Every man she met loved her. And she loved all her men.

//

Clough invited Campbell for a drink over at the Stag & Pheasant, a little fancier for a tavern than Campbell was probably used to patronizing, but out of eye and earshot of Campbell's bosses, Furry & Daggett. For one, the floor was made of wood, not peanut shells. For two, the prices. Campbell quickly realized that he was paying for the honour of sitting at the same table as the one-armed warden of the chain gang, ex-miner, part-time poundkeeper, occasional bounty hunter—Clough listed off his curriculum vitae with practised monotony—and so the prices were preposterous, nickel beers seemed preposterous, preposterous was the only polysyllabic Campbell could think of at the moment.

Why, in that corner over there, Clough said, you can see RH Alexander himself, manager a the Hastings Mill, conversating with his accountant—, Clough hesitated to say: Mr. Erwagen. And his wife, Mrs. Samuel ... Molly Erwagen.

Campbell turned to gape as well. She was sitting there as if that seemed reasonable.

Not even in the hoary days a the first gold rush has Clough seen a lady with such unblemished features, said Clough, awkwardly referring to himself in third person, a slip, an accidental confession of his grand delusions. I wonder what she drinks? he asked, craning his neck until it squeaked. Might she too sup from the Squamish potato? Appreciate the beauty a *that,* he instructed Campbell. She's how we know God exists.

Molly acknowledged the impolite gawking with a mere wince of flattery, then refocused her eyes and hands on the husband at her side, as if to make clear her life, if not her origin.

I'd fuck her, said Campbell.

Clough shook his head, and said: Okay, Jesus, that's enough looking. Stop looking, I say.

What? What?

Campbell, he said. Drink your beer.

They cleared the foam off the tops and drained half their pints. Clough leaned his elbow on the table and wiped his moustache on his jacketcuff, peeking looks at pretty Molly.

Interesting show fight the other day with Litz and Pisk, he said finally.

Campbell, for a man of such middling height, had good reflexes and a long reach, as Clough so quickly learned when he found his collar in Campbell's fist. Tugging, Campbell said: I'm ready to knock their skulls apart.

Clough, unfazed: Those are direct orders from Daggett?

It's what I believe.

You put chickamin on Pisk, eh.

Said I got beliefs. Pisk is the all-round better player between the two. That don't mean he's foolproof. Whatever. Sitting back down, Campbell adjusted his coats and collar bib and finished his beer. Beliefs are all I got. I watch that game, and all I think is those two bohunks aren't half enough man to play that game. Who's coaching them?

Who is coaching them, dammit, cried Clough in agreement.

And why didn't he pick me, not them? I could easily play that game.

I'd bet good money to see you try.

Don't tell Furry and or Daggett I said that.

How old are you? said Clough.

I'm twenty, I'm twenty-uh-seven.

Come on, you're a bunnyrabbit, you don't even shave, you little—

Oh, that's class. How's aboot I punch you in the eyes?

//

Not long after her drink at the Stag & Pheasant, Molly made an unscheduled visit to Wood's on Dupont Street. She arrived as if she were the landlord—unexpected and by unknown means—and sat down in Madam Peggy's room.

My heavens, said Peggy, please tell me you're here for business?

If I may, Peggy, allow me to describe for you exactly how I arrived here.

Please, always pleased to hear the story a such a fateful journey, dear. Sit sit, please. Don't mind me if my eyes close a little, I've heard so many girls' stories over the years. Oh, look now. Careful. Shoo, moth. Shoo, creature. Let me—shall I … well, he was a fast one for so big, wasn't he. Dirty beasts. I'm sorry everything around here isn't up to snuff, you know. The girls stitch up the furnishings one day and the next night things fall apart again. When you deal with men night after night, it's like that.

A moth has the same rights as an eagle to a nest. I should be sorry I disturbed its sleep.

Humour, like the moth, was lost on Peggy at this moment. She was used to seeing a man there across from her, a hungry, lascivious lumberjack or a hungry, lascivious tycoon of great wealth and refinement who wanted to know only two things: the price and the pickings. She laughed if a man asked to kiss her neck. Ha, no. Peggy, shifting her weight self-consciously on her own well-stuffed high-backed chair and watching her visitor with great interest, was keenly aware of the signature aroma of her establishment. She might even admit to taking some slightly cruel pleasure in living softly within the rankness like a pussywillow growing robustly in a sulphuric swamp. Feminine smells, yes, but above all it was the scent left behind from so many thousands of men, few of whom were familiar with soap and even fewer still who came and left without a trace. A rich, throaty tamarind, a plummy sap, coppery blood, and the unmoving salt-air smell found in the deepest recesses of a great big seashell washed ashore. These smells now made Peggy feel more uncomfortable than usual simply by the fact that Mrs. Erwagen didn't seem at all insulted by them.

Tell me your story, dear. Mind if I smoke?

Not at all. Mind if I?

They each lit their cigarettes, Molly first, using Peggy's candle, then Peggy. Your brand, she said.

Stars & Stripes, said Molly.

Go on, you were aboot to say.

I was at the Stag & Pheasant not more than an hour ago, you see.

You're from some completely different place on this vast globe—seen it all—and all you want to tell me is how you got to my *house*?

I was in the Stag & Pheasant only an hour ago …

I'm used to girls coming to me. Ones your own age. Not to insinuate that's what you're doing, dear, quite the opposite obviously. I suppose aboot seventeen, aren't you? Lovely age.

Yes, seventeen. Well, the proprietor at the Stag & Pheasant welcomes ladies as openly as gentlemen, you know. Quite a cultured lot. Nothing like the Sunnyside. I saw a few young ladies escorted by their husbands.

Must be from New Westminster.

Yes, and for a saloon, quite lovely. Fine decorations. A hearth. A clean floor, no peanut shells to slip on, a wheel a cheese, and a choice a liqueurs.

You won't find a drop a expectorate spilled in the whole establishment, yes, I been there.

The ladies drink brandy, the men drink scotch or brandy.

Ahh … don't mind me, Mrs. Erwagen, I'm only yawning from the fullness a my memory. You've taken me back, yes, I can see the soporific place as if I was there.

I went to use the ladies room …

You want to use the—

No, said Molly, squinting and shaking her head, black curls falling off her shoulder. No, in the Stag & Pheasant, I *went* to use the ladies room.

A course you did, dear, Peggy said, sitting back in her chair. Go on.

Compared to the polish all over the Stag & Pheasant the ladies room is criminally neglected. Ladies around me seemed well enough discouraged to use such a befouled anteroom. Mould and mildew and barnacle, seawrack, essentially, in the ladies room. Small white freckled mushrooms on the ceiling. Unappealing, certainly. What most caught my attention though was seeing unmistakable men's bootprints whitening a path on the muddy floor that stopped at the back wall, the clapboard wall, and I did not see a single lady's shoeprint leading to the seat with the hole in it. I found a secret door. The back wall turned like a door and opened. It was very dark beyond. But I could tell from a strange humid breeze that the back wall opened towards a tunnel. Frightened, I fled back to my table and concentrated on my husband and our afternoon together. The whole rest a my time all I looked at was Mr. Erwagen's handsome face. When we finished our drinks and Toronto came to escort us homeward, I begged off and stayed behind so I could return to the ladies room at the Stag & Pheasant. Once I'd procured a candle I was into the tunnel.

Peggy nodded her head. Your curiosity got to you. Yes, yes, you found the tunnels. She leaned forward and put her hands on the table between them and patted the top of a leather book. You shouldn't have been down there.

I followed the draft in the tunnel until I arrived at a ladder that led to your property.

What do you intend to do with this information, Mrs. Erwagen, blackmail me? I got a tunnel that leads to my coach house, so what? I am one a the founders a this town, that is why. I can't tell you aboot the tunnels. There's not much you can do to me that won't embarrass *you* in the process, with worse consequences.

If the tunnels are part a the city planning …

Now listen, Mrs. Erwagen. You look smart. I trust you. But let me ask you a question: Do I poke around in your cabinets at home, do I? First time you came here, I said I liked you. I said I'd help you. And I will. Pass some news around, *Litz and Pisk are in town,* that I find simple, this man game. You put yourself where I can fathom. I can fathom you. Most can't. That's why I have this home. Your courage, I call it foolish. But I like you for it, Mrs. Erwagen. It's a beautiful trait on you. I have it too. You see, for every lucky one, for every beautiful girl like you or me who wakes up to find she's a lady, there's got to be fifty who wake up all trampled. I won't spoil your secret. I might not be able to hold my tongue for a man's favours, but never and I say never has another lady's secret slipped free a these lips. I hope you know that. And if anything should happen to you, I'm right here, you know where to find me.

You protect the trampled.

I provide for a few.

A girl shouldn't be treated like a wildflower even if she is wild.

Wildflowers, eh. I don't know aboot wildflowers. Peggy pressed the tip of a glistening red fingernail against the top of her desk and traced a shape, a ring of connected semicircles.

Peggy always liked being paid attention to. She mused: For every wildflower we got twenty bears.

If there are maps a the tunnels, if you allow me to see them, it will save me the trouble a making them myself, said Molly.

I can't think a anything more boring, Molly. Don't waste your time. Let me show you something that might change the way you look at me. Understand that there is someone for whom even Madam Peggy will compromise. And to show you how much I respect you, Molly, I shall introduce you. Follow me.

Peggy took Molly by the wrist and they went around the corner to the back door of the whorehouse where Molly had entered, and from there they ascended a narrow coiling staircase to the second floor where they arrived at one side of a long hallway with multiple bedrooms all behind closed doors. No one and I mean *no one* goes through this door but me, said Peggy. She quickly unlocked the door beside them and guided Molly into a darkened bedroom. The only light came from the far side of the room where there was an attic window no bigger than a sheaf of paper. Between the window and where they stood was a four-poster bed and silhouetted on it was a slender child, and as Peggy's eyes adjusted, the hood over the girl's head came into focus. Molly's composure remained unchanged, but Peggy heard the moment when her breathing stopped. Here's your wildflower, she said.

//

The clearing on Doyle's land that Litz and Pisk used to practise the man game was walled in by thick old growth, protected from the elements, including wind and rain and Furry and Daggett. It was a natural clearing, not much larger than a boxing stage where no one could see them, and few would even think to look. There was a little rockbed creek that provided fresh water as it pizzled its way to the alluvial fans of the North Fraser River.

At around noon, Litz and Pisk took a breather. They'd been at it all day. Hands on their knees, coughing, spitting, muscles broken, hurting, then stretching their backs, hips, and legs. They discussed the problems that led to Pisk's toppling head over foot and kicking Litz in the face while trying to execute a Wheelbarrow *{see fig. 6.5}*. Molly kept insisting that it was an easy move if only they paid more attention to each other. They were here by themselves to try to work it out before they next met with her. Pay more attention to each other. By this she meant to forget one's own strategy and concentrate on the opponent's. Or did she mean to actually wait and drop the competitiveness altogether? Could Litz still slap Pisk upside the head or was Pisk just supposed to roll with it faster? The move involved a lunging vaudeville stomp alternating with an operatic scissorstep, boldly slashing the crapulent leg off a genteel tiptoeing, building up speed with this half-drunken, half-musical stagger for the inevitable banana flip. Litz was supposed to catch his ankles and save Pisk from a fall, only to have him wheelbarrowing backwards on his hands (indeed, the move bears a fair resemblance to both the Spanish Layover and the Boxing Chinee). But Litz overcompensated with the midget walk and got hamstrung in the knee-to-heel pivot. They'd been practising it all morning

---

FIGURE 6.5
The Wheelbarrow

Calabi's commentary: Any farmer who has competed with his barrow down a rocky slope can master this amusing competition.

with no success and now it was the afternoon and they didn't seem any closer to figuring it out. Meanwhile, they were heavily bruised and cut up, bloody from dirt scrape-ups like the last one and many more like it. Litz sat down, crossed his legs, and began to pack a pipe full of weed. Using the tip of a knife he smudged a coat of black sticky hashish into the pipe and then added another pat of the weed, levelled off the plug to two-thirds a bowlful. The weed glittered and sparkled in the bowl as if sprayed with the finest blood mist. Above, the rainforest sunlight was yellow in the south and white in the north. This was more than a daily regimen. These were men on the cliffs of the lesser-known world. Proper hopes like a family didn't matter. Children, soup spoons, and a dog strangled to a post in the backyard didn't matter. What mattered was gaining freedom.

Litz rummaged in the pockets of his pants, which lay on the grass beside his toque and woollies, with leather suspenders still tentacled to their buttons, looking for a timber to light his pipe with.

After not a long pause, Pisk said: I'd do anything for this Molly.

No shit. She's not even here today and look at us.

I mean, have you ever seen *any*thing the likes a her?

Never in my life. She's so … Litz scratched his balls fiercely, instinctively, like a cat. They'd lost any sense of dignity and paid no more attention to the material state of each other than they did to comparing the sizes of trees. At the end of the day the forest's all made of wood, and there's nothing more to be said about it. Maybe they'd achieved something like animalistic grace, and that may or may not have been Molly's intention.

Dragging on the pipe, Litz nicked alight a new matchstick and puffed it over the bowl to heat it up again. Coughing, he said: Where do you think she gets her ideas?

Taking the pipe, Pisk said: What?

I mean, how do we know what she's got planned for us next?

How the hell am I supposed to know that? Cough cough. I don't know.

If I'm not thinking aboot moves, said Litz, taking the pipe back, I'm thinking aboot why she's putting us up to this.

Like you say, it's a better way for us to make a living than being chased around the fucking woods by Furry and Daggett, that's for damn sure.

Cough cough. Litz spat on the ground. No doubt, he said. But we're still getting chased around the woods and we're not making real chickamin.

Not yet. But pretty soon we're going to be stacking those blankets. This game's going to burn through town.

Let's get up try again to do that combination.

They shook hands and went through the paces.

//

Christmas was rather more of a strain this year on Samuel's boss and his wife. Mr. and Mrs. RH Alexander's life in Vancouver, with its vicissitudes of California snakeheads, the mugger, naked lumberjacks, the opium trade—, it was all very distracting, and kept them from maintaining a stern hand in child rearing. The girls were lonely and spent all their time in their room building and destroying doll families in doll houses, reading literature, and weeping. British private schools took care of the boys for most of the year, but HO and TK were home for the holidays. They were taller, more restless and combative, their parents hardly noticing what for.

Mrs. Alexander had recently plunged into a community project to ensure that the Erwagens were adequately provided for over the holidays. With the work she does to care for him, Mrs. Alexander told her husband, she's practically a nurse. There's not a single garland. It's as spare as the day they moved in. That poor girl. I hope she's coping. Oh, I feel awful for them both.

Invite them for dinner, said RH, to rile her.

Yes, well, she said to her fingernails, I must decide on a plan.

A voice upstairs upset the quiet.

Children, thought RH, are awful things. RH was especially disinterested in his sons, who'd arrived by boat and train from Cambridge with excellent grades and grandly self-conscious of their new opinions.

Mrs. Alexander hid from her boys in the smells and bluster of the season's kitchen servants, actual Whitewomen for a change, and RH locked himself in his study and smoked the pipe.

Through the window of his study he saw the boys in the yard. They took turns chopping wood, arguing as well as working. He couldn't hear the conversation, only the hawkish tone. They talked in House of Commons voices that scaled the threshold of wrath sooner than one ever should in good business. He found irresistible comedy in this attempt of theirs to unlock the mystery of adulthood. Pride and too much condescension in his smile made it feel like a grimace, and if he retracted the focus of eyes to his own image in the rain-dappled glass, he was, in a moment of high truth, pained to see his former self so unflatteringly re-enacted in the actions of his sons. Inasmuch as he loved them at all, he wanted to see them fail early. Such cocksure adolescence deserved to be shivered up the same as cordwood. In a furthering haze of narcotic aphasia, he watched his sons chop and argue. He wanted to go out and discipline them for using foul language, a bar of lava soap for you and you, but he couldn't raise himself to his feet. The pipe was effecting. His eyes slouched to the inkblot in front of him and he completely fell asleep. Three hours later he heard his wife scream. She screamed again.

He awoke just in time from his purple coma to see his wife bound into his study. He swung his chair around to face her. The look of disappointment on her face was typically protective, adoring, and hardly an endorsement of sobriety.

There is a *deer* in the dining room.

His wife got him up and they went together to take a look at the snow-daubed doe.

What's she doing in here? he asked.

How should I know?

Must've come in through the front door, said RH, the boys left it wide open while doing their chore, chopping wood to keep the house *warm.*

The table was nearly set. The flatware was in order. Most of the food was in place. From the smudge on the wine glass it was plain to see the deer had sniffed it over but luckily not broken it. Trying not to startle the creature, RH crossed the dining room and opened the bay windows. He had a plan. The deer p-clopped with nervous balletic steps while RH corralled it slowly but surely around the table, and at the count of three he and his wife charged from all angles and forced the valiant creature to jump out the window—but not before it ate the last of the Christmas pie.

//

Molly and Sammy celebrated Christmas with Toronto that year. It definitely affected *his* life for the better how at ease she was commanding the manservants to do the complicated and time-consuming chores of the household. Without her and the manservants she ruled, the home would be chaos. It was during the Christmas season when Sammy began to realize how selfless she was. Even when he *contemplated* trying to explain how to prepare a traditional Christmas meal to an Indian, a Jewess, and two Chinamen, he got anxious. The Erwagens were a traditional accounting family, where God existed nominally at best. The receiving and paying out of gifts was observed as a sacred transaction. His ancestors were Protestants from the good side of Ireland, and the ordeal of Christmas was not something Sammy was prepared to order Chinamen to reproduce for the sake of tradition.

Ooh, squirmed Molly, but Toronto and I would love very much to experience the Christmas a *your* youth, Chinook. For his benefit, and my own, I want the perfect Christmas for us this year. Besides, it would be foolish not to include ourselves in this feeling a joy simply because we don't understand it.

Toronto looked hopeful. Sammy wasn't so sure. It seemed an absurd task to recreate Christmas in this hoary forest.

In the meantime, Mrs. Alexander was kind enough to make a very impressive laurel and mistletoe wreath for their front door in her spare time, which she brought over herself in the week before the 25th. When Molly invited her in, Mrs. Alexander was distraught to see her laurel was only the Erwagens' second Christmas decoration after the expensive paraffin candles Molly had on the mantel.

Oh my dear, she said to Molly and touched her face, you'll see how Vancouver's families rally around their *own*, you'll see.

Though not a surprise that his wife had never experienced Christmas, Sammy was bemused by how its conventions silenced her. When the mayor's wife appeared on their doorstep the following day with shortbread cookies, Sammy laughed to see his wife stammer for a word. She had no reply to the charity of Christmastime. The mayor's Mrs. was shocked to tears at Molly's speechless acceptance of the cookies and she quickly said: We're all behind you, Molly, and ran away.

It seemed to Sammy as though every reputable lady in the community came to the aid of the cripple's bride. Fearing and pitying the Erwagens, no ladylike soul was quite brave enough to offer seats at her table, but to compensate for this blind spot in their benevolence they united to help Molly prepare the perfect holiday feast of her own. By the third day Molly had accepted three puddings, three pans of scalloped potatoes, a honeyed ham, a bowl of mashed potatoes, a sack of freshly shelled peas delivered by a shy child wearing her father's boots, seven jars of cranberry sauce, a jar of pickles, and a bottle of Canadian rye whisky from Joe Fortes himself, who shook Molly's hand inside both of his and saluted her goodbye as he walked away with a tear in his eye, singing: Hallelujah, brother Jesus. Mrs. George Black promised a turkey with stuffing on Christmas Day, and by the time dinner arrived, the three of them could hardly contain their laughter.

//

Under a starry Christmas night, frost on the windowsills, quiet streets, and empty beaches, two snakeheads aboard crossing ships raised a toast as they passed each other through the inlet, one boat empty, the other soon to be. That's money in the pocket for snakeheads everywhere.

Dr. Langis had lost everything in the Fire that summer, instruments to medical texts, worst of all his skeleton. Over the Christmas holidays he was asked to conduct an operation to remove a mastoid, and he still lacked the proper tools, so he went down to Tom Dunn's hardware shop and bought himself the most expensive chisels available. In the privacy of his kitchen he tested them on an oxtail he'd bought from Joe Fortes, and when he was satisfied that he could indeed chisel precise work he went ahead and successfully performed the surgery.

As was her annual tradition, Mrs. Alexander paid a visit to the poorer neighbourhoods of Vancouver during the week after Christmas. She often came heavy with alms, which she generously apportioned to those she met on the street corner and around the gin houses, coolies and navvies, charlatans and seafarers, all variety of modern reprobate, characters and dispositions and scents she did not—today—object to. It was not normally her custom to visit Dupont Street, for it required she come in direct contact with the poor degraded souls of the girls in the brothels. She could not even acknowledge that such an abomination existed a mile from her doorstep, or that the world around her was a savage, cruel, predatory vista. Such was the stubbornness of her civilized upbringing that she could not adapt easily to madness and anarchy.

But this year she did want to see the poor sad condition of the newly arrived Chinamen. Those who'd set up beach houses over the tide had demonstrated great pluck. She felt it her duty to visit them, welcome them to Canada, and provide them with a little extra that her husband could not afford to add to each and every one of their personal fortunes.

Poor things, she said aloud, not gazing at all at the Dupont Street businesses, avoiding their sight and thinking only of the coolies across the street innumerably dozing inside their shantytown on this rare reprieve from the job. Somehow, though these pulchritudinous women beckoned for savage men, they beckoned for her, too, and Mrs. Alexander was likewise suddenly drawn by the sultry funk of their hearts away from the Chinamen to the door of Wood's.

The girls who smoked, sang, and cursed on the verandah could have been her daughters, her maids, her grandchildren, her sons' sweethearts, but they were not.

SEVEN

> First, what did yesternight deliver?
> "Another year has gone for ever."
> And what is this day's strong suggestion?
> "The passing moment's all we rest on!"
> – ROBERT BURNS, "SKETCH—NEW YEAR'S DAY, 1790"

A cord of wood whistled in the fireplace, then popped, dusting sparks against the blackened stones, then cracked in two pieces, exhaled a gush of fire, then dimmed. Sammy raised his eyes from the hearth and looked at her across the living room, then down at his body in its chair. It was the morning of duck eggs, sweet butter, and rye bread, New Year's Eve 1886.

We could say I bit my tongue? Sammy suggested to his wife without enthusiasm. We could say that I was unable to find a tie to match my shoes? The axle broke on my wheeled chair?

Chinooky, I'll despair if I miss the only official festivity this entire year.

I'll need a bath, he said.

Toronto shifted his feet under his chair. He was reading the Bible at the dining table beyond the cantilevered glass doors, opened to the heat of the fire.

Yes, Molly said, pressed her cigarette to the ashtray, stood and flapped out the wrinkles in her skirt with a happy sigh. I'll prepare the water.

Toronto brought the bucket to the well to pump the water for Sammy's bath. It was six minutes to eleven in the morning. The sun was at last upon the horizon, skating a dim curve around the south as it started the day. The chill in the air was like an ice cube falling down your back. A deer nudged through the evergreens beyond the yard, raised her head to look at Toronto, then gently disappeared into forest shadows. The shadows were long, dark, and slow to diffuse against the muted grey landscape.

Once the bath was ready and he'd been lowered into the warm water, she pinned back the danglets of hair that fell in her face, hustled her skirts up, and kneeled on the oilclothed cedar floor beside the tub. She rested her arms on the porcelain rim and looked at her Sammy, all submerged and immobile.

I'm looking forward to seeing you in the new year, she said.

He stared—not out the window, but *at* the window. With the sun still dipped low, he saw the mysterious commas of fingerprints and the pale notation of dried raindrops on the glass, somehow related to his fascination with numbers.

You see, he said. Even under these conditions, I'm still able to provide for you. And for Toronto.

Yes, I know that. She sponged his back.

What I mean to say is—you remember how my father, how he …

Yes, you've become the bookkeeper that Toronto never would accept.

I've proven him wrong, and look at me. The victory is all the greater for my impairment.

We both knew Vancouver would be much more hospitable to your thinking than he ever was, or ever believed a city could be.

I so rarely admit to a personal triumph, Sammy said solemnly. Thank you.

And still I wish you'd tell him what's happened. And your mother.

He didn't answer. She took a cigarette out and lit it, pinned up a mountain of her hair. She leaned to the sink and ticked the ash. Her body seemed ever so long. She opened her mouth and smoke shimmied up her face. Then she swung forward and sandwiched the sponge between her fists and lathered it in soap and water, brought it up to scrub his neck, behind his ears.

Through curls of cigarette smoke, she said: You understand how I must keep busy? You have your work. In my own way, this is my work as well. But let's concentrate on this moment, and only this moment. I'm so lonely for you. Lonely for your embrace. We never kiss anymore. I want to kiss you, Sammy.

Has it come to that time already … you want a whole man?

She put the cigarette to his lips. How do you mean? She paused once, then twice. Do you mean in the *sense*?

Yes, he said. In the sense. Only in the sense, in fact. He took a few puffs that tasted of her red apple lips before she put the cigarette back in her own mouth. I don't want you to leave me, Molly. You know how much I care for you, I love you. I love you so much that—. Another man for—. It hurts to say it. A man to satisfy what I can't.

She continued to soap him down even more thoroughly, kissed him on the cheek. This is the kind of conversation I've always imagined having, she said with true surprise, and affection he could feel.

I want what's best for you.

What tragic magnanimity you possess, intelligent man. I've often wondered—, she said, and trailed off. She seemed to be ignoring him entirely. Idly, like a slow square creature, the sponge bobbed down his body leaving a milty ooze of soap along the hairs of his chest, her grip squeezing free the sponge's white froth. It came to rest in his pelvic bowl. It stayed there hidden beneath the pearly water while she finished off the cigarette. She scooped the exhausted sponge from the water and rung it out until its wide pores filled with air and it relaxed back to its original shape. Then she smothered it all over again with a damp cake of soap and down it went into the water—sea sponge to meet sea lamprey.

Standing now, she neatly undressed. The bone buttons of her petticoats and skirts came from their slits with ease and soon all her clothes were rumpled on the floor. To Sammy, sunk in his bath, looking up at the vista of her long body, she was uncharitably magnificent—oh, swaying a little at her hips with one knee bent so her heel was off the ground and her big toe could obligingly tickle the hardwood. He felt something stir in him that he related to curtains, perhaps stage fright, perhaps romance. He was a heavy tide to her moon-white skin, and he loved her deeply.

What a tease. She did a ginger impression of a tendu, then brazenly *rond de jambed* the raised leg over the tub for him to get a good eyeful of her wry zone.

You'll catch cold, he hardly said, briefly hating her for what seemed to be some kind of a sort of satanic impulse to fuck his mind.

I want to make love to you, she said. (He was so right, there was a devil in her.)

I don't. I can't.

Sammy, have you already stopped thinking a me?

Don't make me feel this way.

Her lips parted and he could see the edge of her tongue where it floated over her teeth. Don't you crave me?

Don't be cruel.

Her movements were smooth. Basic seventeen-year-old naked beauty. She leaned over the tub to begin her task again, to clean her man. Her carved torso was dappled with soap bubbles. A breast fell against his lips. Preconsciously he licked its hard ruby until his thirst for more of what he could never have was throbbing against his temples.

He had to get this load off his mind: I want you, too. Molly, Molly, he said.

Mmm, she said, wet to the wrists.

The sponge was such a delicate slimed tool, its spoor of lather clouded his hips. She soaped him down between the legs where he felt nothing. She jostled and padded lubriciously over the bagged weight of his former virility where he felt nothing. His bobbing eel, around which the sponge most wanted to grovel, felt nothing. Weep weep, cry cry. He was powerless, nothing but h-h-hot anxiety rose in him. If he closed his eyes long enough maybe possibly he could contain his filthy soul from blurting out and curdling in the tub.

Have you tricked me this whole time, Sammy?

Tricked you?

She stepped into the milky water to share the tub. Her fingers in one of his ears, her mouth against the other, not speaking but still using her tongue. Sure enough, he saw it, there it was, mesmerized, sturdy, poised for her wet grasp. She lowered herself gently and with utmost grace and purpose onto the buoy of his lap, and if anything was possible, then before she left the house to embrace a life with other men, he'd give her all his coagulated love.

//

The sour odour of fish tails boiling forever boiling. Wet grease bubbles landed indelicately on the floor around the miniature cookstove. In the middle of the apartment she sat and stirred and stirred the hotpot. She sat hunched over the boil, dredging cabbage and tofu to the surface of the oily broth. A fishtail occasionally rose to the top of the soup and slid down the bowl edge and back under the simmer.

An infant slept below the hag's bosom, resting in the bend in her arm.

The only proper light came through the window blocked by their overcoats and bobbyhats and moustaches, so she was almost entirely shadowed. The darkened room bore no more resemblance to domesticity than a rotten tooth or a bullet hole.

Smells like something dead washed up on a beach in here, said Clough.

Now you watch here, Clough, said Constable Miller. He put his hand on Clough's shoulder to direct him back to the dirty windowpanes and the street below. He pointed to the fruit stand where two men kept shop: one mangy little old man with a stooped back and a pair of clippers in his hand, and a larger, unmoving figure in a leather apron with a great twisting moustache and pigtails that hung down each side of his chest. You see the big guy there in the apron? said the constable. That's our watchman. Minute he gets a boo we're on the street, he takes one step back, presses the buzzer to send the signal, and everyone vanishes. What we need from you, Clough, are you listening to me?

Say now, I'm listening, for the love a—

Well then quit staring at that old lady, she ain't no criminal.

Staked out along with the constable and Clough were two other po-lice who liked to chortle and cluck, as interchangeable as pigeons lazing on the shoulder of a statue. One held an axe and the other had his arms crossed, letting his billy club swing to and fro like a stiff black tail whenever he moved. In their doublebreasted black uniforms with the two rows of big white buttons, they really were less than pigeons, thought Clough, less than ornaments, they were dominoes.

Pay attention to the street, you old hophead, said Miller. See how this watchman does business.

At first all he saw was Chinamen. Beyond the window and down on the street they crossed to and fro, dodging in between one another, pausing on occasion to greet a neighbour, as indistinguishable as a plague of pharoah ants, thought Clough, like souls without spirits, holding in the grip of their infestation the future of Canadian culture. He felt the urge again to stare at the creep and her hotpot.

See how nobody walks too close to the buildings? said Miller. That's to make way for the runners taking numbers for the lotteries. See, there's one now. See they practically run sideways, they stick so tight to the walls.

I seen two runners come at each other from opposite directions, eh, said the po-lice with the obsession for his cudgel, and the one going that way, he just plain old jumped over the one going this way, and the boy just ducked down a bit to let him go.

They got lotteries going by the hour, said Miller. The fan tans're taking bets and numbers, and their runners stick close to the walls going back and forth. So don't loiter against the walls or you're going to cause a jam. Now look, Clough, how the watchman sees who wants in. He gives a signal, they cross and pretend to inspect the fruit … see, here we go.

Not even a word of greeting before the fiends slipped into the shadows behind the watchman and through a narrow breezeway between wood crates stamped BLUE CHERRY FARMS. A moment later, two others went right up to the watchman requesting entrance, and he turned them away.

You see what's going on here?

Yes, I do.

This is a big operation. There's a lot wrong with the world, and one day we'll clean out the whole mess. For now, we concentrate on the gambling den. I suspect this fan tan rakes in a thousand dollars a day from this one nest.

A thousand …

He understood what he was supposed to do now. The watchman was nothing more than a lock on a door, and Clough would be its pick. So be it. It got him in. The longer Clough stared at him the more completely conspicuous the watchman looked. The coolies themselves took on a sinister pall: not only were they corruptors of tradition, labour, and language, but also promotors of addiction, immorality, and greed.

It's a maze in there, said Constable Miller. You think you're going one way, instead you're going the next. Once they moved into the building, eh, the fan tan rebuilt the insides. There's hidden *rooms*. Whole floors are disguised. One room in there's a *gambling den*. And we got to find it. And I do expect a few collars out a this as well, don't I, boys?

Yes, sir, they said. The duller one heaved the axe off his shoulder and leaned on the handle like it was a cane, his legs bowed like a real lumberjack's boy.

Don't spook the Chinee, the constable told Clough. Like I says, he's got a mean tool, eh. Down his pants he carries a stick a bamboo with a rusty black blade from an old butcher's cleaver tied to it. How drunk are you?

I'm fine. I can do this.

Listen to me for once. You got to be drunk to do this. But you can't be too drunk, you kumtuks? Not so drunk you fuck it all up.

I won't.

You better not.

With his whisky bottle back in his fist Clough was down on the street mingling with the coolies, laundrymen, and mystics, inconspicuous as any drunk hobo looking to sober up at the nearest bar. Even in his ostensible stupor (however close to the truth his performance was that day) he easily passed some poor Chinaman dragging a cobbled-together barrow of fresh fruit and rotting vegetables.

Slow on the road, eh, he said.

The rutted, walnut face turned to him, the eyes intimations of a greater, more profound void. Suddenly the face stretched and he gave Clough a wide toothless smile and said: Kwinnum kwinnum.

Yes, I see, said Clough, how much is it for the cuke with all the mould on it, eh?

Ya ya, kwinnum.

And are them bananas meant to ooze from their skins or is that a—

Then he waited as the watchman stepped away from the fruit store to the edge of the boardwalk where he accomplished two things: a wider scan up and down Pender Street, just by chance failing to see Clough, and the release of a torrent of mucus from one nostril, then the other, onto the packed-dirt road where it was all soon trampled into the dust. As he swept away the remains from his face, Clough was on him. He took the watchman by the shoulder and said in his most wretchedly slurred halitosis: You got any lemons, sah?

The watchman took two steps back, his right hand instinctively reaching behind for the bamboo, but Clough, lightweight and sloppy, was already draped over him again, pulling the arm away from the butcher's axe, harmlessly drunk, unable to stand on his own two feet without help from a stranger.

You got lemons, sah?

Ya ya, said the watchman, trying to steady Clough on his buckling ankles. Ovah heeya, okay?

Hey, lissen, I got a prop-zition for ya, okay? How's aboot if I do your job for an hour and let you take a break, eh, and when you get back, I get myself *three* fresh lemons, sah? Fair deal?

No, no, ha ha, said the watchman, too busy for you.

Oh, I can handle it, sah. I worked in coal mines for five years until my assident. I can sure as spit work in a fruit stand, sah.

Ha ha, ya ya, said the watchman, letting himself be entertained, trying to keep Clough's odour away from his own, ya, you good worker, okay, I see, ha ha.

We're all hard workers, eh, you and me both. Why, I bet you could use a rest just as much I could use them lemons.

Ha ha, no sah—yowlp, said the watchman as he succumbed to a headlock. Constable Miller took the big aproned man to the ground in the matter of a single rotation, whereupon he pinned him no less elegantly than the cowboy does the calf and motioned for his men to move in. He pulled the bamboo axe that rested against the watchman's spine and threw it to the side even as he unravelled the hemp to hogtie him to a post.

Go on, he said to Clough. No time to waste, I'll meet you in there.

With unhurried steps, Clough travelled down the first secret hall in the fruit store, and shortly came to a door at the left that had just been hacked to pieces. The two po-lice could be heard striding up a narrow staircase beyond. Despite the clamour, guests of the building seemed not to have reacted with any noise of their own, which Clough believed must be a promising sign. He waited as the one with the axe took a big stab at the wall. At the first cut a terrified voice howled out on the other side, its owner proceeding to scramble down a secret hall running perpendicular to their place in the stairwell. The po-lice spared no moment. An opening was hacked in the wall and the two men took off through it in search of the gambling den. Who knows what other illicit activities were contained on this single, hidden floor in this unspoken-for building, thought Clough, following right behind with no time to make inspections of his own. He could hear a growing sense of alarm. The inhabitants had caught the drift.

Seems we got the jump on them this time around, eh? said the po-lice, laughing as he reared the axe and struck another wall. While he pried the axe out again, all the other noises in the building went abruptly silent. This is the po-lice. Open this up or we'll break you down.

A single passive voice replied: Okay, sah, okay.

The po-lice eyed each other one final time as they steadied their nerves. The door was unlocked in two places and pulled open. The po-lice were greeted into the room. They came with the billyclub and the axe in plain view, and Clough brought up the rear with no weapon. The po-lice were immediately giving orders for everyone to stay seated and quiet.

Clough was the last to regard the situation fully. Each table was candelit; a single window faced south to the incoming white cold rain from Seattle. The wood-panelled room was big enough to comfortably fit three rectangular tables and smelled like the blankets around a man who'd passed in his sleep.

Every table was filled to capacity with six men, all shoulder to shoulder in silence and submission as the po-lice trolled through them. Clough could easily discern, as anyone could, that the clientele were among the most rapacious, despairing examples of mankind it was possible to import. A whole tableful of men might count a single set of teeth. These were the diehard clowns of the Orient, a criminal class from another earth. But no matter their villainous features, the only thing the Chinamen were doing was drinking tea.

In the centre of each table sat a plain ceramic pot with a slimly curved spout and in front of every man perched a little teacup. A puckish Chinaman took his elbow off the table and with an air of innocence raised his cup for a sip. When he put the cup back down it gave Clough an idea. He reached over and picked up the nearest teacup, took his own sip, and declared: This tea's cold as yesterday's piss.

Take a look over here, eh, said the po-lice; and then, seeing a figure appear in the doorway: Hallo, Constable, welcome to our crime scene. A bunch a tea drinkers.

Miller was holding the watchman's notorious bamboo axe, and when he'd properly assessed the situation, he felt comfortable putting it to rest beside a chair near the door.

How's our watchman? Clough asked.

Subdued.

Take a look over here, eh, said a po-liceman.

What Clough had mistaken for a deeply shadowed far corner was actually a discreet opening to a long narrow corridor, and all the way along it were tables with men seated drinking tea. Heavy curtains were drawn across the windows between the tables, presenting to the street below the impression of a regular floor in a slumhouse. In fact all the rooms were set back from the exterior to make space for this infestation.

Was gambling to blame for the plight of the Chinaman, wondered Clough, or a reaction to it? He hoped to find his answer in the eyes of the Chinamen at the tables, but they expertly evaded his gaze. Each man displayed a stoicism in direct relation to his gambling abilities. The better the gambler, the more stoic. It was not long before Clough figured out which table was the high rollers, the risk-takers, the young or unlucky seeded with a confidence man or two. Clough saw all the same gambler breeds he'd seen his whole life growing up around miners and railroad drifters. The poker face was the gambler's only feature not completely devoured by terror. The soul, the mind, the stomach were all gnawed down to a sponge filled with maggots. All that remained was the face, a rigid mask of pain. Reminded Clough of something he used to hear at the bar when he was a child: Best poker face is a broken nose and two shiners.

The po-lice paced around between the tables eyeing everything and everyone, twitching their eyebrows and moustaches. The room was otherwise so silent and motionless that when a

Chinaman broke the stillness by scratching his neck it brought on an unexpected search. Stand up, said the po-lice. Turn around face the wall put your hands on the wall spread your legs. He shook down the Chinaman for evidence. When nothing was found on his person the po-lice roughly sat him back down at the table. Stay where you are, said the po-lice, nobody move.

Don't think we're going to find nothing on anyone, said Constable Miller, but we can't rule it out.

Should we search them all?

Miller stood at the juncture between the corridor and the room, his sights on the whole scene. His skin looked mottled and flushed and his breathing was heavier than earlier in the stakeout, but otherwise one wouldn't suspect that moments ago he'd subdued an ogre. He crossed his arms and said: Anyone believe this is a teashop?

No, sir, said the po-lice.

What a you think, Clough?

What I see are men who'd use their mothers and daughters to settle a debt, said Clough. If any one a them is here for tea and fine conversation then I lost my sense a smell.

Search them all, said Miller.

The po-lice lined the whole group against the wall and searched them.

See, Miller said, turning his head to speak as if to Clough alone, but in the same bellowing voice, that's how you know you'll get your most rats. New Year's Eve, they think we let our guard down. They unfortunately got another thing coming.

Miller watched the whole ordeal with great attention as Clough wandered the room and up and down the corridor, losing his balance only once. When the thirty-odd Chinamen were declared inexplicably clean, the constable took aside the one dressed as the proprietor and questioned him more violently.

This tea house, said the Chinaman. No gamble here.

When we find our evidence, Miller said, all these men go to jail. And you, sir, for operating a fan tan, you go back to China, hear me?

He left the proprietor slumped in the corner and returned to his men with his nostrils fanning. Where's our damn evidence? growled Miller.

Clough knocked on a nearby wall. Must be in here, he said. Or down here, he said, pointing to the floor.

Miller squinted his eyes as he considered the possibility. The cords of his neck were heaving. He flipped the watchman's bamboo axe up into the air and caught the handle again as it fell. The Chinamen, with their backs to the scene, craned to see as the constable wound up and gave one sporting swing at the panelling next to the end of one table. When the cleaver blade connected an explosion of chips and chunks flew off in all directions, and as he yanked the axe free, as sure as the guts of mankind, a cache of smooth black dominoes spilled to the floor.

A single Chinaman got spooked, and in a paroxysm of madness tried to make an escape through the door, knocking over both po-lice and bumping the nub of Clough's shoulder, but Miller took him out with another swing of that watchman's axe, wedged it deeply into the man's spine, and within the hour the man was dead.

Having fetched the horse and carriage and gathered the arrested in the back with their wrists, ankles, and pigtails bound together in one length of hemp rope, Clough steadied the Clydesdales with the reins as the po-lice carried out the body of the slain Chinaman. The body swung back and forth between their grips as they received him to the street. He was covered in a carpet, but a hand steadily dripping blood from the fingers was in plain view and the darkening stain on the carpet left no question in the minds of passersby. A rising choir of anxiety rippled down the street until the children stopped their play. The watchman, in the back of the carriage with the others, stood to his full height to see the dead man. The watchman's eyes were bruised and red-seamed, and his mouth was smashed. Siddown, said the po-lice, and he did as he was told. They lugged the corpse onto the floor of the carriage.

Oh my oh my, said the unexpected harpstrings of a lady's voice. Clough was jarred sober (briefly) to discover the seraphic presence of Molly Erwagen there beside him, touching a kid glove to her cosmic mouth, beautifully horrified at the sight of the Chinaman's corpse, the hand dripping blood. The two lumpen po-lice stood mid-hoist, mouths agape, immobilized, blood splashing on their boots as Molly moved towards them. Her most humbly elegant fineries tousled about her louche figure; she neither floated above the earth nor ever seemed totally locked to the ground. The same forces that kept a man in his skin didn't touch her. It seemed that at any given moment she could lift her legs and fly away, kill them all, and give birth. She was accompanied at a respectable distance by her skookum ward Toronto. Whatever's the matter? she asked up to Clough.

Dear Christ, Molly, cried Clough. Avert your fragile eyes, I beg you. What sour luck. Aw, Molly, a man's business's never pretty but this one's a mighty gruesome incident.

He's met his fate, she said, drawing closer.

What the—are you doing, Mrs. Erwagen, cried Clough, wasting your grace in these squalid parts?

Errands, she said. A lady's errands. Tofu …, she said ambiguously.

What the—I shouldn't think your husb—ah, dear sweet … don't lift that rug up.

Indeed, she was raising the frilled edge of the carpet as the po-lice fumbled to keep the weighty body off the ground. Finally the whole thing unrolled and the body lay fully exposed upon it like a man asleep on the living room floor, his cold nose in the air leaking blood.

Aw, for the love a—, said one po-liceman, throwing his helmet aside in frustration. Now look what you done.

It wasn't me, said the second po-liceman, quickly folding the rug over the deceased again. Please, ma'am, I got to ask you to step back now.

He must've done something awful for it to come to such an end, said Molly.

Indeed he did, replied Clough. But these are matters for the po-lice and the judges to sort oot. You and I mustn't dwell on the grisly. That's why I beg you to swerve your gaze another way instead a moving closer to the … the way you seem to … don't touch that, for you and myself, we are put on earth to light the path a righteousness and obeisance.

Please don't touch the—, ma'am, said the po-lice.

Don't lift that, hey, please, why, said Clough, Mrs. Erwagen, I beseech you.

My innocent curiosity …, said Molly, each syllable dancing on her tongue. I don't know what's gotten into me. I must be light-headed, for I have such an irrepressible urge to view the face a the criminal.

No, lady, you mustn't, said Clough.

My soul compels me not to ignore this terrible opportunity.

Uhh, said the po-lice.

No, I simply must look, she said feverishly, and quickly turned the carpet off the man's head. Oh, she said gazing upon the Chinaman's lifeless features. His lips were a livid purple and his wet tongue could be seen. His neck was soaked in oily blood. His eyes were ash-white, wide and dry.

He's only a child, she said. He can't be more than … yes, I suppose he's my age. Slipping off a glove and touching the dead man's cheek with her bare hand, looking him in the eyes, his paling horizons, and exclaiming in a trembling voice: His skin, he's still warm.

//

As New Year's celebrations were readied, the lone woodsman Campbell staggered around. In these forests, he was no taller than the ferns. Starlight in the carbon-black sky.Without his bosses Furry & Daggett to break his back, without a female to spend the night with, without the encouragement he hoped to find in the life of a bachelor, a skinful of that mystic moonshine sloshed around in his otherwise empty belly. There in an unfenced yard owned by a family he knew well enough to respect better, he found what he was looking for, an outhouse. He closed the door behind him, stretched the suspenders down from his shoulders and crumpled his pants around his ankles, then sat on the toilet stool. He picked up some ragged issue of a men's journal he found beside him on the bench, awaiting the chance to relax him, and saw it was legible. He was reading the latest installment of a western serial when with a rusty squeal the door swung wide open and a wild-looking man cried: Holy Jesus, and fell straight back in terror. Campbell leaped up and reeled around inside the outhouse with his pants dragging around his feet: What the—, nearly wedging an arm down the hole before summoning his wits about him.

Clough? Clough, is that you?

Campbell? Campbell, is that you?

Yeah, yeah, you totoosh, you scared me.

What the—. I mean ...

Campbell took a breath to relax. It was only Clough, thank God only drunken old Clough. Where are you going, *man*? Campbell asked with practised bullheadedness. Where you off to, man, eh?

Clough said: Where am *I*—? Why, I'm on my way home. I'm on my way right now, home.

Home, eh. A long way to your door, lost lamb. Ha ha. What made ye stray so far?

Nothing, *Father,* said Clough, amused to see Campbell as drunk as himself. No, you see, what happened—.

Let's see the bottle in ye hands, said Campbell, reaching for it.

Clough reluctantly offered up the hair-tonic moonshine bottle hidden behind his back.

Where ye been?

I tell you. I helped bust a fan tan.

That so.

A Chinaman perished during the duty.

Pity. Your work?

No. Speaking a totooshes, though, one who did witness the body was our dear Molly Erwagen.

That so, said Campbell, perking up again.

Damn, after seeing her, I headed straight for Wood's, said Clough. You, where you been, on a stool at the Stag & Pheasant?

Yeah, right, eh. I been to that place, it's nothing special. Oh, except, I did see that lady Erwagen though. Talk aboot your … Campbell took a swig and couldn't disguise his shock at the searing taste. That's *some* poison.

If you got half the troubles I got, you'd drink—.

That's fine, Clough, that's fine. I don't need your confession, thank ye.

Yeah, well, what the fuck *ye* doing?

What's it look like I'm doing? Then in front of Clough's eyes, Campbell finished off the dying embers of his firewater. He gave back the empty bottle, which wasn't of much damn use to Clough now. Campbell licked his lips. I did not mean to interrogate you, eh, he said. And I don't much take to interrogation myself.

You look all shaken up, said Clough. Everything go smoothly in there?

Smooth as stone.

Right.

So, anyway.

Yeah, anyway.

They tested each other out to see who would be the first to say what was on both their minds.

Happy New Year.

Happy New Year.

What time is it?

Was just aboot to ask you the very same.

Hm.

Campbell broke first: … You hear aboot the man game tonight?

Yeah, said Clough. Was just aboot to ask you the very same. When and where? The women I heard it from were soft as candlewax by the time I got to them for the news.

I can't get a good answer from no one either. Before midnight's alls I know. What time's it now?

I don't know. When I left Wood's, it was half past four, according to Peggy.

Half past four? Man, it's been four o'clock for hours.

I agree.

Well, damn, it's going to be a few hours then before we see any action. I'm going to go look for something to eat. See you, said Campbell, and shook Clough's hand vigorously and crushingly.

As always, said Clough.

Clough picked his hat off the ground, and while straightening the hat across his brow he saw that Campbell was already off in some direction or other into the vast, fat darkness. A charge of dynamite some many miles away echoed down the coast from the side of a mountain pass where iron trestles were being fitted by Chinamen.

He started walking through the brush. Up ahead he had to deke left to avoid a wall of blackberry thistle, then switch back to keep travelling west into the forests towards Granville Street. Having nothing else to guide him, he walked towards the orange glow of the celebration's bonfire and the sound of drums ricocheting down the valley. The cedars blocked out the skies above. And with its bears, cougars, and ticks, the forests were not only disorienting but dangerous. But Clough wasn't about to get lost or damaged. Animals never threatened him. Not hemlock nor Fly Agaric had any effect on Clough. He questioned his mortality, he tested it, his life never seemed to hold any meaning unless he pushed at the possibility he was immortal. Eternal as fire, that was Clough. And he *hoped* to run into the notorious mugger. He knew Vancouver better than any man. That's how he felt, and that's why he was so taken aback when he stumbled upon a normally lonesome intersection to see Litz and Pisk round the corner of an old clapboard building that housed an unpopular billiards hall and a half-deceased notary. Pisk was belly-up beside a tractor wheel and Litz was keeping his balance after the flailing toss *{see fig. 7.1}*. He leaped and soon they were rolling and jamboreeing down the alleyway's mossy slope, gasping for air and grunting in pain. They rolled around the corner, gripped to each other, tussling and throttling in a manner that seemed alternately spastic and part of something more. The two men in front of him now, moving in, totally naked and fighting like the dickens.

Good gravy, what in the—is going on? said Moe Dee who happened to be nearby. Who are you? What's this—oh, shoot, that looks like—that must've hurt. *Clough*, my brother, said Moe Dee, what the fuck's going on?

It's a man game, said Clough, smiling broadly. And just our luck to witness it, he said, scratching at the bristle-covered loose flesh of his neck. Thinking to himself, Campbell's going to be pissed he missed it; he looked around, saw many of the usuals among the spectators, but many more who seemed to be congregating out of plain curiosity or rumour.

What's it called? said Moe Dee.

FIGURE 7.1

The Point and Click

Campbell's commentary: If your opponent fails to accomplish his move and finds himself belly up, you are granted a point if you can deliver him a decisive blow to the midsection.

A man game, said Clough for the second time.

A little snow fell. In the moonlight the men were creepy and pale. Clough watched Litz and Pisk shit-kick each other in the most bewildering of ways. No doubt, every time he saw the man game it got more complex. Every time held new surprises, new moves, new countermoves, unexpected plays, and regularly occurring anomalous gymnastic miracles. To inexpert eyes the moves might have looked spectacularly unplanned, but for anyone like Clough, who'd seen over a dozen of these games, every skip, pirouette, and headbutt was recognizable as one piece in a larger choreography. Nevertheless, the logic of the movements contained a certain antagonism that made it more than just a dance or slapstick routine; it was a fully competitive game. Clough was impressed and still confused. The money he understood, but where were these moves coming from? Where was the coach? Who taught them? No way was Clough going to believe these two woodsmen came up with all this by themselves.

Today there was no preliminary pussyfooting around. First it seemed that—was it?—Litz dragged Pisk by the neck across the mud. Pisk kind of camelwalked backwards to keep up with how fast Litz kept dragging. A gout of mud splashed when they rolled through a leaftclot in some meltwater dribbling across the lane. They hopscotched with their legs locked, commenced to turn right, took a small step back, and, hot-stepping leftwards, swivelled right. What seemed a pause in the snow was mere happenstance.

It looked like a social foxtrot except for how they kept slapping each other in the face. Litz suddenly really turned up the heat on Pisk. He started to hammer blows down on the top of Pisk's head with his fist. His head jerked with each blow. As if this weren't enough, Litz began moving Pisk's torso back and forth, bending and stressing Pisk's leg and lower back until the guy let out with screams. Your Cherry Tree Clutch *{see fig. 7.2}* was no good, Litz cried out. Now I'll show you a real thing. Litz held Pisk in this position for several seconds, working on the chinhold and bodyscissors. Finally, he hump-tossed Pisk across the lane.

Litz won five points to three. Clough shook their hands, said: Men, that's the most I ever saw.

Thanks, Clough, thanks, said Litz.

That was some spectacular win, Litz. Why, even just this afternoon I scoffed when boys on the chain gang thought you were the lesser player.

Who the fuck thought I was the lesser player? said Litz.

Well, I—wouldn't, I mean, don't expect me to snitch. Alls I know is there's debate every day aboot the man game. You got Moe Dee defending you both. I tell the bohunks around here they need to pay more attention if they want to go debate the man game. How many games I seen you play now? A dozen? How many d'you think you played in town all told, eh?

I don't know. Pisk tested his jaw with his hand; sure enough he rubbed away blood.

How many, more than a dozen?

Litz stretched his shoulders one arm at a time.

Better than any circus, said Clough. Aren't you cold now?

Not really. You work up a sweat.

FIGURE 7.2
The Cherry Tree Clutch, alternative sketch

See Calabi's commentary on p. 7.

I get cold, said Pisk. I got bad circulation.

So tell me straight, what kind a game is this? Who else plays this with you?

Nobody, said Pisk. His clothes were in a jumble next to an achingly empty beer barrel (Clough checked). His muddy boots lay nearby, one here, one over there somewhere. He put each item on. He beat the dirt off his pants.

I could coach you, said Clough. I watch this game like astronomy. Listen, if you take this betting, this game could be big blankets, fat chickamin, money out your ears, eh. I don't just spectate like everybody else. I can tell there's a lot a work that's gone into this by you two. And alls you need is a little more coaching and I can see this turning very profitable. With just the two a you playing, there's no one to give you that eagle-eye view.

The men both muttered inaudibly, appearing intent on the more important task of finding all their clothes. Eh? said Clough. Then he let the subject die. The snow was falling faster now, and less steam curled off Litz and Pisk's bare backs with every moment they remained exposed. He watched them dress. He sensed Pisk's mood had changed. During the game he'd looked passionate and cheerful, almost baiting Litz. Now there was a grim inevitability to his face. Must be his loss, thought Clough, the boy doesn't like to lose.

When the two men once again stood before him, dressed in their dungarees and plaid wool jackets, Clough thought they looked surprisingly vulgar. Something about clothes fit ill upon them after what he'd just seen—like dressing up a horse or a bobcat in a man's duds for a laugh.

We tried a new move out, said Litz, squishing his fist around his eye. It just didn't work. Pisk should've got out a the hold.

I still think I can do it.

So do I, nodded Litz. He turned to spit on the ground. Jesus H, I'm thirsty now.

Please be my guest for a drink, said Clough. I was just on my way over to the Sunnyside for a refresher myself.

Sunnyside? Is that an insult?

Excuse me, Clough said, shaking his jowls, I momentarily forgot your predicament. What a shame.

Nobody's going to be there anyways.

Why do you say so?

Everyone'll still be at the New Year's Eve dance.

The New Year's … dance …? Clough stammered. Had no one told him? How did two forest exiles know there was a New Year's Eve dance and he didn't? Was he purposefully uninvited?

I'm going home, said Pisk.

Home, said Clough, where's that?

Pisk shook hands with the other two men without saying another word, turned his back, and started walking.

Where's he going? asked Clough.

Back into exile, where else, said Litz.

Clough watched him vanish into the darkness of the vast, violent forest.

Pisk definitely did not like to lose, and was determined to go home to bed early especially because he didn't like to lose. Apart from that the New Year's Eve dance would only make him feel worse, knowing he wasn't included, and knowing that Molly would be there with her husband. Seeing them together would dampen his mood even more, and he was freezing cold and couldn't feel his toes or fingers or eartips. His muscles were all busted and stretched hypertrophically from the backflip, and if he was in a predicting mood, at this moment, despite it all, he'd be skeptical of seeing any improvement in the year to come. The man game was hardly making them enough money to survive. Furry and Daggett continued to pose a serious threat to their lives. They were still stuck out in the woods in a barely habitable fortress hidden from view. Mrs. Litz, trapped there day in and day out, was going insane. As he walked alone through the ever colder night he said to himself: Maybe I'll shave off my beard. Maybe I'll take the biggest knife I can find and cut it all off.

//

While Pisk, a solitary man, tumbled home, Litz, now separated from his partner by a mile, nursed his hairline where he'd taken a knuckle. A pipe was brought out and a plug of tobacco was laced with hashish and a daub of opium. A fire was lit inside the bowl. Litz's expert puffs stoked the embers of slow-burning tobacco before he passed the pipe to Clough, who ignored the sucking hollow pain in his stomach requesting alcoholic remedy and tried to substitute the offered inhalant. It made his mouth dry out as if clogged with cotton.

The more Clough had learned about the man game, the more curious he'd become. Now he wanted to know everything there was to know. With amply fungal halitosis, he asked point-blank questions that took Litz aback.

Why naked?

Keeps a player honest.

Well, how often do you practise?

Almost every day.

Almost every day, why, who's your coach, eh?

I, uh …

You make a living off this?

Hope to.

So you want some competition?

We'll seek out some players, yeah, when the time's right. We got to know friend from foe. That's the thing. We got to be cautious with new players.

These were not questions that Litz felt deserved a straight answer but he was flattered to hear them asked nonetheless. As they traipsed through the underbrush over clumps of snow and avoided the deeper mud, Litz thought about the questions Clough asked him and grew agitated at not knowing what to disclose and what to reveal. As politely as possible, Litz said: You want to pass the pipe or do I have to come over there and—

At a certain point, in a valley of silver ferns, Litz admitted he was lost. Clough said: Follow me. They weren't far off the trail, but they'd reached an unlit patch of undergrowth in a cave of cedar trees. The moon was far gone. The blackness was bubonic and utter and wet. Couldn't even see his one hand before his face. It wasn't the first time a man got lost in Vancouver. They just kept walking, like the walking of voyageurs, fur traders, gold diggers, werewolves into the barbed nest of a black nightmare.

Clough was the first to catch a spot of yellowish light: what turned out to be the letters of the BAR RÚSTICO MONTAÑASO sign, lit by whale candles. The sign's font was made of logs suspended above the bar countertop by two log columns. They walked towards it.

Miguel Calderón had set up his Bar Rústico beside the roots of one of the most paleolithic tree trunks ever seen on the West Coast, a magnificent timber that once rose over two hundred-fifty feet in the air with a thirty-seven-foot diameter. After the tree was cut down and shivered up into wood and shipped away to the Emperor of China, the remaining stump made for a perfect dance floor, which was exactly how it was being used tonight, the last evening of the year 1886. A tree stump beside it measuring fifteen feet in diameter was used as a bandstand, where a few po-lice, coroner McGuigan, and Red and Rosy from Red & Rosy's General Store played tunes on the fiddle accompanied by a rhythm section of thumped-on hollow logs. The beat was as steady as a trance, heavy and true, leavened by the free-floating old-world nostalgia of Rosy the fiddlist, a melancholy optimist. Lanterns swayed all around, and bonfires on either side kept the party-goers warm. Opium smoke was lithe on the air, smelling like coca.

After his saloon burned down in the Great Fire Miguel Calderón had disappeared for a while into a pool of tears, but recently he'd re-emerged with an idea. He decided to build the first portable bar. It came apart and reassembled and had wheels. With help from an ox and carriage he was able to take his saloon on the road to wherever a drink was needed. Calderón's goat had a little bell on his collar, and when men heard that jingle at night they snuck out of their homes for a quick nip of whisky and a smoke of hashish before returning to the safety of their stubborn wives. He served drinks to fishermen at the docks, Indians in the peninsular woods, and he was always busy over lunch at Hastings Mill. All in all, Calderón was doing very well, and the po-lice didn't give him a hard time so long as he didn't park out front of a hotel, billiard hall, saloon, or any churches. For the record, he still had a liquor licence, under a registered address that no longer existed. This seemed to satisfy the city councillors, all good customers with long lines of interest-free credit. And as in any bar, Miguel served Indians or Chinamen only when no Whitemans were around to see him do it.

The bar itself was made from scavenged wood. He'd taken this old cedar, cut it in half like a meat pie, hollowed it out leaving a thick crust, and set down to business. Half of the trunk was used as a bartop, wide enough around to fit five men and thick enough to work as a countertop, where Litz and Clough now bent their elbows. On the bark exterior, Calderón had smoothed flat the tops of five lopped-off branches into ready-made barstools. The other half of the tree trunk Calderón used to shelve all his liquor bottles. Miguel stood inside the two halves of the tree and served drinks, although he'd yet to serve any to Clough or Litz. In fact, Miguel wouldn't uncross his arms.

Hello, goat, said Clough, and scratched the goat's forehead. I don't have any food, I'm sorry. He turned to Calderón and said, But what aboot a drink, man?

The goat clacked his wide yellow teeth and then turned himself around and noodled his way around looking for grub.

I don't even think by the looks you need a drink, Clough, said Miguel with musical diplomacy in his voice.

When has looks meant anything? What aboot the substance a the man himself? What a you say to fraternity? Bonds.

It took Clough a while longer to persuade Miguel that he

owed him a favour and that a drink would call it even. Pour old Litz here a drink too while you're at it, and, Miguel, then I owe *you* one, eh. Clough, needing a quick change of subject, pointed his index finger at Litz. You got mud all down your neck, eh? No, other side. That's right.

Litz wiped his neck. Is it gone now?

Yeah, mostly. Well, cheers.

Cheers.

They clinked tin cups.

Litz had nothing to say. He glugged his beer, watching the couples on the dance floor.

There's a lot a talented people in the jails, eh. I've met a lot a talented people in my years, and if I had my way I'd hire them all up and give them all homes and wives. But that's not reality, Litz. Oh, yeah, I meet a lot a men in there who know my reputation. People exposed to my legacy, yeah, that's true, but that kind a wears off after the first two or three weeks, eh. Then you're stripped down to the man. Every day I got to act like a man.

Litz checked across the dance floor for any sign of Molly. There were tradesmen, real estate agents, scriveners, and bookkeepers, so many capitalists in view, he was sure she'd be among them. Mayor McLean was here with his whole obese family. RH Alexander and his stout wife were dancing gaily across the tree trunk. The butcher George Black was stomping along and hooting low notes across the lip of his moonshine bottle. So many men, so many young eager men, new landowners, new capitalists mortgaging their family fortunes on Vancouver, they all watched from the sides of the dance floor inside the warm embrace of beaver caps and fur coats, eager for their turn. Every man had an oiled moustache and combed hair. Underneath they all wore the same fine black suits with long tails, cotton shirts, and trim slacks that fit inside shining leather boots with shining buckles. Plenty of these men stiffly escorted their feminine partners across the tree trunk to the informal rhythm of the wooden instruments. The ladies were all blushing old hens from New Westminster with elbow-length kid gloves and fur stoles to keep their shoulders warm. They had expansive waistlines and thick, clumsy legs. No Mollys. Where was she if she wasn't here? Not at home. Wouldn't her crippled husband want to attend? Litz shook his head, then looked at Clough, who was staring at him as if he'd lost his senses.

Mind I ask what you're looking at, man?

Sorry, what?

Clough flung his arm in the air. I give up. Why do it? A all the things, man, why this?

Litz didn't answer all at once. He said: I kumtuks how you mean. I do. It looks crazy.

It's seems like a fool's way to waste the days, yes.

No, it isn't. No, see. The man game's more important than logging, or fishing, or any job. For me. The man game's the test. Even taking down a tree don't compare. When I'm out there in the game, alls that's going to save my skin is my own strength. Strength in my body and in my mind, eh. My stealth. My strength and my stealth. I never even thought aboot it until I started to play. If it weren't for the man game, Clough, I wouldn't be standing here with you right now. Probably be dead. Or in Alberta. Me and Pisk risk our lives every time we play. Because this is what we're meant to do in Vancouver. But right now we don't know who's going to come after us. Furry and Daggett want to tan and hide us like bisons.

That's all I'm talking aboot. Why don't you skedaddle, leave town?

Leave town? Who should leave town? Who's a menace? Furry and Daggett come after us with saws and axes—and us, what do we have? Nothing, not even our skivvies. I don't wonder who deserves this town. Who do you think?

This was Furry and Daggett's town before you could spit. Leave and be done with it, I'm *beseeching* you, eh?

Who you think's got more courage? We'll stand up to them, or anybody else, any day. Try us in the man game and see what I mean. Pretty soon you can bet me and Pisk will be sitting in their seats at the Sunnyside. Believe me.

Believe you, eh.

Alls I got are my nuts and my word, said Litz, hunched over his drink, elbows splayed across Miguel's conveyable bartop.

Clough chewed at the inner skin of his cheek, meditating on the hypnotic drums of the celebration. The dancers trotting along four-legged like prize ponies to the rhythm of the log band. Such hopeless pleasure was good for the soul of a new town. Clough said: I respect you, Litz. For a kid, you work hard. I just don't like to see you in trouble.

Trouble's the easy part, said Litz.

Okay, I can tell your ears work as good as my right arm here invisibly choking you, so you know what? said Clough. One sip a this beer and I forgot all aboot how badly I need to piss. Save my branch.

While Clough was away, Litz returned his attention to the dance floor in hopes of seeing her face, her olive green eyes, that softly sexual, sarcastic smile, her thick black hair, her stiff-backed rump, the heaven of her somewhere waiting for him among other men. He straightened his tie, dusted off his shoulders, rubbed his hair flat, and checked again for mud. Crazy to play a man game before meeting Molly this way. He listened to the music and studied all the shoes travelling in time to the rhythm, watching patterns of skirts and pants coalesce, cede, and transform. The atmosphere was perfectly frivolous.

A part of him still held out hope that when she arrived she'd come straight to him and that would be it, they'd get married. There the fantasy abruptly ended, as if forecasting beyond that moment was more absurd than even he would allow himself permission to explore.

Clough said: Now I'm freezing. Miguel, a whisky. You in pain, Litz? Looks like a good cut on your forehead.

Litz found the long cruddy spot, dabbed it curiously with his thumb, and brushed some crumbs of dried blood off his cheek. No, he said. No pain. The opium and hashish … Finally he caught sight of her. Before he thought to keep it to himself, he said: *There* she is.

Who?

… Oh, well …

Who, you mean Mrs. Erwagen?

Hm.

What aboot her?

Nothing, I, only I … think she's, I mean, ain't she *be*autiful?

Sure, Mrs. Erwagen is, hell, why … Are you … say now, do you mean you …

No, what? No.

She's the—. Your—. Is she your *coach*? Litz?

Litz looked in his glass of beer at the bubbles on the head slowly popping out of existence.

Are you a fool?

You tell a living soul aboot her—

'The fuck, I—

—and I'll personally tie you a noose with your own gizzard like a chicken, hang you, then axe your head off.

Molly Erwagen?

Was her whole idea.

You *talk* to her?

Said it yourself, she's our coach.

How often do you see her?

Look, I shouldn't a opened my smacker in the first place, it was dumb as fuck and I don't know why I told you, and I can't tell you any more, so let's drop the subject and carry on with our drinks, I got to—

Clough put his hand on Litz's shoulder: You tell her this has got to stop.

You come to see every time we play. Why should I tell her to stop?

A lady shouldn't be involved in such activities—

Clough, it was her whole idea.

Fine, so it was. I suppose we all took the bait. That's a lady's beguiling skills. Her powers a persuasion. For women, men are all marks. Have no confidence in her. But what she's invented, this is a man's domain. A lady like her does not belong involved in this kind a sport. She knows she's trespassing. She's not invited. I don't like her for it. It being her idea. I don't approve.

She's never even seen a game you played, has she?

Not yet.

Because she *can't*. If I believe you and she's your coach, she can't even be there when you play. That's not helpful. She knows she can't. What with her reputation to upstand. Spectators wouldn't stick around if she were there anyways. Men wouldn't go near the game with her around. Spoil it. How's she supposed to be your coach like that? Not able to conversate with you aboot how you played. That's a deficiency worse than one arm. That's worse even than being a lady. I'm at every game, Litz. I watch it all. I seen every time you played. I know how you move. I can see how you get your speed and where you're still clumsy. I know why you lose to Pisk so often. Don't look at me like that. You know you do. I can see what you do to win and I know how you lose. I watch you both like a hawk, as if I were your coach. I should be your coach.

You? said Litz, incredulously.

I could tell you advice that would burn your ears off to learn. Your whole game style would change, Litz, if I was your guys' coach. He gave Litz a hard shove on the shoulder and said: Listen to what I say, not how she looks.

I'm listening, said Litz as he watched her make a slow, partnerly circle, rotating along the circumference of the tree stump towards where he sat at the bar. She seemed to be carried along the age lines of the tree, a shimmering needle, touching the floor with only the diamond tips of her toes. She smiled, but not at Litz, at some face he couldn't see. The dancers separated into lines of men and women, then he saw old Mr. Husband Erwagen, seated under a tartan blanket. He had his ward Toronto behind him, sublimely Indian under a hood of natural darkness. Litz's features backed up, crinkled before he could resist the expression. What was he supposed to feel for this handicap who got all Molly's love?

She's teaching you how to play this game? said Clough, still trying to grasp. Since when?

I guess it's been since she saw Pisk that day with Daggett.

The time Pisk ... is that why you play in the, what, buck?

She says it keeps the game honest.

Keeps it honest. My fucking lord. I'll have another drink there, Calderón, but make it a real whisky this time, and a double, I'm feeling reality.

And who pay?

It's New Year's Eve, for crikey. Put it on 1886's tab and forget aboot it.

//

What's the matter with you, eh? What's in your head? Take *more* time when you next go. Never come back. How aboot that? Where you been anyway? What took so long, eh? Where you been so long? And where my husband, also? Eh? Where is he? Not with you?

By moonlight they argued. Nothing but wild animals within earshot. Pisk shook his head and walked past her to fetch the axe. Shut your trap, why don't you?

The fire out for hours. You chop no firewood before you left. I told you chop some firewood, eh. I'm frozen. Go chop some wood now. Right now, eh? Don't look at me. Don't look at me, dummy. Where's Litz, that bastard? Where's Litz?

Jesus, woman, would you just shut up?

You got to chop some wood, eh? Can you do that? I'm freezing cold.

What a you see me doing? Now just shut up, all right? You're shrieking right in my ear. I'm chopping, I'm chopping. Jesus.

Where's my husband? Where is he? Is he gone to the dance? You know I can hear it. Drums like Salish nights. All night I listen to it. Did he leave me here? Where's my fucking husband?

Stop crowing in my ear. And don't use that language on me, hag.

You shut up. Get to work, *man.* Get to work, lazy Whiteman.

Stop screaming.

Where is he, eh?

He's nowhere. He's, I don't know where he is.

Wa.

I was with him, Jesus. Don't scream in my ear. You're driving me nuts, woman.

Where did he go? Keep chopping, not enough. Not enough. The shack is freezing cold. Where did he go?

He stayed in town, is all. He went for a drink.

You work all day. Then you leave me alone at night. Gone for a drink. Bullshit. He's at the dance. He forgot me. Wa. Let me out a here. Let me find him. All day you log. When are you supposed to make real chickamin? You expect me feeding you, little Whiteman?

Shut the fuck up, woman.

Mrs. Litz was close to tearing her own hair out or clawing Pisk's already bruised back. She howled louder than he'd ever heard her before. He's at Wood's, she screamed. He went. That it, eh? He's at Wood's. He's at Wood's. Tell me. Don't push me away.

You're screaming in my ear.

Is he with a woman?

No woman like you.

Take this fucking wood to the house.

You take it to the house.

I said—

You take it to the house, Whitemans. Go warm my house before I feed you.

You stupid bitch.

I hate you. I hate you both.

He swung the handle of the ax and hit her in the face with it. Jesus, you just don't shut up, do you?

He picked her up over his shoulder, took her to the house, and threw her on the bed. After going back outside for the firewood, he stood in the door and looked at her laid out on the bed just as he'd thrown her. There was a big cut on her face and a lot of blood. Her eyes were closed. He dropped all the firewood. She didn't stir. He wiped his face and set to work on the stove.

About an hour later she awoke to find she was in a lot of pain.

What happened?

You fell.

She gingerly touched the gauzy blot on her forehead. No. You hit me.

He handed her a lukewarm soup that she drank in hesitant, queasy sips. The house was warm again. She was shivering.

I'm going to be sick. She ran out the door.

He waited for her.

When she came back in he was on his chair, leaning over and jabbing the fire inside the stove.

//

As the hours grew later, he came and lay in bed beside her. He lay on his side facing the wall and a draft kept whistling across his eyes. He couldn't move, he couldn't sleep. In the starkness of his transgression he'd completely forgotten his New Year's promise to himself to shave off his beard. He would let it grow now until it concealed his entire face. He would no longer be Pisk. He would become Beard. He lay on the mattress with his hands under his hairy cheek. Of the four choices he had between moving, falling asleep, ignoring the pain, and not moving, choosing not to move was the one he knew was the wisest and worst. He listened to her halting breaths, as if she was on the brink of sickness or tears. She was certainly not asleep. He heard her throat constrict and tenderly swallow. He couldn't slow the punches of his heart against his chest, nor his constant lip-chewing, nor the loud sound of swallowing the saliva that kept filling his mouth while his tongue and palate somehow remained sickly dry. The wood in the stove hissed and cracked apart. In a minute he'd have to get up to put more in so she wouldn't get cold. The thought of what her reaction might be when he moved was unbearable. Of all things, he didn't want her to flinch.

Should I—.

She stirred.

Should I get you some opium? He wiped his face.

Please.

//

Her cold-pinked skin was near the bonfire. She tipped her scotch to her mouth and it gave him a chance to contemplate her bosom, moist and heaving from dancing and gaiety. She said: Did you practise today what I told you to? How did the game go?

Yes, the dance …

Did you see me dance?

Yes, Molly, but—

I mustn't stay long. My husband, he needs me.

Molly, yes, but—, he looked at her.

She didn't want to hear anything else yet. Her smile reflected the pleasure she took away from the dance, not her new joys at seeing Litz.

Yes, he said, thinking to grab her attention by talk of the man game. Yes, yes, we did practise, and the game went well tonight.

How—?

It, uh …

Were you able to convert the Whistle into the Hatched B—?

Molly, yes, but …

It's wonderful. I'm so pleased. I knew it would, I mean, I knew *you* would—

Molly, I don't know how to, see … But I love you.

You what? Well, a course. I love you, as well.

You do?

And this air, this fresh, cool air.

No, I don't think you—. He paused to collect his thoughts. I know I love you. I promised myself I'd tell you tonight. I'm sorry.

You mean … you? She looked away from him, concentrating, her head tilted like a bird's with one ear to the tremors of worms.

In no time at all her shock was reduced to something domestic. She said: Why, if anyone I thought Pisk.

Pisk? Why would you think Pisk?

He's rowdy. He's a bachelor. You're *married,* Litz.

Hm?

I thought you loved your wife.

I do. It's not … but why? Do you love Pisk?

I didn't say—Litz, listen, darling. I love you both. I love you both very much.

Don't love me like some pet, said Litz, brushing her hand away from his bloodied temple.

Litz, that's not fair.

Show me. Show me fair. Marry me, Molly.

You're lovely and mad, she said. She kissed him on the cheek. I have to go to my husband now. We'll talk in a while. You'll still be here?

I'm sorry, he said, hiding his face. I've taken some opium for the pain.

That's fine. Don't worry.

And some hashish.

Litz, don't worry. I'll see you shortly. I'll come back. Stay here. Don't move. Don't think aboot anything.

And I'm blotto.

She blew him a sympathetic kiss and looked back to her husband.

There was a moment of silence while Litz dryly wept. And then another moment just like it, giving Litz the chance to contemplate whether or not to scratch out his heart.

//

How would you feel if you were my husband? said Molly when she returned, leading him by the hand as they gingerly made their way farther into the forest, away from the party, away from her husband.

If I was your husband I'd feel great, said Litz.

No, you misunderstand. How would you feel if you were my husband and I left you when you needed me most? Because a course I love you, Litz, but I love my *husband*. Don't you kumtuks, Litz, it's not possible. I don't even want it to be possible.

He couldn't argue with that because he felt a little winded. Okay, said Litz in a lesser voice. Then don't leave him, but come with me now.

She kissed him on the cheek. Oh, Litz.

Wha—? he said. What?

Stop here, she said.

What? He spied left-right.

She said: Careful for that branch.

Then she edged him back against a mossy pine and kissed him on the cheek. Pomegranate. Between the outlines of so many trees. The trees made an army in the darkness on a night of intermittent snow. Behind the chirruping of nearby raccoons Litz could hear the New Year's Eve band beat their logs. Their rhythm nearly competed with the blood pounding in his ears. Pounding so hard it numbed his kissed cheek.

A man is known by his actions, she said. Let your actions be natural. Do not think aboot how you look to others. Recall how difficult it can be to follow your movements when you look in a mirror as you scissor your moustache. When you are guided and not leading your actions, that's trouble. Be at ease with yourself, Litz. This is who you are. Don't guide yourself, but allow your actions to speak for you.

I don't kumtuks, he said. I won't kumtuks. I want to … how do I say it, I want … to make love to you.

She sighed with pity for him. If we made love there'd be nothing left. Tell me why you feel this way?

Oh, Molly, he said, jumping at the chance to explain himself. Don't you know. The way I look at your. And I'm wanting you. Missing you. I think aboot you no matter what I'm doing. Wouldn't you like to be my wife? Wouldn't you like to lie down with me now? You and me, right now?

No, she said, simply, and without unnecessary cruelty.

But he was crushed. There were plenty of women who loved to do it in the woods. In coming to the dance tonight, Litz had very much hoped that Molly would be one of them. Lovemaking in the woods was one of Litz's specialties, where the fears vanished and the entirety of his passions and prowess was available to him in all sorts of ways. Mrs. Litz had married him not for the love he showed her in the bedroom of Wood's, but for the richer expression of it she saw when he took her in the woods. Litz was instinctually drawn to women who loved to do it in the woods. That's why he expected Molly to already be on top of him. For some women, that's what the forest was for, private discussions with men. Litz assumed by his popularity with women that he must be attractive. Molly was defying this expectation, but he didn't believe her. Litz believed that Molly wanted it, but couldn't admit it. Molly wasn't a frigid thing. She bit her bottom lip, very on purpose, and batted her eyelashes.

And here was Molly with Litz in the woods, on New Year's Eve, no less. With a kiss on his cheek, she dipped away without so much as a wrinkle on her skirts.

Where are you going? he said.

I have to go back to the dance again, Litz, she said.

What? Again? So soon?

I just realized it's almost midnight. Sammy will be expecting me.

Almost midnight ...? I thought it was ... what time is it?

He kept working to get his erection down as he watched her subsume into the terminality of 1886. Seeking if nothing else then at least to kiss her while she sought to kiss her beloved husband on the big fat midnight. He couldn't even bear to go back and say a proper klahowya to Clough. He walked, instead of anywhere else, home.

Back at the portable Rústico saloon, Clough was still marinating in the news he'd just learned. I'll be damned, he said as he rubbed his entire face. I need a drink. I said I need a *drink.*

//

He opened the entrance to the hideout, a mere silhouette of her former husband. At god-knows-what hour Litz stood in the doorway and didn't move farther. He was late enough that the wildlife was already uncurled and waiting in secret shades for food. Late enough that 1887's first sun was rising behind his back. She couldn't even see her husband's expression. He, on the other hand, could see her well enough, purple across the face. She couldn't even muster the energy to bawl him out. Litz tried to react. His eyes were burnt-out, hardly open, as from opium addiction. He walked over to the bed. He stared at Pisk asleep. He swallowed. His wife looked up at him with wet, sorrowful eyes. One eye was swollen and bloody. He sat down on a canewood chair next to the bed and unlaced his boots and she shifted to the middle of the bed without waking Pisk. Litz lay down in the warmth she left behind. The ceiling beams above his head were spotted by a black mould. And he turned, held her until they somehow found the energy to fall asleep in the cold sunshine through the door he forgot to shut.

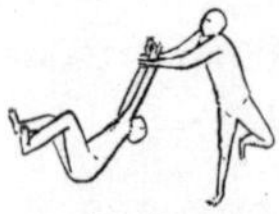

EIGHT

> When unappeased, violence seeks and always finds
> a surrogate victim.
>
> — RENÉ GIRARD

When the Litzes awoke it was already evening, January 1, 1887. Night in the forest. Above the treeline the clouds were a perfect ceiling aside from one small hole, as if made from a flame, breaking it open to show a view of the deep black universe where the stars hang to dry. One dead tree, as dead as any star, exhaled a thin trail of smoke like off a forgotten cigarette next to a window. At the base of the dead tree, the shanty cabin. Food cooking. The stovepipe fitted into the trunk of this tree. The room was warmed to the smell of fresh Canadian bacon, a dozen eggs, griddlecakes, coffee on the stove. Pisk was frying up breakfast for dinner.

Litz separated himself from his wife, making sure to avoid upsetting the food when he cold-cocked Pisk hard across the jaw. Rolled him to the floor, pushed him out the door for the last straight-up fist fight of their lives. They stood with fists raised. Pacing around, trading blows. Pisk defended himself enough to take what he had coming to him. Once Litz had him down on the dirt, the fight turned into punishment.

'The fuck you think you are?

Pisk blacked out when Litz smacked him across the head, got his ear split in half, and his nose broke flat when he fell to the ground. Litz knocked him around a bit more until his partner was beside the door, falling limply against their home like a cord of firewood that had toppled over.

Litz went back inside and poured three cups of coffee, gave one to his wife and brought the other two back outside, slapped

Pisk awake with a soaked shirt and helped get him to his feet. The men cleaned up together at the creek then sat on logs until they'd finished the dregs of their coffee before going back inside where Litz's wife served them up breakfast for dinner.

Afterwards, she filled the net with the dishes and went down to the creek and slung the net under the running water. She hooked it to a peg so it wouldn't get dragged away—nature's dishwasher—and went back to the shack where two bastards treated her cuts. That night in bed—Pisk against the wall, Litz in the middle, his wife on the outer edge of the mattress—no one got much sleep.

They thought about what could not be said.

She wondered why she still believed she would be happier if permitted to sleep in the middle.

Litz mentally repeated a shoulder roll he'd done earlier in the night, going through the moment again and again and gauging when he'd reacted against when he should have reacted.

Pisk asked himself why he agreed to so much pain in life. He wanted something to happen that would change the course of his fate. His problem, he figured, was he avoided success. He was cruel when he should be kind, laughed at mercy, and feared women. His hands could break a cow. He kicked open doors. Opium never once made him drowsy. Metabolically he could take anything. Not long ago he was a boy. How did he go from being a boy to being this? He'd agreed to try the game—why? Because Molly was beautiful and it was impolite to say no way. Imagine you turn a rock into an eel. You turn a mosquito into a monk. You take mud and moss from the forest floor and you shape that into a man. That's how he felt. No one ever taught Pisk the words for when you had good feelings. All he knew was that the man game was something more than Litz or himself. Above all else, from this day forward he would obey the game.

//

Since Dr. Langis's moratorium on prescription renewals for laudanum, RH Alexander and his wife had decided on scheduling a private room in the back of Ming's, a popular den that smelled of cold sweat, coffee, and human feces (after the first puff you didn't even notice). Pale inebriated Chinamen in silk booties, long smocks, and porkpie hats were at your disposal. They cooked your opium on the tip of a wooden pin and fit your lips to the end of the pipe to inhale its smoke. The pin the Chinamen used was beautifully carved. Dragons clutched in their talons the top of a scored poppy bulb. Another pin was silver decorated by an inset jade leaf. A ball of opium the size of a pea was jabbed on the pinpoint and held over a candle until the stuff went from a defecatory brown to a limpid honey yellow. You inhaled. Who could say no to such a thing? They were both quite sure this was the ideal way to say goodnight to the first day of the new year.

I can see why they sometimes refer to them as Celestials, said Alexander.

... China-ese, said his wife, sleepily.

Because here I am deep in a basement and I can see the stars as clearly as if I were floating in a canoe on a lake, looking up.

Mrs. Alexander gazed up at the ceiling with her husband, wondering if her mind would conjure up the same zodiac as his. Yes, she said, I see it.

But he was already asleep. And so was she.

They awoke moments later from vast dreams. The Alexanders lay together on a long, wide, very flat sofa carved with scaly dragons, poppies, and pyres. Seeing them stir, a Chinaman silently put the pipe back to RH's lips and dropped a melty nugget off his pin and into the pipe's glass bowl where it was hot enough to vaporize with just a little more candleheat and RH's deep inhalation. He passed the pipe to his wife, who accepted China's gift to the imagination, leaned into the candle, and sucked the flame towards the syrupy shag. She held the world inside her lungs for twenty seconds before exhaling.

That fool Langis—he was a clown. This was real medication. This was poetry. This was the tabernacle. This was the mind's histrionic death scene. Opium was a theatre as yet invisible to the naked eye, a silent squall of profound and blissful drama.

Only China knows how to sleep, said RH.

That's the word I was trying to remember, his wife said. Sleep, she said as if the word meant ecstasy.

The walls were thick. RH didn't feel anything and the only thing he heard was the ringing in his ears. RH was on the other side of the helix. Beside him, his wife seemed preoccupied with swallowing something perpetually in the back of her throat. His wife was the tongue on the owl of time, licking minutes. Despite them, the temperature in Vancouver dropped two degrees and made all the nothings sound more succinct.

//

Sammy watched her tusk-handled hairbrush slide down her hair, smooth as a night's river for that ivory boat. He was enamoured of her. Her long black waters shone in the candlelight against the buttery stone of her tilted neck. The hairbrush was decorated with a maple leaf. He saw his country against her nape, where he alone ought be pressed. Even the inanimate left him jealous.

He was lying on his side in bed, facing her, and just a glimpse out the window. Until she came to bed, this was how he preferred to lie. It was how Toronto set him up at the end of the day, unless Molly was already asleep, in which case Toronto sidled his crippled body in edgewise and laid him on his back with a thin pillow under his head.

She placed her brush beside the silver cuticle wedge on the doily. Also on her bureau was a framed photograph of her and Sammy on their wedding day. Two things about the picture he never failed to notice were how terribly beautiful she was in her bridal gown and that he, her husband, was not yet crippled. Tall man. Upon reflection, he could see that he had a certain handsomeness in his stature. Foolish to hate himself. He distracted his mind with the soft seam of an undergarment creeping out her dresser drawer. The perfume of her. The salmon glint of her nightdress moving against her flesh. Mustn't sink into the horror, the horror of himself, the horror that even suicide was impossible. Her gaze drew back from her reflection to his outline in the mirror while she tilted her head to remove each earring. She smiled. He smiled back, without sign of horror. She would soon be in bed. He could see her daub on the creamy white face creams that came from shallow tortoiseshell cups there beyond the wedding photo. Don't be so jealous, he told himself, you're her husband.

She moved through the room without even so much as a hint. She sat on the side of the mattress tugging at the frilly ends of her white nightie as he looked out the window for hints in the sky of something, anything, an image of his future in the clouded darkness. Her white nightie. Her white skin. Like light shining through a pristine sheaf of paper. Beguiling picots of thread dangled against her calves where her nightie ended, adorned with pearls or was it his imagination? No, his imagination, but still.

Should we sleep? he asked her.

She didn't answer, she pressed a hand across the coverlet and took a breath. Her back was to him.

What's wrong? he asked.

Nothing. I'm just tired.

The window looked out over the freely ranging wolves, the dangers of everything not domestic, the physical world. She collapsed her head against his chest, and began to weep.

Love; his palate leaped and his tongue thickened in his mouth. He exclaimed: Oh, darling Chinook, what is it? But did he want to know the answer, or did he only want her attention? What's the matter? he asked in a bruised whisper. She held him, body so close so very close beneath the thin nightie, the snowy caps of her vertebrae against the silk, the wintry smell of her hair furled under his chin.

It's nothing, she said. I'm fine.

She sniffed, lifted her chin, and petted her nose on a white knuckle. She blinked, then to look in his eyes, she turned and smiled for mercy. Oh, darling, he said. The smile faded at the sound of his voice. She quieted, her breathing, her pulse, her air. She was suddenly absent. He said again: Dear Chinook, what's the matter?

She gazed at him as though he wasn't even there, right through him to the wall or something beyond him, or her mind's inner wall maybe, but she kissed his chin wetly, and then his lips, wetly, and she was still in tears when she pushed him down and saddled on top of him in the bed in the night not talking not speaking so quiet aside from her sobs and kisses on his many numb spots while she undressed him a little further and a little further until the cold moist air and her fear made his nosetip tingle, not wanting to stop and consider what was happening or why, but to just let it, let her, let himself, be, again, if possible, seduced.

As if talking to someone in a dream, she asked her husband: How old are you? with a quivering voice, her neck stretched out and chin up, her mouth cold to the kiss from a draught coming from the window, —and her belly, a blueberry in the night's light.

I'm never old when I'm with you, he said.

You're always so old. Can you feel anything?

Nothing, not a tingle.

Tell me what's happening …

We …

No, don't tell me.

//

The wind started before dawn. Sammy awoke. She stirred. A giant boom so loud it shook the loose boards of the porch, startled the house. She stirred awake. He watched Molly's eyes unlatch and open. Fishermen, he thought, listening to the echo decay across the inlet. It was the signal to start the day's fishing. Just beyond his view he knew fishing boats were creaking off into the inlet, and the same thing happening down in Steveston where the fattest smelt swam. He listened with disinterest to the intestinal groan of the cedar floats paying out over the gunwales of the tugs, the floats separating in the scupple of the waves and blooming with nets. The line used was of the best hemp, slightly vapoured with tar, not impregnated with it. All those fishing boats, they scooped salmon by the thousands, even when the canneries' limit per boat might some days be as low as a hundred fifty. Sometimes the beaches below Hastings Mill were strewn with carcasses idling in the waves of the tide. The air stank with their rot. Some mornings he wished he could sleep forever. He was afraid to wake up, but something soulfully prompted him; daft love. He said her name: Molly.

Before he knew it the city was quiet again, the fleet awaiting its gather of fish. She stirred but did not wake. He went inside himself and stood at the window in his mind's kitchen, made coffee, and meditated on the view.

A minute later he was still in bed, almost too warm. With latent desire he studied the pressure of the blood coursing through her jugular. Her pulse was steep. It fluttered the skin of her neck and cheek as the blood surged up behind her ear. For a while he contemplated what could be going on between her gorgeous ears, inside her intimidating and inscrutable head. She was asleep, all the better. Was she, in dreams, contemplating him, the way he, in torment, contemplated her? Was it all love?

He heard January spit on his roof. It was a new day, a new year, and all that, but it was still dank, and the forecast was for more dankness in the weeks to come.

She turned to face him, smiling with contentment, stretched and squeaked, and said: I love you.

He said: I love you, too. I was just thinking about how much I love you. I wish I could go back in time and love you from the moment of your birth. I wish I could experience all that you have experienced, to love you more completely.

I want to go back in time to give you the first banana you ever ate, she said.

He laughed. He said: I want to go back in time to leave a chocolate at every corner you walk past, for your entire life.

I want to go back in time and find your first kiss and steal it.

When Toronto returned from errands, they all drank coffee and ate Calabi&Yaus in the living room. The Calabi&Yaus were fresh and soft as mousse. Chocolate with banana. Blackberry jam and cream cheese icing. Cheddar with raspberries. Maple-dusted confection of the gods. This Byzantine shapelet of marbled pastry. This outrageous delight. Toronto fed Sammy bite by bite. Molly blew on her coffee and drank it black. In effect, this was 1887. It was pointless to argue. Take your bites and leave as little as you can for the next.

At some point she stood and opened a drawer and removed a tin of her cigarettes, popped the cover, extracted, lit, and smoked a fresh Stars & Stripes. Smoke went aloft in the still morning air, hovered, and in a moment of poetic contemplation he imagined it as another of the sails he could hear distantly crack and flutter. He asked her why she did it. His whisper didn't even startle her. She told her husband that she wanted to *inspire the bohunk.*

//

Silas and Ken competed for a still unknown (to Minna and me) objective. Ken struggled to instigate a different move among Silas's knife-hand throat chops. Ken ducked, spun on his right heel, knocked Silas off balance, handstanded up and pushed off and landed on his feet. Silas accomplished the same feat, only with his legs over his head, swinging up and over and tripped, pivoted, alley-ooped and landed just a few yards from his opponent. Then, with dustpowder upturned behind his steps, we watched Silas charge Ken and force him through an aggressive kind of New York cha cha, every step so trippingly tight that bare millimetres separated each ankle *{see fig. 8.1}*.

Whoa, said I.

Eek, said Minna, squirming with pleasure. What a move, she said.

Ken was the one to crumple. A paff of dirt rose quickly at his fall and settled around his head. It didn't look good. It looked like 911. Something about the angle of his neck said 911. I can't say it looked like a death blow that Silas had dealt there. But at the end of this impressive wheeling catenate came a splendid calm … and then worry, and our eyes for an instant grasped the retreating motions of Silas away from the loser's crumpled body, and just as quickly we returned to the body, for the first time seeing that the possibility was officially in the air that Ken was dead, and that Silas was a murderer. This was how it felt at the instant when things went from good to bad. The core body temperature in the yard rose and fell in sync as we all waited for signs of life from Ken, there on the ground.

Minna laughed despite all the drama. I needed her amusement to hide my anxiety.

And then finally I heard Ken wring the last bubbles of air from his lungs and inflate his chest again with a giant sucking fatigued wheeze. He was deeply, utterly winded, but not dead. The game was over. His gasps were huge. His eyes were completely bugged out and cracked with blood as he gasped

---

FIGURE 8.1

Rook Takes Pawn, alternative sketch

See Calabi's commentary on p. 10.

for air while we applauded. Ken was being held up by fans because he kept doubling over to catch his breath. Coughing, with thick ropes of saliva dangling off his lips, he finally fell to his knees, wheezing at the ground. Silas watched him without enough compassion. The idea of calling an ambulance started to circulate through the crowd after I posed the question to Cedric and someone overheard me. Eventually the idea was passed on to Ken that he should seek immediate medical assistance.

No ambulance, wheezed the defeated between gagging pukes.

Death, I said. I don't want to see it today.

You won't, said Cedric.

I saw bruises and welts as they appeared like rainclouds. Not to mention the gashes and blood, and now the filthy brown-speckled line of vomitous spittle up Ken's cheek, the bleak winter clay trapped in the plentiful hairs on Silas's chest as they started to walk around shaking out their limbs, looking very tired, slouching way over, necks out like invalids. This was as bad as it looked.

It's theatre, said Cedric. Ever seen theatre?

That's fake blood? I asked.

If an actor is cut, he bleeds just like you and me.

Silas came up beside Ken and put his arm around his neck and helped carry him inside while we all clapped to see them out. They were gone. The show was over. For the first time, I realized where I was, and just like everyone around me, didn't quite feel ready to leave yet.

I'm impressed, I said.

Make a donation if you like it so much, Cedric said, running his pink eyes up and down Minna's body, all the way from flip-flops on up to her seasonally thick, long, naturally tousled brown hair with salon sunlights.

The guys are good, I said. It looks like an insane amount a practice.

Like all day every day, Cedric said.

They made this up or someone else? I asked.

No, man, said Cedric. Someone else. Long time ago. Fuck, said Cedric through clenched teeth, never taking his pink eyes off Minna or the game.

So that's it, I said. When's the next?

Patience, child. We go inside and discuss matters. Plays. We break down the plays. We conversate. We digress.

Who's this *we*? Minna said. I'm ready to call it a day.

I said: Do you think anyone here is packing heat?

Don't whisper in my ear, she said, it tickles.

//

The middle of January was as cold and crisp as a single handclap. The city was already humming a different tune. Behind the cedars, firs, and anomalous arbutuses, away from the prying eyes of eastern civilization, Vancouver men were safe to grow their hair out, live and die on instinct alone.

Litz and Pisk met for their regular lesson with Molly in the forest clearing on Doyle's land where black bears lived. When they arrived Molly was already waiting for them, sitting on her Hudson's Bay blanket with the bulk picnic goods. Over the months this once grassy patch of open land had become a mud-packed floor. Her first order of business was to inspect Pisk's hands and toes. Sure enough, the palms and soles were splotchy red along their sides, the fingers and toes rich pink at the top.

All numb with needle tingles, said Pisk.

You don't have a problem with the cold, Litz?

Nope, said Litz. He sat naked cross-legged beside them with his face leaning on his knuckles, elbows on his knees. I can feel the cold on my lips and my ears, he said, but my chest feels warm and my arms and legs are usually hot by the end.

Molly said: Men on the street are enjoying the man game, aren't they? I feel that.

Yeah, said Pisk.

It's too early to come out a hiding …

Oh, a course, Litz, said Molly. Yes, I don't believe your exile is over yet. You shouldn't dwell on that. Exile is not an article of clothing you wear then take off. It is more like a burn. You live with it always. But I agree. If you bought a house in town tomorrow you'd be dead. But the man game has won some hearts, I do say. There is no arguing that as you play, no one will trouble you. I doubt that even Furry and Daggett themselves would stop you now.

Scratching his neck, Litz asked: Does anyone else know aboot you?

The secret remains safe among our trusted accomplices, said Molly, grinning at the pleasure of collusion.

Who shall remain nameless, said Pisk.

Who shall remain nameless outside this circle, yes, said Molly.

Pisk shook his head.

What's wrong? said Molly.

Nothing, said Pisk. I'm just tiring a the secrecy. You still like it, he said, nose pointed at Molly. All the secrets. I don't see the fun. Alls I know is we got to make some real chickamin and we got to get out a the hideout.

Soon. Soon, Pisk. Have patience.

Litz didn't know what to say. Whenever he opened his mouth it dried up. Should he admit he'd let slip the secret to Clough on New Year's Eve, or hope that the one-armed man had been drunk enough to forget it? That seemed impossible. Clough remembered everything, especially gossip. Drunkennness had no effect on his memory for secrets. He collected information like stray dogs.

Peggy knows, said Molly, for the safety a everyone. Calabi and Yau know aboot me. My husband, a course. Four other than the three a us. A total a seven, which I like. Seven's a beautiful number. She kicked up her legs as she sat, as if to make of herself the number.

People are damn curious to know who's our coach, said Pisk, sitting down next to her on the Bay blanket, naked. I can hear it.

Litz stammered, then fell silent, walking a few steps back and facing the treeline.

What is it? Molly said.

Nothing, he said, flushing red from the neck up.

Really, what is it?

Nothing, he said, now fingering shy circles on the Bay blanket.

Pisk rolled his eyes. Instead of one-upping Litz's flirtations, he kept it strictly business. What's your take on that imp Campbell showing up at every game?

She shrugged. Very promising. If there was a risk in his presence, we would have encountered it already.

Do you think he's telling Furry and Daggett?

No. He deceives himself to excuse his behaviour. Campbell, the child, he believes he's playing spy.

Spying on our scene.

But in fact, he is fascinated, said Molly. When Furry and Daggett are eventually confronted with the popularity of the game, Campbell also hopes this will give him an advantage over his colleagues.

Ha ha, he must be sore always biting his tongue like that, said Litz.

It's true, said Molly, touching Litz's hairy, red-spotted shoulder. With Furry and Daggett he can't talk aboot us, and at our games, he can't discuss why he's there.

Y-yes, said Litz, drymouthed.

These winter months are the most ruinously boring for the working man, Molly said, choosing to ignore Litz's blatantly sudden change in mood. Our matches are bound to start getting more and more attention. And if we take enough bets, the gamblers will protect you from anyone who wants to disrupt.

I can protect myself, said Pisk.

I know you can, she said, picking up and massaging his giant hands. Oh, they're as cold and hard as ice. We need to pay more attention to how you use your hands and feet. You shouldn't be this cold. Well, she added after concentrating on his hands for a while, squeezing the thick muscle between his thumb and forefinger, perhaps we'll finally meet some new competitors. Let's send word out that you'll perform a man game tomorrow and see who comes out a the woodwork, shall we?

Tomorrow night? said Pisk, quietly and happily, a bit blissed-out from the hand massage.

Expect Furry and Daggett will hear aboot it, said Litz.

How's ten?

Ten works for me, said Litz.

Fine by me, Pisk said.

//

The next day there came from the train station in New Westminster a surprise New Year's guest to the Erwagen house. Toronto was charged with escorting a man from the train station back to Vancouver, just as he'd done for the Erwagens themselves. Seven moons. Two and a half seasons.

Truth be told the trip back and forth from New West' to Vancouver was becoming more than a little burdensome for the Indian. Whenever he set off, it was with a cramp. He rode every time in a little more pain. If he were asked to locate this pain for a doctor he could only have dropped his hand between his legs and pointed up. Collecting the mail was one thing. Meet the postal clerk at the mail car when the train pulled up, take the sacks from him, hitch them to his dray, and be on his way. But Toronto had begun to notice that every time he was charged with meeting someone at the train, that person brought some new evil. It was as if they'd brought along a hidden set of matches and, once in Vancouver, dropped them on the ground, alighting it, transforming his home again and again. His home. Every time he brought guests to his home, it burned away a little more. Soon it would vanish completely and some new crystallized aberration would appear, the way blood, after soaking the earth, dries to a dark, cracked stained glass.

Last Sunday Toronto had found a Chinaman businessman from San Francisco waiting for him at the postal drop-off in New West' wanting a guide to Vancouver. The Chinaman was something to look at. Inside his fat smile, his dentistry was all gold nuggets. His eyes were blood-misted. He dressed like a Mexican banker, complete with the black and yellow fingernails and six-shooters holstered across his chest. Their ivory handles were inlaid with jade cobras. He wore Shanghai boots. Along the way they witnessed the sight of three men beside a disembowelled grizzly at the side of the road. A fourth man was inside the animal, dumping out the intestines. Whitemen, gone mad. When the men saw Toronto and the Chinamen, they all took to their feet. The one man inside the guts lurched out and, wielding a cleaver, chased them down the road for miles, his naked erection covered in bear blood. When they were safely out of sight the Chinaman looked furious enough to cock the hammers and leave Toronto's corpse behind.

Around the Vancouver settlement the woods were high risk. Toronto felt it his responsibility to duly warn a visitor, such as this one today, a cleanly dressed and barbered Whiteman from the American west, that Vancouver was a known destination for Wanted types.

Thank you, boy, said the guest, I already heard plenty. I spent last night in a New West' hotel and saloon eating verminous pies and listening to slanderous and libellous talk. According to what I hear, Vancouver's infrastructure is gripped by a confederacy a whores.

True, said Toronto.

Tell me, I heard a strange story last night aboot the Hastings Mill. Why, I heard the bookkeeper there's a man with *no* body.

No *body*? said Toronto. Impossible.

Wife pushes his face around in a wheeled chair, so the gossip went, said the visitor, riding a lively adolescent horse next to his guide on his aging wildebeest.

Toronto fell silent. He was weighed down with a week's worth of letters, plus a paper box of sweet-smelling, cooled but freshly baked blackberry Calabi&Yaus that he ate while riding, not even so much as offering his visitor a peek let alone a taste.

Even from the underbrush, where a mugger might hide for extended bouts of mugging, Toronto's pastries smelled like cream heaven, pacifying any urge to strike out with the blade.

How much longer? the guest asked.

Toronto, looking ahead, speculated three hours. They'd been on the road ten minutes. The trees began to close in on all sides, especially above him where the canopy had blocked out most of the sunlight. Toronto kept pulling the fragrant pastries from the well-folded box and eating them all himself, a bite and a half at a time. It made the guest's stomach complain. Eventually, after non-stop staring, Toronto did pass one over, but only once he'd eaten ten of them by the visitor's own count.

The pastry was quite doughy, with a slightly sticky, crisp surface of sugary brown. It was heavier than he expected, owing to what he soon realized was an inner cache of blackberries. Perplexing shape. What had seemed a straightforward brocade knot of ribbonny dough turned out to be a puzzle. On closer study, the pastry seemed to refract its own surface, as if it were a jewel and not a pastry at all. From nearly every angle it appeared to be as flat as a cookie, and yet its own knotwork and interwovenness changed as he turned it in his hand. It was like a multitude of curls in a bow, capable of maintaining from all angles the illusion of being as flat as a disc. By the time the visitor felt it was ludicrous to inspect the pastry any longer and just break down and eat the mystifying thing, Toronto had already eaten two more, making it a baker's dozen, of which this precious example was his only taste. The Indian reflattened the paper box and flicked it into the ditch, where a mugger was perfectly hidden and got whanged right between the eyes with the flying blade-edge of the Calabi & Yau box.

They clopped on down the street with too much left unsaid. For one, the visitor's impression of the taste of the Calabi&Yau was so profound that it made the relatively long trip seem like a minute. Secondly, the visitor didn't want to admit to the Indian that his wallet had gone missing since before he went to bed the night before. His wallet stolen, he accepted it. He couldn't recall the men at the New West' bar, only their punk stink, their policy of bear hugs, shoulder punches, and spontaneous chanties. His throat was sore at the thought.

Nine Avenue, said Toronto, gesturing to the corduroy road intersecting their path, as if to explain the calamity ahead. North of this line, the earth was scorched black for miles in every direction. Livid green ferns were already growing. The land was spiky and raw and blemished. Thousands of trees were blackened to haggard, dwarfed stumps. The logs in the road were black as coal, covered with brilliant emerald mosses. The tall narrow houses in the distance with their peaked roofs leading to the northern inlet some five miles away, where the Hastings Mill was located—their earnest construction was not impressing the guest. All he saw were a lot of desperate three-storey post-and-beams raised over scorched earth. Houses seemed eerily cloistered in this landscape, isolated from their kin. A fenced yard might not include a garden but rather three enormously wide, jagged, hollow stumps surrounded by a complete mess of broken branches and red-capped white spotted mushrooms, yellowy green, dysenteric moss growing over it all. Some of these stumps were thicker than horse and carriage both. As Toronto and his companion passed one junction, the raised sidewalk on their left ended abruptly in a giant mound of wood chips tall enough to live or die in. The electrical posts at their sides were wireless, long-legged crosses at perfectly imperial intervals, shedding nothing, not light, not guilt, not even the sacrifice of God.

Toronto and his latest guest, this strange new shifty visitor, clopped past the Greyhound Hotel where a man tipped his hat to them from the second-floor verandah. He put his hands on the iron railing and called down to Toronto: It's a man game tonight, ten.

What did he say? asked the guest.

Toronto thought for a moment. It's Monday tomorrow, he said.

The guest shook his head, despairing at the mounting evidence around him that life here was rats, it was outhouses, it was Indians on this corner and Chinamen on that. The ground looked blasted. Hunks of tree root lay scattered all about. Moss and fungus everywhere.

Vancouver is on a lower steppe a hell than Wyoming, that's for damn sure. Hey now, boy, is that smoke a grease fire, fish burning, what is that?

Toronto said: Always smoke. Always men working. Always new capitalist arrive like you. You look like my boss, he decided to admit.

Ah, so the stories are true. He is a man with no face, a wife who pushes him around in a wheeled chair, and *an Indian ward,* the visitor said. I remind you a Samuel Erwagen?

Toronto winced a nod.

He's my baby brother. I'm Dunbar.

Was this good or bad news? Toronto was unsure.

... Whitemans call me Toronto, he said.

They shook hands across ponies.

My name is Dunbar Erwagen, said the guest. I'm fourteen years Sammy's senior. Surprised? Oh, yeah, I keep my youth because a my vegetable farm in Wyoming. Cukes, potatoes, tomatoes, cabbage. Goats for milk, chickens and eggs for the table. I require only the grace a God and my wife at my command. Not another soul do I rely upon to feed and clothe myself. I might go a month without speaking to anyone. Bless the silence. For I need no one. Ask nothing a anyone. I might say a prayer to the hen before I butcher her and before I sit down to eat, or I might say a word to my wife before bed. Or I communicate through my habits. Language is man's greatest source a pride. And pride is a sin. The Bible is all the company I need, the only words I need to hear.

Toronto made no comment. Then he said, Amen.

Amen, said Dunbar.

//

Ken and Silas were long gone inside the house and the kids around us started to accept that the man game was done. I kept thinking it must be an intermission, but from the way Cedric said goodbye to the people in the crowd he knew personally, I began to accept it was over. Before I came here, when I was going purely on rumour, I understood more than I did at this moment. Now, having seen the man game, I knew much less. Minna looked ready to leave. We seemed to teeter-totter, who wanted to leave, who wanted to stay. I wanted to stay and learn more so I tried to stall Minna by making conversation. She wasn't listening. It didn't matter that she wanted to leave, she was already making new friends. Some of the spectators talked with Cedric for a while, eyeing Minna from top to bottom, disregarding me entirely.

Quit your job yet? said one ballcapped fellow with razor burn across his neck.

No, said Cedric. I'm still writing that mathematician's guide to Vancouver. Where you been?

I'm still at home. The guy tipped his ballcap to Minna.

Hi, I'm Minna.

Hi there, he said, and shook her hand while looking at her daintiness. I'm the kind of guy who tags around local sporting events, he said. You know what, let's do more than shake hands. I feel like we've been through something together today. Let's hug instead. I think it'll feel better.

She was simply amused. When he opened his arms to let her out of his clutches he held on to her hands as if finished a dirty dance, grinned all down her body and said: Damn, baby.

Suddenly I had to scratch my neck. I stared at the clouds and felt foolish. I didn't introduce myself to the new guy. It didn't matter.

Cedric suggested a group hug. The three of them made a disturbing sandwich. Minna waved for me to join in. I declined the offer.

I'm just aboot to take Minna here, and her fri*en*d, on a walking tour a the home, said Cedric. You want to join?

Nah, he said, I should head.

Powerjuice?

Nah, man.

Well, said Cedric, this calls for a goodbye group hug.

They sandwiched up again, with Minna in the middle

again, same as last time, knees and big toes together and a creamy smirk on her face. I saw Cedric pat Minna's butt. She swatted him away with her style of gaiety. It all seemed a little unfair considering how recently they'd met.

Cedric mated his fingers, stretched his arms out with the tendons flaring at me. He said: We need to clean this place up. Kat, would you mind helping stack up those plastic chairs over there?

I nodded sure. I'm usually willing to pull my weight. Some of the chairs didn't need to be stacked because they already were, some were turned over, and some were clotted with beer-wetted paper towel, and so I prepared my shoulders for labour. I looked up from the mess and saw Cedric with a hand on the small of Minna's back, guiding her into the house. Minna turned and shook her head at me and said: Come on, Kat. She gave Cedric a reprimanding smile.

They went inside together with those faces on, unwilling to wait for me.

I contemplated going to my car and just leaving her. My Chrysler Dynasty was waiting a block and a half away on a suspicious crescent. And I was sure I'd forgotten to trap the club inside the steering wheel. I took one step towards my Chrysler Dynasty. It wasn't that I didn't want to learn more. I did. But even though the chance that this whole event had been staged to create an opportunity for three men to gang-rape a girl was pretty slim, still I couldn't up and leave. But if that *was* their plan, then I was in trouble also. I was no fighter. I wanted to be a fighter but I wasn't. It was one of those times when the only smart thing to do is smoke a cigarette. It was one of those times, but I don't smoke.

The grass in the yard was foot-ruined. My bladder was beer-filled. My tie was on straight. I felt ready.

I scraped my shoes' soles on the broombristles of a terra-cotta hedgehog beside the entrance, flattened my shirt, and creaked open the screen door. They'd waited in the foyer for me.

I realized why I was thinking about cigarettes. It wasn't just the old Siwash sweater hanging on a coat hook next to my face, the whole place reeked of dead soggy nicotine.

The back entrance was little more than an architectural pause between the upstairs and the downstairs, but it was enough to have coat hooks and a tree of family pictures. A stern family of seven in layers of shirts and jackets in a park on an autumn day. It was difficult to make out faces in the pictures because of the angle everything was on, the westerly keel due to the home's sinkage. It was hard to figure out much of anything at this angle. The sinkage was dramatic from a distance. It was unmanageable inside. It almost felt as if you'd have to walk upside down to get to the basement. Even the four stairs from the foyer up to the kitchen were a hazard, dangerously thin steplets each with its own corrugated aluminum lip guard on a wonky angle.

I noticed that the house seemed exceptionally loud. Maybe water was thrashing its way through old lead pipes or hissing about in a water heater right below us. It was an incessant churning white drone that nagged at the overnervous part of my brain.

Oh, I said, super place.

The house was dressed with senior citizen's bric-a-brac. I was discomfited by the loudness and ever-present nicotine smell. The kitchen was long, narrow, carpeted, with a stove built into the wall and a breakfast nook that hung off the end, and the whole room had its own smell. It was the smell of moist homemade cookies baked with socks, cigs, and hair tonic.

The incline in the kitchen seemed much worse, almost an embankment. In the corner nearest the entrance at the bottom of this embankment there was a lazy susan. That most mysterious of cupboards, a merry-go-round hidey-hole for delinquent bags of dried apricots, coconut, and jars of beets, burrowed in its rotating core on the seat of its rings.

My focus broke when I saw Ken and Silas rear up from the corner of my eye, coming through a hallway towards the kitchen, wiping their necks and ears with terrycloth sports towelets.

Ken walked in after Silas, both freshly showered. They wore vintage prototype athletic sweatsuits. They charted the floor's tilt with the ease of seamen. Silas flew into the kitchen's corner booth. Ken finished drying his hair on the slant. I appreciated the piping on their velour outfits. The dark green piping on sky blue for Ken's suit was an agile combination. Silas's gold piping on velvety black was total karate. It was a good way to dress.

There was a kitchen witch dangling aslant from a curtain rod over the sink, bopping Ken's ear as he scrubbed out a couple bowls in the double sink. All the dishes on the counter were made of unbreakable Cold War plastic in the now-faded hues of our planetary system. Ken cleaned out the bowls, a Saturn pink and a Plutonian blue. There was built-in bench seating with the coarse-spongy carpet growing up the wall to the bottom edge of the wood seats.

Ken brought over the bowls and slid one to Silas. The breakfast table was fastened to the floor in the booth. *Nook.* Silas sat on his side of the nook and lumped his oat cereal with sugarcubes.

I stood there dumb as a nail waiting to be hammered as the men ate cereal in the nook. A long uncomfortable silence. Cedric remained too impolite to introduce us. If, as he later defended, he was in some kind of a brief alcoholic *walking coma,* some people might consider that an acceptable excuse, but not me. The athletes were in no visible hurry to make friends either by the look of it. They poured more cereal. Therefore I was just getting ready to go.

'The fuck are you all looking at? said Ken between spoonfuls.

Ha ha ha, said Cedric.

History repeats itself, I said.

No, said Cedric. History repeatedly hits himself.

I said no more. After a long, quiet interlude listening only to the slurping noises as the players scarfed down bowl after bowl of cereal, the talking began in earnest. Even then Ken and Silas downed three more bowls of cereal each before we retired to the heavily doilied living room.

I took the opportunity to check out the facilities. There was nothing out of the ordinary about their peach bathroom except that it was virtually impossible at the kind of altitude the toilet bowl hung at to get any piss in there. Even with my full bladder I hardly shot high enough to wet the carpeted seat. I was afraid to wash my hands. The panic of watching the toilet flush at forty-five degrees was enough for me. I did find it odd to see there was no shower nozzle or curtain, only a fluoride-stained peach tub. Dry: How had they showered?

When I returned Ken and Cedric and Minna were sitting next to one another on different cushions of an eight-foot-long lily-patterned davenport sofa from the Hudson's Bay. The faded teal green was not unattractive, considering the sofa was likely more than forty years old. They were already nine-tenths of their way through a conversation Minna knew I wanted to hear.

Most moves are classic, said Silas. Circa hundred years ago. We started making new ones.

Inventing moves is why I—

Do you want to see the diaries? asked Silas. Most people don't know aboot—

—Ink brush drawings circa a century ago. Old wilted paper. Really cool.

I sat down next to Cedric on a doily-backed sofa in this veritable retirees' boutique of a room.

You try to lead, mumbled Ken.

In other words, said Silas, the man game is a—, you know, who within the dance is the woman and who is the …

The what? I said aloud.

So wild, tweeted Minna at the idea of what Silas was on about. She straightened her back; craven eyefuls of her bust; file under Kat's dreamlife.

I said, The facilities sure are on a wonked angle, don't you think?

We don't use *that* bathroom, said Silas.

I told you to use the one in the master bedroom, said Cedric.

I didn't hear you say that.

As I was saying, said Silas to Minna, the man game is a competition to see who leads.

Cedric was reading a magazine that featured teenage girls from the city dressed as ranch hands. He didn't so much gaze or study the magazine as adjudicate. When something about a scenario displeased him he thrashed to the next page.

You want to force your opponent to do your move.

So the points are a distinction, not the purpose, of the game? I asked.

What?

I mean in contrast to ..., I said, and muttered the rest: In contrast to modern dance.

'The fuck? said Cedric, flapping the glossy pages of the magazine together in irritated disinterest. Modern fucking ...? What? Who *are* you, Kat, who?

I'm here, I said.

Whose house is this? asked Minna.

It's mine, said Ken.

Why is it decorated like—old people style?

My granddad got pneumonia in the hospital after a bypass, and a couple years later my grandma died of cirrhosis. They left me the house. I kept the place because I always liked it here.

Who keeps it so clean? I asked.

Silas tossed his head this way and that, said: Mothers, sisters, girlfriends.

Ken said: We don't drink either, so.

Cedric said to me: I drink. I drink constantly. Name a combination I drink it. Powerjuice with vodka. Vodka with rum. Rum with champagne. Champagne with grapefruits.

So who lives here? said Minna, ignoring him. Just you, Ken?

I also live here till I get my life together, said Silas.

Ken picked his nose in front of everybody as he read the liner notes on the back of a twelve-inch record cover. The title was: I *Heart* Airplane Noise.

Are we listening to airplane noise right now? I asked.

I bought it at the flea market.

Cedric said: What you are looking at, guests, is two poor folks. These boys are netting single-digit incomes. Silas is hoping to parlay the man game into a lucrative endorsement contract with a major carbonated energy juice brand.

That's right, said Silas, presumably in-joking. First I have to invent Powerjuice, he said, and after that become its spokesperson.

Spokes*man*, Silas. You *can* call yourself a spokesman. No one's going to think you're sexist for calling yourself a man.

Silas didn't answer.

Until he can stuff his mattress with filthy lucre, Cedric added, he sleeps in Ken's room. Ken, I should add for purposes of clarification, sleeps in the master bedroom.

The man game?

It's called that.

I'm sorry, baby, Cedric said to me not Minna, no women allowed.

Gazing away away, away from it all, I noticed handprints on the ceiling.

Of the two, Silas, the taller bigger hairier one, seemed denser on first impression. Ken, though smarter, was more insane. They treated each other like brothers, ones who trusted each other, whose rivalry was based on an unbreakable bond.

//

You can't fool a brother. Brothers can't be lied to. You can't hide from the facts a life, eh. You can't hide from your family, *Sammy.* No matter how far across the country you go, even to the farthest reaches a humanity, living among the lowest most base filth a humankind, he said.

Dunbar sat crossed at the knee, smoking, and without so much as a pause to take a breath (so it always seemed to Sammy), he began to describe in arduous detail a stalwart father and an aged, ailing mother. Millicent Erwagen, born 1816, a healthy child in her youth until her own father died of a wild rash, then she herself became weak, easily fainted, and indeed the mother Sammy knew growing up was always prostrate and dying, had been now going on thirty years or more. Dunbar rattled off the problems. He never doubted her condition. Never mind the cracking, seeping blisters, he said, the humorous pallor of her dry dusty skin, the dizzy spells, the loneliness, her dying wish, need I remind you, is to set eyes on her baby Sammy one more time before she leaves this earth. Lord, her baby boy who won't get up the pluck to answer pleading telegrams. No reply. What did you do with the letters? And your personal manservant, added Dunbar, is the mailman.

Sammy was swaddled in a Hudson's Bay blanket to keep him warm while he sat in his wheeled chair. His face was all by itself atop the wool cocoon, exactly as the tipplers in New West' had promised. A head without a body. His brother's wife Molly had vanished after their first greeting three hours ago, and there'd been no sign of her since then. Dunbar looked at the bottom of his empty tumbler, rolling one final drop of scotch along the edge, back and forth, until it seemed to vanish. He said: I'm absolutely mortified by your state a affairs. Where's your wife anyhow? What kind a society is this where your wife's not present?

Sammy let him jaw on for a while longer. He knew his brother. What a mouth. There was no regaining these wasted minutes. Playing dead was the best you could hope for. Sammy was in no mood. He didn't tolerate unexpected guests, family least of all.

How dare you conceal all your misfortunes from me?

My wife is on important business, and I have some a my own that needs attending, if you please.

What kind a important business does a wife have? Tending to her cripple, I should think. It's as dark as midnight out there, by god. Brother you don't know this city at night. Everywhere I looked, Chinamen. Hopeless starving Chinee on every corner, with pigtails and yellow eyes and fangs. Like wildcats. Not entirely human. Savage life on your streets. I witnessed it. You don't see the hunger in their eyes, Sammy. Stuck in your chair. It smells of them. This is no place for an unaccompanied lady, and—

When Dunbar paused for a breath, Sammy said: We don't have room for you. You'll have to find somewhere else to stay to-night.

Dunbar relit his cigar. It had the acidic coal-black smell of legendary Ontario tobacco, slave-picked. Father Erwagen sent Dunbar cigars. He sent Sammy telegrams. Dunbar clacked shut the lighter and regarded its silver case. Molly had bought it for Sammy as a first wedding anniversary gift. Engraved on one side was the word *olam* and on the other side *Samuel & Molly*. I had no intention of staying with you, Dunbar said. I made other arrangements a course. In advance. Won't you answer any a my questions?

I sincerely doubt it, brother.

Stubborn as ever. I can't see how this outpost could be sensitive to the needs a your dear young bride, said Dunbar. Ladies need to socialize with other ladies, don't you agree? Her health, I trust that she's doing well in the climate. Although in Spain, their winters still have the cold and damp.

She's not *from* Spain.

Dunbar pretended not to hear, fetched a tidbit on his tongue, dabbed it away on the ashtray, said: You know, after the in*i*tial shock, I'm not saddened to see you. I've always known fate was against you. Didn't I tell you when you were just my little bratty brother that you were destined for punishment?

But *you* were the punishment, Dunbar. That was always going to be my destiny around you.

So long as you cut yourself off from your family you'll continue to be *pun*ished. I know what your situation is, Sammy. I can help turn you around. Take you home, first, and see your ailing Mother, see your *family,* get some rest. Clean you up, let you grow your moustache back. I'm sure the paralyzed part a you is temporary. I'm certain. It hasn't affected your vitals has it? Whatever has you numb—. If we take you to see Dr. Billings you're certain to make a full recovery. The doctors *here* aren't aware a the newest advancements in medicine. You live here in this little hell in your condition with a wife who—, and the Chinaman within *spit*-ting distance, and all these ailments?

I don't understand you. Why won't you at least speak your mind? Don't be a coward. I'm your brother for God's sake. Come to your senses.

If I had anything to say to you I would.

What aboot *ai*ling Mother?

Sammy whisked the issue away silently.

I'm going to tell Father.

It's not your place to interfere, Sammy said.

It is my place, brat, absolutely my place. You're still such a brat, aren't you?

Sammy's face was unmoved.

I'm your brother.

You've tried to be my *father,* said Sammy, but I don't remember you ever tried to be my brother.

Then, as if a rhetorical fog was cleared, the grandfather clock chimed eight—hours had passed and Sammy was still facing down the intrusion of his brother. Not another moment went by before Sammy heard the one-armed drunk outside on the street singing in the woods, probably on his route lighting the lamps. Dunbar's demeanour quickly changed. No longer was he impatient. Now he was ready to go. The bell chiming had the effect of rousing him to his feet, and as quickly to the door. Instead of shaking hands, the brothers merely regarded the other with disgust.

Good night, brother, said Dunbar.

Sammy blinked.

Clough's voice, even through the shut door, was the loudest frog of all the nights' choir, and running behind schedule to light the lamps. He was, among so many other things, never on time. Without another parting word between them, Sammy watched Dunbar turn his houndstooth collar up against his cheek as he stepped quickly down the porch then along the planks to the street and, in a run, disappear. It was dark but the temperature was unexpectedly warm for January. A purple cloud had descended across the city over dinner and, once bundled, started to warmly fog it up. The weather couldn't have been better for the night's man game, thought Sammy with some dismay. He and Toronto waited awhile longer, on the porch, to finish a smoke.

Right to send him from home, said Toronto. He not your brother.

I only wish I'd known that as a boy, said Sammy.

//

Dunbar didn't know where to run. He ran, that's all. A lot of pride, no money, where did that take him on these vile streets in these ruined shoes? He'd have to book himself into some flea-bitten hotel over a saloon and sleep to the sound of billiard balls clacking like skulls. Where was he going? He lost his bearings and was out of his mind with fear even before hearing the gun blast through the trees with a flash that briefly exposed a wide logging path only two yards from his left foot, where he saw an Indian man soar down the incline towards him and around a corner into the trees and the po-lice following in hot pursuit, yelling ahead to Dunbar: Where'd he go, buddy? Where'd he go, eh?

What? What? He went—

They ran into the forest yelling: Halt, it's the po-lice, halt. Halt.

He stood there in rigid worry. He lost track of time. Eventually he heard the police thrashing their way back to the road, gasping for breath. When they reached the edge of the woods, Dunbar saw they had the Indian worse for wear.

Thanks, buddy, said the po-lice and tipped his hat to Dunbar as he and his partner dragged the perp down the road to the city jail. He killed a man, the po-lice said, broad daylight. Poor Siwash, I don't blame him. A cuckold. They held the murderer under the armpits.

A crime a passion, hollered the broken Indian.

The po-lice turned back to Dunbar and said: Say, are you hurt?

I'm new to town. I don't know where to get some rest.

Take this road down three blocks, turn left you'll see a house with this bright red lantern. That's Wood's. Peggy will set you up.

Thank you.

The Indian's head was hanging back; then, after further beatings, it slopped to one side, bleeding, and rolled down towards his chest as the po-lice dragged him along.

Dunbar decided to follow the recommendation, though he knew where it would take him. The po-lice's tone of voice said it all. A cat house. But he *did* need rest, and this Peggy woman might know of a vacant room, if not one to spare herself. He was a married man in a difficult situation with no alternative.

//

It was an eventful night. Besides the po-lice apprehension of the Indian who earlier in the day had put an axe in a Whiteman's shoulder right there in the middle of Hornby Street, there was a man game.

Across the logs from the Hudson's Bay store's construction site, hidden from plain sight, Molly whispered to her men: Don't think a them as people. In the circus, tightrope walkers and acrobats, have you seen them? There is the rope and there is the net. Tonight you have a safety net. The net is there for the acrobats to use, learn with. The people will be your net tonight, and you can use them. Kumtuks? Don't be afraid to take the risks, she said. The people will catch you if you fall. Do you understand? Pisk?

Pisk was exercising his top half, shoulders and arms especially, doing windmills and rolls in repetitions of ten. You bet, he said.

Litz paid attention, sitting on a mouldy log, worrying his ankle in his opposite hand. She was so beautiful. He said: Do you mean I can fall at the crowd?

Pisk laughed at him and scratched his belly, but Molly said: That's what I mean exactly. I mean trust the safety a the crowd. Take risks. Trust the crowd to catch you, yes. They are not an audience, they are a soft fall. You are warriors now. Impress them, scare them.

Wish you could be there to cheer us on, said Litz, remembering Clough's words to him only a few weeks ago as they'd watched her dance the year out.

This isn't rehearsal, she said. I can't be there. There's simply too many men. We have work to do before a lady can be present for the man game. Then she clasped the slabs of their hands in her own, as best she could, to say: We've made something no one has ever seen before. You know why people come to see you play? Because they want to be you, but they can't. No one can. You're the first.

She waved goodbye, and was quickly out of sight. They listened to her footsteps recede and then regained their composure. Part of her mystery was the sad milky features of her face. Each of her eyes was the lens of a microscope searching for the fundamentals, which resided deep within her.

When Litz saw from high up in his hidden vantage point that a huge crowd had formed, what most unnerved him were those associates of Furry & Daggett. There were a lot of them in attendance. They'd chosen this place for good reasons. The Hudson's Bay construction site was a significant piece of neutral, remote, and familiar ground. It had never been logged by either Litz and Pisk or Furry & Daggett. Nevertheless, he espied at least a few of the men from F&D's crew in the crowd tonight, and that was what he reported to Pisk on the ground. He said: What a you want to do?

Pisk thought about the question as Litz slowly climbed down from the heights. Unfortunately, since Molly had left them alone for their final preparations, he couldn't ask her. He attempted to crack his knuckles, and then tried his neck. His shoulders and ribcage wouldn't crack. Nothing cracked until he got to an esoteric divot in his lower back where a miraculously huge pop released countless tensions, beginning in his hips, thighs, the cartilage in his knees, and then hotly ascending into his whole chest, throat, and skulldome.

Litz swung and dropped to the ground, dusted himself as he got up. What a you think we should do?

We do what Molly told us. We use the crowd. We impress them. There's none like us in the motherfucking world.

Litz was motivated by her cursing tongue, shivering in the forest without a stitch on, and about to do a backflip into a crowd of enemies, because he was in love with her.

//

If the po-lice hadn't pre-emptively subdued him senseless, the Indian knew in his heart he'd have the strength to bend wide the bars separating his little jail cell from his neighbour's. He would climb through and strangle to death Miguel Calderón, the Mexican who sold him the whisky that blinded him to the fact that a Whitemans had been raping his wife every morning for six weeks while he lay in his own pee in an alley, scared, humiliated, angry, and most of all, a fool. But he was exhausted, beat up. He could see the Mexican with only one eye, but that was more than enough.

Miguel Calderón put his head in his hands and scratched his hair.

The po-lice came over and stood in front of the cells and squeaked his ear. Look, boys, I don't know. But maybe you *do* know. This is tough shit. We have a way a handling matters such as, you know, murder. He rubbed his moustache, said: Miguel, we try to help make your life easier, let you port the bar around ... but serving drinks to Indians ... the law don't stretch much ... that's more illegal than portability.

I know, I know. Ah, if only—

When a man commits a crime, said the po-lice, he got two choices. He turned his attention to the Indian's cell: When a man commits a *murder,* he already made his choice. His choice is death. Around here, when you commit murder we put you to death by hanging. Do you kumtuks, buddy?

The Indian nodded, said: I—

Okay then, said the po-lice. That matter will be taken care a tomorrow. In the morning you meet the judge and once we get our gallows built, we hang you ... We'll put you to death by hanging. He thumbed his belt. Now, when a man commits a crime ...

Miguel Calderón raised his eyes.

A crime such as selling whisky to a Siwash. Then a man has three choices. He can either serve his sentence in this cell here. Thirty days. Or, he pays the fine.

How much? said Calderón.

Twenty dollars.

Wa, might as well be hundred dollars, ah, if only—sir, the mugger got me today. I no money. The mugger.

He eludes us, buddy. That mugger's a fast one, a real fast snake. I sympathize, I do. In 'at case, you got the third choice. You take him up the plank. And you hang him. Do that and it completes your sentence. Means you get out today and we see you again when the gallows is done. We been so busy with everything we haven't time to ... anyway. The po-lice crossed his arms over his chest. What a you choose, buddy?

If only I know, Miguel Calderón said, holding his face in his hands. If someone tell me ... I never ...

Sir, said the Indian in one last vain attempt to save his life. Whitemans rape my wife, thirty-seven days.

I know, buddy, said the po-lice to the Indian. You said that before. I never doubted you. He gripped the bars of the Indian's cell. But when you killed the bastard in broad daylight with all them peoples staring at you, that is when you made *your* decision. What are we left to do? I sympathize with you. I do. But you wrote this yourself.

NINE

Develop the dragon spirit; establish a dragon culture.
— THE BLACK DRAGON

The Erwagens weren't the only couple in Vancouver society hosting an unwanted guest. The week before Toronto brought Dunbar to town he'd brought the snakehead from San Francisco. His business here was unknown to Toronto, and frankly, he didn't want to know. The snakehead settled quickly into Chinatown and set all its residents' nerves on edge. The hustle of money quickened. The fan tans worked their boys hard on the streets, speeding the lotteries and doubling the sales of opium. The laundries and tofu shops all became engrossed in criminality. The snakehead, jewelled as he was by bullets, weapons, gold teeth, and greasy hair, walked the boardwalks at night with his head held high and his moustache antennae sensing fear wherever he went. The Chinamen were almost all indebted to this man who'd financed their transportation from the backwaters of China to this coast, where they were required to work off their debts at half the wage of a Whiteman. They took the jobs the Whitemen preferred not to, clearing stumps and slash off construction sites and working in perilous stone quarries, in the baddest bowels of the least safe coal mines, and in the Hastings Mill next to the sharpest blades. Clearing land earned them thirty cents to the dollar, hardly enough to live on, to say nothing of what they owed. The po-lice were aware that the San Francisco snakehead was in town, and, intimidated by his many connections to both the underworld and capitalist society, kept away from Chinatown while he visited. He tunnelled through town, searching for debtors who eluded him. His perceived immunity allowed him to act without discretion. He pistolwhipped drunks and addicts and stole their belongings.

RH Alexander was obliged to invite the Chinaman to his house for tea. As manager of the mill, Alexander couldn't resist the financial rewards of a coolie labour force. In hiring coolies, he saw a mutually beneficial plan, even if it sometimes required that he make alliances with gentlemen whose social standing wasn't equal to his own. If a snakehead believed he was a nobleman and saw no difference between his riches and Alexander's, so be it; it was not necessary for Alexander to prove the snakehead wrong. He also wanted to be given a personal tour of the big new construction site his indentured servants had been hired to clear for the big Hudson's Bay department store on the old Granville logging road.

Almost a week went by before the snakehead heard anything from Alexander, and during that whole time the city was in a state of panic, or so it seemed to RH. No one looked him in the eye for six days. The streets, usually busy but not brisk, were in a frenzy of activity. Men screamed and cracked their whips, sending ox carts loaded with goods back and forth down Water Street in the mud. The billiards rooms were empty. The bars were scarcely populated, and those who did drink were of sullen mien, worried gents with the forlorn look of the damned. The Asiatics kept to Chinatown's streets and sprinted from door to door, never stopping to talk to one another save for the occasional cry of strange and speedy polysyllabics. Business at the Calabi & Yau Bakeshoppe ground to a halt: no one wanted to alert the snakehead to the sublimely sweet pastries, fearing that some ill might befall them. No one wanted to draw attention to the sacred oven. For six days Alexander avoided his duty to the snakehead. Then on Saturday his supply of opium ran out. Now he needed to make a call to Chinatown. There was no way around that. He knew it would lead to an encounter with the San Francisco snakehead, so he cleared some time on Sunday and, along with the request for a tin, promised the Chinaman a visit to his very home.

That morning RH awoke and gazed out the bedroom window with fear. It felt as if everything was compressed into this single morning, and that the reflection of the mountains on the inlet told his life story all at once. What a terror to lose sight of alternatives. It was a beautiful morning.

Darling, he said. Over the misty-lipped water of Coal Harbour a single duck flew just above the crests of the shore, rumpling the fog. Across the water, the dark green limbs of the cedars grew as thick as wolf hair up the pack of mountains that blocked the city from Alaska frost and kept their mirrors warm. The greenish-black smog hanging loose from the brick smokestacks at Hastings Mill. The whole scene filled him with dread.

Waiting for the teatime hour to arrive, his wife gathered her energy. The house was prepared for the man's arrival. RH went around and checked that all the rooms were locked save the kitchen, the living room, and the library, in case RH wanted to take the snakehead in for a private viewing of some of his rare antiquities. RH claimed that his pornographic works, imported from Bombay and Constantinople at great cost, dated from the medieval era, although telltale signs on the page suggested they were no more than a hundred years old.

For her part, Mrs. Alexander was concerned with maintaining another sort of filth. Before the tea was made, the silverware was not polished. The carpets were not swept. The curtains were not beaten. The furniture was not oiled and buffed, but left dull and dry. Her single act of rebellion against this intruder was to not dust. The whole week she'd let a fine white layer settle over everything, commanding her servants to leave it all. Even the mirrors were stained with grime, fingerprints, and a ghostly fog. Nothing in her house would shine for the Chinaman.

As a gift, the snakehead brought the lovely tin free of charge, filled with a heavy dollop of legendary mud. The Alexanders thanked him, bowed their heads, begged him to enter their home. They led him into the living room where everything was set out for his arrival. From the tips of his boots to the whiskers atop his lips, the snakehead presented himself behind his guns. He never took them off. In their greetings, RH apologized for the late invitation, claiming work at the mill had required his attention during a mechanical emergency. The snakehead agreed that RH had been very impolite this week and he was glad to see there was still a chance to reconcile their friendship. RH was flustered. He promised he meant to harm. His wife looked on with terror as she watched the snakehead treat RH the way RH treated Mayor McLean, as a nobleman treats a salesman, as definitively as a snake treats an egg.

Tea was served. They drank in silence. Mr. Alexander buttered the scones.

The snakehead watched Mrs. Alexander eat. He impulsively touched a bullet in the chamber, tickling it. To a woman approaching sixty, his lecherous gaze was unwanted and distasteful but also surprising in its effect: she was suddenly conscious of her every motion. RH was keenly aware of the man's strange power over his wife, much the way a hypnotist controls his subject before she knows it and long after she's assumed herself free again. Mrs. Alexander had not been courted more than once until this day—if that was even the word for the squamatic eye that watched her. As his wife shifted her weight from hip to hip, munching toasted crumpet, RH was having great trouble swallowing and kept needing to find excuses to stand.

In all my travelling, said the snakehead, I never taste salmon so delicious as ones spawning Vancouver's waters.

I'm delighted you enjoy it, Mrs. Alexander said with a bow of her head. The Alexanders never served Whitemen salmon, never would dare. For the snakehead they made an exception and ate the blasted fish to spite him.

I love salmon meat cut from living fish, he said. You try it?

Y-yes, she said, a lie out of timid politeness. Her husband shot her a frightening look. She looked at her lap where she discovered her hands made into fists.

At my home I have tank with Pacific salmon for the purpose, said the snakehead. See them swim with my bites in them, yes.

RH sucked bravely on the walrus brush hanging over his upper lip. He was vexed at himself and feared for the safety of his wife. She was brave, too, likely braver than he, but excitable. It was within her character to do something rash. She might leap from her seat and slap the snakehead across the cheek. She might be capable of murder. RH didn't know. He did not know his wife in anything but domestic situations. He did not know her when life might be threatened. He was not so brave as he thought. His wife's neck was flushed to the ears and, if he knew her body, all the way down to the navel. Looking at her, the sight of her fear, terrified him to the core. His heart, weakened by mud, palpitated.

The snakehead accepted a second cup of black tea. The minutes ticked by. He sipped without quite opening his fat lips. When the conversation fell into a morbid silence, the claustrophobia didn't seem to bother him the way it bothered the Alexanders. He put the teacup down with a squeak as porcelain touched porcelain, reached to his side for the shelf of the four-legged chess table, and opened it—the one drawer they forgot to lock. The ebony and ivory players rattled around. He picked through them and produced a deck of cards. He looked the deck over and finally, with a disgraceful show of ardour, sniffed it.

Shall we retire to my library and talk in private for a while? said RH, smiling.

The snakehead ignored him. He took pleasure inquiring about the provenance of her furnishings. When he caressed the leg of her teak tea table, she rubbed a calf against a shin under her unattractive blue dress. She gripped the shiny glans knob of her oak armrest. RH felt an intensely encroaching fear and began to talk aimlessly about the weather in stilted phrases, saying the word *rain* upwards of ten times in as many observations, pretending to enjoy the sight of a slave trader with his wife, hoping not to faint as he watched a Chinaman-servant spread butter on a fresh crumpet.

Polite society be damned. We should be on our way if we're going to make it to the clearing before it's too dark, said RH.

RH was more than relieved to see the snakehead out and to kiss his wife goodbye as he shut the door. They walked to the gate, heard her lock it, which they hardly ever felt the need to do. He knew his wife's habits, and could've guessed what happened next. Her manservants prepared the pipe, cleaned the tar out with a coarse-haired little chimneysweep brush, and practically poured the sweet smoke into her.

Walking through the forest with this madman, this rabid sensualist, RH regretted bitterly the tea. Having such a creature in his home was as wise a move as inviting in a demon, an evil faun of the woods, a trickster spirit such as the Indians spoke of. Once the man was in his house, something of him would stay forever as a sticky, ectoplasmic residue. The wallpaper would bubble up now. Their mirrors would never again return a proper reflection. They would have to burn the chess table. RH shivered involuntarily at the thought.

The two men began the hike through town. They passed tradesmen who whipped pairs of ox from atop full carts being heaved along the road, loaded with shipyard tools and blacksmith junk and barrels of lard and everything else you could think of. The men at the corners eyed them with deep suspicion. Alexander avoided any conspicuous routes. He stayed far from the Calabi & Yau Bakeshoppe, Red & Rosy's General Store, the Oppenheimer factory, George Black's butcher shop, and most certainly City Hall. The last thing he wanted was for the mayor to see them. Alexander would show his guest the construction site of the Hudson's Bay six-storey department store and be done with it. He'd employed many Chinese to clear the land for excavation, and his responsibilities ended there. He might even give up hiring Chinamen altogether after today. He'd already lost the mayoral election to his decision; he wasn't about to lose his wife. Sammy Erwagen was a good enough accountant. Together they'd find a method to make back the money from employing more Whitemen as workers. This was where the snakehead wanted to be taken. As they trekked down Hastings at dusk and then to the edge of town and up the stiffening incline into the awful dark wilderness, neither businessman enjoyed the company of the other.

Ah, said the snakehead, what beautiful mushrooms.

A pace or two in front of the snakehead, RH saw a patch of muscimolic mushrooms. Their bright red caps were flecked with white and ranged in shape from flat as a table to conelike rockets. RH didn't see the need to waste any more time on the matter. The snakehead looked at the mushroom patch without so much as lowering his head. He smiled but it didn't appear to be from joy.

Ah, the fine shaft on that one. Or there, that pie …

Fly Agaric, I believe they're called, said RH.

Indeed, said the snakehead.

RH turned to walk again, but the snakehead remained still. RH sighed and shifted his weight, combed his fingers through his beard, and waited.

When I see rare mushroom, said the snakehead in that cruel accent, part Oxford, part Shanghai slum, I never know if I want to eat them or kick them to pieces.

At least, thought RH as he crouched behind two rotting logs in the pitch black, he wasn't still at tea. Except that he'd inadvertently trekked the snakehead all the way to Georgia Street, just outside the light of the four torches wherein Litz was after his third point against Pisk.

I say, I say—, said RH, and in great haste broke certain codes of conduct and tugged the snakehead's coatsleeve, ignoring speculation about leprous pathogens, hoping to get him to turn back from the spectacle before he saw too much. Too late. The snakehead raised his arm away, saying:

Move move, and stepped onto the log for a better view. His cufflinks—silhouettes of concubines in their lustre—flashed back moonlight in RH's eyes.

I'm afraid we shouldn't have made the trek …

On contrary, said the snakehead, peeking between the logs, I did not realize so much to see at construction site. No, I'm very interested to see what Whiteman does when you not looking.

I think we should leave, for our own safety.

If I was afraid for safety right now, said the snakehead, you would be dead.

I hardly think—

The inky evening combined with the flickering torches made the crowd seem to RH and his guest one black seething mass. The snakehead shuddered from neck to tailbone. Through the red cedars that concealed them, RH and the snakehead saw only a few slavering faces lit from the torchlight. Smouldering orange faces. They saw raucous gap-toothed mouths opening to shout and scream and make maniacal sounds as caves will make in a terrible wind, surrounded by moss that was their beards, skulls as thick as stone. Neither man assumed the crowd was made of anything other than Whitemen. It didn't occur to them that Chinamen were present as well. If they saw any Asiatics in the throng, their minds denied what their eyes took in. Racial commingling at an event like this, and of all the places, did not seem feasible. RH saw two men, two exiles, Litz and Pisk, wrestling like rabid incarnations of the figures from Greek pottery. He was thoroughly disgusted. When pirated-wood shipments from the CPR-owned land had stopped coming in he'd assumed Litz and Pisk had left town and contented himself with the fact; didn't give the boys another thought. Instead they'd been playing this game right under his nose the whole time.

I abhor this kind a behaviour, said RH, dusting himself clean of specks of the man game that had drifted through the night air to land on his shoulders.

If you permit elements like this to continue, said the snakehead, if you permit deviance. If it continue unabated, sir, Whiteman will turn on you sooner or later.

I think my Whitemen will turn out to be *your* problem before they turn on me.

This is your opinion?

Yes, that I foresee, said RH. Great ambition resides in the Anglo-Saxon spirit.

There was a troubling pause. In the snakehead's opiated stupor each of RH's words lay on his head like cold coins, drop-drop-drop, and it took a lot of thought to tot it up. He fitted his palms together at his chest, covering his pistols in a gesture like jaws shutting. He said slowly and gently: Don't misunderstand me, sir. Kumtuks. I protect my investments.

When RH made no reply, the snakehead continued: I trust you know how important it is for our mutual investments to be protected? It is only way to do business. Your Whitemen, they are not my concerns. They are not my investments. I retract my advice on matter your Whitemen with great apology, sir. I do not mean to look like it is *I* who undermine your authority.

Realizing his error, RH leaned ever so slightly forward in nausea. Yes, he said.

//

The fists popped at him one by one. He ducked the left and swooped to avoid the right. He wasn't losing much ground when Litz circled in boxer stance and popped a fist at him. Litz wasn't giving it his all. The fists popped at easily dodged intervals. One came high, he zigged left. One came low, he narrowly zagged right. Left popped then the right. They scuttled in harmony through the cold mud. Pisk was relaxed. He was in control. He was all dodge. Tried to block one but his balance made it impossible now that he was steadily backing up. Had to kind of bounce like a fish to avoid a slow gut punch. Litz skipped to the left and cornered Pisk in his own strange gliding momentum and in order to miss the punch he had to contort in the opposite direction, again with a fish's determination. What was Litz up to? For a guy who wasn't as smart as him, Litz had a swift mind for strategy. What never failed to deke out Pisk was Litz's ability to whip a new move before Pisk even recognized that he was playing along. Litz got points off Pisk's own damned obliviousness. It was happening again—but how? He thought he was bobbing and weaving, zigging and zagging, ducking and jiving. He thought he was saving energy for a big comeback. Tie it up three-three. Whatever it was Pisk thought it was, it wasn't. Somehow the tides had turned on him. Pisk was used to winning. He was used to winning against Litz, and now he had no choice but to give away points. How was it possible that the only player he'd ever played, the one man who constituted the entirety of his opposition and whose moves and actions he knew as well as his own impulses, had somehow suddenly one-upped him? Litz was suddenly the better player. Pisk was, to be honest, furious. He was furious with himself. The moment finally came when he heard everyone snapping their fingers to the rhythm of Litz's fists popping and his own dance-like ducking. Those fingers were goddamn snapping. It was another point. Three-two for Litz. As the crowd cheered him, Litz bounced on the weightless power of his newfound glory *{see fig. 9.1}*.

FIGURE 9.1
Beat the Fish

Calabi's commentary: When the great coho spawn every autumn finds you kicking at the fish beneath your feet, concentrate on your movements and repeat them in your next game.

Concentrate, Pisk said to himself. Look at each one a the men in the face. Every man. Look at him. He is your opponent. Fear not the opponent. Destroy him. See every man for who he is and destroy what makes him real. Who am I? I am Pisk, the greatest athlete the world has ever known. I swing the moon on the end a my rope. I am not going to sit here forever in the mud. Look at every man. Stare at his eyes. The dancing Chinamen. The woodsmen twirling their hats in the air, the old faces, familiar voices. There was Bud Hoss and Calabi with the books keeping track of bets. Bud Hoss beamed at Pisk with a son's admiration. Get up, get up, Hoss seemed to say with his expression. Calabi was unmoved. His focus was the chickamin in his hands, conscious of potential pickpockets. There were so many men. Loudmouthed Moe Dee, and that ol' so-and-so Terry Berry talking and talking with his bud Vicars; the cowboy RD Pitt with his arms crossed looking unimpressed. He heard Pitt say in his weak Alberta accent: Where's the fucking whisky seller Miguel Calderón? He's supposed to be here with his Bar Rústico, no?—all these *Chinamen* here, *damn,* it spooks me out—I need a fucking drink. Standing next to the cowboy was the dipso Clough, all laughs, slapping his knee: A man should always bring something in case a emergency, eh. Clough showed the cowboy a bottle full of liquid clearer than the very firmament that exposed the spilling stars. He passed Pitt the bottle. He took a swig and reeling, almost falling over, hooted with a squeaky voice: Oh, that's fucking good hooch. And between RD Pitt and a twenty-foot-tall stack of wet two-by-fours stood three of the bohunks who worked for Furry & Daggett. The tall one with the monobrow, Boyd. At his side, Pisk saw that little seal pup Campbell, as usual. That boy never missed a single game. But it was unusual to see his woodsmen colleagues here. Smith with the balding scalp. Meier, the giant one. Were the others here too? Were Furry and Daggett in attendance then?

As he studied the crowd, Pisk remained seated in the cold black mud. All the attention was on Litz who was flapping his arms to get everyone more and more riled. The rabble of the canneries, the shipmates, the loggers, they were here too. Pisk spotted Joe Fortes with the little Snauq boy Jack Khatsahlahno sitting on his shoulders. These people weren't so special. Pisk knew because he was one himself.

He smeared his icy feet with mud and leaves to insulate them then scraped off his crusted soles. He rubbed the heels dry. He loved the soles of his feet. You couldn't get a nail through those calluses. But his feet were so cold that when he tried to make a fist of the toes he couldn't do it. He blamed his feet for why he was losing. Far too early in the game to have lost sensation in his toes. He dusted off, clutched his nuts, scratched his beard, caught his wind.

I got a score to settle with you, he called out to Litz.

Wa, cried the coolies in the crowd, whipping their pigtails in every direction. The bohunks who rooted for Pisk made some dog noise when they saw their man spit to emphasize he was open for business.

Yeah, said Litz, you got a score to settle? So that mean you going to make my last point easy or what? You been beating me for too long, buddy. It's time to move over. Or are you still going to be a real fucking pain in the ass?

I'm going to kick *your* ass straight to Ontario, and put your face on the next train to meet up with it two weeks later.

That right?

There's still a lot more man left in Pisk before this day's over.

Really, said Litz, where'd Pisk go then? I heard he's pretty tough.

Ha ha ha, said the mob. Wa, wa, wa.

Even your ma's going to be jealous a the whipping I'm aboot to give you.

Swells of boo wove through the crowd. It was undeniable. Litz did not have the same body as other lumberjacks. Speculations ran the spectrum, but one thing was for sure: Litz was the specimen of a peak athletic regimen, every muscle at its most versatile.

His game is strong tonight, said Hoss.

Looks to me like odds is riding on those *mus*cles, said Moe Dee.

Litz is swift.

Pisk is a fucking pillar a marble. You can't break that man. Woo-ee, I do love me a man game. Moe Dee took a moment to unpucker the dome of his bowler hat, study the interior; then, fixing the hat again on his skull, he said: If I was Pisk, I think what I'd do is grab Litz by the hair on his head, pull him down, knee him in the face. Then when he's dazed, spin him around and pull a dance on him.

Litz has muscles, he's stretchy, he's loose and limber, but he'll bruise up fast.

A loud voice cut through: You're shit, the *both* a you.

And then another: I'm going to tear you a new—.

A third: You guys're nothing but liars, cheats, and fire-starters.

Litz, recognizing all three voices, withdrew his arrogance and dropped his shoulders, said: Aw, shit.

Three voices. Count four men. Furry & Daggett's toughest, swaggering into view in their plaid lumberjack coats and greasy moustaches. They stepped out from the crowd and into the circle with Litz and Pisk, crossed their arms. Within spitting distance. Campbell—all these months the peaceful spy—stood the closest, too short for comfort. The second man was a blushing behemoth, Smith. His hair was as transparent as celery strands. Beside him, the monobrow named Boyd. Where was Meier? Ah, Litz saw him finally, bringing up the rear, towering over them like an obelisk, wobbling with a bottle in his fist and a wet-lipped drunk on. His watery eyes caught the flickering torchlight. The entire crowd fell silent.

What a you bohunks want? asked Pisk, standing upright

and brushing the muck and dead leaves off his body. His arms were as massive as coho, covered in scrapes, open bleeding cuts, old white scars, and finished off with two sets of massively swollen fingers throbbing as if each digit carried its own heart pumping in tandem.

Interrupt a man game, said Pisk, you might get your throat slit. Lot a chickamin on the line tonight.

Why I oughtta …, said Boyd.

Easy easy, said Campbell, holding back his friend. He pointed to Pisk, said: We're here to challenge you.

Challenge us, ha ha? In what?

In this, in *this,* you fucking poltroon. In the man game. What I been watching you do for the last fucking months.

Pisk scrunched his features, clawed at his beard, and thought carefully about the guys in front of him. Since when d'you all know how to play? This isn't something you make up as you go. Maybe you think what we're doing is nothing but a waltz with a clap in the face, but it's not.

You going to take the challenge or what? said Campbell. Let's play. Let's do it. You know me, Pisk. I'm going to kick your fucking teeth out.

Said Pisk: I thought you wanted to play the man game.

Said Campbell: That's right. We're going to show *all* these folks how to really play.

How to *really* play? What the fuck do you know aboot how to really play?

We learned. It's easy.

Since when's it easy? said Pisk.

Since we came along, said Campbell.

Who the fuck coaches you?

Should ask you the same fucking thing, said Campbell.

Okay then fine, fuck, said Pisk, taking a step back. We're waiting. We're all waiting. Strip. Let's go. Let's get this over with. Strip.

Campbell turned to his crew with a cocked eyebrow. The other three shifted and touched their necks and sleeves noncommittally.

What are you waiting for? It's fucking cold out, said Pisk, dancing in place, hugging himself to reiterate, a steamcloud with every breath. You're wasting time. Hurry the fuck up.

Campbell swallowed, said: All right, yeesh, we're getting undressed, already. Come on, boys. We're used to it now, remember?

At Campbell's lead, throwing away his monkeyjacket, skinning off his bowtie and collar, and unbuttoning his longsleeve undershirt, the other three men, if a touch reluctantly, also started to peel off layers of wool sweaters, shirts, hats and suspenders, mildewed undershirts; off with the pants, wads of socks in bootheads. Standing in a naked row with their white knees pinched together, they were enduring it no better than well-trained altar boys, and Pisk was going to fuck them all.

I'm going to come at you and just keep coming and coming, said Pisk. Don't think I take pity on a novice.

Tomorrow? said Campbell. You're going to be picking teeth out a your morning poo.

With one pant leg on and one off, Meier hopped around drunkenly trying to get his stovepipe free of a bony heel.

Yeah, yeah, just hurry up. What we're going to do, said Pisk, is you each get one shot. One-point games. Whoever wins gets to play another round. Whoever loses, they're out. I don't want to waste time with you. This is our game. You're interrupting a real match. Until I see some proof you know what you're doing, there's no point giving you time. Agreed?

Campbell switched to mouth-breathing, said: Uhh …, and looking around, waited for some kind of message he expected to find in the crowd, Pisk couldn't tell from whom exactly but he had a pretty good idea. F&D.

Can't make your own decisions, little man? said Pisk.

Fuck you. Yeah, yeah, agreed, fuck, okay, what?

The way you guys look, said Pisk, pacing in a small circle, rubbing his palms together then scratching his beard, I think this'll take me and Litz aboot ten minutes. You motherfuckers interrupted a *man* game. Calabi? said Pisk, looking for the baker.

Yes, said Calabi with a nod, I'm ready.

Hoss, too, signalled that he was prepared to take new bets. What aboot the game you and Litz were playing?

Pisk waved a hand as if to slap the subject out of the air around him. It's over. An interruption ends a game. Whoever has the most points wins. Smooth as a mink. It's Litz.

Who's your first? said Litz. Me, I'm the first. Pisk plays second.

I am, said Campbell.

Fine. Everyone here going to bet on Litz? Cause otherwise your blankets aren't going home with you. And I promise if we see any funny business, Pisk said, pointing his finger at each and every man in the crew, everybody here today is going to rip you apart. Am I right?

Campbell agreed to the terms.

Wa, cried the audience.

The Chinamen lined up in front of Calabi and the Whitemen in front of Hoss and the betting began again in earnest. As the money followed its paths of hope, Pisk stood by, disgruntled on the whole, though he did enjoy seeing Campbell's legs tremble. Pisk was not trembling even though he couldn't even feel his feet, his persistent bad circulation. No matter; his legs were as steady as cedars. He watched Litz put his hand out to greet his first new competitor.

I don't care if Litz wins this game because he will. I want a chance. I want the next guy.

Suits me, said Litz, and turned back to Campbell. Klahowya, he said and held out his hand.

Klahowya. Litz noted that Campbell's hand was cold as an iron hammer, while his own was still raging hot and slippery from the last game.

The woodsmen in the crowd boot-hooked up the trees for bird views, sat two or three per branch up the pillars of two-thousand-year-old cypresses, firs, cedars—in all directions Pisk saw the forest was covered in lumberjacks. Behind them, blinking in the dark: Salish Indians, uncertain if they should enter the inner circle.

A man's hat fell from a high branch, spinning and flipping before swooping down into Pisk's hands. He read the ink on the inside of the rim: Terry Berry.

The instant the game started Litz's eyes shrank out anything that didn't pertain to Campbell. If the ground was uneven, he registered unbudging sticks and natural lumps with a blind man's memory. He noticed Campbell's sweaty wet sideburns and how his shallow breathing was restricted to his upper chest and neck, saw Campbell's uncertainty over the uneven terrain and the firelight shadows flickering in and out of sequence. But what spooked Campbell most of all was the disapproving snarl of the men in the audience who'd come here of their own volition in order to hate and despise the players they bet on. For Campbell, as Litz saw, this was the hardest relationship to comprehend. Whoever coached them, if anyone did, hadn't trained them for this moment. Campbell shrank even as he came towards him, like a wool sweater drying out.

Do it, Campbell, said a bleak voice of encouragement from the branches above their heads.

Let's see some fight.

Yeah, Campbell. Do so*m*ething.

A drop of water fell from a needle on high and landed on Litz's shoulder.

Hear the people? said Litz. Isn't that nice. Don't give up, little Campbell, said Litz in a swooning feminine sing-song, don't be afraid, little mink Campbell. In his own voice: It won't take long, just close your eyes.

That what you said when you burned down—

Litz grabbed for Campbell's legs, then somehow had him in a headlock. When Campbell fought back he increased the pressure. Campbell found an ear and tried to tear it off Litz, who promptly kneed him in the face and chose to liberate him with a burning red neck-wringer. Campbell gasped, *whuorked,* rubbed his eyes, and walked it off for a couple steps hunkered over studying his nose for blood, which there was, then abruptly felt Litz shove him from behind, whiplashing him to the ground. Through teary eyes what he descried from his place face-down in dirt was the finish to Litz's forward somersault, which had been vaulted off his own fucking back and landed perfectly, impressing the woodsmen to no end *{see fig. 9.2}.*

Litz saw a window of opportunity in a flinch of time when he was out of Campbell's peripheral, and in that rush of adrenalin he nearly snatched his point. He intended to sneak up behind Campbell and pirouette him through a move that finished with a spine-ruining pile-driver. But just at that instant Campbell's head slumped back. The knuckles of his limp hand touched his forehead. Campbell said: Oh, mah lord, as he promptly fainted. Litz found himself in the unexpected

FIGURE 9.2
Gone Fishin

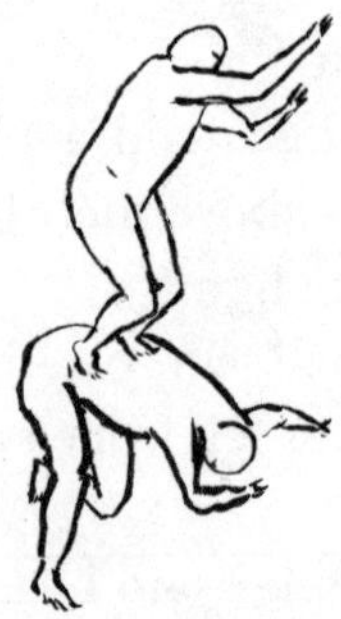

Calabi's commentary: Your opponent's face should be as firmly planted in the earth as you are free a any gravitational impediments; airborne versatility will surely impress the court a public opinion.

position of having caught Campbell in his arms *{see fig. 9.3}*.

Why thank you, declared Campbell, I didn't know you're such a gentleman.

Litz dropped him. The audience blew their tops off.

Rising from his faked woozy spell, Campbell saluted everyone with the pleasure of a true trickster princess. It was no move. Good for a laugh, but anyone could pretend to faint. Not a point. Campbell thought he'd whipped a new move on him, which was not the case.

Get, said Litz.

What the fuck, said Campbell. We're tied. One-one.

You don't get a full game. You heard Pisk. One-point games. You interrupted a game. If you don't get a point, you go back into the crowd, eh.

That was a point.

Boo, said most of the audience. Nah, you didn't.

Yes I did. With the Faint.

The Faint. You and your names, said Litz. Doesn't mean it's a move just because you did it.

That was Campbell's point, claimed a minority of the crowd. Campbell got you with the Faint.

Guys, said Litz, not so much pleading as shaking them

FIGURE 9.3
The Campbell, aka the Faint

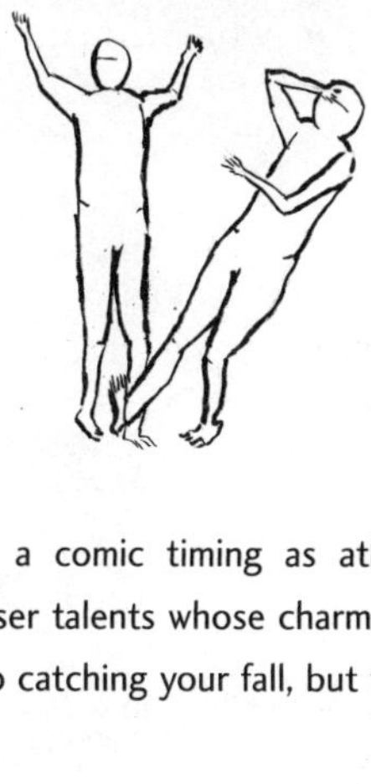

Calabi's commentary: As much a matter a comic timing as athleticism or strategems, the Faint is popular among lesser talents whose charms lie in their persona. Few opponents will be tricked into catching your fall, but the laughter a the crowds can be its own reward.

down. That's not a fucking point. That's too easy. If you're expecting to come in here and win games with minky little points like that, no. No, that's not how we play. Look, I did a thing over his fucking back. We all agree, no point. This thing he did, it's not a point any more than that, less even.

Campbell said: I pl*an*ned that move.

Don't matter. Not a move. You could never trick no one to catch you again. It's just a thing you did. And you shouldn't a gloated aboot it. You already *lost*.

I'll do that move again, Campbell said. Fuck, I'll show you it's not so easy. Campbell shook his head and walked back into the crowd to collect his clothes. That was my fucking point, he bellowed from behind friends.

Litz saw his opportunity and couldn't resist: he chucked the dumb kid through a fast Medical Breakthrough that included an elbow three times in the face, worsening the shape of Campbell's bloody nose and losing him the game *{see fig. 9.4}*.

You aren't ready, said Litz to his fallen competitor.

Moving on, said Pisk, pointing to Boyd.

Boyd's arms instinctively flexed a wrestler's pose, his palms up, amounting to the confused gesture of a praying delinquent. He brandished his arms expecting Pisk to cringe. This was not a beast, it was a child. Pisk half expected him to flee the scene. It all depended on what Boyd did next. Pisk waited to see what the ignorant kid thought wise and then

---

FIGURE 9.4
The Medical Breakthrough, early sketch

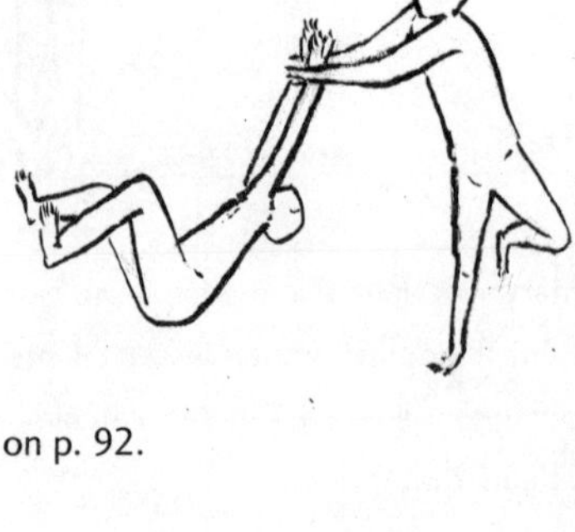

See Calabi's commentary on p. 92.

he'd take him to school. Every hair on his body was ready to strike from any angle.

Boyd leaped forward. Pisk limbered. He saw Boyd falter midway between steps one and two and decide to throw a punch instead of whatever plan A had been. Off balance, unprepared, and slow, Boyd's arm swung past Pisk's face. He'd lost count of how many times he'd practised the move he did next.

Take a punch and turn it into ballroom dancing, that was Molly's original idea. She made them do it at least five times a day. Thursdays it was the only thing they practised. Not that they complained. It was the basics of the man game. Plus she loved to watch them do it, now that they were both talented dancers. Helped to have a good teacher. Either of them could warp a speedy knuckle sandwich into a delicate Irish lilt. Ha ha ha, I'm surprised it's so easy, she said. I thought you'd hit each other in the face more, but no. Even Pisk's most brutal punch looked like the opening to a Parisienne tango. In hindsight, Pisk's fancy pattern of footwork had been modified to accommodate his partner's stumbling. And seeing Pisk transform his own uppercut into a majestic triple twirl was something she wanted to show more and more people.

Not tonight though. What Pisk gave them was the original promenade from in front of the Sunnyside Hotel. He took Boyd through a basic waltz then tossed him at the audience.

As Pisk threw Boyd free and watched him skid to a crumpled finale, the men in the front rows who jumped to dodge his body stepped on him. They went spastic with cheer, and when Boyd scrambled free of so many steel-toed boots he was berated by a circle of his buddies.

Pisk felt this great relief, a comeuppance of historical proportions.

That's the exact same damn move, Joe Fortes cried out. I saw it myself.

He pointed his finger at everyone in the audience,

screamed at the top of lungs: We call that the Pisk *{see fig. 9.5}*.

The Pisk, cried all. Wa, cried all.

Pisk and his partner met again for a warrior's handshake, full of winning's strength. They looked into each other's animal eyes in almost hysterical excitement. This is really happening, Pisk said, as if to say, There's no turning back.

Litz shook his partner's hand with fingers like icicles, turned to the three contenders and pointed to the pale, nearly albino behemoth. Smith, Litz said. You going to meet me? I'm looking forward to this.

Smith lumbered into the space created by the light of the torches and the shape of the audience. He and Litz were the lone figures of attention, two naked spectres in orange, and Litz, half the weight of Smith, had hardly a sense of where this was going. If Campbell's loss in any way affected Smith's mood, there was no way to tell, for his face was thick and his eyes were small and his hair was white as frost, not to mention he was a mouth-breather.

They met at the centre of the ring and shook hands.

Fuck it, said Litz under his breath and ran at the cretin full speed.

As expected, Smith didn't move an inch as he ran at him. Litz's taking the offensive was the sort of tactic he guessed Smith understood, and sure enough Smith stood his ground, calling the bluff. Molly's voice in his head: It is a bluff. He reminded himself to watch for the arms. He was within five running steps of Smith when he saw the big man's little eyes widen. Four steps and his arms started to brace up. Three steps and Smith's knees bent as he put his weight on his left leg—the last thing Litz needed to see if he was going to try the move. Meant that Litz would

FIGURE 9.5

The Pisk, alternative sketch, the moment before the thrown punch is transformed into a ballroom move

rotate left. Two steps remained.

The last step was more of a spiking jump towards an ever more unprepared Smith. When he landed, his grip on Smith's squishy massive shoulders was unfamiliar, un-Pisk. Litz's weight was forcing Smith back. He was almost vertical himself, and if everything went well that would bring them to equilibrium. With his hands on Smith's shoulders and his toes scraping thirteen feet into the air, he did the first rotation, moving his hands from shoulder to shoulder, facing the opposite direction with his legs still vertical, and prepared for the next rotation while Smith was at a loss to fight back. Litz completed a three-sixty in a handstand on his shoulders. They were face to awed face the whole way. Smith was so hypnotized he didn't feel his knees giving out. Litz remained in a perfect handstand as he fell to the ground.

Ohh, said many men just when Smith landed flat on his back. Men found it incredible to witness because Litz was still in the handstand. Honestly, he could have held the handstand long after he'd flattened Smith. One of the talents the man game allowed Litz to exploit was his indestructible sense of balance. As Smith fell back Litz began curling down from the handstand, aiming his left knee into Smith's neck.

Whiyaugh, said Smith's mouth being forced open *{see fig. 9.6}*.

FIGURE 9.6
Sausage Links

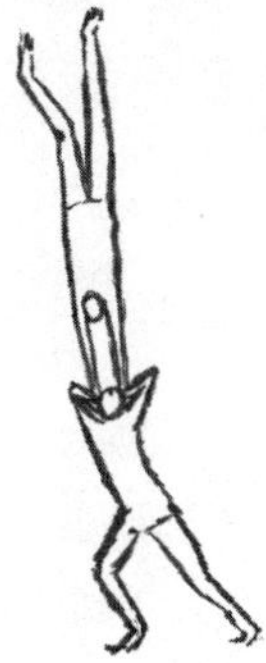

Calabi's commentary: Molly once told Litz to strangle Pisk upside-down. This move requires the strangler to maintain his balance while the victim must complete an entire tai chi routine. In the event that both players complete the part in the Sausage Links, no points are awarded.

That's *p*oint, said Litz to the fat, dumb dude on his back, and kicked a clod of dirt in his face. Litz walked away and asked the audience: Who got d*u*sted, eh?

Wa.

We're way ahead a schedule, Litz said.

But I don't want no break, said Pisk. Now Meier, come here you little prick-eater. I got something special I want to try. Better be ready. You're number three, Meier, and we haven't seen nothing.

I'm ready, said Meier. I'm so fucking ready. I'm ready I'm ready.

Ready for this? Pisk swung a testing left. Meier dodged it with ease. Hoisted a fist to the right. Meier ducked it. Popped another. Meier had to narrowly jive around it in order to keep his balance. Shit, said Meier. One more, said Pisk aloud, and almost punched him in the gut—*hoip*—if Meier hadn't bent over on one foot just in time, though altogether too late *{see fig. 9.7}*.

Hear that? Pisk asked his opponent. It was the sound of fingers snapping and one fak you. He punched Meier in the gut as hard as he could, doubled him over the fist itself, felled him to the side like only a logger knows how. He let Meier puke his eyes out like a stuck pig while he trotted around the crowd saluting folk. It wasn't all rehearsed theatrics. Some of it was improvised. Some of it was real. Meier's broken ribs were real.

FIGURE 9.7
The Litz, side angle view, winning punch

See Calabi's commentary on p. 145.

You see that? said a spectator.

I saw it. He did some fine work on him.

Yep.

Yep. How aboot that? Three punches earlier just like you heard me suggest.

I like the fact Litz did a Pisk and Pisk did a Litz.

That's true.

An ol' timer hollered: It's the Litz. It's the Litz. His voice had the sound of bad plumbing. He was waving his arms to gather attention to his plea. His body a flea-bitten edifice, a bony shambles with a memory like a hollow tree, amen. It's the Litz, Pisk did the Litz.

The Litz, cried all the woodsmen as they clapped their hands and spun their hats above their heads, hooting, hollering, kykying and chucking each other. The cliques of coolies giggled among themselves, discussed the play in their own language with frantic, joyous gestures.

Wa, cried the lurking Indians, not to be mistaken for nesting herons, unable to conceal their rejoicing.

Call it the Litz then, said Pisk. He nodded his approval and saluted.

Litz brushed his shoulders off and he and Pisk bowed a little to the sustained applause. With that in mind he walked handsomely over to Pisk where they had a laugh and clapped chests and patted each other on the back. But when Litz touched Pisk and almost stuck to his frost, he knew something was wrong.

What's wrong, man? You're ice.

Could be I just need a cup a tea.

Get us a cup a tea, said Litz to a circle of men sharing a pipe of Campbell River weed. One of them tipped his hat and split, went off to find some Lipton's.

I'm freezing, said Pisk.

Can you feel your toes?

Wasn't sure I still got them, he said, when from the corner of his eye he saw a familiar beard. Don't look now, he said to Litz, but Furry and Daggett are behind you.

Litz swung his head around and Pisk rolled his eyes: Jesus Christ, man. I just told you not to look.

You fuck with our men, stated Daggett from the other end of the field. You fuck with me, he clarified.

He was naked. So was Furry. They stood stock-still on the pitch with plumes of steam rising from their nostrils. They were as filthy and pale-skinned as two tusks pulled from the mouth of a giant mastodon. In the flamelight Daggett's eyes were corn-yellow. His partner Furry kept his chin up, pointed his thick, mossy beard at his opponents. Each man seemed to carry an extra fist hanging off an extra arm hanging down from a gnarly forest of oily pubes.

It's time for me and Furry to take you down. Pisk, you hoodlum, you common criminal, come here and take me on. Argh, I'll tear you apart like a dead timber. Daggett beat his hairful chest and strangled the sky between his clenched hands. Let's play your fucking man game, he said.

Furry stood behind and to his side, arms crossed, and said nothing. Definitely he was the more dangerous of the two.

What a they want? Pisk said.

They want to play the man game.

Now?

I think so.

What are you talking aboot over there, screamed Daggett. I just challenged you goddammit.

I heard you, said Litz.

Well let's fucking—

Shut the fuck up, Daggett.

What the fuck—

I said shut the fuck up. We heard you. Hold your horses, eh?

Hey, asshole, I don't think—

We just finished buggering *four* a your mink pals, Litz reminded him, so you can wait your motherfucking *turn*.

I don't care who the fuck, fuck I'm going to—

Will somebody shut him the fuck up for once? asked Litz.

Okay, said Daggett. What?

Litz said: We got to take care a something before we do any man game with you guys. Pisk here's been out in the cold like *this* for a long time, longer than any a you ever been. He's freezing. We sent for tea, all right, and once he's had some a that we'll see. In the meantime—, (already the Chinamen looked antsy to place bets)—In the meantime, Litz said louder, we need some blankets over here right now.

Whatever, how the fuck—, said Daggett.

Feeling in his hot-faced drunkenness to be an instrumental player in the survival of the man game, Clough staggered forward to learn more about Pisk's condition. Now what in the fuck's going on here, eh? There's folks with plenty a pay on these games. Don't tell me you all are cowarding out on us.

Shut your gob, Clough, said Litz. We don't need your opinions. Leave us be.

Why, if you let me know the situation, I can pass around the information to the crowds is all.

Leave us. Can't you see he's blue as ice?

Shit-bird. Only trying to help, said Clough, backing away, muttering and pulling at the linty emptiness of his evaginated pants pockets. I got an interest in this same as you.

He walked back to Furry and Daggett's crew and quietly conversated with the men in a private circle. Campbell didn't even want to listen to Clough talk. He indulged in his dejection, leaning against a plank wall that snaked around the construction site, smoked his cigarette and spat, didn't even care if some of it stayed in his beard. He looked between the slats of the wall where a big pit was to become the basement for the Hudson's Bay. It was a moist cube-shape three storeys deep into wet grey earth, held from collapse by a tight apron of wood scaffolding. A puddle on the ruddy floor of the pit wasn't reflecting anything.

Ma. Ma. I might been more a this. I miss you, Ma. I might be more, Ma. Ma, if you let me. If Ma let me, said Pisk through bluing lips.

What?

Here, drink this, said the baker Calabi, coming to their side with a cork thermos, handing Litz a tinful of tea, who took it and rested the warm liquid against Pisk's mouth and drained it down his numb throat.

Oh, Ma, he said, after coughing the tea up. D'you love me, Ma? I wrote you letters. Did you read them, Ma? I try hard. Did you know?

Keep quiet, said Litz.

D'you still love me? Ma?

Keep drinking your tea, said Litz.

I can't hear you, Ma.

Pisk, Jesus, hush, he said, looking to and fro to make sure no one else heard.

I can't hear you, Ma.

Pisk's ice delirium began. The teeth-chattering started in earnest after his first long sip of the steamy tea.

//

Exhausted, frightened, and humiliated by everything he'd seen at the man game, RH had suggested to the snakehead a nice place he knew. And now, not far away, concealed behind the better establishments, past the liveries and hotels, deeper into the Chinese ghetto, beyond a set of greasy doors, through the kitchen of a dim sum restaurant, up a flight of stairs, down the hallway past all the rooms stacked full of coffins as beds, down four flights of stairs to an unlit dirt basement with a cave dugout of the earth extending in three directions, following the left fork of the moist tunnel, up a yellow ladder and into a mystic room imported straight from a thug's dreams of Beijing, RH Apparition was entertaining his business associate. The grave realization that his life was in danger, that the snakehead might finish him off as fast as a mushroom, had meant coming straight to the opium den for a restive. He should never forget that his associate was a murderer and slave owner, slithered up from California, presently enjoying the transmundane effects of the Afghani poppy delivered to him with great delicacy by a spicy-smelling girl named Ling from the province of Sze-Yap, a place where his reputation thoroughly preceded him, where arid farms and impoverished villages feared him, the all-gold teeth in his smile, the white knife-scar straight across his neck like a second, evil smile, gem-inlaid snakes on the ivory handled .38 Specials that never left their holsters on the belts across his heart unless they were used to kill, a born alone die alone man who made his fortune selling heads.

The mud was of exquisite quality: it smoked evenly, tasted like coca, and its high lasted into the astral plasma. Only the finest, to ensure the prolonged pleasure of everyone's worst debtor. Ling knelt on one knee beside him, head bowed and concentrating on keeping the pipe's bowl warm while he inhaled, exhaled, the guns tied to his chest, one hand on her breast as he rocked his hips and laughed out a sweet brown fog.

However many worlds later, the proprietor invited them to smoke another and another.

RH was basically asleep. He hadn't slept properly the whole week the snakehead was in town. Lucky he was leaving soon. Tonight had been the worst night yet. Negotiations were nothing compared to this. Oh, but what a run-in earlier in the evening, thought RH. Of all the places to take the snakehead. To watch as the men he'd fired for immolating the city used construction sites to gather mobs of his mill employees, Chinamen among them, to watch that? To watch them wrestle naked? It was not at all what RH had in mind. Without being seen, RH had followed as the snakehead circled around the audience, had listened with growing anxiety as the spectators discussed anti-social strategies. Or was that all a dream? He delighted in the lack of restrictions at the border between memory and invention. He took another deep inhale off the pipe and let the smoke circle his organs. Had the snakehead actually said, as they departed the man game after Pisk's collapse: Your Whitemen damage my property, my imports, I make sure you pay personally, with a life a your own, sir. If you kumtuks? Yes?

Please be a dream, thought RH, exhaling … please let that threat be a dream. And this intimate experience, an opium high, shared with a man who had just threatened to—, and—, have mercy—, this harpy from the underworld, this San Francisco snakehead wanted to frighten him.

The snakehead on the cot beside him put his hands on Ling's cheeks. A tiny pulse of shock ran through her and she quickly bowed to him. He didn't take his eyes off RH as he gently told her to leave. She scurried out and once the door was closed again and it was only the two men, the snakehead continued the conversation they'd begun in the woods that RH had spent the last five seconds trying desperately to deny was any more than a dissolute fantasy.

That's right, said the snakehead, we share investment of my Chinese. Do you understand, sir, why I expect you make sure that, in my absence, our investment is protected to best a your ability?

I do understand that.

And yet you tell me Whitemen will turn out to be *my* problem, my cost.

No, I'm very sorry. A foolish—

—That another *Chinaman* might end up a boot hanging for a month in the sun? Sir, forgive me for not being amused. I made very difficult journey up here to tell you personally that if Whitemen kill my employ*ees*, I will *sever our* business relationship in equally unpleasant way. I am not content to lose property to inactivity, British inbred. I as soon—

I'm fully a-aware a the circumstances, said RH.

Whitemen, Whitemen, you all the same. I make circumstances.

TEN

> A man bows down before another man
> And sucks his lust
> — HAROLD PINTER

Back in the day when you were out logging for months on end, the lumberjacks got used to sleeping *eight* in a bed. And those guys who lived in boarding houses in the city, it was the same thing. The Chinese slept in *shelves*. Shelves like the kind in a dresser. To stuff in more men per room. A Whiteman could expect to make a dollar a day. A snakehead hired out his Chinamen for thirty, thirty-five cents a day.

You're interested in history, I said.

Sort a, said Silas. We're interested in the man game. Back then it was a popular event. Me and Ken and Cedric want to bring that back.

It's chilly in here, Minna squeaked, hugging herself.

We're trying to cut expenses, said Ken.

Cedric stuck his neck out, said: What? What does that mean, cut expenses?

No heat.

Who needs heat? said Cedric. You need *body* heat is what you're telling me.

What aboot blankets? said Ken. What aboot sweaters and socks and toques?

It's a way to improve our game, said Silas.

It's a way to connect with the past, said Ken.

It's a way to connect your—, said Cedric.

It *is* very cold in here, I said.

The whole lifestyle, said Ken, reseating himself on the plush armrest of the davenport. We want to know how they did it, he said. You know, how they got by, how they *dealt*. Those guys back in early Vancouver, Litz and Pisk and so on, they lived off their share a winnings from man games. It was all they did to get by. Times were tough.

Because I didn't know yet, I said: Who what? What's a Lizzanpicks?

But Ken, you live off your in*her*itance, said Cedric. You're just being insane. What aboot indoor plumbing, get rid a that, too, and eat bear meat?

It isn't much inheritance if I keep the house. I can't afford to rep*air* it ...

So what, how do you plan to make money? I asked.

The man game.

Couple hundred from the bets, said Cedric. Twenty bucks off the beer maybe.

Like I said, we need to cut expenses.

Cedric grunted dismissively and scratched the back of his neck, rolled his eyes, and smiled dumbly at Minna, as if looking for confirmation. But I could detect something else in his critique, as if he felt, like me, that he wasn't being included in some important part of the world, the society of the man game.

Cedric dug into his pants pocket and dropped a few mushy old twenties on the coffee table. Noticing the bulky mahogany thing for the first real time, I absently opened one of its doors and saw a shelf stacked with the bamboo-yellow spines of vintage *National Geographics*. I was tempted to check out the more creased and worn-out issues, but I didn't want to be caught looking at the breasts of exotic village women *in situ*; still, the issue I ended up choosing seemed to have page after page of them. It was the wrong time to be confronted with faraway beauty when here I was so close to losing the woman right beside me on the shag carpet.

What aboot girlfriends? Minna asked. Do they—? A second question seemed to linger on her tongue, a more explicit question she was too coy to ask.

Girls don't seem to care, said Ken. Some like it.

Silas said: Do you want to see, we have a picture of Furry and Daggett and their crew in bed. It's a really wild picture. They've all got their nightshirts on and their faces are filthy. I don't know why, but they used to take pictures a logging camps. Do you want to see? Silas stood up to his full bulk.

Where is it? I said.

Oh, it's in the basement. You should come down, I'll show you. It's really wild. We have *so* much stuff down there related to the man game. We've hardly scratched the surface.

Ken said in a mumble: Why can't you respect the decisions we make?

Who, me? said Cedric.

Yeah.

Cedric said: Oh, come on. I'm busting your balls. You know that's why I was put on earth. We all have a special purpose, and mine is to bust balls. I promise. And if you guys want to sleep in the same bed in the cold and eat bear meat like it's 1886, it's your lives. Hey, you know what I always say.

No one did. Silas and I scaled our way down the kitchen and waited for the rest to meet up with us at the tiny stairs. I remembered when I first came in—when was that? half an hour ago? seemed like forever ago—standing on that scary tipped-over entryway between here and the steps to the basement, worried that I'd let go of the banister and slip and fall down that dark, serrated tunnel. Here I was *volunteering* to see the basement, actually *wanting,* despite my reservations, to see the basement, for the sake of a picture of men together in bed, and a strange curiosity for a sport I was increasingly unsettled by, largely because of its effect on Minna.

We got a whole shelf a my forefather Samuel Erwagen's journals, said Ken, and all these handwritten receipts from the Calabi & Yau Bakeshoppe with Toronto's name on them. Things like that.

Things a that nature, said Cedric.

Who? said Minna.

Conversation was a little stalled by us all having to gingerly navigate the weird angle of the staircase. I had to keep in contact with the lower wall as I held on to both banisters, taking a step and then redistributing my weight, taking another step, and so on. The passage to the basement reminded me of pictures I'd just seen in *National Geographic,* not the tribeswomen, but the pictures of people hoisted into spelunking chasms.

I waited in a foolish position on the seventh stair as one by one the other guys let go of the banister and landed on a nerfy chair, there for the purpose. Minna was in front of me and she didn't hesitate. Her landing was not graceful. Her nose almost slammed against the armrest. She didn't need quite as much assistance getting to her feet as the guys seemed to believe. I was last to jump, and owing to a lifelong love for the freefall, my land was faultless. I have, for whatever private irrelevant reason, always loved the suicidal grace of a good freefall.

Once I stood back up and objectively checked out the area, I was the first to comment. What we had was a fire hazard. It wasn't a basement anymore because of the steep angle of the house, it was more of a wood-panelled well that led into a septic tank for paperwork.

Nothing basic down here, said Ken as he slid between two handmade bookshelves and patted a row of slim, wrinkly spines. He said: This is like three-four generations a my Erwagen people not throwing anything away. This is the Erwagen legacy. All this you see. My grandfather's grandfather, Samuel. He kept a lot. And my grandfather's father, he kept everything and stowed away as much old stuff aboot his dad as he could. And my grandfather was out a his mind. He kept train tickets. Slowly getting more and more, over the years, disorganized. These are …, Ken looked at the small type, ledgers from Hastings Mill intermixed with … looks to be old magazines aboot cowboy life.

In most ways the basement wasn't all that different from the crammed-full used bookstore downtown that I sometimes visited when I felt lonely and needed to be around things that were older and more ignored than me. The difference of course was that this wasn't a priced inventory but rather a pack-rat's intense problem. Whoever was responsible for this basement was the same kind of intellectual as my favourite used bookseller. The back or lowest wall was stacked floor to ceiling all the way across with yellowing newspapers crisp as wasps' nests. That was a little more unsettling than you'd expect.

Ken flinched when he saw me gawking at it. He said: It's two rows deep.

Oh god, I said. Fire hazard. Why not recycle?

Ken wrung his hands, said: I know, I know.

I can't find that picture. Silas searched in dresser drawers filled with leather photo albums of black construction paper, those corner tabs for every picture of one's unsmiling loved ones. Silas said rhetorically: I wonder where I put it then? He searched more with his fingers.

One day I'll do something with all this, said Ken. He seemed honest enough but I doubted him.

What blocked my path was a weedy green brass chandelier from the Cold War. After I uprooted the chandelier, I crept below a door and scaled a stockpile of Hudson's Bay catalogues. The basement was a library of digressions. A wooden file cabinet to my right was labelled CALABI & YAU BAKESHOPPE ~ RECEIPTS 1884–1941. I didn't touch it. Fear of dust. The bookshelf at my left was used for a long-held subscription to a monthly magazine on experimental bookkeeping from the nineteenth century, and when I opened one dusty volume to the masthead, Cedric told me that Ken's grandfather's grandfather was a member of the editorial board. Samuel Erwagen. The dust on things had plant-like texture. So daunting, where to start looking, where to hide. The sheer amount of paper sapped my curiosity. I wondered: Why me. It was a choice between asthmatic claustrophobia or going home.

Ken revealed to Minna his special cache of musty letters that required going down on their hands and knees and crouching close together. I found myself reading the same sentence over and over, about how a legendary coyote urinated on milkweed and turned it into hemp, for what that was worth. I returned the manual where I'd found this true tale to its wrongful place among the wrack, and lo and behold, spotted the picture we'd come to see.

The picture was smaller than I'd expected. It was on top of a cardboard box on the shelf in front of me, at waist height. I looked at the picture discreetly to see its value. Indeed, it showed six men in a bed in a weather-beaten shack. One was very small, another two were very huge with only three eyebrows between them, an average man of average looks stuck in the middle, and all of them bookended by two savage creatures, mannish beyond belief, snarling. Coming from every known region of an impoverished planet to share a bed, suffering a life of no privacy to escape a life of no hope. I turned the picture over. The cardstock was heavier than today's memories. The elegant handwriting's faded pencil lines listed the names Furry through to Daggett. I turned it over again. I looked at their condition. They were so foreign, yet I shared their streets. Furry's beard was something to behold. It spanned his cheeks right to the eyebags. With the dark rings around his eyes and the downcast mouth, he was looking tired or rabid, not in the mood for daguerreotypes. Campbell held his chin up; that is, he held Furry's chin up, while they took the picture. Perhaps, despite the serious faces, this was a joke. The other possibilities were that Furry was too drunk to hold his own head up, or that he was dead. Boyd lay there beside a dwarfed Campbell, mid-puff of a cigarette, cocking his monobrow. Half of Daggett's mouth smiled, the other half was showing off a long wolfish incisor tooth. Smith looked ready to go to work even though he was in woollies and a sleeping cap. No matter that there's a huge hairy surly Meier to share the bed with, it looked to me like they all expected to get some rest. The sheets and blankets were arranged. Toes still needed to be covered. Stiff pants hung on bent nails on the slat walls around them. I tipped the photograph behind a shelf. I didn't want to start more conversations today. I wanted to leave. I was sleepy. The picture only reminded me how Minna and I still had to pick me up a bed before I could go to sleep tonight.

You have to see this, said Minna, waving for me. From my vantage point all I could see was her slim tanned arm waving above a rubbish wall. I was glad to have hidden the picture.

I switchbacked my way through piles of unsought-after history to Minna's position between the two formerly naked men. What is it? I said. I couldn't even muster up an inflection.

It's a map a the secret tunnels under the city.

She handed me a notebook open to a scribbled-upon page. At first blush all I saw were paired sets of numbers, *358 - 224*, and so on. Ken explained they were city addresses with tunnels below linking one to the other. Usually the tunnel's entrance was concealed in the backroom a some reputable establishment, Ken said. One tunnel started at the address for the Stag & Pheasant, a respectable parlour. For a man of RH Alexander's good taste (as an example), manager of the most successful lumber mill in town, who loved to entertain, an evening at the Stag & Pheasant on Water Street was just the thing for his wife's spies to see him doing. It was a pleasure to sneak away from normalcy, kiss the cloakroom girl, and unlock the secret door behind the rows of topcoats to the staircase down to the tunnel that led directly to a private room in a reprehensible men's lounge named Wood's on Dupont Street, where he scheduled his time with lush Peggy, a bottle of bodega and a pinch of hashish, a late game of stud-horse poker against *Mayor* McLean and George Black and the capitalist Oppenheimer while Siwash princesses and Chinagirls massaged their shoulders.

Do you think the tunnels still exist?

Ken said no, he didn't think they did. They were like the workers' tunnels for the early sewers, he explained. They had the Chinese labourers and the prison chain gang make the whole thing.

Did you know, he said to Minna, that your mouth is shaped like an infinity symbol when you smile?

Who, me? said Minna, wrinkling her nose. Her percipient mind still enjoyed shallow compliments. I knew the bowl of her vanity was deep enough to hold many more gushes than that clever little sputtering compliment. My only chance was to get her away.

Moving upstream, I started to say: Actually, I just remembered how I got that bed—

Ken cut me off: Check this out, I found this a little while ago.

We peered into an old tin can. Inside it was something made out of clay or the like.

What is it? Minna asked.

The mummified body of a canary. It's wrapped in old newspapers, he said.

That's so biz*ar*re.

I found it all in a small pink purse—from around the 1880s, Ken guessed, by looking at the can. The newspaper had long since faded and crumbled into illegibility. When I poked my head in and took a second look I realized that it was indeed a small bird. Its eyes were shut. Even more delicate in death than in life, with just the slightest shade of yellow left on its dried body— I was visibly moved.

What a you think it is? I asked.

Ken explained that he believed it was the pet of a girl at the Wood's brothel. And he knew this because of something to do with one of the tunnels, but I wasn't listening carefully enough to understand how the path that led from the Stag & Pheasant to a VIP gambling room in the coach house behind Wood's whorehouse had anything to do with a mummified canary.

//

The day after the man game RH celebrated the snakehead's departure with a day of opium and hashish in a slumhouse, and then, after stumbling across the street, celebrated further with a poker game in the coach house behind Wood's.

He heard the canary in the distance, peeping from a window on the second floor. The Whore Without A Face's canary. It whistled a brief melancholy scale once a minute. No man had ever set eyes on the bird, nor on its owner.

RH played poker with Mayor McLean, the successful Jewish capitalist Oppenheimer, and George Black, the local butcher. Weak competitors, weaker men still. His mind was stretched like a cat's cradle between their hands. It was chilly along the floor and too warm around head level. The cigarsmoke was a mask. He had to think fast. At the moment he had a pair of Queens in his pocket and the ante was high.

Quite a riot your city's lumbermen held not long ago, yes? said RH, looking to his own chipstack. Right under our noses. Fools and their pranks. Disturbs the semblance we once had a order and discipline around here. And all these men stomping around on precious real estate. Almost wondered if these activities are being condoned.

The mayor, seated at RH's right, knew the comment was intended for his ears. He said: What's that supposed to mean, eh? Now, listen, RH, I just heard aboot this myself only a few hours ago. Asking around, by all accounts what you're talking aboot was just some whisky party with a bit more dancing than usual. Ha ha. Your riot. You make it sound like we're all going to get our throats slit because a couple guys started lobbing fists.

The mayor was a rough man underneath his thin skin of political pretense, and Alexander enjoyed flushing out his true self, a salesman.

Perhaps you're right, and what would I know aboot the mind a these woodsmen? I've so little experience. But these gatherings seem to be more and more frequent, if I'm not mistaken. If memory serves, said Alexander, the paper reported six hundred citizens out to cheer the departure a those twenty coolies last month.

I read the same. Old news, grunted the mayor.

The round of betting done, everyone paid to see the flop.

Quite a fearsome group, I dare say, said RH. Why, I dare say there wasn't six hundred *teeth* among two hundred ruffians that day.

Ha ha, said George Black, that's a laugh.

I remember more support, though I hardly worry, said the mayor.

Twenty Chinamen received more public support than the vote.

What?

The total, what was it again? Five hundred, give or take the men you convinced to vote twice.

More old news. RH, please, play cards. Why bring this up again, after all? Do I come *here* to talk aboot the el*ec*tion, no. Your theories don't hold water with me, never have. Let a sleeping dog …

Ah, yes. What was it? We're all North American *China*men.

You *said* it, not me, said the mayor. Well, al*as,* popular opinion wasn't on your side. What can I say?

Oppenheimer slid four more red chips in after his first three and leaned back fraudulently.

George Black squinted at the flop, the cards remained wrong. RH's mouth was dry and he broke a sweat. He was about to trap them all, in cards, in life, all of it in his pocket. Even his enemies would do as they were told. Lying to the mayor, he said: I never *said* it myself, but it has a certain eloquence. It's true, isn't it? I can at least appreciate … and—, well, regardless a the words exactly … one can twist any words to smear a man with magnanimous intentions for his people.

The mayor squeezed his forehead. Time stands still for you, does it, RH? The vote is over. Try again next time. At least a hundred men heard you say those words, and were—

Again your numbers. Twenty-five men at a union meeting.

And they hear—

They misrepresent a comment I made, foolishly attempted to reason with your klans—. Does this mean you're going to hold a parade every time you run another dozen Chinamen out a town?

I believe it's worth the effort, said the mayor, scratching his unnecessary cummerbund. I'm sorry we disagree on the issue, my friend. May we continue—

A handful a Chinamen? Hardly worth the blink a your brown eye.

An inferior race overrunning our country? Never happen on my clock.

I'm a capitalist, not a Cassandra, said Alexander. I only know they have inferior bargaining power, which my accounts department approves of.

You're completely backwards. This must be why Hastings Mill is plagued with strikes. It's your own damn blood you've given inferior bargaining power. And I shouldn't need to remind everyone how your accounts department is a disembodied head.

Oppenheimer choked on his hair tonic.

All this effort to rid us a our best economic asset against Ontario, said RH. It's interesting, and yet you ignore the threat posed by dissidents within our White population.

Men, said George Black. How's aboot some poker? Alexander, it's your—

Yes, I'm tired a prattle, said the mayor. If I wanted prattle I'd be home with my wife.

Yes, ahem, said RH, feigning a last look at the top corners of his cards, seeing Oppenheimer's raise, and doubling it. If he read his mates, they weren't expecting him to go large. He had the cards. His nerves hit full gallop as half a minute elapsed in no time. Not giving the mayor a chance to think, RH said: So am I to assume you know aboot this lurid game the men in this town are at, very indecent and anarchistic, I should add.

Yes, I had the unfortunate occasion a seeing it one time a while back. Heard it's pretty popular with skid road types. The mayor spoke while he fondled his chips. All this talk, RH. What barn are you circling? This game you keep talking aboot, I've wanted to mention the same to you—. Say, what are you up to?

I should ask you the same.

Aren't the crowds mostly men from your mill? Including Chinamen in the gambling, too, I hear. And Litz and Pisk, the players, aren't these bohunks your employees?

Former, said RH.

George Black sloughed his cards across the table after a torturous decision no one noticed. I fold, he said.

Ah, *my* responsibility? Alexander was irked by the moisture around his collar that made him twist his head. Does *my* jurisdiction suddenly extend beyond the—the—

The mayor was stacking and restacking his chips, said: I see now what you're after. You want me to take care a this mess for you? He shook his head with fatherly disdain. Why not say so?

Pardon?

Don't come walking in all proud to me when you're pussyfooting around for a favour.

I beg your pardon?

You want me to clean up your mess, right? That's what you're asking?

I'm not in charge a the *law,* said Alexander, stiffly. If you're content to see mobs a men gambling openly in the streets, and the indecency. This is crime, not a mess. My employees are your citizens. What they do—

Ah, said Oppenheimer, to see a strong man broken by a criminal habit, that's a sadness, that's a pity. He shook his head. The easy way to money never pays. Nothing saves like hard work.

RH agreed vigorously: Indeed, indeed.

The mayor muttered and punched himself in the head. You deal with Chinamen, you deal with snakeheads … I don't know, RH … He measured his chips in smacking stacks of five. He saw Oppenheimer's raise and Alexander's raise, pushing a few paltry chip towers into the middle of the table. The mayor looked Alexander in the eyes and said: All in.

All in? said Oppenheimer. His head fell back. All in, ay-ay-ay, I'm all in. One thing I hate is all in. Yeah, you heard me, I'm all in, too, you bastard.

George Black said: Glad I got out when I did.

Oppenheimer said: I want these steamers to battle it out. This kind of poker isn't what I came for anyway.

Ha ha ha, said George Black. That's right. Let's see some blood. Come on, Alexander, call. Put your money where your mouth is.

RH made a quick estimate. If the mayor won, he was out. Was it worth the risk? He'd liked his hand a lot until the mayor went all in. On the flop, Oppenheimer started the betting after they all saw a Queen of spades, as well as a ten and an eight of spades. Alexander knew from memory that his pocket cards were Ace, King of spades—beautiful black royalty. A flush on the flop, he felt quite confident to bet high and see who got scared, see who was still chasing. It seemed to Alexander that the mayor was using the off-chance he had the straight flush to make him fold a strong hand.

RH said: All in.

The mayor nodded cosmically, and said: Good, let's see their faces. He turned his cards over, Jack and nine of spades—straight flush.

All told, RH lost two dollars. It was getting late he had to go, klahowya. It was on to Peggy for yet another chance to spread open his wallet and get fucked out of his money.

While the mayor expanded his empire of chipstacks, Alexander's knees cracked as he stood to leave. The mayor said: Pleasure to see you as always, RH. *And* I will consider what can be done aboot your problem.

They shook hands.

I'd recommend the man game be outlawed, RH said from the doorway as he casually beheaded a fresh cigar.

You would, eh?

Yes. First, it is indecent, and second, it promotes gambling.

Promotes gambling, the mayor said with a chuckle, twisting his own cigar in his mouth. Promotes *assimilation* more like … well, I'll look into it.

As he left the coach house, RH took a moment to breathe the night air. It was a night of daunting shades. The barebones trees pleaded for leaves. They wore raggedy crinolines of fog. Weather was a greater force than any other on earth. This morning he'd predicted to his wife a cold evening. Instead it was relatively warm and foggy. He walked up to the porch and opened the back door to Wood's, stood in the cloak room, and held his breath. Going from the pure clean air of British Columbia to the smog of human lust, even for a regular, took some acclimatizing. As the eyes required adjustment to the darkness, so did the nose.

In the smoking parlour at the other end of a house decorated in King George's castoffs, RH Alexander heard the rowdy talk of axemen.

Swinging crouching dancing kick. It was a swinging kick. Like the beam a your schooner swinging by on deck, knocking out legs.

It was point after point for Litz and Pisk. I don't know aboot Campbell. He's too small. He can't move, he's thick. His eyes, he might be blind the way he squints all the time.

I think it's he's angry.

That squint's anger? If that's anger, he's in trouble. Never bet on him. Never. His one move. That Faint. No. Pisk could do five Cherry Tree Clutches *in a row* to get him a win against that naive bohunk Campbell, shit *{see fig. 10.1}*.

Damned near invincible. Brute strength though. Not finesse, character? Muscle. The man game is aboot *more* than muscle. It's aboot strategy and, you know, not just aboot muscle.

Who coaches?

A gust a wind. So far's we know they make it up themselves.

Listening to the men talk, it seemed as if no matter where he went RH Alexander couldn't shake yesterday. Men might conversate for a few days, but the *issue* of the man game's long-term future was, he believed, resolved, so long as his discussion with the mayor bent to his influence. He checked his reflection in a convex mirror. The narrow staircase coiled

FIGURE 10.1
Cherry Tree Clutch, alternative sketch

up to the women's bedrooms. As he inspected his face, he thought about his plans. Along the intricate carpet of his thoughts he hit a lump where something unswept remained in his strategies with the mayor. If nothing else RH was meticulous. What was kinking up his strategy? Enough thinking like that, he told himself. He would put an end to it, that's all there was to say.

He mounted the staircase. The hall on the second floor was papered with a design of red roses. The hall smelled of years of perfumes, skin, and today's exhaustion. The candlelight was borne in flowery sconces, and the unsteady light was accompanied by all the muffled and murderous noises of coitus. Six doors, three on either side led into private rooms where it happened. On the other end of the upstairs hall was a sacred room. Behind its door lived The Whore Without A Face. Her only companion was that singing canary. She was feared and desired in equal bouts. The Indians said she was cursed. Her allure for Whitemans was her invisibility. In her studied drawl, Peggy always said: If I let you all go inside her walls I'd be out a business. One fuck you're done. She's a manslaughterer.

I'd like to slaughter her, Alexander thought toughly. After years of coming to Wood's—since before there *was* an upstairs—, that sacred door to her room still made Alexander's heart quaver. The Whore Without A Face. Rumour was she was Snauq.

Six more doors, each assigned to a woman, each presenting her *origin of the world,* as it were, and he'd visited them all. Except her. He was not a man who fell for whores, but Peggy was a delicacy, a truffle among yams. She lived behind the door marked P in gold filigree at the end of the hall, right beside the sacred room. He expected her to be in bed waiting for him to arrive. He took off his hat and pressed his ear to *her* door—not Peggy's, but the one adjacent. The Whore Without A Face. Quiet, not even the bird. Strange. He backed away. He took one last look at the door, and saw it shudder and start to open.

At that he froze. From the shadows of the room he saw a man's profile emerge, and in an anxious hurry RH turned the brass knob and swung open Peggy's door to hide. He shut the door and heard the other door shut just as fast. Now both men were hiding. What folly. But as he caught his breath, he realized he'd just seen the face of his crippled accountant, Samuel Erwagen. An impossibility. The man was a total cripple. Impossible. This golem, standing and walking, some flight of the imagination, thought RH. Bah, he thought. A trick of the mind. I thought of Sammy only a moment ago, that's what caused me to see him just now, yes.

What are you doing? The voice startled him. He'd forgotten where he was. He was safely inside Peggy's room. He looked over at the door that connected hers to the sacred room. Locked in there with her was an able-bodied double and in bed with—. His eyes bulged. He was seeing spooks. He feared the door would open.

Honey, said Peggy. You're scaring me.

What? Peggy. I—nothing, I—it's nothing. Indeed, he saw that the door was locked.

What if I was with a customer? Then what?

Yes, I'm sorr—

Come here, you, she said.

Yes, but—I saw, I think I saw—

You saw nothing. Peggy squeezed his cheeks in her hands. My crazy opium addict, she teased. What did you think you saw?

Nothing, nothing.

Did you take care a your little problem? she said.

I insisted the mayor outlaw the man game.

*Out*law?

Yes, why do you say it like that, like you disagree?

Nothing, I just wonder if—. Nothing.

What is it?

No, I see why outlawing it is the only way.

A course it is, dearie. It can't con*tin*ue.

How much did you lose?

Two dollars, he said, knowing he'd have to tell his wife it was six to include the forthcoming cost of Peggy's routine.

Two dollars? She shook her head. Wasting your money. You're the worst gambler in the world. Why do you do it?

To relax.

Actually, I must admit, what I meant when I asked if you'd taken care a your little problem was if you saw the snakehead.

Ah.

You did, I trust?

I did. Yesterday. A fine afternoon, a terrible evening. I had him in my pocket. Then we stumbled upon the man game.

You resolved …

I resolved nothing. Please, I don't visit you to talk business.

Baby, sweet thing, who, then, if not me, is your confidante? Do you talk to your bookkeeper aboot strategy? Certainly you don't speak with a cripple. You consult with no one. You think you can take it all on alone. You know I'm not just a mink. I'm a businesswoman. My profits exceed yours.

Doubtful. Now shush, come here and put your hot breasts on my face.

Shush yourself. Your costs are higher. My margins are better.

I love your margins.

You buy me, but I could buy you.

How dare you speak to me this way, Peggy.

It's just that I'm so terrified for you, sweet RHA. That snakehead … if he ever visits again, I believe your life, *our* lives are on the line. We won't survive without his help.

I'm fine, we're safe. I took care a things as quickly as—. Now don't move a muscle, unless it's to undress. I need to use the head.

Go then. Quietly.

//

For the second time, Dunbar Erwagen was a shoe into the hallway at Wood's when he startled again at the sound of the next door opening. Instinct told him to shut his door, and the other man—RH Alexander's instincts told him the same. What a shameful sound: two doors slamming in a whorehouse, both wanting the same thing, to micturate. Why should I be shy, thought Dunbar, when no one in Vancouver knows who I am? I have no one to hide from here. He was about to step back into the hallway with his anonymity but remembered his brother, Sammy, and their disgraceful similarity. This put him in a spot. Meanwhile, he heard the other door creak open again and a man's footsteps walk down the hallway and open the door to the very facility Dunbar so badly needed to use.

He turned around to find his lover had disappeared. The Whore Without A Face: where was she? A moment ago she'd been on the bed clutching the serpent of blankets twisted between her pale candlestick legs. Her sweetly tapered legs wrapped around this veined rope of linens. His own manhood had never touched such bliss as this. They'd spent hours enjoying the crests and surges of euphoria that marked their style of love. He'd kissed her on the collarbone and neck. She seemed to like it. If not her face then he wanted to kiss the hood. If not the sight, he wanted to feel. He'd grown to adore her black silk hood. But on his first attempt to kiss above the neck she'd pushed him away with a strict hand.

One of the other girls had brought her a dozen Calabi&Yaus, which were sitting on the dressertop with her other perfumes. Before going to the door, he'd brought the box to the bed and suggested she eat a few while he went for his break, but to save him the one with chocolate and goat's cheese. She undid the knot and clapped gaily when she saw the pastries. They looked imaginary and they smelled amazing. Knowing how delicious they were, he craved them even more now than when he'd first had one with Toronto. She poked off a baked scallop stuck to the sugar on a sweet one.

What variety do you have there, my sweet?

You want taste? she asked.

She wore a slip that suited her figure from every angle. The hood itself was brutally sexy. He loved to watch her breath push and pull the silk around her mouth.

When I return from my lordly duties, he'd said to her. He'd turned to the door, opened it, shut it in embarrassment, turned around, and she was gone.

Da-arling? he said now.

Wa, she said from behind the wardrobe. Scared me. I think you left—

No, not yet. What are you doing? He tried to see her between the slats of the wardrobe.

Eating, she said. Please, no look at me.

A-a course, he said, and nosed in for a snoop. It was impossible not to be curious. He could smell the pastries and hear her eat them. Through the slats he saw a little of her head where the skin was a paler complexion than her body. Perhaps that was all he could really say for sure. It wasn't even possible to see her chew. How serious was the deformity? Actually, he didn't really want to learn the reason she hid all day in a room in a whorehouse and wore a black silk hood locked around her neck with a leather collar. Some horrors were best left unseen. So he turned around and walked out the door, crept down the hall to the piss-pot.

Indoor plumbing, he said to himself. Not bad. He shook off and stared into the empty porcelain, unsure if he was actually finished. There was a framed crocheting of a King James verse hanging on the wall. In a bright floral arrangement, it read: *Jesus saith unto them, Verily I say unto you, That the publicans and the harlots go into the kingdom of God before you. For John came unto you in the way of righteousness, and ye believed him not: but the publicans and the harlots believed him: and ye, when ye had seen it, repented not afterward, that ye might believe him. - Matthew 21:31, 32.*

Dunbar didn't know that this toilet was a local secret among a cadre of sinners. Wood's was the first house in Vancouver with indoor plumbing. No doubt Dunbar appreciated it this minute going on two. No such luxury on the farm in Wyoming with the heavyset wife. Every day he looked at her, she looked more like his mother. Invalid. Skin like encaustic. Sand in her hair. He never wanted to go back there. The outhouse was twenty-five steps in the frigid silent cold. He heard the wolves howl. His wife howled. His stomach howled. Wyoming was the worst place on God's crumbling earth. His family home in Toronto had had indoor plumbing all along. That's comfort.

He chalked up the sudden upspike in his sexual activity as the reason why the piss was not flowing proper. Months and months of nothing and then all this fucking, a little stammer of the bladder was to be expected. Squeezing out jot after jot of urine, Dunbar thought a little about The Whore Without A Face. Peggy had been a true visionary to recommend this mystery to him. When he first arrived at Wood's, Dunbar had been all eyes for a couple of the squaws in the smoking parlour.

I know she's a girl for you, Peggy had said. Peggy's fingernails were always fixing up the pins in her mungo hairstyle. When I see a man come into Wood's I know what girl is just for you, she said. Some men get this or that because anything will satisfy them tastes. Not you, I can tell aboot you. She changes your whole life, honey. I see a brave man, ain't I right? she said. Dunbar nodded. It was true, he'd helped capture a dangerous criminal only moments ago. Honey, she said, not just any man gets to visit my Whore Without A Face. I protect her and I protect her and I keep her safe from all them out there, right? She's my flower. My little broken wildflower. They're all my little flowers, but I love her too much. More than my own daughters. Oh, I keep her safe. I can only trust certain men with her, right? Men who deserve what she got. Men who *need* to appreciate her and what she got. A spiritual man. I think you're a man like that, don't you? She unlocked the door to the sacred room and guided Dunbar through.

Dearest Huldah (his wife), wrote Dunbar the next morning, *I hope you remembered to slaughter the chickens before the cold. The news said it hit Wyoming in the night. I'm concerned that the meat will go to waste if they die of exposure, placing me in the unfortunate position of once again crediting that against your monthly allowance. We did agree the chickens were your responsibility. Take care. I must return to Toronto again to tell Father and Mother how far Samuel has fallen since he left the nest. I mustn't go into the details of his predicament now for fear that it might provoke another of your debilitating phantasies. Your husband in eternity, Mister D. Erwagen.*

//

The following morning Dunbar escaped from Vancouver. The moist savage cage that had imprisoned him for three days in January, 1887, finally set him free. It was not without mixed feelings. Tears, his own; and The Whore Without A Face, she too, if he heard correctly, had wept. A kissless farewell and he was gone. The Whore Without A Face remained in her cloister at Wood's and he boarded a train in New Westminster heading east. He didn't bid his brother any kind of farewell. He didn't even call on Toronto. He rode in the back of an applecart, shivering, while the farmer complained the whole way there about the Chinamen.

On the train, his sleeping car was compact but royally accessorized. Yet still he felt like a real peasant: letting his emotions overtake him. He already missed her. There was a girl, and he had met her, who knew love when she felt it rubbing against her heart. She was a glorious hydra with no true face, and their time together was so short-lived, so punishingly short-lived. He didn't know how he would survive not having her. Was he in despair or just incredulous? Life to Dunbar was a series of worsening associations. It was so private between them. No one would ever know that he was ever in love with her because his love lived in a sacred room, a dark room. He realized he might find some satisfaction in cherishing a deep regret and harbouring it to the grave, his secret love, all the while living in Wyoming among cows, a wife like a chicken coop on fire, and who knows how many children he'd eventually have to feed. The image of his brother Sammy, the man who was only a head, floating around in his wheeled chair with an Indian at his side—it all came back to Dunbar in a rush of queasy vertigo. He decided right then and there that from this day on, he would grind like a mortar and pestle, and his labours would provide for his life, and he would ask for no more than what he reaped with his own hands.

Please, Ma, Father, I mean no harm, for it is I, your loving son. I have returned with foul news aboot Sammy …

As Dunbar prepared his words, he became aware that many of the passengers and crew aboard the train were watching him. Until he found out why, he wouldn't let on. This was how he always lifted his hand to his chin. Why was that woman leaning back in her chair every minute or so to search for something in her handbag? And why did her eyes always dart up to look at him with the most unflatteringly serious face? Her face was quite similar to the train conductor's, who came again to check for tickets. Another suspicious goon. His brother is living with a woman who controls his every move, quite literally, while she seduces what appears to be every drifter in town, right under his nose. To make it worse, they live with an unstable, or perhaps he should say fiendish Indian, since his parents will never visit. And two Chinamen act as houseboys, creeping soundlessly over wood floors that scream when any other foot touches them—the floors that is. The real culprit of Sammy's predicament was still definitely Molly, a conniving woman after the Erwagen fortune sure enough. Sammy was virtually incapable of rational thought with her around; her every gesture left him senseless with ardour. Sammy was so thoroughly seduced by Molly's hypnotically green eyes, soulful and yet so proud, that he himself defended her innocence while she plundered the good name of the Erwagen family in plain public view.

The fur traders on board carried weapons under their skins. Dunbar saw a big man straight off the trapline flash the black double barrel at him and laugh. If he changed from one car to the next, the fur traders always followed him. When the train conductor asked him for his ticket again, he was afraid to show it. How you feeling, sir? he asked, a shockingly inappropriate question coming from an utter stranger, a mere ticket-taker. All these questions were getting under his skin. He didn't answer any of them. Instead he shut himself in his private, seven-by-three sleeping cabin, and washed his face with the new bar of Ivory soap, shaved with the complimentary Kampfe Brothers safety razor, quite an invention, and rolled up under the Hudson's Bay blankets for what he hoped was long enough.

He slept for two days. Three more days into the voyage, and Dunbar was howling and thrashing and not unlocking the door, though he could reach it from any place in his room. When they liberated him, he was clammy beyond belief. According to a doctor he'd succumbed to a kind of fevered paranoia brought upon by infection, and if kept under watch, his health should improve within the week. For safe measure, he was opiated heavily and quarantined. Influenza was no laughing matter. They fed him milk to relax him and he did indeed say some queer things about lumberjacks while under the fevered spell. With good-hearted intentions or pity, the doctor prescribed for him chicken soup and lots of rest.

An intense bladder infection quickly turned into gushing venereal sores overnight, all over his genitals and mouth. The slightest movement Dunbar made cracked open a sore. In the hours before the train reached Fort William, the crew recommended they stop for real medical attention, Dunbar insisted that the only doctor he trusted was Klinx in Toronto. Klinx, he's the only man in the world I trust, he said. But as his temperature dropped, he kept saying the same thing. Klinx. Take me to Klinx. These were his final lucid hours. The Erwagen family doctor's name was Billings.

His parents, Mr. and Mrs. Erwagen, took him straight from the train station to the hospital. The first thing he said upon seeing their faces was that they were milky devils.

Dunbar had developed a full-blown case of catatonic mania brought on by a breed of super-syphilis, according to Dr. Billings. He sees nothing but devils, the doctor surmised.

Herpes sores ravaged his genitals with craggy and volcanic scabs. The gonorrhea doubled him over with bee-sting pain that throbbed across his entire pelvis. He was unable to stretch out his legs to full height. Rank mucus streamed in green rivers from his eyes. The colour of his urine alternated between dark red, oxidated copper, and muddy grey, and dribbled all day. The last stage of his journey through life came when the syphilis gained complete control of his nervous system and started to mutilate his features. In an hour, he went bald. Once the hair was gone, his entire head deformed until, in about a week, it resembled cauliflower. His nose and mouth sank between the gutters of ruddy white vegetable flesh. His veins poked themselves to the surface, almost on top of his skin.

Before anything could be done, the Toronto medical establishment stepped in and requested that Dunbar be allowed to live under a prolonged spell of morphine for the opportunity to study him as a rare and valuable scientific specimen of rampant venereal mutation. The mind was lost, but his body was a boon, said the men of medicine.

A monthly stipend was offered to the Erwagens as compensation for their loss. His mother was bedridden again. The idea of her son living out his years as a morphined freak, cut up and inspected by avid surgeons, attacked her overnight like scarlet fever. Father Erwagen looked at the cheque and started to guiltily daydream. The cheque's amount was good, it bespoke the gravity of the matter at hand and was, after a time of calculating deliberation, accepted. An Erwagen is taught never to argue with numbers, he told the doctors, who seemed to find the credo disagreeable. They wrote a letter to Dunbar's wife in Wyoming but she was already dead, frozen to death in the latest storm. What happened to Dunbar next is a story for medicine. Photographs were taken and discreetly reproduced for private collections, including at least one in Vancouver.

Instead of telling their son Sammy the whole horrid story of Dunbar's illness, and whose own health his parents knew nothing about, they wrote him a telegram to let him know that his brother Dunbar was dead.

//

On the same day Dunbar left town, two days after the man game, Vancouver's general practitioner Dr. Langis received a panicked-sounding note:

Please, doctor, we must meet. Be at the post office 5 P.M. Man needs help urgently ... etc. etc. ..., he read through it quickly, searching for any sign ... *bring your instruments - Mrs. Samuel Erwagen.*

He read the note again. It was written as though by the hand of someone new to English.

Man needs help urgently—as if dictated.

He said aloud: A man?

What man? he thought to himself. She must mean her husband, not me, he thought, putting aside his own feelings and studying the note further.

He checked to make sure his pince-nez were in the breast pocket of his vest—they were—and was on his way.

In Vancouver there was steady work for the Whitemen's doctor. Why, just the other day, a young man up in the branches of a red cedar had axed his hand in two, fainted and dropped a hundred feet to the ground, landed on a bed of chanterelle mushrooms, dislocated a shoulder, woke up, used his mouth to prepare a tourniquet for the cleaved hand, walked ten miles into town and dingled the office of Dr. Langis, let himself in, sat down at the doctor's side and showed him the bleeding wound and the wonked arm. All a problem like that required was gauze and a drop of laudanum. Now and then stitches were needed. Dr. Langis was an even-tempered man, that temper being serious and impatient. Never looked you in the eye. Wouldn't remember your name. He heard only what ailed you. Among these salmonbellies he was an eel, quick-witted, never sympathetic.

The note from Molly left him curious ... hopeful, if he allowed himself such luxury. Which he did not. As he walked down Cordova, he walked into the pall. There was snow in patches and the fog bleakened everything. He could see into it as much as a block ahead. According to Dr. Langis's pocket fob, it was twelve past the hour. Late as usual. Fine then, he thought. He knocked steadily three times.

Molly hurriedly let him in, studied the street with her green eyes (moted with brown), slammed shut the door. The post office's clapboard facade trembled as if struck by the back of a hand. Inside, he allowed her to remove his topcoat and scarf and find them a place on the rack. Her lips were the colour of a sweet plum, her tongue hiding between them, strange fruit, peeled.

And how have you been, Dr. Langis? she said politely, leading him past the counter to the back room. She wore a modest frock with a seasonal lily appended to an open buttonhole, but this didn't smell like romance. Dr. Langis felt the blood to his fingertips ease back. She walked too quickly for this to be a secret rendezvous.

I-I'm w-well, said the doctor, pressing around his face for his pince-nez.

He followed her through the door to the back room. There before him sat a bearded gentleman, charmless and hulking across a sofa that leaked sawdust. His bare, ravaged feet were up on a table. Doubtless, the feet were the matter.

Why had Molly sent this urgent message for him to meet her here when it was only to amputate the feet off this unrepentant bohunk? Surely her husband must be in the room and he was just too blind to see him. Well, the other person in the room turned out to be a second young man who stood dumbfounded next to a tube of brown newsprint. With a moustache for a face and ball bearings for eyes, his expression was of calculated sheepishness, the manners of a pugilist or lummox.

The doctor fished pockets in search of his pince-nez, wondering if he'd left them in his topcoat, but no, here they were, where they always were, in the right breast pocket of his vest, wrapped in a handful of blue silk.

Molly gestured.

The doctor focused.

Pisk's feet were laid out in the light coming through the south-facing window. There was a candle-powered frosted lamp as well. These feet, they sat on the table like two gruesomely overdue loaves of raisin bread waiting to be thrown out with the rest of him.

Worst frostbite I've seen in I don't know how long, said the doctor to Pisk's feet, which were black, flaked, and glassy. He gingerly lifted one and turned it to the side. Pisk didn't acknowledge, no sign of pain or awareness. When the light touched it, the black showed through to a layer of green, scaly, and metallic skin like exposed mica. The heels, ankles, and patches on top were hot pink. The knuckles were a molten shade of red surrounded by the blackened silicated crust. They'll both have to go, he said.

What? No. Do something, said Pisk in a hoarse, fevered voice. I can't lose my feet. I can't lose them.

I've no other choice, young man, I'm sorry.

Don't be sorry, fucking don't amputate.

Nothing else I can do.

You don't get it, doc. I *need* my feet. Look, Molly said you'd be a better fucking doctor than *this*. I'm not going to let you amputate. If I leave this room without my feet, you will, too, doc. You will, too. So. What else can you do?

The doctor sighed, rubbed the irritated bridge of his nose, the pink indents where his pince-nez sat. He looked to Molly for support, for another voice of the rational. To prevail against this man's fervour with the aid of a woman's logic. Instead he saw someone who expected miracles.

Bloody hell, said the doctor, flushed. He checked his watch again, by reflex. Sixteen minutes past five.

He said: What did your boss have you doing to get your feet in such a state?

Said Pisk: I don't got a boss. I got frost-bit in my spare time.

Spare time? said the doctor. No boss? he said. The doctor dabbed his forehead with a kerchief. He unrolled the leather purse that held his chisels and tools. They glinted. Pisk clenched his teeth. The doctor took the sharpest chisel, gave it to Litz, and ordered him to assist in the preparations. From a pouch the doctor unslipped a stainless steel flask, twisted off the cap and took a swig, passed it to Pisk, who took three swigs, then another swig, then passed it to Molly, who took a swig. She passed the flask to Litz, who declined when he felt the weight. Save the rest for Pisk, he said, leaned to give it back to the doctor, and saw engraved on its side the words *Adveho valetudo vel altus unda.*

What?

I shouldn't have any, Litz said. Spare it for Pisk.

There's more than one raspberry on the bush, son, said the doctor, take a pull if you want.

Litz nodded boyishly and took two swigs of the warm brandy.

I better have some more then, too, said Pisk, grabbing and slugging down.

We get this over with fast, said the doctor.

Faster the better.

Molly took Pisk's hand in hers and patted his rocky knuckles. He let her go and said: You better not hold my hand, I might crush it.

Dr. Langis said: Where do you want me to start?

Pisk looked at his feet. He took another drink. He said: With the big toes and work your way down. Fuck.

Might not be enough, the doctor warned. These feet …

Cut the feet off, I kill you with the stumps.

Yes, yes, said the doctor, enough out a you. Have another drink.

The doctor lopped off the big toe in a swift two-fisted jab with the large chisel, and said: Bring it.

Litz opened the door to the stove and pulled out the wood-handled iron pick, well-reddened like a cigarette, and applied it gingerly to the wound. A noxious cooking smell arose from the hissing flesh and blood. Hold still, said Litz. It really fucking hurts now, said Pisk. All right, said the doctor, and waved Litz off. The wound cauterized shut and Dr. Langis slathered the nub with aloe lotion. Holy shit, said Pisk. His face was pale and wet. Keep going, he said. Keep going.

//

The doctor walked Molly home, for it was quite late by the time it was all done. Past midnight. The fog lifted into the trees. The ceiling of the world wasn't much higher than the rooftops they walked past, silently, fatigue keeping them silent despite all the things a man would normally inquire of a lady in such a scene. Like who the hell were those guys back there? And why does she keep company with them and not himself, if she's grown weary of the paralyzed company of her husband?

When they reached her verandah, he paused on the walk while she ascended two stairs. Then she turned and looked him in the eyes at last. They were indeed brown moted with green, so said his heart.

M-Molly, he said.

Yes, Dr. Langis?

Not certain what to do with his hands, Dr. Langis touched his chest for his pince-nez. He said: Worst of all is knowing that you mustn't love me.

Oh, she said. Her cheeks were flushed and plump. The swirl of her mouth was imploring him to recant his words. She was tracing circles around his desire. But I do love you, Dr. Langis, she said. I do. Look what you have done for me today. How could I not love you?

That's not love, my young thing, he said, with misted eyes under his pince-nez, that's gratitude you feel. I was only doing my duty.

What you did for Pisk, that was not for me, said Molly. I'm aware of that. What I mean is, you have respected my dignity. Dr. Langis, she said, you know that I love you. You know how shy I am around you because of it. Your intelligence brought you there, to help another man, another good man in need of help.

You've shown *me* your strength. My husband, Dr. Langis—, well … Klahowya, dear doctor, she said and turned and ran up the final stairs with an irrational titter to her step.

Yes, but—

Klahowya, she said, and eased in the door and out of sight.

But how was I supposed to know that you loved me? he thought to himself with growing, ascending, impending nausea. One denies the face of love as often as the skull of death … Ah, Langis exclaimed, curse my intelligence.

//

Inside night's jewelled mouth, under a forest of bacilli on the tip of North America's tongue, saved from the jaws of gloom by the flames and sparks and embers of the campfire, Daggett hacked a message into a tree that would remain there until the construction boom of 1952. In giant wedged-out axe script, the message read: KILL PISK.

His men watched him carve out the message and laughed and, as Daggett seated himself back by the campfire, fell into silence. The cook came over. Furry & Daggett hosted their logging team to a late dinner of beans, flatbread and butter, coffee.

When dinner was over, Daggett took a deep breath as he prepared to begin the evening's soliloquy with a bold declaration: Vancouver's going to learn *our* crew's the better. Woodsmen *and* man game. Bohunks are going to want a coach, and that's us. Open up a Furry & Daggett's Coaching Association.

Furry, who usually never said a word, lifted his beastly face from staring at the firepit and said: Don't forget, Campbell is our first. Campbell's the man on the street.

That's right, said Daggett. Campbell is the first in line. No one starts a game except Campbell. Don't let bohunks and peons and poltroons get your goat. Don't get set up and let your pride get you a fight. That's for Campbell. You hear? I tell you straight, this here a lesson for me. Alls I know is a good fight. But shit. We got to push this game. Every day practise.

What do I do? said Campbell, chewing his lip.

You wait. You wait and listen to see who wants to compete against you. If it's Litz, so be it. If Pisk is still alive, you stomp his toes, that stupid bastard. I don't care aboot how they play. I can tell how much they practise. We got to practise twice as much.

Tired a waiting. I want to call out a man game.

If you can stir up some others, I don't know who, then do it. Daggett smoked his hash cheroot and paused for thought. No one interrupted, no one dared derail his train of thought. At last he said: If Moe *Dee* is looking to compete, fine. I suspect he is. But everybody can't be on the street looking to start something. Campbell's our representative for now. If someone wants to battle Furry & Daggett, they got to go through Campbell first.

And then it's Boyd, said Furry.

And then it's Boyd, agreed Daggett.

Why Boyd? Why not me second? said Meier. I want a shot.

You're still too clumsy, Meier. Don't argue here. We know what we're doing. So don't start something just to start something. It's Campbell then Boyd, and that's how it's got to be.

And no way me or Furry go up against nobody but *them,* said Daggett. No way I'm a showing a single one a these nuts before I use them on Litz and Pisk. If Pisk dies, I'm gonna curse God till the day I die for not giving me opportunity for revenge. I'll curse that motherfucker God he gets a spur up the ass so deep he gags. I'm one thing, said Daggett, and that's vengeful …

He paused.

He smoked.

He continued: That's why I don't take a wife. I got a vengeful soul. I'd strike a woman as quick as I would a tree. Women and whores fear me, ladies scared a me the same as a grizzly, and, you know what? I don't care. Anything aboot who I am strike you as caring what a woman thinks? You think a lady gets a load a these tattoos and this beard and expects me to support her? You think the girls at Wood's look forward to my visits? I'm the unluckiest number in the room, always.

He paused again, his chest heaving with phlegm.

While the men enjoyed the silence, their Chinaman cook rinsed the dishes in the rushing creek nearby, spying intently on their conversation and trying to understand their words—he regularly attended man games—, and they all smoked copious amounts of purple-haired weed inside cheroot leaves.

On the subject a women, Campbell said: I want to get married, marry me a plum girl like Molly Erwagen and make some childs with her.

If I were your teacher, Daggett said, raising his elbows off his knees and swinging a fist through the air, I'd whip you for saying that. Campbell, my friend, don't get involved with a lady.

But that Molly ..., said Campbell.

You see any other ladies around here like Molly? None that I see. And do any a the wenches calling themselves ladies around here, do any a them say word one to a fuck like yourself? You ever conversated with Molly Erwagen? I'm asking you a question, Campbell.

... No, said Campbell.

You're so full a shit, Campbell. A lady like that shows a man like us no interest, I can promise you that. Marriage, Daggett scoffed, marriage is for one a them pencils who needs an eraser, them men who keeps making mistakes and rubbing them off. We're not pencils, we're not even fountain pens, men, we're goddamn axes.

Wa, cried all the men, raising their drinks for clinks, inspired as much by Daggett's words as their fear of displeasing him.

Daggett pointed a finger at Meier, who braved a harsh woolpack of firesmoke to meet his boss eye to eye. For instance? Daggett asked himself (implicating Meier, perhaps), name me one married man who wouldn't *dream* to trade lifes with you. This taking care a the kids business? Do I look like I'm rearing me no kids? These women get it put up in their heads by their mothers. Think if they can marry you then they can control you. Make you do all this backbreaking work, take all your chickamin, spend it on rearing. Know what I'd rather spend my chickamin on? Hash, whores, horses, and hooch. That's what blankets are for, spending at the saloon, the billiards hall, the cat house. What use do we got for families and childs-raising? What good's all that? No, she got babies because that's her sex.

As Daggett paused to catch his breath, Campbell said: I do, I want to find me a smart lady, good with money, marry her, have some childs. That's why I'm here. Raise money for a family.

Daggett stared at him. He received the weed, inhaled, gave it to Smith next to him, and exhaled.

Furry got the pipe next. He took two long pulls one right after the other, as if his lungs could take the entire plug at once. Their boys sat on the overturned logs around the fire, getting hazier, all ears at their age, young and impressionable and afraid of a belt whipping.

If I could marry a lady such as Molly Erwagen, said Campbell, I'd never want another thing in life.

Oh hell, said Daggett, calming a bit, I wasn't talking aboot Molly Erwagen. You find yourself a Molly Erwagen, Daggett said, and I don't say nothing to you. Go right ahead. But that girl's aboot as common as a blue cherry. You'll see one in your life if you're lucky. I'd say any one a us might be crippled to some degree by her loveliness.

Aye, said all the men. A faint silence came upon them, and Smith, in a good mood, donated the cherried joint to Campbell at his left.

Presently, a strange puppet-like grimace overtook Daggett's face. With eyes unblinking and glassed, his mouth thinned and spread from ear to ear. He said: Fucking if wives didn't want some childs I might change my mind. But she wants a family. I'm telling you you don't want a family. Fucking you know what a family is? You want some freedom to—Jesus Christ, do a damn job wherever, whenever, *with* whoever you damn well please. What's the point a wives?

Daggett threw a pinecone into the fire and watched it crackle and explode, and said: I'll tell you. None.

Campbell shook his head and spat into a flame to hear it hiss. You're a godawful sonofabitch, you know that, don't you?

I might be, Daggett said, straightening his back, but you're the one who likes taking orders from everybody all his life.

There's no comparing us, said Campbell.

No one moved. Daggett was slow to respond. How you know that? he asked.

What, in the span of fortunes, was the difference between the two? Added up, Campbell was dozy and incomplete. His boss Daggett was fierce and patient. The two of them were equals in every way. They may have stared at each other like a world of difference had landed them together in this forest, but that was mere pride. Life had subjected them to the same worsening. The shades of their personalities were no more constant than the play of light on the leaves of the trees or the fire in the pit.

//

I believed wrongly that to the alien eye there'd be no comparing Cedric and me. When it came to Minna, his warring tactics were no match for my funny conversations, but she seemed to like him just as much. Every so often Cedric looped one of those hands of his around her waist, or her shoulder. She giggled and squirmed away ... Oh, it wasn't so much that I hated him per *se*. In school we were taught to respect all creatures on earth, even the lower primates. His fingers without any nails truly sickened me, I confess, but so did the expression on the face of a baboon.

So you two aren't ...? Cedric asked me in semi-private, ... bunkmates?

No, I said.

Then, turning to face Minna, Are you ...?, he said with impolite ellipsis, implications galore.

Minna slouched on her heels. Cedric, she said and slapped his bare, reddish pimplish shoulder, I told you, I'm not and we're not.

Cedric open-mouthed a smirk and said to us all in a quiet, spiritual voice: So this is what it sounds like when doves cry.

Ha ha, well who do *you* go out with? Minna asked Cedric. I can't even imagine who'd think so little a themselves.

Me? Cedric asked. I can make a flower bloom in winter, you hear?

I'm feeling allergic, Minna said.

Don't get me wrong, Cedric said. I'm still interested in hooking up for some c*a*sual.

Haw-haw, Minna said.

They began to talk about the man game again, and I, exhausted by jealousy, tuned out.

You know I'm just fucking with you, right? Cedric nudged me.

Yeah, yeah, I said, being nudged. I know that.

Everything in this basement has something to do with the man game, said Ken, on his knees in front of a stack of ledger books. I just don't know what yet. When I started looking I didn't know what I would find. I found some pretty weird shit down here, too. Ken turned to Silas and said: After we found the book with all the drawings of the moves, that's when we sort of realized what was going on.

Silas turned to Cedric and said: Ken wanted to figure out why his grandparents had all this stuff before we threw it away. To keep the important stuff. Turns out—

Cedric turned to Minna and said: It was an intergenerational search for nothing in particular.

Kat, Silas said to me, you should really see this book a drawings upstairs. We use these drawings all the time, hundreds a moves drawn by a pastry chef using a brush pen. We use these drawings in this book to learn new moves. There's so many. Some we can't figure out yet. There are like hundreds a drawings a man game moves, all glued into this yellow leather scrapbook.

Sounds great, I said, instantly regretting it. I'd love to see it, I said.

Where's the book? said Minna, yawning. My heart danced at her boredom. She covered her seductive mouth with her hand. A tear glazed along her eye. We'll go home soon, I thought to myself.

Silas said: It's upstairs. It's definitely a great book for inspiration. We look at it every day. I think after we looked through it the first time we realized right away that we wanted to revive it, didn't we? All these pictures on this old paper.

I wasn't so concerned aboot getting naked as you were, said Ken.

No …

But I was afraid a getting hurt.

Yeah, me too, said Silas. Ha ha ha, I was not comfortable with the—. And I didn't want to get hurt, either.

Why aren't you in the man game? Minna asked Cedric.

Silas said: It's not aboot showing my … It wasn't aboot showing at first. I think if just *I* was, had to, and you guys didn't have to, I would have been comfortable. But it was, ha ha, you have to make the comparison.

You have to make the comparison, agreed Ken. So be it.

Right, but.

Even though like …

Yeah, I mean, said Silas, a course I don't *care* care. What the fuck do I care what you look like? But it was not going to be easy, I knew that when we saw the moves …

Ken patted his fist into his palm, said: We weren't ready to touch.

Uh, no.

Cedric said: I was ready to touch right away.

You were.

Seriously, Cedric said, these guys were *so* lame aboot it.

We were.

Afraid to be buck, afraid to be hurt. I had to slap it out a them.

You're way bigger than either of us, said Silas. It was intimidating.

Yeah, said Cedric in an unfamiliar voice, now you beat me almost every game.

Only recently, said Silas.

Only recently does not bode well for King Cedric.

We'll see.

So you *do* play the man game? Minna said, getting even more excited.

As a way to excuse myself from a conversation I was already not a part of, I began to rub away the ink from an old newspaper's headline. Mummified yellow paper from February 14, 1887's edition of the *Sunday Advertiser:* PREPARE FOR 1500 CHINESE TO LAND ON VANCOUVER THIS MONTH.

ELEVEN

> I felt then, I feel now, that it was not the impropriety of my discovery but its explosiveness that disconcerted him, and that he had, in my absence, joined the ranks of those new men who feel that truth is no longer usable in solving our dilemmas.
>
> – JOHN CHEEVER

February already; and yet, still only February. She kissed her husband goodbye for the umpteenth time, and then, with an actor's confidence, Molly swept up her skirts and promised to be home for dinner.

And how does the thing go? he asked. Is it developing as you'd like it to?

You don't really want to know, do you?

A course I do.

Well, I can't tell you. It's a secret surprise.

A secret surprise?

Yes.

Tell me you won't see the hanging today, Sammy said. At the least, please don't include yourself in that pitiless business.

No, she said, pouring herself and finishing a quick glass of water from a sweating glass jug on the table. No, I won't. That hanging, it's a pity indeed.

But isn't *your* sport … well, is it so violent …?

It's not. It is an imit*a*tion, an extraordinary imitation. You'll see.

Well, at least tell me where you're going.

Why?

For the fun a it.

All right, I'm going to visit John Clough.

Why ever Clough?

A thought.

It pertains?

It does, she said, and he read in the wet flicker of her eyes that she was covering up an emotion she didn't like. Apparently, your foolish boss RH Meddling Alexander has seen to it that the po-lice put the word out that anyone caught playing the man game will be fined and jailed.

First I've heard, said Sammy.

Hm, yes … And now, she said, no one plays. My hope is we find more players.

Po-lice you say?

Nothing to be alarmed …, said Molly, as if his concern over *criminality* was beside the point. Your boss sees the entire world as his factory, she said.

Yes, I've noticed, said Sammy.

Klahowya, my love, she said in the penumbra of earshot.

Klahowya, Chinooky, he called back, straining to see her in the fog before Toronto wheeled him back inside.

Not only days had passed, but most of a year had passed, and he was still unable to use anything below his mouth. It was February for a quadraplegic. And Molly was still as unfettered as a bird.

Anger, aimed mostly at himself, had sweated away to admiration for her. Jealousy over her new friends had faded to a sick fascination. Molly was the rare breed. He was not. It struck him that if he wasn't paralyzed he might still have stayed home today, watched her from the porch as she blew him a last kiss before doe-stepping along the raised sidewalk to meet other men. She had an appointment with other men.

And then Toronto wheeled him back indoors where his life was of no consequence. The day had hardly started and he was already exhausted. His morning cup of coffee had yet to make its powers known. The sun, if it existed at all, was somewhere above an opaque white void.

I got message from post officer aboot your brother, said Toronto.

When did you get a message?

Toronto blinked. Little while ago, he said, when I—.

Fine, then, Sammy said, suddenly very irritated with Toronto's slowness and constant anxiety. Have it your way, you always do. Don't explain anything, just read the damn letter.

Y-Yes. It say: Brother arrive home on deathbed stop your loving father stop.

Well then, what does that mean? What a strange message. Well, he must have contracted something while he was here, but how could he have done that? He couldn't have been in town much longer than the night I saw him or he surely would a tried to come back here. Deathbed, it says. How ominous.

I heard your brother stay at Wood's, Toronto told Sammy.

Sammy didn't know what Wood's was. What do you mean, man? he cried. Please, you drive me mad. Simply mad. If I had use a my arms right now, man, why, I'd—I'd, why, oh. Panting now, out of breath, Sammy continued on just as strenuously. Ah, Toronto, he said. You always do this. You leave me so confused. I try to tell you what I want, what I need to survive this way, and you never listen. You never listen. What do I have to do? Now, you come to me with news, and you say you know something, but how the fuck am I supposed to know what Wood's is?

Wood's.

Wood's. Yes. That's what I heard you say … and then Sammy thought about it a little more, and quickly fell into a deep silence.

Toronto, wisely, said nothing.

Why Wood's?

First all the pieces fell into place, then Sammy had to look at them to make out the picture, and then he had to find what was missing.

Toronto chose this moment to speak. I think brother Erwagen visit Whore No Face.

A whore no— Whatever do you mean?

Very special. What she do, her love take away. No man live. All the Whitemans become a devil after her.

A devil?

Brother a devil now, eh? He not living on earth no more, no, no more.

I see, said Sammy, too stunned, too crestfallen to correct grammar. He said to Toronto: Molly and I never spoke aboot what I should do with Dunbar, since he was bound to tell everyone back in Toronto aboot my infirmity.

Why not tell Erwagen family aboot life?

Well, I don't know that I wanted him to go home and spread his malicious gossip around, and yes, I don't want him to talk to my mother and *fa*ther aboot my—. Dunbar is an unreliable witness. Dunbar is obsessed with Dunbar. Sammy's eyes shut. Not for tears, for his emotions were too conflicted.

Does Molly know aboot Wood's? he asked.

Toronto couldn't resist a shudder. His body convulsed. In his eyes, Sammy saw the guilty look, sheepish, caught, cornered. Molly did know about Wood's. Another secret surprise. The Indian was normally such a safe, quiet presence, and far better at disguising his thoughts than he or Molly. Treelike. Then he felt that the giveaway in body language was beginning to seem less telling. Toronto was still shaking. His shoulders twitched, his hands and legs were trembling.

Is something the matter, Toronto? he said.

Mr. Erwagen, he said, tearfully. I think I am dying again.

//

Hallo, she said, klahowya, wake *up*. Tell me aboot the tunnels.

Clough stiffened in his cot. Tell me aboot the tunnels? What did that mean? He wasn't sure yet if the female voice was real or imagined. He didn't believe there existed a voice of such chocolate consonance. The right side of his brain ignited. The other lobes wouldn't quite. Hello? Clough? The familiar crusty bleb that had formed in the eyeducts made it sting to even think about opening them; plus the daylight was pure violence; luckily the sound was imagined; dream; he was pretty sure of that now.

Wake up. Coming to what remained of his senses, he still hadn't opened his eyes. His first thought was disconnected: Erwagens' house to light the lamp? He dreamed Toronto and Sammy outside on the verandah, watching as he raised his iron javelin to zippo the lamp. Squeaked open the lamp door and buzzed the javelin's flint to light the wick on the little glow worms and shut the glass again. He loved to watch the wick catch and the trembling flower of light grow just wide enough to lead him to the next lamp.

Wake up, *you.*

Seeing *Molly* seated on the edge of his bed ... why, he must be asleep still. He scrubbed his dream-face from eyebrows to beardends and when he pulled his hands away, she was still there and he was definitely awake.

Tell me aboot the tunnels, Molly said.

Tunnels.

With her bosom contained in undulations of pleated cotton and her hair in a Siwash beadworked ribbon, Lord, wasn't Molly pretty, posed at the end of his bed like that while he cowered naked under the blankets.

Well, the tunnels, he said, blinking strenuously. What a you heard aboot tunnels, Ma?

She rolled her eyes, said: I'm not here to scold you. Wake up, man. Be honest with me. I'm not so easily fooled so don't waste your time. Let's talk. Your men play well, considering you probably only had a few weeks with them.

Why, what the—I say, ma'am, what're you on aboot, eh?

I must know if my men, *our* men can use the tunnels.

Our men? Your men? What's this aboot *played well*?

Are you even awake? She looked around the shack, said: Do you need a drink? How can I bring you to your senses? Get out a bed, you foolish man. She started to tug at the bedcovers and he squeaked with indignity, so she stood, crossed her arms, and waited for him to dress. Quit your poor acting, she said. I've no time for you to deny it. Listen, man, our mutual friend RH Alexander is threatened by the man game. Doubtless you know he's convinced Mayor McLean to outlaw it, and this should make you as unhappy as it does me.

Clough put his feet on the ground, and if he got the blood to finish tingling in his left, he'd stand up and slap her. His equilibrium didn't immediately follow his need, and for what seemed far too long the world persisted in feeling horizontal. Gravity was pulling on the left side of his body. He knew that if he stood up he'd fall that way and if he lay back down he'd feel like he was standing upright. So when he did fall he really felt the mistake he'd made. It was an unfortunate side effect of being a drunk. He knew that. He weathered through it, waited it out, on the fence there for a minute or two whether or not to vomit, shit, or die, but when it was over and he was normal again he pulled his pants up and secured his tremendous belt buckle, lit the stove, and cooked a pot of coffee to start the afternoon. Overnight the westerly draft under the door had brushed his evaginated wool socks into a corner where dust and animal fur nested together. He shook out the woollies, and amid a rank odour, tugged them on.

She sat down on the table, faced him, and said: Does Alexander know about the tunnels?

Confidential information, eh, Mrs. Erwagen. Scrubbing his face with his hand, he sighed heavily, releasing a noxious odour, and said: Oh, yeah, he uses them, a course, what a you think? Clough stared into his tin billy at the coffee grinds inside, and using some timber, lit the stove to reheat the water. When it looked ready he poured out two cups full, took a sip off the hot surface, and placed the mug down. He said: We built them precisely for Alexander, the mayor, Oppenheimer ... people on that level, not yours, with all due respect.

She looked at her palms, as if for better answers. Her eyes were devastating, but her bosom was tremendous. She said: They use them at night, then?

No, I wouldn't say that, no, he said, there's a tunnel *right* from Hastings Mill that leads in one direction to an *opium den* and in the other to the coach house in back a Wood's. Matter a fact, I've got the chain gang working right now on the tunnel that'll connect the *court* house to Dupont Street. Fancy that, eh? Sorry to be the one to break it to you, Mrs. Erwagen. Ho-ho, I'd say your highfalutin friends use them day and night.

Who knows aboot them? The po-lice?

Hell, no, that's the whole point.

Constable Miller?

Well, now … I mean, no, I don't think so.

Can our men use the tunnels? Will you give us access?

Our men, why, who do you mean by *that,* our men? Our men for what, eh … for … He scratched and tugged his neck flesh as his defences failed. He said: Listen *here,* Mrs. Erwagen. I don't know how *you* knew that *I* knew, but …

Only observant.

Observant, eh. Why, Jesus, let me tell you, Mrs. Erwagen, I expected you to be *right furious* when you heard Furry & Daggett challenged them that night on Granville.

Not at all.

And how in tarnation did you figure it was *me* coaching them?

I thought to myself, Who else?

He was suspicious. No one said a word? Not Campbell, not Litz?

Why would Litz know?

Well, I mean, for example …

He watched her reset the pleats on her skirt.

Who would be your traitor?

He said: Damn you, lady.

Whyever?

You need to be put in your *place.* You're coming in here talking aboot—and *I'm* the one who named the damned sport, after all. Not you. You didn't even name it. I was the first person to call it the man game.

You? I hardly think so.

Call me a liar? Was it you who named it?

No. But—

At the game behind Calabi & Yau's Bakeshoppe.

I heard a vagabond, a sailor, never Clough.

You need to be put in your *place.*

Put in my place, she said, calmly. I am in my place. And you are in your place. Why be furious? These are your motives. Fine. Kumtuks. But you must a known that we've been waiting for you. All along I wanted more teams. Litz and Pisk have been waiting. I waited patiently. I was surprised actually, to see you out so soon. I thought it would take longer to convince Furry & Daggett.

So soon—

When you practise for only two or three weeks, it was going to be difficult to ever win, but I'm so glad you tried. How is Meier? His cuts sounded quite awful.

What a you think you are, eh? This little game of yours is not right for men.

And thank you for asking aboot Pisk, hm, she said. He's *dy*ing, by the way. So you might never get your revenge. Not *my* game, I should add. Litz and Pisk are not my marionettes, if that's what you believe. I don't control them and I doubt you have much control over Furry and Daggett. Don't exaggerate my role. We want competition.

Well, you make it sound fine *now,* but I don't like your influence. I got to say it. This talk a competition, eh. In all honesty, Mrs. Erwagen, I never trusted a gypsy.

I'm not a gypsy.

Nevertheless, alls I meant to do was teach you a lesson. That's it. That's where I saw eye to eye with Furry and Daggett. I never told what I knew. I appealed to their vengeful, murderous nature. I'm not involved in—. It didn't go according to plan. But a *wife* meddling in the affairs a men. Why, you're just liable to get yourself hurt. Why don't—, now, wait a minute, did Litz and Pisk know aboot us, too? And from who? Who'd you hear from, eh?

I taught them from the very first day to attract competitors. It's been months. We beat you. I hope your men will be more prepared next time.

His hand started to shake. For some reason, she seemed downright pleased. What's so funny? he said. Mrs. Erwagen, he said, I don't know who you are, but Vancouver is no place for a lady a your calibre. Say to yourself, I'm not going to *med*dle no more, I'm going to—what I mean is stick to your other friends, and there'll be no trouble.

She played with her full tousled locks of black hair, then broke into a full smile that showed her top teeth. Set him back in his chair with that smile. Hair dolloped on the left of her face like that, a single ear poking out. What a grand spanking smile. He was dizzy from love's sudden apnea.

I don't know ..., he said. If the mayor outlawed the man game ..., he was losing her smile with every word. He said: My guys want to keep playing. But I'm not going to make them break the law.

I took you for another kind a man, she said.

Why, what's that supposed to mean?

She lowered those eyelashes, said: That's fine. If you prefer to quit after such a humiliating loss, that's your business. I just assumed your pride would insist you receive a rematch. That's what it's all aboot, isn't it? Especially with that contentious point against your man, what was his name? Clampon?

*Cam*pbell.

I didn't come here to talk aboot cowardice, she said. I didn't expect to. I asked you a simple question, Clough.

What the fu—? What's so special that you got to know aboot the tunnels? Figure it out for yourself if you're so keen.

For my safety, for the safety a my invalid husband, for the safety a our men who play an illegal sport. The tunnels, she said. I ask you a favour. I owe you and I promise I will repay you plenty. Allow *our* men to use the tunnels. With the po-lice, it's the only way.

Was he going to let this lady push him around just because he decided moments ago he loved her? He didn't think so, but maybe he would, maybe what he needed was a push. His confusion was so intense he felt it in his hair. He put his fist down on the table, said: I've heard enough. No way I'm taking orders from a—, he bit his tongue. Protecting her from his urge to strike her left him exhausted. He contemplated his lap. He didn't want to raise his eyes. Tears risked flying out.

Ma—, he said.

Darling, Clough, she whispered. You silly fool. She petted his single hand with her soft fingers. Among all the methods of torture in the books of God, none matched the touch of a lady's hands on the hand of a one-handed man. Her feminine side on the craggy knuckles of his fist was more than his soul could bear. At last a bosom to accept all his secrets.

I'll get you maps, he said.

No one must know aboot our meeting, said Molly in such a way as to suggest hot intimacy, and she added: Needless to say, I want to remain anonymous for as long as possible. Please ask any a your acquaintances who know my identity to keep my participation in the man game a secret. For my dear husband's sake. He knows nothing a what I do, how I occupy my time while he's at work.

Nothing? said Clough.

Nothing at all.

Poor daft man, said Clough aloud.

A single deception to save a man's soul.

Clough stared at her until he felt ready to pass out. He let go of her hand, and like a bird it immediately returned to her, and he rubbed his entire face over once, scratching long and hard at the beard. When I saw the game, I felt a kind a passion and fury that nothing has stirred in me since my boyhood. I'd a torn my clothes off right then and there for you. I admit. I wanted to play.

//

He was alone again in his one-room house. No time to lose. Stepping outside, he was pleased to see the sky was starting to clear. Blue sky, sun casting actual shadows over the earth. Shadows of clouds. Italicized shadows of a picket fence.

Came across a Chinaman sitting knees up, nothing but bone and rag with ten dirty claws outspread in a plea of mercy, and the tiny teeth of the dispossessed. His eyes lay somewhere far back in his skull, his lips were minuscule, and his hair was clumpy on his blue scalp.

Coolie life, eh? said Clough.

The Chinaman agreed for the sake of small change.

He walked through lumpy muskeg, over skunk cabbage, weather-whitened elk antlers, and ancient middens, and over the dappled paws of ferns circling the trunks of massive oaks and cypresses. Absolutely no sunlight poked through the forest canopy. The air was cold and humid and fresh and hell on his joints, the ghost elbow included. The course he stuck to was a muddy log road carved by ox-handlers who used it to haul great logs from English Bay to Hastings Mill. They called it Granville Street. It wasn't much. No road signs, no stop-lights, no sidewalks, no sun for a kind of compass, Granville Street might be the future centre of Vancouver, but Clough thought it was bunk. He liked the forest. He liked the privacy of the forest. He liked the loose morals of the forest. The forest was made for men. The forest was a drunk like him. The forest lost track of itself.

He watched his step around a thicket of rusted bent-out nails. Granville Street saw curiously high foot traffic that afternoon. With a bit of work Clough acquired rolling paper, weed, and as sure as smoke leads to fire, there in front of him were Terry Berry and his friend Vicars, who kindly supplied the light Clough needed to share some of his weed.

Terry Berry mentioned how they saw Furry & Daggett's men that night a month ago, and what Vicars wanted to know was how did they ever learn to play the man game. Clough only shrugged, and Vicars wondered aloud how a shrivelled baby prick like Campbell ever thought he could play. Clough wasn't going to apologize for the loss because he wasn't yet sure if he wanted to reveal he was coaching them. So he gave these two dudes the old rigamarole and tried to say goodbye.

Vicars wouldn't give back the burning weed, and stood beside him and smoked. Said Vicars to Clough: Did you see this poster? Says here the mugger is wanted for a fifty-dollar reward.

So you know who it is?

Me, nah.

Neither did Clough, but he said: What a you want to bet me I catch him?

Bet you, hell, I *should* bet against you, Vicars said, I might get some better luck.

Then Terry Berry changed the subject. What he really wanted to know was why Campbell lost. I had a *fee*ling about those guys, but no.

Clough didn't alter the rigamarole one bit. The guy kept asking questions. You think Meier's got talent? I sure would a loved to see Daggett versus Pisk, eh, when you think that might happen, 'cause, boy, that was some flogging those guys' asses got, eh, ha ha ha, but seriously, you think Daggett or Furry could a won against Litz or Pisk?

After Vicars finally passed, Clough snuffed out the worthless butt and started walking, wondering aloud where everyone was going. Paying closer attention, he heard a faraway thunderous clamour of Indian voices.

Hey, he called out to a group of Westminster ladies in their Sunday finery. Hey you, he said, who's all that jabbering and kykying, eh? With their tartan bows on their straw hats, milk-fed bosoms, petticoats, and skirts upon skirts. What's the shindy? Where's everybody going?

They snooted their noses at him.

He didn't walk more than seventy paces when he spotted the ruckus. It was the execution. Clough pushed through the crowd watching for more people to avoid. Hundreds of Salish Indians from the nearby reserves were here to plead for the man's life. Besides them, most of the audience was a race of liver-spotted bulldog-jowled lady from New Westminster's Christian Temperance Union here to protest the wrongful execution. Vancouver, as they shrieked, was in a spiritual crisis. Clough kept his distance. He watched from the back of the crowd.

An Indian man was on the wood stage with a rope around his neck. His face would be covered soon. His eyes were getting their final sights. Perhaps these would be his final memories, if God allowed for him to replay even the scene of his own death in the final second. Or are there scenes from life that one represses to the end, and is the death scene one of them? The Indian did not appear reconciled with fate. There was hope in his legs. He said goodbye to his family over and over. The audience was in pain. The women from New Westminster berated the po-lice with King James. If the decision to repeal the execution came at the final hour, the Indian's legs were ready. No one wanted to blink, fearing the end of seeing. The Indian's young wife, stricken in the arms of her relatives, was enough love to imagine he might slip through the noose.

His executioner arrived. The Christians shrieked at him to spare the Indian's life and the po-lice told the ladies to calm down. The po-lice were armed with nightsticks to use only if an outburst needed to be quelled. But no one wanted to a quell a mother. They shrieked until their faces were red and spittled.

Polite phrases, like The Indian's trial is hardly fair, were screamed at the top of their lungs.

Calm down, lady.

Why, it was only a month ago he was caught, shrieked one lady with a fur collar.

A judge denied him life and that's that. Easy, ma'am, easy.

They were all from New Westminster. Vancouver had no ladies this genteel.

His wife is r*a*ped, cried an Indian. Now she has no one. Wa, wa.

Stand back, ma'ams.

Give them a few more hours with their son and father and blood. To make amends and say goodbye.

Don't shriek in my ear, ma'am.

Oh, please, please, po-lice, do not kill Indian for crime a passion. Think a wife and children.

Okay, granny squaw, that's enough out a you.

Think a wife pain. After all she endure, take her husband, too, no.

What I say aboot—, ma'ams. He brandished the nightstick.

Wa, wa. The Indians cried in their language.

It was beyond the po-lice or his executioner to show mercy. By law, the Indian was destined to be hanged.

His executioner was as meek as a golem. Miguel Calderón, the whisky seller, who a month ago had been ordered to perform the act in retribution for having sold this very man the drink that had put him over the edge.

Calderón pulled the eyeholes down so that he could see through his hood to watch his step as he crossed the stage. Every board creaked underfoot. He paused to collect the convicted man's hood off its bench. The po-lice looked at him without sympathy—of the two convicts here tonight, thought Calderón, I should not be the one let off the hook. For his mistakes he too deserved a stricter, more lasting punishment than an iron vacation or a pittance fine. In the book of what's right and what's wrong, if the Indian on stage today was supposed to be hanged, then it was Calderón who deserved the grim honour of setting it so. The hinged floor where the Indian waited was an uncompromising pedestal. They heard each other breathing hard. He brought the hood up and over the Indian's head and trembled fiercely when he covered the Indian's face. Feeling the Indian's sweat on his knuckles overwhelmed Calderón with terror.

Now they were truly the same. Calderón was shocked to see the Indian in the hood, breathing, the hood sucking in and out around his mouth. His breath's steam in the cold air went aloft for the heavens. Calderón was about to say a word. But what word? No, it was over. There were no words. It was too late for words. The hood was on and the noose was secure. He had done this, tightened the noose around the Indian's neck, without consciously seeing to it. He realized now: the hood—the executioner's hood—was an alibi before God, and with less effort than opening a door, he took the Indian man's life out his neck.

There it was, tied high above the crowd. A single flayed actor, a dangling corpse, another dead Indian.

It's too late for crocodile tears, ladies, Clough said as he walked away. You failed, the Indian is dead.

You terrible boor. How can you—

There's nothing left to do. That's what a hanging does for your mood, eh. As Clough sat on a log and nursed a bottle of cloudy hair tonic, he realized he was already committed to the man game.

//

It was late in the morning when the lumberjack Bud Hoss got himself out of the bush and into Vancouver. It had been a month since he'd last been seen or heard of, not since that fateful game back in January when Pisk had lost all sense. With nothing for him to do as bookie, he, along with others like Calabi, had returned, somewhat reluctantly, to the life he'd led before the man game was invented. Hoss did a few odd jobs. He loitered around town. He began to feel a loneliness sit on him, heavy as it was, like a burden. He was once again a free man, tied to no one, no job, no time. Felt good to be him.

Hoss continued on, a big man swaggering on his buckles and fluffy young moustache. He made his way to the East End, a stumpy neighbourhood where pioneering families of all race and creed mixed with dormitories, hostelries, bordellos, and drug and gambling dens. Hoss knew his way around. He skipped over a red picket fence and followed a creek down Union Street. At the corner he took off his hat, then stepped into a Methodist boarding house and dropped his sack on the first cot they had available.

I been living in the cold for weeks, he told the widow of the house, and you touch my skin it might have a bit a warmth to it, but my bones are ice. Alls I need's a bit a time by the stove, maybe a cup a coffee if you got it, and a blanket that covers my neck same time as it covers my toes.

Well, she said, then I can do you. There's no women allowed and that's final. I'm sure you know better than to do that. I catch you in your room with a bottle a anything and you're out. I don't care if you say it's cider. That's the rules. There's no smoking in the rooms neither and I catch you you're out. You smoke on the verandah if you have to. Breakfast's at seven A.M. so you missed it, sorry ... but regularly we got back bacon, strip bacon, porridge, griddlecakes, syrup, butter, fried potatoes, boiled eggs, and fresh bread, jams and compotes, and that's included in your quarter a night, so you can't complain to the boys at the bar I sent you out in the day with an empty stomach, eh? But you're all oot a here by eight-thirty A.M. so I can change them linens and do up the cleaning. Takes a woman my age quite a *while* just to do the back and forth along the clothesline unpinning and pinning clothes, eh?

I hear you.

We open back up at five and there's a dinner at six. That's a nickel extra. Understood? God bless you, son, I hope you'll avoid the bootleggers and cat houses and keep to yourself. Be strong, young man.

Yes ma'am.

Having unencumbered himself, Bud Hoss was back on the streets, casual strut amidst intermittent rain. The ruffled mud was moistly glinting. There were ponds of ice-cold water. He had to watch his step. Banana slugs sopped along the boardwalk leaving behind a webby trail of ick. Seeing frost on the lowest shakes of the homes gave him a shiver to the backs of his ears. Even the air was icy wet. The clouds around the sky passed in thin perspirate bands.

A leafless cherry tree quivered with sparrows. Walking past he startled them into the sky.

If he thought about it, he probably could've predicted he'd start a fight today. As he walked through town he shook hands with friends, including Moe Dee.

How the fuck are ya, eh?

Doing fine, thank you.

Heard any news aboot the man game?

Nothing, said Hoss.

On Alexander Street he ran into two bohunks he knew from his early days shimmying spars, one named Terry Berry, the other Vicars. They were coming out of Sprigmans & Co., specializing in flour, feed, hay, grain, and poultry food, the relatively new competitor to Red & Rosy's. Vicars had on a new black hat and he'd got his face cleaned since he last saw him. Vicars, who always had to keep busy doing something, sat down on a stack of firewood next to the store and rolled up more weed and the three of them started to smoke it. Taking the cigar from his friend's fingers and puffing on it; coughing, he said: Hully gee, that's weed.

That's church service and hell's delight all rolled into one, said Terry Berry.

Hoss took another long pull, coughed out the words: Just finished a clearing in the forests north of Squamish. Ever since they outlawed it I been bucking and slinging, chuting logs down to the bay where a tug dragged them back south to Hastings Mill, eh. Got back to town and hooked up with this ol' feller living way the fuck south a Cougar Canyon. I'm talking the old logging chutes kind a area. Chutes and flumes. Hell, I worked for Furry & Daggett, but there's no way I'd work for them now that I got a taste for freelance.

Uh-huh, hey pass that here, said Terry Berry, watching Hoss smoke the thing down, taking a puff at every pause in his story.

And I worked for them canneries for a week. Easy work it was *not*. Look at my hands, they're twice regular size.

And salmon pink, said Vicars, whistling.

Pass that damn timber.

Hoss, marvelling at his big hands, said: Heard anything aboot the man game?

Nah, said Vicars. We were just talking to Clough this morning before the lynching and—

The what?

Same ol' story aboot manslaughtering. Some Whiteman raped this Indian's squaw wife. So the Indian killed the Whiteman and the court killed the Indian.

Damn, that was this morning?

Why are you babysitting? said Terry Berry with his fingers out to the weed in Hoss's hand. Pass it along.

Hoss listened, casually smoking as Vicars said: Talked to Clough this morning anyway, trying to get something out a him if he knows anything.

Aboot what? said Hoss.

Well, if the po-lice are going to lock up anybody who plays or not, eh. And he was acting pretty cagey, eh?

Yeah, said Terry Berry. He would not conversate on the topic.

Why wouldn't he? said Hoss. He's usually the first to talk shit and act up when it comes to the man game.

I just want you to pass it along. You been hanging on to that bitch for damn near a quarter hour.

Do you think it's the law that's got to him? Hoss wanted to know.

Yeah, that's what I'm trying to say, Terry Berry said. You're fucking the rotation, man, pass that weed.

Said Vicars: How many games has Clough seen?

You're holding up the *train,* Terry Berry said angrily. Don't derail that lumber.

Quit jawing on, man, said Hoss. Well, I don't know. Clough seen a lot a games. At least since the first time I was bookie. You boys missed a lot a good early games, that's got to hurt. Amazing games between Litz and Pisk. Clough? I suspect he's been to all but one or two. I been to them all. I saw every game so far. If Clough is taking the side a the po-lice in this issue … the man game, naw, I can't see it. Clough's like me, he sees what Litz and Pisk are trying to do and he wants to support that because a his love for his home. So I don't think Clough's taking the side a the po-lice on this issue, the man game.

I can smell it in the air, but where the hell's it coming from?

Then what's he doing? said Vicars.

Look at him with the weed in his hand. The rules are still the same when it's yours as when it's mine, Hoss. Don't make me put my foot in your ass knee deep.

All right, all right, calm the fuck down, Hoss said. He finally passed it to Terry Berry. I just didn't want to get *mine* behind *Vicars* is all.

Look at this. You smoked half the spar. I'm sorry, but I'm gonna have to revoke your privileges.

Whatever, that's a fine klahowya, eh. Thanks for fuck all, TB. What's Clough doing? He's not telling you because you're a couple a bohunks is why. Jesus Christ, you seen one man game and you think you even know what the fuck you're talking aboot?

Hoss bid adieu and walked on to Westminster Street, turned and went down the middle of Hastings. He could see all the way to Coal Harbour and across to the squatters' shacks on the government land soon to be Stanley Park. If he knew to look, John Clough's cabin was still visible in the clouding light. Innocent of secret plans between coaches concerning the fate of the game he loved most, he walked on. He was careful down the plank road. Sometimes the posts underneath shifted, the planks leaping and twisting or pinching together and squirting up mud when you stepped on them. Save for a trio of scarred-faced Indians in second-hand suits and porkpie hats, Bud Hoss didn't see anyone till he got to the kerosene lanterns on Water, where a horse and cabriolet buggy rattled by with the merry laughter of a gentleman and a lady inside.

After the dray passed he saw Campbell, that little punk-stick who worked for Furry & Daggett, leaning against a wall for a piss.

Campbell looked Hoss over and gave him what for. Fuck you, he said. 'The fuck you think you're looking at? He shivered involuntarily and his piss stream dashed in all directions. He said: I never liked you when you worked for Furry & Daggett anyhow. Waste a everybody's goddamn time. Ask me, I'm glad they sacked you.

Go fuck yourself. I never got sacked. I quit.

Bullshit.

Forget it, said Hoss. What's news in town?

Campbell shook off and buttoned up. He said: You hear aboot the lynching?

Yeah, I already heard that. So what?

Well, that's news, if you're interested in seeing another Indian get strung by the neck so tight the eyes fell out a their sockets ...

Jesus, said Hoss. Well, that's nowhere near close to what I meant when I said news.

Jesus yourself, said Campbell, gripping Hoss's collar in his wet hands, is all you think aboot your own affairs? Don't care one pity for a—this Indian, man, I witnessed it all—

Ah, forget it then, said Hoss, and brushed Campbell off for being a nuisance.

Tell you one thing. Furry & Daggett are serious. Seeing what they do in practices these days?

Practices? said Hoss. You all are practising?

Listen, eh, we don't *log* no more, we don't cut timber. Alls we do is practise the man game every day. That's the fucking news, Hoss-boy. Furry & Daggett are serious aboot the man game. We're the men who're going to run those turds out a town once and for all.

That's what I call *bull*shit, said Hoss. How'd you expect to do that?

Hell, I heard up until they outlawed it, Litz and Pisk got at least three dollars a day they played. *Ea*ch. That's what I was told. Because a the Asiatics who bet so much—talk aboot Jesus fuck, that's good chickamin. I could stretch out with that kind a income.

Hoss did a mental tally. Yeah, three sounds aboot right. And how do you expect to make that much?

Pisk's dead, said Campbell, you heard that news already?

Don't believe that.

You seen him?

No, but—, well, besides, fucking Mayor McLean outlawed it like you said, so what's the difference.

Ah, fuck that. That's nothing. Listen, Campbell said. We take over the man game. That's easy. Me and the others with Furry and Daggett. Not just Meier and Smith and Boyd and myself, but everybody. It's time to lay down the axes and make some chickamin the easy way. Look now, Campbell said and jabbed Hoss's chest with a pointed finger, I give it to you, you're strong for a fat kid. You interested?

With you, C*a*mpbell?

Sure, that's right. Who else?

Where's Litz and Pisk if you got all these takeover plans? It's their game.

Hell, no one's seen them since they took off from that game. For alls we know Pisk's dead and Litz is gone for good.

No way, said Hoss, unable to conceal his distress. His fists and jaw impulsively clenched.

Well …

So you think the man game's been left up to you ball-smackers, is that it?

Unbeliever. You're just another poltroon, aren't you?

Who the fuck is poltroon?

If you aren't yellow, then you must be tighter with Litz and Pisk than I thought, eh?

Litz and Pisk? said Hoss. You aren't worth one tick on my ass compared to them. Campbell, I wouldn't team up with you if you were the only man in town with legs.

Campbell stepped back. Why, you still walk ass-first, don't you? I know you, Hoss. You're nothing special. You're just some starving kid from a starving farm squat in the middle a starving Saskatchewan. You're nothing if not a pain in the fucking ass. What a you want from life, Hoss?

I know one thing I don't want is some boss belt-whipping me because I want to get to bed instead a listen to him jaw on.

Never mind, eh. Forget I asked. Better yet, get yourself out a my sight, you proud piece a shit.

Yeah, said Hoss, and fuck you back. I never wanted to work with all you anyhow. All your mothers are guttersnipe whoores, and none a you know dick aboot the man game.

Arrr, Campbell ran back at him with his fists raised, but Hoss didn't budge. Sure enough, he stopped short of taking Hoss down. Campbell growled, I should split your face open.

I'd as soon kill you, said Hoss, stepping straight up to Campbell's face, grizzle to grizzle.

You're some fat fuck, aren't you? said Campbell. Where's your stones?

Send word you want a man game, and I'll see you there.

Is that so, eh? You better learn up fast then in the next fucking blink, so I can show you what's what. Klahowya, Campbell said, already across the street at this point. That was enough of that. Campbell washed his hands of Hoss and walked away down the frosted mud road.

Whatever, Hoss said, watching him go. He looked at the lights, garlands, and verandahs of the saloons within a stone's throw. The Stag & Pheasant was an establishment with a real piano player. In the evening they required you wear a collar and Hoss didn't have one. To the left, the clamour of voices from inside the Tremont Saloon meant there'd soon be a fight. He preferred to start his own. Although it might mean running into Campbell or others from Furry & Daggett's crew, he could think of nowhere else to go but the Sunnyside.

Raising his head for a moment from the rutted trail, he studied the mountains in the distance, rising above the north shore of Burrard Inlet. Caped in woollen fog cover, they were even-tempered, aristocratic, and loyal; strengths Hoss felt he lacked. These mountains, with their staggering composure, were more like royalty to him than any faraway monarch on a stool. This world was the world of mountains; they had seen generations of Indians live and die here, and now this. The salt off the inlet and the rich sturdy smell of cedar filled Hoss's lungs, and his heart, with ghosts. The ghosts of the long dead, whose ungathered chains and hanging skirts and tattered, feathered wings were what keep them tangled up in the branches of the trees. The forest, the mountain's big beard—the biggest, creature-infested beard of them all—bristled with millions of trees. Vancouver had a *living* smell.

He took the stairs two at a time and pushed open the door to the Sunnyside, where the glory days of wild drinking were still alive. The player piano in the corner *rink-a-dinked* a slow instrumental bootlegged from Ireland and turned American classic. He went up to the counter beside a bruised girl he recognized from Wood's, greeted Joe Fortes, bought him a round, and turned to face the room, see who was here.

Not you all again, said Hoss aloud to the crowd in the bar. You're still here.

Of all the people, the first he picked out was RD Pitt, that horseless cowboy. There was Moe Dee again there near the back, well ahead of the rest in his drunken stupor with five empty shots in front of him, but Hoss barely noticed him or anyone except that bastard cowboy RD Pitt, troublemaker of a different sort altogether.

Pitt was sitting at a table nearby with his arm around a green-stained bronze bust of the Queen. He rested his elbow on her neck. Beside him were the usual men he was seen with, the group who were organizing a Knights of Labour union in town with Pitt's aid. In front of him on the table was a big stack of leaflets.

What's all that? said Hoss, pointing affectedly, showing off how uninterested he was in what Pitt did with his time.

Pitt turned to Hoss and said quite loudly: Alls I want for this city is some decent, honest ways for a Whiteman to make a living.

Hoss immediately turned around to face the bar, and Fortes, and ignore Pitt completely. The woman beside him seemed to find his style charming, and took a step towards him in a way that suggested even more steps had been taken.

And with his nose squashed to the side of his face, as it always was, RD Pitt nodded and nodded, beckoning in the ugliest, chin-first of ways to this prostitute at the counter next to Hoss, and then loudly whispered: The Wh*ore* Without A F*ace*.

Hoss winced, then looked at her for her reaction. She raised a thigh and jammed the heel of her shoe in a barstool rung, swished open the wide slit of her skirt, took a cigarette out of her garter and put it to her pale blue mouth, lighting it off the match Hoss provided.

You hear me? said Pitt.

I heard you well enough, she said. She adjusted her tongue, singled out a curl of tobacco between her long yellowing fingernails, and flicked it away. She said: I've known men like you. Lame on your feet and worser in bed.

Give me some a that, Pitt said, taking a swipe at her rump. Hand it here, you selfish bitch.

Scared to even speak aboot her, or her name, said the woman, swigging her snifter.

What aboot it? said Pitt. That *crea*ture you hide up in there? You think I'd fuck her?

I *know* you, she said, turning her backside to him, pointing and swaying her silken fanny at him. You all do, shifting her weight from one cheek to the other and waving a fingernail at the men. You all want to crawl up her walls. Because she sweetest you ever get.

You spend all your time with your stomach to the sky, you lost contact with the world, said Pitt. I'd no more fuck a mollusk.

The whore dabbed her finger into her beer and sucked it off, and said: I know that's plenty a room for you, baby boy.

RD Pitt said: Bitch, I pack a horse dick.

That's funny, said Hoss, dabbing his eye now, *plenty* a room in there, that's right.

Not a word from you, said Pitt to Hoss, pointing at the door. Either get right or get left.

Why don't you try lefting *this*, Hoss said, grabbing himself.

You fat peon, said Pitt.

Hoss patted the loop on his belt where his handaxe would normally be, said: I'm sick a hearing your voice.

Pitt stood up, honking back his chair.

The whore said: Boys, boys, don't waste all your *ener*gies.

You crazy mink, said Pitt, touching himself. Come sit your mouth on my lap, eh?

How can you talk like that? Where's your mind? You a Christian or a heathen? cried Hoss.

Pitt pounded his fist on his table. I'm Christian, he screamed.

Look at this, said Bud Hoss, hoisting himself to a standing position. It's not even the PM and already you got my scrotum up. I'm sick a coming in here to listen as you jaw on forever aboot one thing or another. If it's not your hated Chinee it's your sore loins. You aboot as useful to me as a wood tick.

Pitt mustered all his fury and leaped from his seat, reached for Hoss, and a table fell on its side. Pitt stumbled, his fists swinging full simian. Bud Hoss looked ready to pounce. Fortes tossed his towel over his shoulder and slammed a closed fist on the counter so hard that the chandelier wobbled its candles. He bellowed: That's enough out a both a you.

Pitt turned and said to Fortes: Nobody asked you.

Fortes started around the counter.

Hoss said: Step outside and settle this like a man, Pitt, or's a cowboy afraid to fuck with something besides a heifer?

They tumbled out the doors onto the street and everyone inside followed, including Fortes, a small crowd forming around Hoss and Pitt on the road.

Huuorking a loogie in one direction, Pitt spun his hat to the other side where it rolled to a stop at the feet of Moe Dee. He rolled up his sleeves, adjusted his belt, wiped his hair out of his eyes, and put up his fists. He waved his fists in the air. He stood like that for a moment waiting for Hoss to get ready; then, reluctantly, he lowered his fists to his sides and straightened his posture, looking at Hoss with disdain.

'The fuck are you doing?

'The fuck does it look like I'm doing?

Hoss was undressing. His hat was on a nest of shirts, denims, and woollies. He tried not to seem troubled by the cold mud on his bare feet and the jagged little stones he endured. His body was pale and undefined like heavy dough. Nutsack the only tight skin on his body. His giant pink fists were unnerving on this soft ball of a man. He was young enough to be grinning, but with a seriousness, to show he wasn't fazed by his own nakedness, which he was. All eyes were on him, sussing up his ability. Based on what, mind you, he thought. The gut's deceiving, Hoss knew. He was a force to be reckoned with.

If you think I'm going to play the man game you got another thing coming.

You better meet me at the circle and shake my hand, Hoss said, pointing to the middle of the ring. He appealed to the informal circle of men for support. Come on, men. Let's hear it for the man game. I knew you were a poltroon, Hoss said.

A what?

A *coward*, you illiterate fuck, said Hoss.

No. Sorry, Bud. You can't threaten me. I try to get a punch in now you're going to make a fool a me, forget it. I know how this works. I seen the man game.

Then play.

C'mon, whined Pitt, loosening his boxer stance.

No way.

C'mon.

Fuck you.

Moe Dee putted a clod of dirt.

Whatever argument Hoss pressed on him, Pitt held his ground. As the conversation dragged on the other men grew impatient and Hoss felt the blood in his head start to burn the rims of his ears. Whenever he thought Pitt failed to give him his complete attention, he'd lunge to push him in the chest or slap him across the face. RD Pitt took the shoves without losing his balance. He dodged the slaps and didn't fight back, and meanwhile remained stubbornly clothed. When he had a chance he even went over to the boardwalk and picked up his hat. The nerve on this guy. He frisked the bowl of his hat, and no matter what kind of threat or insult Hoss shot at him, Pitt dusted it off.

The way things were going, Hoss was a naked man in the middle of the street with people around him. It wasn't even dark out. Luckily people weren't drunk enough to make a scene. It was quiet for the birds. The light was bright enough through the clouds to make Hoss feel like people could see him too well. The flab of his hairless arms. There were sore pimple clusters on each of his shoulder blades and they never went away. Upper lip notwithstanding, he was a young man still.

I said I'm not going to fight you, Pitt said. I don't like games.

Why're *you* whining? I'm the one in the buck. Get stripped or I'll do it for you.

Listen, kid, Pitt said, take wisdom from the wise: not everyone who rides a horse is a jockey.

Hoss lunged chest-first and bellowed: Let's fucking showtime.

Pitt stepped back to avoid getting physical. The crowd didn't approve of Pitt's cowardice, to the point of booing.

A guy in spectacles said: Let's see you play, and Pitt snapped at him, almost hit the guy upside the face.

Who the fuck asked you? Pitt said. Holding his temples, the guy cowered away, stumbling on a chicken neck as he went.

And then Hoss spotted Mrs. Erwagen in the middle distance. Molly. She was standing at a half turn, just past the door to GG Allin's Boots & Saddles. Her skin was shaded, her head was at rest on the stalk of her parasol.

Oh no, Hoss mouthed and blushed tip to toe.

Pitt checked to see what—and quickly, automatically pulled off his hat again and held it over his heart.

The rest of the crowd of derelicts turned to look, and repeated Pitt's gesture one after the other, in guileless deference to the finest lady ever known. In his cowboy way he apologized, trying to find the words to express what he thought might elevate him from the situation in which he was a central figure.

Please continue, she said, causing jaws to drop.

W-what? said Pitt.

Hoss, blushing from wrinkled scalp to toenails, was closer to her than he knew. His nudity mortified him, but little did he know what she really saw.

The delicate expression on her face; she was the kind of lady you toiled for. Her figure in profile was as beautifully curved as the *f*-hole on a violin. The box hat atop her head was aglow with a yellow flower. Beneath her pleated skirt and fur-trimmed coat the sharp tips of her leather boots were as sensual as entire legs. There's no way any man would guess that such a dainty creature made of silk and honey and mothers was responsible for the man game. With her kid gloves whiter than snow on her almond arms, the fragile plumskin of her lips, the glimmering jade visculent green eyes, the slipperiness of her licorice hair, she looked to be the nourishing opposite of the man game. But she was the man game. And if she was its invisible centre, its boiling lava, he was its crust.

Those fresh green pools. She looked Hoss straight in the eye. Later, he would realize his good fortune. At the moment, his shame was thorough. She was an impossible ideal and he was gutter reality, an ineligible bachelor living in a shack. She was a pearl and he was a geoduck, a formless slime to her perfection.

He was no more than a young Canadian boy. He didn't know what else to say to her so he apologized too. I'm sorry, he said. I'm sorry.

//

The young Chinaman translator said to his host Mr. Erwagen: The doctor, he want to—, then paused at his loss for the English, used the Chinook word: three *bath paseesie,* please?

Sammy immediately saw to it that a Chinaman servant retrieve some towels from the closet. He brought them back and spread them out over the sofa as the doctor ordered. This wasn't precisely what he expected the towels were for, but it was too late for correction; with the language barrier and the urgency of the call, the deed was done, and if Toronto ruined the sofa, it was beneath him to fret. Whereas if it was his brother Dunbar, the sofa might come first. Priorities. The doctor swept his finger across the room for Toronto to follow. It was an all-meaning finger. It drew a picture of Toronto removing his dungarees leg by leg and lying on the sofa, stomach down. As Toronto reluctantly began the doctor studied his kit, where all variety of glass phials clinked in their felted leather holsters. Each of their corks was graced with a Chinese character that named what was inside, from bear this, to tiger that: the doctor was well stocked in the remedies of the day. Toronto looked to Sammy for reassurance, and Sammy duly blinked. To see Toronto shaking and sweating even as he unhooked his suspenders and rumpled down his pants and undergarments to the floor was not the kind of equity Sammy had in mind. Money was enough. He was sad to see the daily chore of their friendship reversed, with poor ailing Toronto the one ashamed.

Oh, you *are* sick, said Sammy, dry-mouthed when he saw the problem.

Toronto was a mess.

Why he no see Whiteman doctor? asked the translator as per the herbalist, who muttered in timpani as he administered.

I am bad luck to Whitemans, said Toronto feebly. As the translator explained, the doctor cocked an eye at Sammy. Bad luck to Whitemans. He looked Sammy up and down with a queer expression. It was malice or annoyance that flexed the doctor's lips just so. His hands were on the bloody danglers.

Why he no see Salish doctor?

Toronto didn't answer right away. To Salish people I am dead. I am ghost. They will take no care a me now. Ghost, bad luck.

Just as the translator spoke, Sammy interrupted, said: The Indians, your *fa*mily, they won't help you even in a serious case such as this?

No, said Toronto. Sammy knew the story, and it was not one Toronto liked to share. The doctor, for helping him, was going to hear it. Three year ago I went very sick, said Toronto. In sick days I went into deep state a sweat. Then, I was convert to Jesus Christ. For outside world, I look as dead. Up the cedars near Snauq village, my family make a burial. I lay for many days up there. Many blankets, much respect for my family. I was strong boy at potlatch. Many blankets still owed to me. I remember trees blow to and fro. One day I wake from dead. Very weak. I open blankets. Put me in high up tree. Great cedar. I know I am alive. I know what happen to me. But I hope Snauq believe me. Return to Snauq, families screamed and afraid a me, they ran. And elders came out with gun and yell. I am ghost. I am never touching on Snauq ground again. They scared a me till I die again. Never speak to me or help me. I am a ghost to my own peoples. Wa!

The translator's face sank through the holes in his skull. The cold room felt a long pause while this superstitious man recuperated his professional skin. After a glass of water, he told the doctor what the Indian said.

Ba, said the Chinaman herbalist, who got down to work. While the translator watched, the doctor removed a pestle and mortar from his case. From one phial he drew out a darkly gangrenous claw and broke a knuckle off. Toronto recognized it. It was the licorice root that climbed from the earth by gripping the bark of maple trees. The sap improved its flavour. The doctor added five or ten aging grapes that oozed from their thick skins. He left the remaining shrivelled grape cluster on the Erwagens' table. A more foreign and hairy item was ground into the unsavoury gunk. When Toronto saw him add the witch-hazel bark, he got the bad feeling he was going to have to open his mouth.

Doctor say to ingest tincture twice daily with water, said the unhappy translator. When Toronto got a whiff it smelled like muskrat.

The doctor also lay a small jar of *long-life mud* on the table. The translator said: Very good. Highest quality. No expensive for Indian.

Anything if it will help Toronto.

The doctor set to work preparing a new set of ingredients for his mortar. As he ground down the peony and sulphur the pestle dully clucked against the bowl. Toronto lay there, bum up, the clucking sound of stone on stone a calming medicine of its own. The phials in the doctor's pack were nearly empty, and the cream in the mortar had a powdery metallic finish. It was made with more than just St. John's wort, a mound of flaxseed, and the dried rhizome of butcher's broom, but those ingredients alone were enough for Toronto to know he wasn't going to eat this cold paste.

Doctor say apply to dangling chilblains two time every day. Must be sanitary at *point* before, yes?

Everyone understood what he meant.

The doctor will bring back more each remedy tomorrow, yes?

Yes, absolutely. In fact, tell the good doctor I will have a man pick up the remedy from his office.

Ha ha, the doctor thanks you, Mr. Erwagen. Before we leave, may the doctor inquire to your own health, sir?

My health? Well, ha ha. Under the circumstances I'm doing very well, thanks. Toronto is a godsend. He is more than just my ward. He is a friend. I hope he recovers quickly and that I do, too.

The doctor say he may examine you?

Oh, no, thank you. That's quite all right. I have a fine doctor, another doctor, I already have a doctor. I'm well cared for. Thank you for the offer, doctor.

He say there is old Chinese remedy might cure you.

Oh, said Sammy, what's that then?

It is not medicine as Whiteman know. There are no phials, no pestles. Nothing is for ingest or apply. Doctor use, you see, very light pins, to your skin.

Needles, oh my. Acupunctures, I've heard a it.

Yes, acupuncture.

I'm not sure. I'm deathly afraid a needles. But Toronto, what should he do with himself?

The doctor say Toronto must now see own people's doctor, Indian doctor. Chinese remedy not solve all Toronto ailments. Much risk to health for Toronto. Piles worsening greatly. Imperative Toronto visit own Indian tribe doctor or risk death.

TWELVE

> I know I'm part of history, just a tiny stone in a very big wall.
>
> – LOUISE BOURGEOIS

A man game's broke out, said a squirrelly young kid whose head popped in and out the door of the Hastings Mill store to share the news. That's where Clough was, a bit drunk, a bit lonely, staring at saddles he'd never live to afford. Gorgeous nubuck calfskin saddles in the milkiest browns in the spectrum, smooth as a lady's inner thighs, with pure merino wool sweatbands.

A man game, cried the dirtiest men in the store, and just as quick shoes and boots scraped and honked across the hardwood floor and all these bums rushed out onto Powell Street, asking: Where, where?

Whoever it was playing, Clough thought, their timing was spot on. What with everybody still jawing on about the man game and a month gone by without a sign of any players, no one wanted to miss this chance to see what was all the fuss. He saw more harsh sailors and plain thugs lurch out of door stoops and saloons on the corners and add their scent and heft to the growing mob. The dirt road underneath Clough's feet was stamped solid and flat and made for relatively easy running despite the occasional rock and people choosing different speeds and no small amount of jostling and shoving to get there. The Indians stayed by the corners, watching, disappearing. By the time the man game rumour was fully spread across town the message was so garbled no one knew anything for sure. So after Calabi and Yau's initial panic at seeing a red-faced mob of Whitemans descend upon their humble shop unannounced—no small worry for two prosperous Chinamans, mind you (a rifle under the counter said it all)—their bakery became an impromptu meeting point. Who else but the chefs would know for certain where the man game was, especially considering Calabi was often the Chinamen's bookie? The first wave of men who stormed the doors stopped short, and instead of plunging in, just the first guy, the fastest, most eager of them all, dingled the bell and opened the door, knocked back by the warm aroma of fresh pastry.

Where's the man game do you know where the man game is? said the dude, with a squeak of childish alto in his throat.

Yau, alone in his shop, flour-speckled and sweating as he wiped his hands on his apron, came to the counter from where he was working the Dutch oven in the back room. He looked at the man, and at the men on the street crowding at the windows. He kept his hands below the counter on the rifle and calmly said: The man game at False Creek shantytown.

False Creek shanties, the young man called out to the bohunks, and at least seventy maybe a hundred men took off at a sprint, while another mob of ten-twenty ironworkers and lumbermen lagging behind came to confirm with Yau the words they were pretty sure they'd just overheard. Even the fact that Yau was up in front at the counter signalled that the rumours were true. Calabi was obviously already at the site of the game.

So, it's true, said Clough.

As he and hundreds of other men clogged the blocks, the windows opened in the businesses down Cordova Street, and not a few moustaches poked their noses out to watch the rabble. The printmakers and copy editors took pause from their toil to see what the fuck was all the commotion. What's the scoop? A man game. A man game, eh? calling inside to his union men: Hey, boys, let's go, it's a man game.

The spirit of Vancouver is goddamn invincible, thought Clough, walking at a brisker and brisker pace. He wasn't much of a runner, what with the chronic stomach pains, emphysema, and recurring indolence to contend with. But today more than yesteryear, Clough believed, the noble pioneer must speed to his proud fate. A man even rode by on a penny ha'-penny bike. What a marvel, a two-wheeled transporter. How the devil did he climb aboard that thing? Vancouver's men were boisterous and thick-skinned. They cursed each other out of respect. Vancouver wasn't just a city, it was a kind of fate, a destiny rock for dreams that needed ledges. Why, even the new buildings on Cordova were damn solid, why, he helped brick some of them himself. These buildings could last for an eternity if God and civics allowed.

I hate to go through Chinatown, said a man with a burn scar across a clouded eye.

Why don't you complain aboot it then? replied Clough. I mean Jesus.

What's stuck in your craw, eh?

I don't see no reason to grouse on like that when you know well enough as anybody what we're aboot to see.

They saw now, approaching the shore, that the Chinamen had built up full buildings and worse shanties on the beaches of False Creek across from Dupont where the ladies of the night used to enjoy an unobstructed view of the water. Now a block of fragrant buildings sat above the tideline, chop suey cafés and laundry houses disguising tong offices, fan tans, gambling and opium dens.

With RH Alexander's help, local capitalist John McDougall had hired Chinamen from the California snakehead to help clear land on the northeast side of the Burrard Bridge. And already every room in Chinatown was rented. Some of those apartments were sleeping fifteen-twenty men per room. So when MacDougall's employees arrived from their weeks-long transoceanic voyage, this vacant space beside an already expanding Chinatown at the base of the railroad tracks on the beaches of False Creek became an overnight slum.

The outward appearance was of a leprous hive of tents made of scrap wood, cloth, leaves, bark—whatever could be found. They looked no better than rat holes, where these young male immigrants from Sze-Yap lived, on this skewback, with one knee up, their rice steampots sneezing over log fires. As the Whitemans crested the sandhills and saw the size of the village, it came as a small horror.

The Whitemans were uneasy. They were an uneasy people. For their part, the Chinamen were quiet, heads down, meant no trouble, not proud of their fleas. They were here to work, and more specifically, ready to place their bets. The crowd was thoroughly mixed, half Chinamen, half Whitemen. Shouldering up to one another left everyone stiff, assessing their collective safety. The sun touched upon the men's hats; their faces were shaded masks. They spread out along the beach and up the incline. Many were cock-eyed, some were browbeaten, others merely young. There was an unashamed grizzliness to them all, a clear sign of the times. Clough picked his way through the crowd, shaking hands monotonously as he passed. Holy smoke, he said to himself, this's an even bigger crowd than January. In the distance he squinted to see one naked guy, definitely Campbell.

Move out a the way, get out a my way, Clough said, elbowing ribs and more, pushing his way through the men to get to his player. That was unmistakably Campbell, but until he was closer, the other physique wasn't ringing bells. Didn't look like Litz so far as his bloodshot glaucoma could tell. But he knew one thing. This time his boy had to win or they might as well leave town.

He walked directly up to Campbell and patted him on the back; then he saw the other man.

Is that you, Bud Hoss? he said. What the fuck you doing here?

To Clough's eyes, it looked as though Hoss was built like the bear at the bottom of the totem pole. Fat, stout, solid, the last thing you'd expect to see topple.

Hoss said: I'm going to man game this dude until he looks like my sister.

Haw, said Clough. Not my man Campbell, you're not.

Listen here, said Hoss, clearly incapable of moving in natural motions while naked, pointing at Clough while turning and taking two steps. Campbell made us wait a quarter hour for you all to show up. What the fuck's all that aboot? Everyone was ready to say he forfeited. It's luck you showed up when you did, eh.

Pointing his only index finger back at Hoss, Clough said: Hold on to your ponies, tough guy.

Let's hear it for Hoss versus Campbell, shouted that spitter Moe Dee. Who thinks this game don't look a little lopsided? he spat, raising and lowering his hands in the air to show the discrepancies between Hoss's size and Campbell's gnomish stuntedness. A dozen men with no role models applauded with wolfhowls, hat spins, and handclaps. Yeah, said Moe Dee, let's see some new moves, he said, and the crowd duly roared.

Campbell groomed his licey beard, leaned on Clough's shoulder to talk in private. Man, I'm glad you're here, he whispered. This motherfucker Hoss was trying to start a man game with RD Pitt.

RD Pitt, said Clough with bugged-out eyes. Who thinks he'd play? I saw him in the crowd just now.

I know. So I'm eating some jerked beef over by George Black's and minding my own business. One fucking hour ago, eh? I hear this news aboot what's happening and run down the street to catch him. Because you and Furry and Daggett agreed I'd be the one to go first and take every opportunity I could.

Clough gave him a slap on the cheek in a loving, fatherly way. Good kid, Campbell, good kid. So what did Pitt think a that?

Didn't give him a chance to think. I could see that fool cowboy Pitt wanted a way out and I just came in spitting mud and I knew from talking to him this morning that all Hoss wanted was to play, so easy.

Good to hear, said Clough. Hey, now say, you talked to Hoss this morning?

Yeah, and he was ready to fight me then and there, I swear.

Why didn't you? You should a called him out.

Well, I …

Cold feet, eh.

No, I …

Forget it. No time for that now. Listen, I got something to tell *you* …

Are we going to fucking play this or what? cried Hoss from across the pitch.

Give us a minute, will ya? You can dump the routine.

Who are you, Clough? Do the books if you want in my stead, but what's with all the gossip?

Why, hold on, son, said Clough, I'm just talking to the man here.

What difference does that make to me? Might as well talk to me if you feel like conversating.

Listen, Hoss, who's seen as many or more man games than you? I have. I'm your local expert on this. Campbell, let me tell you, Clough said, pulling Campbell back into a huddle, this is going to be easy. Let's grease him, let's grease him good. Look, you and me together, said Clough. We been training. Maybe not as long as Litz and Pisk, but has Hoss even practised once? No. This is what for. This is a chance for you to swagger with the man game. What, do you think Hoss can do this? You think he's been tr*ai*ning like we have?

No. Hell, no. Hoss likes the attention. He wants to be more than a bookie is all.

That's what I figure. All right then. Let's get me some meaty bets and take gold teeth out like the dentist's in, all right?

All right.

Coach and player shook hands.

Calabi, said Clough. How's bets?

Calabi nodded, closed the book, slipped it into his coat pocket, and nodded again.

Okay, said Clough in the buffalo roar voice he used for crowds, we're ready to go.

Finally, said Hoss, cracking his neck and hup-hupping his legs.

In the middle distance, on a crinkled scaffold at an abandoned factory, Molly espied the whole scene from beneath the word *BLUE* in BLUE RIBBON TEA CO.

Let's fucking showtime, said Moe Dee, the loudest voice in British Columbia.

//

That lean pale cowboy, RD Pitt, driven by a powerful cause that wedged him between men and their idle time, walked through the crowd around the man game catching Whitemans' eyes, saying in his most amicable and least honest-sounding voice: Oh, say now, hey, I'd like to invite you all to a very special meeting in the community we're having down at the City Hall next Sunday afternoon.

Terry Berry, already instinctually backing away, said: What's this all aboot?

Well, see, said the cowboy, leaning back on a hip to give Berry some room to think, a lot a us in town are concerned aboot the unwanted ele*ment* invading our city a late. As you can see it's all around us as we speak, and, we fear, might aim to take our town over completely. Like locusts. You catch what I'm drifting?

Yes, I do, said Terry Berry as he regained his original footing. And I believe I might sympathize with your cause. Me and a buddy plan to open ourselves a dry goods store and ...

The cowboy smacked his lips and said: It means a lot to us to know we have your support. It's been nice to meet you, my name's RD Pitt.

Yeah, I see you around, Pitt. I'm Terry Berry.

Klahowya.

Vicars, said his buddy.

Klahowya, Vicars, said Pitt.

They all shook hands with their calluses, reading each other's honesty through the roughness there. Pitt, soft-handed but for the hard yellow palms from his horse's reins, gave the good men a poster, which read, in part: *DO YOU WANT FOUR HUNDRED MILLIONS OF CHINESE IN YOUR BACKYARDS? IS THAT WHY WE BUILT OUR HOMES AND STAKED OUR CLAIMS? TO HAND IT OVER TO THE ORIENT?*

Men, said Pitt, it'd sure do a lot for the cause if you all attended our meeting next Sunday, and show them how us're working men.

Well, by the looks there's only twenty or so, said Vicars, eyeballing the beach where the shantytown had cropped up. I'm not sure I agree all that much with your cause for …

Pitt interrupted, said: I heard a vanguard a *fifteen hun*dred or more are *on route*. Should be here by the end a the week. Think that's something to speak up aboot?

Fif*teen* hundred. Well. Sure as hell do.

Can't encourage slave labour a any size, is my thinking on the matter. We already got a Chinatown, you think we need another one setting up? Besides the unsanitary conditions, alls we have with Chinamen is them helping fill coffers a the industrialists, magnates, and railroad capitalists.

I hear you.

Eroding the strength a the labourers, making obstacles for unionization. Me and some a the other guys in the Knights a Labour are starting an anti-Chinese league.

I'm interested.

Good to meet you, said Pitt, shook Terry Berry's hand again, and moved on.

When the cowboy came around in his direction, Moe Dee expectorated a cheekful of tobacco at Pitt's cracked leather boots, said: Get that shit out a my face.

You're a real and true pissant, Moe Dee, said Pitt.

//

Big crowd that day, lot of money on the line. It was a betting crowd. Everyone had a stake. Those cast along the last ring of the audience couldn't see a damn thing and resigned themselves to smoke and banter over employment and wait for game updates to trickle back. Miguel Calderón set up his Bar Rústico, and business was brisk as usual, but Calderón was not his old self. What was once his jovial face was now a pale skull draped with what might have been wet paper. His eyes were set back as far as they could go inside bleak, dark, cavernous bowls. He broke into song now without warning. Along with his mangy, long-horned goat and ice-cold ale there was now his husky voice singing Mexican folk ballads, the ones that always began with a filial murder and ended in revenge. He waved his arm and his tenor shook his jowls, the songs from deep within the gullet of his cowardice and sorrow. He was a good, powerful singer, untrained as a mule, but with heart in it. A lot of men sat on the stools just to listen and try not to weep. Men with broken noses listened and thought of their mothers. It's hard to believe the private loneliness of strangers together.

Campbell and Hoss shook hands and introduced themselves *{see fig. 12.1}*.

FIGURE 12.1
The Handshake

Calabi's commentary: So often misinterpreted by novices as a lampooning of formality, a veteran player reads his opponent carefully in that last peaceful salutation before the brutality begins.

Campbell.

Klahowya, it's Hoss you're aboot to taste.

As the salty water splashed against the beach, Campbell and Hoss paced through the packed sand and tubular clods of old goosedung. A tremulous silence appeared within the circle of devoted fans. People inspected the players like racehorses. Hoss, though unshapely in this respect, was surprisingly a threat when shucked of all his husks, the jackets, vests, shirts, and slacks. Campbell lacked the size of his opponent, but his stomach was a solid shield and there was real beef in his biceps and forearms. Campbell made up for size and slowness with accuracy. This was also what he was known for in the bush.

When Hoss worked for Furry & Daggett he'd done slash and burn in Cougar Canyon. Thinking of those chutes and flumes he remembered how solid on his feet Campbell had been, as unbudging as a tree stump. An average brain with barnacles for legs, shouldering rocks and heavy branches as they tumbled around him. There was no point in Hoss testing the guy's balance.

Hoss was a potato with bulky arms and a seaman's complexion, pale pink and burnt, with a loaf in his belly as inert as a giant wad of bread dough. His legs were short stones wedged in the sand. He was born to throw an axe; those arms took down trees in half the time of your father. Strength was one thing, but unlike Campbell, he also had speed. Hoss kept his elbows locked at his belly and his fists out like a boxer's. And when Campbell walked up to him, sure enough, Hoss danced back.

What's wrong? said Campbell. You hurt?

Hoss walked gently on the beach, checking everywhichway for obstacles, so deep in concentration he wasn't aware of his surroundings at all. Campbell was enjoying this easy bit of intimidation. The crowd was ridiculous, and it startled Hoss the way it had startled Campbell in January.

A shrewd voice cleared his throat and said: Hoss, you got to get your arms in there and start looking for an *a*venue.

A wave of agreement, then Hoss said: Do what?

The voice said: First, take a swing at him, and when he tries the Daggett see if you can't take it into your *own* whatever, pirouette fuck. Just do something.

Yeah, said another bohunk. Then you chuck Campbell to the ground.

Yeah, that's good, said the first voice. Then throw him to the ground.

What the fuck? said Campbell. Will you all just shut the fuck up, we're trying to play the man game here, eh.

Yeah, I got some advice for you too, Campbell. I'll tell you; besides, Hoss don't have to listen to us.

Yeah, he does, said another fellow, or he ain't gonna win.

Shut up because we all got to listen to you all.

Hey, fuck you, too.

A debate was ready to break out instead of a man game, so Campbell got his running start at Hoss, who did not budge, then, predicting the worst, turned and ran. Campbell was catching up. From his vantage point, Clough received a jolt when he realized how Campbell planned to take his first point. Campbell raced Hoss down the beach as the crowd swarmed. He sprinted to catch up, his toes scratching at Hoss's heels, until in desperation Hoss lost his balance. A muscle memory pulsed through Campbell; it was of Clough saying: Your opponent loses balance on purpose. In that slow moment before Hoss tripped and fell, Campbell grabbed his wrist and, with solid footing and tremendous momentum, swung him around in a complete circle. Campbell was bent over backwards so far that while Hoss swung and stumbled around him he had his free hand on the ground, turning in place on the mucky, leafy ground. In Hoss's last few steps to complete the three-sixty he was doing everything in his power to avoid falling flat on top of Campbell. And just when it felt like he couldn't hold out any longer, Campbell reversed the momentum and yanked Hoss straight down, dunked him on his face *{see fig. 12.2}*.

It was Campbell's first point in the man game. The clamour was tremendous. All the men of Vancouver tolled his name: Cam-bell, Cam-bell. With profound new humility, he bowed his head. The sensation in his palms and temples, it was a kind of glory he thought was possible only in Biblical days.

He's a real Galileo a the man game, cried a walleyed gentleman with money on Campbell.

It's best out a five, eh? said Hoss, killing the boo-ya. Long way to go before you deserve that smile on your gob, he said.

Before long, Campbell took another spin at Hoss. Hoss dodged it, not surprised by the attack; seeing Campbell's ribcage was yellow from bruises as he flew by, he noted it duly. Hoss twisted under Campbell's falling body, going in for a sprawling fireman's-style carry with hopes of *turking*, or wheelbarrowing him. In the lichen and stones and sand they randomly shoved and bumped and choked, Hoss's elbows and fingers leveraged against the thigh hitting his stomach, a butcher's sound, the wet snapple of meat against fat, all the while Hoss aiming to get those legs of Campbell's under his arms. When he succeeded in

---

FIGURE 12.2

The Flywheel, aka the Tonearm

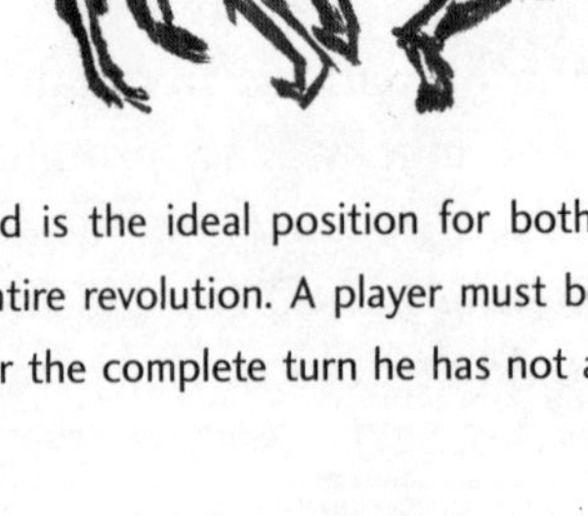

Calabi's commentary: Fully extended is the ideal position for both arms, but rarely can it be sustained for an entire revolution. A player must be sure that when he releases his opponent after the complete turn he has not allowed the man to get a grip on him.

tricking Campbell into letting him put a lock on his thighs while his hands were on the ground, Hoss knew if he didn't start running that very instant Campbell would catch wind of the plan and squirrel his way out.

Hoss went for it; he started to jog. Duck-slapping the ground with his hands, Campbell did his best to strategize as he ran, though he couldn't see a smart way out of the wheelbarrow except to cram his head against his chest and try to roll Hoss over him.

Campbell was getting creeping suspicions. He did the roll because it made sense, yet it was playing into Hoss's plan. Hoss had a plan? When the tread of his spine hit the ground, the only thing Campbell saw was Hoss's legs, so he lunged for them, grabbed his ankles. Hoss changed his hand-hold and his new grip was Campbell's ankles. Now they formed a hoop that looked a lot like the one they'd just made in the last move. And thanks to the experience, Hoss made them roll around the yard doing two three-sixties before ellipsing to a stop like a giant coin flat on its side. For two or three beats the two men just lay there, in position *{see fig. 12.3}*.

The next thing Campbell did was take Hoss by his wrists, throw him over his head like a mallet, and thwack him on the ground. That winded him of his boastfulness. Hoss spat out a shard of mushroom and some dirt. In his weakened state it

FIGURE 12.3
The Dirty Penny

Calabi's commentary: It is in our appreciation a the barbarism, the irrational genius, that we see how the man game has reinvented the wheel.

was easy for Campbell to do it again, thwacking him another time like a mallet *{see fig. 12.4}*. That was a point and made it two-one for Campbell.

Okay, that aboot does it, said Hoss, I'm sick a you. He ran up and aimed his kick for Campbell's face, who dodged it and crossfaced him in mid-air. It was almost a kicking version of the Pisk, and people all through the crowd tucked the same bright ideas under their hats—future plans for their own attempts at the man game. On the ground, Hoss struggled through Campbell's legs and arms. These axemen fought with Athenian formality, coming up with the same cliché reactions and stolen opportunities three times over until it was clear what they really wanted to do was compare versions of a move called the Cobra. The Cobra was a move Pisk did best, a kind of snaking helix on his hands, rolling on his shoulder and head every twist to keep up the momentum, his legs swooning through the air above like the winged head of a spinning cobra.

These men got *bad* brains, said a dude who worked at Sprigman's & Co. He'd never seen the man game before today and after all the noise he'd expected something different. What are you all trying to do? he hollered. Come on, Campbell, smack the bohunk and give him what's what.

Nah, said his neighbour. They want to do their Cobra Twists in the exact same spot. I seen Litz and Pisk do this. They try to get two Cobras going in the same spot, but so

---

FIGURE 12.4
The Ballpeen Hammer

Calabi's commentary: This powerful move will ring soundly familiar to all the men working for the CPR on the railroad.

the legs spinning don't hit each other and they don't trip each other.

You seen that? Pretty tricky. Impossible, I'd a thought.

It's been done. I seen it. Double Cobras.

Double Cobras. Nice. Who gets the point?

Whoever falls first loses the point.

Nice. Come on, Campbell, he screamed. Double Cobras, he yelled.

Where the fuck *is* Litz and Pisk? asked another fellow.

They ain't here, said another.

Think Pisk kicked it?

Dead? Nah, he can't be. I don't want to believe that.

He ain't here.

True, but still ...

Double Cobras, chanted the crowd in rhythm to the men's legs spinning in such proximity, four feet narrowly avoiding mishaps and collisions in the wingspans of their rotations. It was a matter of trial and error to get here and now the men had to deliver serious. The longer they sustained Double Cobras the more hectic the crowd wanted to get. People were jumping in the air. The loser here, especially Hoss, was going to kick himself. If anything was going to throw Campbell off his rhythm, it was his incredulity. He'd practised for a week to perfect a Cobra, and here he was jumping way ahead in training with someone he didn't even know knew how to play at all. And Hoss was keeping up with him. He was losing, but he could do the moves. Where had he learned. Who taught him. Campbell was winning, but it was not as assured as his coach Clough had guessed.

It wasn't just Campbell who was a little stunned by Hoss's abilities. If this was from practice, Hoss's training was a total secret. And if it was beginner's luck, Campbell was going to be furious. The Cobra. It was baffling enough when Litz and Pisk did it. The possibility that any other man could compete in the game at this level instantly roused the minds of these impressionable Vancouverites, these lost men, lonely souls, angry labourers, unemployable crazies.

The Cobras lasted all of ten seconds. But when counted aloud—while these two men spun their legs in the air clockwise and counterclockwise, going through each other's orbit without knocking legs or feet, neither man known as anywhere near an expert—it didn't really matter who won, it was mind and eye boggling. Thousands were present, yet the silence was such that all could hear the two men grunt and huff as the seagulls called out dibs, casting shadows over the stones by the water.

Hoss was flopped on the ground with an arm stuck beneath him as he scrabbled to a dirty stop. Ouch-*fuck*, he said, and hoisted his face up from the muck to confirm he'd lost the point *{see fig. 12.5}*.

Yes, he had.

What was he thinking? He beat his fist on the muck. He looked as far away from the crowds as possible and saw the Blue Ribbon Tea Co. building. It was with a shock that he recognized Molly, seated on the staircase outside the empty factory with her dress pulled up over her knees. From a great distance, even the distance of different orbits, seeing her tan exotic limbs was enough to blow Hoss's concentration for the second time.

The audience, but for one important guy, was really in a ruckus for the point. Calabi was giving Campbell a stern

FIGURE 12.5
Double Cobras

Calabi's commentary: Two skilled players must continue to spin three-sixties on their shoulder blades while each man attempts to knock his opponent off balance by slashing at him viperishly with the nails a his big toes.

gesture, an alert. Campbell knew just what to do.

Hoss, with his eyes still firmly set on Molly, heard something swish and felt a hand take his wrist and grip it hard, yoink it harder back, almost whiplashing him as he stumbled to catch up with its pace. He heard Campbell say: The *brass*.

People scattered. The po-lice arrived in a bluster of apprehensions, entrapments, and near-misses, reaching out their arms to collar a few guys in every row and moving in quickly to get at Hoss and Campbell, whose escape route had been planned to the step. By the time the law reached the sandy muck even their belts and spurs were gone. The money box was gone. Clough sat on a pale driftwood husk and rolled a cigarette. What he really needed was—

Okay, buddy, 'fess up. What's going on?

—a drink. A group of eight sullen men waited in their boots to find out what the po-lice would do with them. Drifters. Hobos. Inebriants. These were runts among runts, buttonless, hats so cheap Clough guessed they were made of paper. He recognized their attitudes but no faces. Good thing, too; it meant Campbell had done as he was told and used the tunnels to escape.

What're you doing wound up in this mess? asked Constable Miller, rubbing his moustache. I don't know what to do with you, buddy. No matter where I look. I give you the benefit a the doubt and the responsibility and what a I get in return.

Now listen, I didn't do a thing, friend, said Clough. I'm just here all by my lonesome smoking when these bohunks show up, start performing this—

All right, all right, if that's your story, then maybe we can knock some sense into all your guys' brains about man gaming. Come on, boys, let's get these lowlifes back to the mews.

The po-lice turned to the men they'd rounded up and said: It's illegal now and these crowds gotta go. No more. We don't want to see any a your guys' faces at more a these man games ever again, you hear?

And Clough, said Constable Miller, who stood silently beside the po-lice as usual. I want to see you help *end* it, not bolster its numbers, you kumtuks or what?

I kumtuks but I got nothing to do with this, said Clough.

Then why's it you're the one I want to arrest?

Clough shrugged, said: Force a habit?

Remember, I don't got to be so nice, eh. I'm sure no one's going to complain if I take you all in and fine you a dollar. What a you think a that? No laughing matter, eh. Hup to it then, buddy, you come with me.

Clough massaged his neck and tossed the butt on the sand, stood up and said afternoon to the goblins and walked with the po-lice back to the station.

I remember when it was trees here, said the po-lice beside him, and none a these houses existed. Big black cedars right up to Dupont Street or damn near close if I recollect. This whole area was forest.

Clough wasn't in a talkative mood as they walked the boardwalk on Cambie Street, where the occasional slat, slippery from greenish sea bacterium, caused him to lose his footing. And the pale crosses every twenty paces remained wireless for the time being, nothing more than empty totems. It creeped him out.

Clough said: You should be worried aboot that mugger.

The mugger. Humph, said Constable Miller. A myth more like.

A myth? Hardly. I'm disappointed. I'll catch that mugger and show you wrong. That's my mission in life as a today.

Stick to mutts and mules.

Mugger's no different than a missing animal. It's all aboot your nose and your instinct. I got both in good order. You see how on his trail I am. I smell him. Any day now. Last time I almost caught him.

When was that?

I never told you? Oh, I had him almost. When you're guilty like he is, sooner or later you let yourself get caught. It feels pretty bad otherwise, to feel unwanted.

That's no strategy, eh. That's just you talking big fish. I'm trained for this.

My strategy is to feign indifference.

Yeah, right, what my wife pulls on me.

Same principle. I apply it to the mugger. Why, in this wife-forsaken place, what counts for desire is simply what I can't get. And so far this mugger I can't get. So, what a I do, I lay low, pretend I'm interested in a different game.

Oh, I *see* …

I'm not sincerely … you think I'm involved in the man game? Oh, buddy, ha ha, you really got me all wrong. I'm just an observer. I'm hiding in the crowd to catch the mugger.

Sure, so why's it that I heard you're involved on a more executive level?

Executive level, Clough yipped, looking at Constable Miller, who was staring back at him hard. Clough put his fingers to his nicotine-yellowed beard and scratched with fury. No, no, sir, you heard all wrong. Who told you that?

Streets talk.

They walked another block without further conversation until the po-lice sighed long and hard, and said finally: This city's changing. Used to be the po-lice and the crime weren't all that unsimilar. Now I got to punish people I don't even understand, eh. I know you Clough, but I got to lock you up for reasons above my head.

It's true, said Clough. Why, three years ago the treeline was that close.

Tell us who started the man game and we let you go. That's simple, right?

You want to know who started it?

If you don't tell us we arrest our prime suspect.

Who's that then?

You.

Right, said the po-lice.

They returned to the jail with Clough and locked him up. Eating the first of a dozen candied-salmon Calabi&Yaus, the po-lice talked with his mouthful: You know where they're hiding?

Litz and Pisk?

Is that who started it?

I didn't say that, no.

Who?

Mrs. Erwagen started it.

The po-lice paused mid-bite, regarded Clough's sleepy mien, and swallowed. Fingering a second pastry, the po-lice said: Nice try. I don't think so. You'd think that was real funny us banging on Mr. Erwagen's door. That'd be a riot. No, I don't think so. Ah, Clough, he said, and wiped his pinkish forehead, sat down on his chair, and crossed his legs. You know the law—. If it weren't illegal, happy to turn the other cheek.

Let the boys have their games.

I don't get you, Clough. Ever think it's not always your job to stick your nose in?

This isn't no crime.

We ought to revoke your job here.

Ah, you don't want to do that dirty work.

Listen. Look where you are again. The wrong side a the clink. You're supposed to be guarding the chain gang, instead look, you're one a them, eh.

If I didn't sleep on your flea-bit cots most nights you think the boys in chains would pay me a lick a respect at a ditch or cracking stones? I can keep them working because they respect me. They see what I must swallow every day just to survive. They see into my face. They see that life is hellish tough out here and they better start to shape up now or they won't survive another year.

Well, alls I meant is it's a shame to see you drink away all your good fortune.

Some souls are doomed to be deaf their entire lives, said Clough, bemoaning.

What a you mean by that? Hm, then I'll give you some advice. The sooner this man game ends the better. This town can only tolerate so much anarchy. You don't want trouble, eh? Tell me who. Tell me who and we'll go buy you a drink. You look like you could use it. We don't want to have to put it on the books we nabbed you for this … how's it supposed to look, you, mixed up in all this illegality?

He leaned over on his cot and faced the po-lice. Who's to say you don't turn a blind eye? Must you uphold every idea the mayor gets in his head? Why, it's croquet, eh, totally harmless. It's no bare-knuckle event. And it sure ain't some damn union meeting or worse, or worse yet, those men the Knights a Labour. It's a sport, not some rabble-rousers from the Klu—

That's their political right to do so. You're no friend a the Chinaman, said the po-lice warily.

You know me better. Clough was getting riled. But you know who I'm really no friend a? I've said it before, eh. I'm no friend a the cowboy RD Pitt.

Yeah, well … let's just say I hear you, but at least he's obeying the law.

Now how's that for laws, eh? Neither'm I a friend a folks like McDougall there, or RH Alexander. These are both a type a Whitemen, you see? You can count them on your fingers. RH Alexander, Mayor McLean, Oppenheimer, and John McDougall who brought this latest batch over, and all those other starched shirts in the CPR for hiring them yellow slaves in the first place. Why do you think they're swarming over here if not for those Whitemen? But both a these sides get your protection.

So long's they obey the law.

If they do, is how they obey the law worth protecting, while what these boys do with this sport hurts nobody and deceives nobody? Is my question to you.

They want to turn our country into more a their big Chinaman's dynasty, said the po-lice, targeting his main interest from among all that Clough had said and discussing that. They aren't aboot to be our slaves.

Might as well be.

We'll be their slaves soon if we don't watch out, said the po-lice. You can't assimilate them. Believe me, I tried.

//

After everyone was long gone, the cowboy RD Pitt and his colleagues in the Knights of Labour returned to the scene of the man game. Here was an opportunity to pay a visit to this new pestilent shantytown with little expectation of po-lice intervention. Pitt and five others, his usual entourage of halitosical greybeards with starched collars, with the usual speeches and rants and logorrhea about the rights of the peasant, outweighed the twenty Chinamen, shanties included. They surrounded and intimidated them. They hectored them in English about the unsanitary conditions of the shanties. They uprooted canisters of waste and slapped the Chinamen in the chests for all the mess. They tore the door flaps off the shacklets and kicked over soup pots, cut the laundry lines. The Chinamen tried to keep at a distance, protecting the feeble. They were real peasants, real starving peasants. Back home in Sze-Yap it was much worse than this. China was death, cold death. Escape from China was the only solution. And any inhumane treatment could not be worse than the only foreseeable fate back home. While China imported Vancouver's lumber, Vancouver imported China's people. This was easy to see, and not, in RD Pitt's estimation, a fair trade.

We can't allow you, said Pitt. Mongols on our beaches, said Pitt. You kumtuks? Get out a here. Get.

No one else was around. It was just the Knights of Labour and the Chinamen, and there seemed to be no other intelligent choice for the Chinamen but to suffer one deep indignity so as to avoid a more permanently disabling outcome. They chose to accept a living fate, and peaceably followed their escorts to the ferry dock and waited with them in chilly silence to be taken back to Vancouver Island. Bamboo bindles across their shoulders were weighed down by heavy sacks tied to each end. Each Chinaman was loaded up with his portion of the basics. That one boulder of the spine at the base of the neck was stretched against their skin while their chins were pressed to their chests. Pigtails were about to fall out of fashion among John Chinamen. They barely spoke. The Whitemen continued to insult them as they brought up the rear, lashing belts at the slower ones. They moved in bursts of running followed by unhesitating steps followed by swift queues of Chinamen heel-to-toe down the gutter. They were barked at if they talked in their own language.

No slave's eating my bread, taking chickamin out a *my* pocket, hollered RD Pitt. They wished the Chinamen off with good riddances, waved their hats at the ferryload destined for Victoria, with sounds of great cheer that echoed over the waters of their half-mooned evening departure. The celebration marched back into town for rounds of bragging at the Sunnyside, from where the news travelled fast: the Knights of Labour had taken matters into their own hands.

Furry, who was present in the Sunnyside along with the rest of his famed crew, stood from his seat, came walking across the bar. At every step he caught the eye of another drinker, until by the time he got to RD Pitt's table most of the men were watching him with half their attention. The orange-pulsing candlelight chandeliers reflected abstractedly in the mirrored blackness of the windowpanes. Smoke hung purplish throughout the room. Furry stood above Pitt's group and put out his hand to shake theirs. He said: Good work, brothers.

Today the Knights a Labour shipped a whole fresh batch a Chinamen off our shores. Let me tell you, we're not finished till every Chinaman's gone. To celebrate this historic occasion, Pitt said, addressing Joe Fortes behind the counter, how's aboot a round a drinks for the entire Sunnyside?

And no one pretended he wasn't listening. The roars of approval rang across the room.

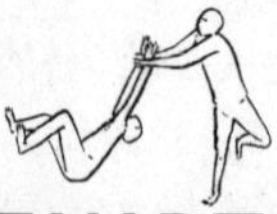

THIRTEEN

All that matters is what you said, not what you meant.

— MICHAEL IGNATIEFF

Where you going? No, not now, are you crazy? I don't know your excuses, Litz. You can't go. I can't take care Pisk alone. Why go now? Please wait. I need you. He need help. Look his feet, terrible. Wa, she cried.

If I don't get us some more wood the stove's going to go out. We need the ...

Please, no. I can't be alone.

Let him go, Pisk said to Litz's wife. He was lying in bed twisting feverishly, red swollen eyes and waxy skin dripping with milky sweat, a beard lathered in days of dry soapy perspiration. His feet were loaves of bandage.

Should I bring back the doc? Litz asked his partner.

No, said Pisk, pausing to inhale wheezily, so that Litz couldn't be certain Pisk knew what he was talking about. Finally he got enough oxygen into his shivering frame. I don't want to see that damn doctor again so long's I live.

You promise to take me to my sister, cried Mrs. Litz. You keep me here with Pisk. I don't know what you do.

He scratched at his greasy hair under his hat, brushed the dirt from his beard, and left the shack.

Pisk's feet were slathered in fresh aloe and rebandaged twice daily. When Litz's wife unravelled the gauze now to get a good look, they saw that one foot was still the colour of salmon meat. The other was a lump of bleeding coal. The toes were gone. The headache was getting worse; the shriek of angels between his ears, it was almost time to meet them.

To think he was once a boy who liked to throw snowballs into the frosty Okanagan Lake and go home to watch his mother do the mending while his grandfather kept himself occupied. Gramps never smoked a pipe like most men his age, rocking in a chair. Instead he rolled tobacco and played guitar, hummed and tapped his foot to keep himself company. When Pisk grew up, which was fast, he was more of a cigarette man, too. What a short childhood it was, a day or two, then his gramps had to take a job and died doing it, and his mother was older by the minute, and before he could bat his eyelids he was out working, not a moment of rest to look back on it all until now.

Wa, wa, Pisk, why you cry? Mrs. Litz said. No, no, no cry, Pisk. Me promise, me save you, no worry. All good. No worry, please, Pisk. Me hold you. Me hold you. Hold me, Pisk. Please, no cry, no cry. Hold me, Pisk. Wa, is terrible, and Litz gone. Why he go? You answer why Litz go? Face, what happen? Why feet this way? What happen?

//

She asked if they could meet at the hollow tree near the Whoi-Whoi village. From their hideout, Litz had a long way to portage. Two miles at least, he thought, with at least two long walks. There were plenty of creeks where you could travel quite a distance before needing to cross land. Still, he expected the trip would take him the better part of an hour at the very least.

With the canoe over his head, he stepped tracelessly over the forest floor. His concentration was solidly on Molly, on her radiant beauty most especially. He made his way down the course of old streams, the sweat of emotion already upon his skin. A dread trembling overwhelmed him, and feeling paler than slush, he almost suffocated in the sudden avalanche of madness. The hollow tree was big enough to hide him completely from view; no one, not even an animal happening to traipse by, would detect his presence. Raindrops pattered around him on the ground inside the trunk; its bark, long deceased, had turned an ashen grey, and wrought as the skin of Moses, its massive wrinkles buckled and bent open to form a mouth. He was cold, and scared to feel unloved. Scared to go another day without love. His wife, he knew, had turned on him. Every night as he slept he could feel her beside him, her hate pressing down on him like shovelfuls of burning earth.

Molly entered the hollow. She looked at him seriously, and said: How is he? Do you think he'll recover?

Oh, sure. Guy'll probably grow himself a whole other set a toes.

She looked better to hear this news, so, hoping to weaken her, he continued: The right foot's a bloody mess. And the left foot's all black and flaky. He'll be okay though. But, Molly—

I'm so relieved, she said. You don't realize how worried I was all this time. Oh, and you won't believe what I saw today down by the shanties—

He tried to kiss her. She flinched, he moved closer, she raised her arms to fend him off, and he held her in a form of capture that was also an embrace. She was young enough to be thin and not wasting away, light on her feet and a rigorous squirmer. Please, she said. Sweet Litz, you're feeling emotions.

What a you mean? He let her go. She flattened the creases at her hips.

What I said. It's emotions. It's been a difficult month for all a us.

Well, said Litz angrily. I can't stay long.

It seemed to upset her that time was brief. I know that, she said, and chewed her wetted lip. Don't tell me aboot the rigours a time.

I loves her, Litz thought, but she's married to the paralyzed bookkeeper, so.

Come on, cheer up, she said, and pushed him on the shoulder. He laughed and recovered his footing, scratched his neck and pretended to brush away his foolish bloody desires. She laughed, too, as if the matter were concluded, while he searched in vain for the right words to stop his heart's wild hammers. He stared at his own footprints on the ground. Didn't she realize? Standing beside her, rapt at her sight, he felt so high he was a peer to God. He seemed the happiest man, but inside he was aflame. For all the pleasure she took in her own gently laughing voice, he was even more blissed to hear that sweetness.

When I only ever see you so little …, he said, I'm sometimes … and from there Litz was bereft of words. His tongue was useless to him, capable only of uttering dull fragments of the timeless exalted poem that formed his wolfen soul.

I *do* love you, Litz. Please don't misunderstand me.

He wanted to say that a tingling fire rushed through his veins, and his eyes were stricken blind, and his ears were filled with nothing but a turbulent scream, and this feeling led to nowhere but blackness. He found instead that he was saying: I got to go.

Do you have to leave so soon? she asked.

Yes, Molly. He pleaded for attention with his hand this time, touching her arm, just to touch it, but also for the opportunity to brush past her breast. He gazed into her emerald eyes, the girl who'd found the game in the man, and inspired action from ardour.

Litz, please. Are you telling me the truth? Will Pisk lose his feet?

What? No. No. My ah, wife. Saving him from more amputation.

Good for her.

Yeah. That would sure be the end if he lost them. No more man game.

It *would* be simply terrible. I worried his bad circulation might be a problem. Strange, it was so warm that night. This circulation problem simply mustn't continue. But I have to tell you what I saw to-day—

Yes, and—

She didn't have to say anything to interrupt him. She lit a cigarette and took her first drag. Because I wouldn't be so sure, she said and exhaled, staring to the sky through the rim of the trunk above where lichens grew in resplendence. I think the man game will survive. I saw Hoss challenge Campbell today down by the shanties. Oh, Litz, I didn't realize until it was happening. This was the first time I saw an actual game.

Litz's gorge rose. She was supposed to watch *him*. He suddenly realized that a great part of what drove him to play was imagining the day when she would see him and be so proud. And now for her first time, her first experience, all she'd seen was a couple mere imitators. Stammering with jealousy, he cried: What? You *saw* a man game? Molly, who? Where?

Hoss and Campbell played this afternoon, yes. I saw it all from beginning to end. How wonderful. My heart was pounding and my legs were weak. I sat on a staircase outside the tea factory. Such a dear sweet boy, that Hoss. I always knew he wanted to play. He's really and truly coming along as a player. I only feared that the law would scare him off.

How did it start?

She described how Hoss had pulled RD Pitt out onto the street in front of the Sunnyside, just as Pisk had challenged Daggett in the same spot so many months ago, and that Pitt looked to be just as unlikely to compete that day.

So how does Campbell fit into all this?

Out a nowhere he appeared, she said, and with almost no effort convinced Hoss to challenge him and suggested a more private location where the po-lice might not find them.

Say, how did you—?

I followed the pack, and found a hiding spot by the Blue Ribbon Tea Company. Watching from a seat on an old narrow rickety staircase. Litz, it was simply glorious.

Those two? I can't believe you saw them. Litz paused to fathom. Who won?

Campbell, a course.

Shit. Was Hoss any good?

Yes, he was fine.

I never thought he was practising.

Molly nodded. She said: Oh, yes, we've been practising

for the better part a the month. I approached him shortly after Pisk's accident. I saw that Furry & Daggett outnumbered us and might soon overtake us for good. I have coached Hoss almost daily since Pisk's injury in January. He is learning, not as quickly as my other new student, but now that Pisk is healing, I'll invite Hoss to train with us.

Hoss train with us, Litz said. *Other* new student? A moment ago he was going to ask sporting questions like what kinds of moves they did, but before he even found the spit to say the words, his heart plummeted. Hoss train with him. The darkest submarinal part of Litz, his inner beard, decided that if he must share her, then she should not exist at all.

The anger came from his stomach and hardened his knees and arms, flushed his face with blood. A flooded river's scream behind his eyelids told him he couldn't share her anymore. It was unfair. The message was so loud, the only way to imagine how to end the roar was to punch out. The hollow tree was red. As he scrambled to control his feelings his worst fear was that he'd already killed her.

When he sobered up he realized the blood in his eyes was from her knee in his face. The other knee was ground like a spike into his shoulder blade, and she had his left arm strained so far back that if he moved more than to breathe it would shred from its socket. And if he moved his pinky finger even an inch it would break in her fist.

I'm sorry, he said. I'm sorry. I'm so sorry.

It was not quite what he expected to hear, though she said very gently, modestly: I don't want you to ever forget. I love you, Litz. You mustn't try to *make* me love you. I already do. I love you more than you can ever imagine.

I'm sorry, he blubbered, insanely hurting. I'm so sorry, Molly. I love you, too.

Oh, darling, she said. You must be patient or we'll never succeed.

She wasn't heavy, but her knees were very bony, and the arm hold she was using meant that if he tried to move in any direction his shoulder, elbow, wrist, and fingerjoints would all simultaneously dislocate. Her thighs were spread across his back, her flowerpetal breath was in his ear, and the flowery frill-edges of her sepia skirts brushed against his swollen nose as if to mock him with their loveliness.

I didn't mean to lose my temper, he said, it's just that when you told me Hoss was—

Everything happens for a reason, Molly said. It's up to *me* to decide what that reason is.

There was no more fight left in him. The knee in his face was excruciating. The arm hold was everlasting. She leaned down close enough that he could smell the exotic fruit of her skin, and freed him from the lock. They stood together a moment longer inside the tree while she watched him regain his composure. He was getting tougher inside against the burns of love. She touched his cheek with the warm palm of her hand and said: Yes, go now. Go home. I'll be with you. I'm always with you. Go home and think aboot your wife who loves you.

//

At Mrs. Litz's recommendation Pisk left the bed and slowly made his way on crutches outside to cool off his soaring fever. While he sat there, steaming in the crisp air, he could smell the coffee she was brewing to warm him up again when he inevitably broke into unbearable chills. Clinging to the threshold, hardly aware of his own actions, he thumbed a punk of tobacco blended with opium mud into his pipe and struck a match, seeing and feeling in her silent ministrations that Litz's wife was trying not to say something. Whenever he wheeled around and looked at her through the open door she'd be looking back at him, never concealing it. She seemed to know not only his fate, but that it was tragic.

Litz knew. And so did Molly. And because Pisk could never bring it up, he couldn't force her to tell him. It is the Tragedy of Healing that the sick man most fears he is dying when his loved ones most fear having hope. And so the sick man strives harder to live, and when he recovers everyone rejoices.

While the shag smouldered with a rustic cocoa scent he loved, he puffed, and finally let his stomach relax. Along with the sweat pouring off his nose, neck, arms, and legs, his stomach had been folded up tight for so many hours, always on the brink of unfolding in a spasm, bursting open and thrusting the worst bile up his throat. Now, as if unrestricted by fears of death, he was able to reach a peace with his organs, and this aided his fever as well. Smoke from his pipe went aloft in the still morning air, hovered there for a moment of poetic contemplation, Pisk imagining it as another of the sails he could hear distantly crack and flutter. She was right, he thought, all I needed was a breath of fresh air. And then, accepting that his impression of Mrs. Litz had been partly a feverish, emotional hallucination, and that her concern for him was no more or less than it should be, Pisk realized he might still have hope. This brought on his fear of death doubly strong, the anxiety screwing his stomach fourfold, the fever burning him another degree. Finally, when the sweat all over his body got so cold it was nearly a layer of ice, he lost all control of his senses, threw the pipe in the air, and collapsed into a pile of shivering limbs and chattering teeth, begging. She came and brought him in, wiped him off, set him in bed, and fed him the coffee. Eventually he came back to consciousness. The bandages were all but useless now, and she began to unravel them to clean the feet and swaddle them back up again. He looked at her with a kind of pity because no matter how much she helped him he couldn't tell her how it had happened. Tears came to his eyes.

Don't cry, she said, wiping away the streams down his face with the thick palm of her hand. Soon you be healed, she said.

How can you say that? said Pisk.

Look-see, she said, motioning at his feet. And despite their monstrous appearance, now that he looked more closely, he could see she was right. The scars where his toes used to be were healing nicely. All the pain he was in meant that feeling was returning to the stumps.

Just then a giant boom shook the loose boards of the house, and that, along with Litz appearing in the doorway at the same moment, startled him so badly that he leaped to his unprotected toeless feet, screamed out in pain, and promptly fainted.

//

Litz saw his partner collapse and ran to his wife's side.

What happened to your nose? she said.

A branch.

Your neck, too? she said. All bruised.

Hit a branch, stumbled and fell.

He sat on a chair beside the bed and looked at Pisk lying flat on his back with the covers pulled up to his collar and his eyes sticky at the corners. He was swollen and pink and sour-smelling, dipsomaniacally breathing heavily as if he were running as fast as he could in a dream.

Is he going to be o-kay? He looks on the brink a—

Yes, she said. He will be o-kay. Where you been all these hours?

He quickly and deeply apologized and she fought him at every turn, raising her voice no higher than a whisper. Everything she said about what kind of person he was he saw was right, or that she was right about who he was to her, and this made him break into tears.

Don't cry, she hissed, and turned away from him to see if there had been any change in Pisk's condition. He was still out. She daubed his brow with a cold, damp rag. This seemed to soothe him.

Coming home, Litz hadn't been sure if he should tell Pisk that Molly had witnessed a man game, and that she was secretly training Hoss and some other fellow, but he'd made up his mind that he would. He planned to tell Pisk. Now there was no question: the information would have to wait. This was not the time.

Today I must see my sister, she said.

We can't go and leave Pisk looking like this. What are you thinking?

There were already tears in her eyes, and he knew that hers were more honest than the ones he was wiping off his own face. Very cruel to me, she whimpered. I hate you, Litz. I hate you.

Shh, said Litz.

Take me see sister. You promise me many happinesses. I say o-kay to you. See how many months? Nothing. So lonely. Wa, wa.

What can I do? said Litz.

What you hide? What you lie aboot? You hide *wo*man. Wa, it is me, Litz, *me* you hide. She crouched at her husband's feet, sobbing, and she hugged him around the neck so that he had to look her in the eyes. I miss sister so much, Litz. Wa. We must go.

Yes, he said. Yes, we'll go.

//

Evening's descent was swift. Cold stars above Vancouver. Furry and Daggett were seated at their corner table at the Sunnyside Hotel pounding back the beers and hollering to Fortes for another round. Fortes tapped out four more pints and brought them over on a tray. The tray looked like a saucer in his hand and a shield on anyone else. There you go, sirs, said Fortes.

Fortes, said Daggett, I swear I never met a finer man than yourself. He called for a toast to Joe Fortes, their bartender. Let's hear it for the best goddamn man in the world.

All the men in the bar raised their glasses, cheered mightily, and swigged. They all chimed in with lines from popular songs in choirs of two and three. He's a jolly good fellow. May he ride the golden chariot to Heaven.

Joe Fortes blinked to express his appreciation.

Next round for the house is on me, said Daggett. The bar toasted Daggett with much the same enthusiasm as before.

The round after that, said Moe Dee, is on me.

Wa, cried all. When the bravado quieted, it was Moe Dee who spoke up again. Too bad we couldn't get to see your moves back in January, eh? I bet you would a showed them what's what. Am I right?

Who the fuck are you anyway? said Daggett.

Getting right to the point, I never seen either a you at a single other game, said Moe Dee.

What aboot it?

All this goddamn chit-chatter is distracting us from an evil right in front a our mugs, said RD Pitt, from his same seat at the back. His arm was hugged around the old green-bronze bust of the Queen of England. After successfully shipping off twenty Chinamen and before that narrowly avoiding a fight with Hoss, Pitt was well beyond drunk at this point. He was almost done speechifying for the night. In his corner, surrounded by cronies, he looked as crumpled as a document's unframed first draft. His colleagues in the Knights of Labour were all just as pasted. Their anti-Chinee party was over, and Furry had toasted their success at least twice, Daggett more than that, and what began as something diplomatic had ended in a loud buzz. I say it again in case you forget it, said Pitt. The Chinamen are why we got to look so far and wide to get a decent wage, decent hours. And not got to slave twelve hours seven days a week like one a these Chinamen here. The solution for a capitalist is a problem for a labourman, eh.

Furry looked at Moe Dee. He put his glass back on the table and said with almost unbearable steadiness: Only someone born and raised in Regina goes to a man game that he ain't planning to compete at.

That right? said Moe Dee, not a man easily intimidated, for he was an orphan born and raised in Regina. He said: You mean if I got down to it right here—

I'd a got five points on you before you had time to shrink your dink, said Furry. Are you ready for that?

Moe Dee was seen to contemplate the challenge.

We sharpened our skills, and now we're ready, said Daggett. We're going to turn this game around. You think you seen something with Litz and Pisk? They're weak dick-biters compared to us. If they aren't dead already, we're going to run those fuckers out a this city for good.

That's your plan? said Moe Dee.

I hate them more than the Chinamen, said Furry.

Bah, said Pitt.

I like your man Boyd, said Moe Dee. I think you might a got something there with him. He can be fast and footloose. I liked him on his legs. There's cat-blood in him. I'll tell you one thing, though, said Moe Dee, undeterred under the influence. He almost lost track of his thought. He said: That little walleyed boy you keep with who always sticks his neck out like to-day. Campbell is it? That boy can't play a lick a the man game. To-day versus Hoss? Hell, I never seen anything so funny as Campbell. What a treat. Oh, he beat him. And who's so impressed aboot that? Hoss never played before. Once Hoss has spent another month practising … man, Campbell blew it completely. Kid's got no good instincts.

Furry took a drink. Another month, eh? he said, but left it at that.

Daggett rocked on his chair, said: You thought that was funny, eh? Think you could do better?

Hell's bells, yeah, didn't I just fucking tell you that, you dumb fuck, said Moe Dee. Hell, I think a plucked chicken might beat Campbell. Besides, I'd rather call you out.

That's not how it works. You don't call on me. You call on my crew. You play our first man out, and if you beat him, you play our second man. Campbell's our first man. You think you could beat him?

I could take the man game to him fast and easy. I'd put him in knots. I'd fuck his cherry. I'll teach him to talk with no jaw.

That right? said Furry.

That's sure as fuck right, said Moe Dee, blushing hard.

//

Hearing the door in the front entrance whine open on its colicky hinges and shut with its familiar stained-glass rattle, Sammy Erwagen waited to hear the steps of his wife on her leather heels before he relaxed his jaw again. He sat in his wheeled chair next to the sofa. He explained roughly what ailed Toronto, and what had been prescribed.

Medicine is medicine, she said.

Nevertheless, said her husband, there he is.

I was going to tell you all aboot my day, Molly said.

I don't really want to hear aboot your day at all, dear. I've had plenty enough day on my own.

Are you upset at me?

No, he said.

You still love me?

Yes, yes, a course I do.

You do? Are you mad at me?

You've been gone all day, while I had to take care a—and look at me. Yes, I suppose I'm mad at you.

I'm sorry. I know, I shouldn't a been gone all day without stopping in to check on you. It was just so busy with—

Sammy felt his hair fall out, a follicle here, a follicle there, a ticklish pluck as each one let go. Surely if nothing else transcends the generations, jealousy does.

//

With Ken, Silas, and Cedric content to look through rubbish for hours, it was time to make an exit. What did Minna see in them? Seeing them *play* was one thing. But with jumpsuits on, looking through trash, they were like every other. In other words, what did they have that I didn't have in spades? I was feeling less and less threatened and more and more competitive. We were in search of a history we were sure to mistreat. As if a city would ever store its proudest moments in this dipping cellar. As if we could floss a story from all this mealy worthless scrap. The file cabinets were rusted around the screws. Every shelf was a heavy wedge of information, scarily not organized. When I randomly picked up a letter on paper that fell limp at the hardworn folds, I read the words *Campbell v. Hoss, False Creek*. Did it mean what I thought it did? Was this her handwriting, *the* Molly Erwagen, Ken's kin? Or was this elaborate prank going to end halfway to a three-way, and me in the corner with my pants still on? It was a perverse basement, and according to Ken, most of its floor-space was devoted to paper that predated Mackenzie King. I decided, once again, to conceal rather than share the letter.

While they scavenged, I stared with confused curiosity at a painting on the wall behind the pile of bordello lampshades. The frame had acquired a layer of dust and the wrinkled canvas was in poor condition, but I nearly shook my head with incredulity when I focused on the subject of the work, two men engaged in a Greek position. It was everywhere. This really was a subterranean altar. Even the artwork down here was man game related.

Ken was in a corner between two shelving units where he'd hit a real gold mine of material about the 1887 riot. Not the first, the last, or even the biggest riot related to the man game, according to Ken's research. He looked like a little boy sitting there cross-legged in the corner reading Grampa's yellowing news for information about himself. Silas was still after the picture I'd flicked behind the shelf, and as he thumbed at cardboard and paper his fingertips were growing blacker and blacker. I could easily imagine that behind the floor-to-ceiling stacks of crusted newspapers was a hole in the wall that tunnelled straight to 1887, straight into one of those secret tunnels under Vancouver back then, constructed by its founding fathers as a discreet route from their respectable saloons, offices, government buildings, and, in RH Alexander's case, from the reading room in his own home to bordellos and Chinese gambling dens and opium caves. I preferred to imagine things like that, the possibility of an irrational portal, because it offered me another viable escape from the ever more confusing present-day.

//

Litz could tell by the way his wife gripped his arm with both hands and talked incessantly in her language as they tread ever so carefully through the trees that she was possessed by the forest. He was susceptible to these spirits as well, but not as much as she was. He reminded himself that she was still just a girl, hardly fourteen.

All's still the same, she sobbed. All's change.

It's only been what, eight months, said Litz, pleading with her in a voice he was unused to, and so quite poor at delivering.

By the time they arrived at Dupont Street her mood had turned. She'd gone from trembling, babbling reverence for the forest to something less attentive and more intent. Litz read from her silence that he was in trouble.

Careful over the—, he said. Whenever he tried to speak she flinched as if at a snake she'd spotted on the ground, and he wouldn't finish his sentence. She was no longer holding on to his arm either, far from it, and when they took the secret staircase from the coach house to the second floor of Wood's, he knew he was no longer her keeper.

One of the other girls in Wood's, as slim and sweet as a candycane, happened to flit out her bedroom door at the same moment as the Litzes passed by on the way to Peggy's room. The two young women squealed, embraced, shared a tearful moment, touching each other's cheeks as if to confirm their realness, speaking in a hush; and Litz, rubbing his moustache, hanging back, was relieved when he was finally allowed into Peggy's room to wait.

He sat on the softest surface of the room aside from the bed—in this case a red velvet chaise longue with a mahogany back in the shape of a woman in repose. He patted his chest absently for the stub of a cheroot he carried in his pocket, whiffing the pipesmoke of a previous customer … His wife strode past him coldly and sat on the edge of the window. She was a fierce wind in his life. But now he saw that her expression was entirely different. Nothing icy about her. Gone were the histrionics, panic, and constant demands. Instead she wore the sleepy, tolerant expression he'd first fallen in love with. And that lovely, resilient, nearly invisible smile—he'd almost forgotten it, having laid dormant for the past eight months—returned.

Mrs. Litz got up again, finally choosing to sit in the highback chair at Peggy's vanity, and now he couldn't see her behind the chair, he was way over on the other side of the room in his jackets and thick hair, hamfists and big knees. He didn't look capable of the smoothness and ease required of this chaise longue, though he was. He not only looked like a clumsy peasant, he felt like his former self as well—the man he'd been before the man game, the man who scratched his neck incessantly, hunched his shoulders, and bounced one leg while he sat. These were all the mannerisms that Molly had trained out of him. So …, he said, hopefully.

To which she replied with a firm: Hm.

They did not speak or make eye contact. There was enough noise from the other chambers and the parlour on the main floor that it was impossible to ignore how alone they were. Every time Mrs. Litz moved, he moved, and then, seeing that she'd only recognized the cries of a friend, both resisted any further movement. When at last Peggy arrived to see them seated in her bedroom she cried out in joy, and without hesitation went to Mrs. Litz and embraced her. Litz blushed, his neck went moist, and he scratched around his collar and turned on his seat so he wouldn't have to watch.

You sweet thing, said Peggy. How I missed you. You're as lovely today as the day I set eyes on you. No wonder Litz keeps you to himself, what a pinnacle a beauty you are. Look at her, eh. Oh, I miss seeing your face, I do, I do. Come here, let me give you another kiss, my heart is beating so fast. It's my old tendency. Never feel safe aboot my girls unless they're under my roof. And why do you look so sad? It's the only thing aboot you I see that's different. Girl, you can talk to me. Don't start to cry. Look at her, Litz, this is sorrow on her face, sorrow as genuine and beautiful as a flower in the shade. But tell me, my girl, where's this sorrow's stem?

Mrs. Litz was unable to stop crying so Peggy shooed Litz from his place and sat his wife down beside her on the chaise. She pushed Mrs. Litz's head into her bosoms, shushing her sobs, combing her fingers through his wife's black hair. She cooed in motherly tones. All the while she stared at him, up and down twice over, with stern disappointment.

You don't stand when a lady walks into a room? Peggy said to him crossly. Come now. Where's your manners. How are you, Litz?

I'm sorry, he said, and continued to back away until he found a comfortable corner in the dark.

Now please, someone tell me what's the matter, said Peggy.

Mrs. Litz looked up with that same look of fright Litz recognized from their walk through the woods. Her gaze was fixed on the other door in Peggy's room, the door that led to The Whore Without A Face. I must see my sister, she said.

Naturally, dear, whenever you like, said Peggy, a course you can, my sweet. She's very well, asks aboot you often, I always say you're stronger than ever.

You did, said Mrs. Litz, wiping the tears off her long eyelashes with her wrists, trying to compose herself.

But your sister, that's the cause a these tears, no?

He keep me in a prison, she said, quietly, maybe with less confidence, thought Litz, as if the memory of those days had changed along with her.

I see now what happened, Peggy said, looking at him. I had no idea, Litz. Didn't you see this little biscuit was crumbling? Oh, look at my dear, dear girl. You were scared out there, weren't you? Yes, all those months … I had *no* idea.

Miss you, too, Peggy, she said.

I missed *you.* We all did, baby. But I see now. You paid the biggest price in this whole debacle around the …, she faltered intelligently, looked to Litz, who was pleading with his eyes for her not to mention the game, so she did not, … *Fire,* Peggy said, and who did *what* to *who* with a … donkey engine, *what*ever. Bores me to sleep. Oh, but sweetheart, you mustn't put all the blame on Litz here. Alls I know is Litz here, he and Pisk worked their tails off these months to get your home back to you. Believe me, I saw what these bohunks did, eh, and no one else would dare do the same under the circumstances unless …, and there Peggy faltered again. She was finding it difficult to avoid the subject of the man game, which she obviously realized would do more damage to her girl than to sheepish Litz in the shadows. To regain her sense of control, she checked her face in the vanity, pursing her lips and studying her profile.

Mrs. Litz kept her head hung down. Litz hoped and waited for her to meet his gaze, but she didn't, wouldn't. When she moved it was only to embrace Peggy again.

Might a guessed eight months is too long for such a delicate sweet morsel to be kept from her family, said Peggy.

I do love her, said Litz, and trying to keep the words in the air as long as possible, he waited without breathing, and then, failing to get any response, his throat dried up so badly he started to cough. There'd been a day not long ago when his voice made her cling to him. When he was still a lumberjack and he and Pisk would come home after work, sometimes after stretches as long as six-eight weeks, they were usually pretty rowdy, and as they approached the house she'd hear him and would rush to meet him when she heard his voice. And Mrs. Litz has excellent hearing, and Vancouver was a much quieter place back then, and so she'd run to meet Litz who was sometimes a mile-two miles away, and they'd see or hear her coming. Litz would be well and ready for her by the time she got to him. He'd put down his axe. Pisk would even back off, give them space not to embarrass themselves, sometimes walking past her as she ran to her new husband and pressed herself against his chest with her arms clenched against her breasts. He embraced her, his arms looped tightly around her. He her cocoon. Inside his arms. Calling to him: Tight. Tighter. And he, squeezing her with as much tenderness as he could without breaking her, until her giggling started to wheeze up. Then he'd release her, blissed and gasping for air, letting herself fall back close to fainting so that he must catch her, swing her to and fro at the wrists. He remembered times like those. They'd met only two years ago, a couple doors down from this room.

He wiped his eyes.

Peggy took his wife's hand, guided her to the door, and with a key tied to a ribbon on her waist, unlocked it. As the door swung open Litz could see her there in the dusty unlit room seated on the bed with her legs crossed to one side under a nightgown. The black hood over her head turned to the sound of the door hinges, silken cowl to disguise The Whore Without A Face, and Mrs. Litz cried at the sight of her and ran to embrace her sister. Peggy shut the door and locked it again.

Let them talk awhile. How are you, Litz? Why don't you fix a drink? You look like you been to see a nun. I swear I should knock you out the door on your heels for making that face at me. How's Pisk doing, he o-kay?

Healing, said Litz.

People got bad luck around you, Litz. Boys in town think he's knocked off completely.

Well, he's not.

My advice to you then is to dispel that rumour. I don't know for how much longer this town is going to stay so bored. All eyes are on you, Litz. You and Pisk. If Pisk is gone ... your wife here ... there's nothing to say you can't still go.

What, up and leave the city?

She prowled around the room, adjusting trinkets, and said: Shame doesn't travel with you. The steam engine hasn't managed that yet. You're a good man, Litz, but at least if you don't have brains, you got to know when to move on. That's the nature a man, the kind a man you are. You roam like dogs, all you men in this town.

Litz stood up. He reasoned with himself that if he walked towards her at his full height, width, and breadth it would show her he wasn't afraid of her and she would quit giving advice. So he got in close to Peggy, and it was almost as if he was going to put his hands on her hips and kiss her. She leaned back onto the table and propped herself up with one arm and stuck her chin in his face. Her neck was perfumed by estrus and extract of damiana. Blood rushing all of a sudden to his extremities, Litz had a bone to pick with the madam's opinion. He said: Listen, Peggy, I never wanted to *hurt* her. My own wife. I love her like the moonlight. But I couldn't let her go to town, my own wife. If I did her wrong, you know what the people in town here would do. Think a what guys around here are capable a. Much worse than being stuck in the forest behind huge thickets a blackberry bush. Much worse shit could a happen to her if I let her go.

Didn't you see her? How could you say no to that face?

I'm trying to *tell* you.

I just love the dear thing so much. I hope you won't expect her to come home with you again tonight, to that horrible cave you call a home. She won't want to.

Why not? I saved her from you.

Please, said Peggy, with a knowing, catlike smile, you can't save her. You don't know the half.

I'm her husband, said Litz firmly; then he looked at his mucked boots and petted his moustache instead of confronting the freezing glare of her eyes. Chewing the inside of his lip, he said: What do you expect me to do? Me and Pisk are woodsmen exiles. You know how different things are since the Fire. This year's different in every way. Guys around here get bored real fast like you say. If we didn't make this happen, we'd already be gone.

She doesn't know, does she?

Aboot the man game, no. There weren't any choice in the matter. I kept her behind the blackberry bushes because a the situation. I want the same as you, Peggy, for her to be safe.

Litz throated two fingers of decanted whisky then poured two fingers more and held the tumbler swishing before him. He looked at it for a long time, then said: Clough told us aboot the tunnels.

I heard, said Peggy. Good thing, too, she added. You infuriated RH so badly, he called in a favour to the mayor. On top a Furry and Daggett now you got the po-lice watching you.

Something cracked in her voice, like a flowerbud between sheets of ice. He felt the temperature in the room rise again, so he feigned a look at her. In fact, she wasn't paying attention to him anymore. She was studying herself in the mirror. Taking obvious pleasure in smoothing the filmy silk scarf that lay across her voluptuous bosoms, she asked his reflection in her vanity: What makes a good player, Litz?

He gave the question some thought. A good memory, he said. Like a bear trap. You got to remember how a man moves so you can set yourself up to catch him out. It's not even memory you store in your dome, it's in your fingers and knees.

When will you play again, sweetheart?

Soon, I hope. I don't think we'll stay where we are for much longer.

You say Pisk's healing.

The stumps aren't much to look at, but he's on crutches, so.

Litz took a final swig. He contemplated pouring another double, did, and said: Even Molly was worried. Not me. But I seen him in the woods every day so I know what he's capable a. For instance he sliced his hand open one time with a cablewire that got loose on him. Split wide open. Blood everywhichway. Alls he did was wrap his shirt around it. Next morning at breakfast we look at the wound and alls there is is a scab. Next day there's nothing to see at all. Healed up completely. Not a scar. When I saw the toes come off I wasn't thinking, Will he die? I was thinking, When are they going to fucking grow back?

He drank. He relished this mouthful more than necessary. She told him he'd had enough and he knew she was right so he poured one more. He heard the occasional murmuring voices. He knew it was the sound of his wife and her sister in the other room. After that, he put the cut-glass tumbler back down on the silver tray and stood there fuming, wanting to defile her. But she might as well have been pointing a pistol at him for how impossibly foolish he knew it would be to make a move.

It'll be so much better now, said Litz, now that we feel safer to tread in Vancouver. Wouldn't you figure that sentiment in the city is on our side?

Me? said Peggy, facing her vanity, reapplying the paint to her lips and eyes, touching up her hair, turning her head from side to side, and massaging her neck with cream, all very passively. When he wasn't aware, she watched him in the mirror as he grew more agitated.

Yes, what do you figure? If men saw me escort my wife into town, what would people do? Litz shook his head. The old whorehouse itches were back. This time they started in his wrists and itched up to his armpits and finally his neck, and he clawed at himself as he spoke. Neither you or me is any good for this beautiful girl, and we both know it. I got to get her out a here.

You don't remember the last time you were sober—, said Peggy, but there was a knock at the door just then, and they both waited.

They heard a voice on the other side: Darling, it's your old burgundy banana. Let me in.

As the man rattled the ceramic door handle, Peggy hissed to Litz: It's RH, you must *hide,* quick, and then called to RH Alexander, I'll be right there, dear.

Litz found himself crammed into her oversized custom-made wardrobe with all her dresses and slips, forced to stand in a very awkward position as RH Alexander, the man who'd fired him nearly a year ago, moved swiftly into the room and took Peggy in his arms and kissed her full on the lips.

I missed you, said RH, wetly.

I missed you, too, said Peggy, no less sincerely than she'd sounded when she said it to Litz's wife. You look distressed, my sweet.

Yes, I am, said RH.

Whatever's the matter, dear, is there anything I can do?

//

While RH enjoyed a private, sudsy bath in Peggy's suite, a gang of men smoked hashish and tobacco down in Wood's parlour on the first floor, easing into a splendid night. Most of the men wanted to talk with Campbell, whose reputation had improved significantly since winning the game against Hoss. This evening he held court like a king, and if not a king then a prince, for what it was worth *here*. Campbell, by all accounts, felt himself a success. He worked for the toughest logging concern on the coast. He held his own in the forests as well as he held his liquor. And he was a player in the man game. He wiggled his foot balanced on his kneecap and talked as if to himself in a mirror. The basic questions about the man game that Campbell had answered countless times over the last few months received big long speechifying answers tonight, answers full of bad advice, in bad breath; Campbell was the kind of expert who made a man want to learn how to play the game just to shut him up.

An adjoining circle of skunky men, among them the leaders of the Knights of Labour and the cowboy RD Pitt, stubbornly discussed other, more pertinent issues.

You can't assimilate them.

Can't *trust* them.

Occasionally the two conversations collided.

Why don't you shut your mouths? said Campbell from across the room. 'The fuck you know aboot assimilate?

Fuck you, said RD Pitt, his shirt unbuttoned to the belly. I'll knock you flat if you so much as—(realizing he was again being led into a trap to play the man game)—all's I'm saying is mind your business.

I am, said Campbell. It's you who ain't. I found myself a way to make some chickamin without your problems. I even get paid by the Chinamens you say stole your job, eh.

You're all so eager to do this man game, said Pitt. Me, I'd rather just shoot you dead. None a this fancy-footing. And didn't I hear Moe Dee called *you* out, too? Now he wants to play. You're all as smart as a bag a nails. Instead a recruiting more bohunks to share in your distraction you should be out here with us trying to save this city from the Yellow Peril.

You saw him? Where's Moe Dee? said Campbell.

By now the argument had set off other, smaller arguments throughout the parlour and it was clear to all that the Knights of Labour were outnumbered. What the men wanted, now that cigars were plentiful, opiates and medicinals available, women affordable, and drinks came on demand, was something that gave meaning to these distractions. Because, as Campbell saw things, as did so many others at the time, ninety-five percent of life was back-breaking misery.

And RD Pitt saw this, too. He cottoned on to how Vancouver men gravitated towards the man game and not his rightful cause. For the sake of his pride, he found a way to avoid what most of the unshaven men in the parlour seemed to want from him, which was to see him compete.

Well, I seen him. Your Moe Dee. You and all your lumpens.

Is Dee here? Is he with Sugar, Dixie? said Campbell. Who's with Peggy?

Naw, said Pitt, he ain't with *her.* He's with another gal.

Campbell stood and brushed himself off, shoulders to kneecaps. All the bohunks in the room watched him eagerly. I'm gonna go up there and find that boy. He thinks I'm too tired after besting Hoss … got another thing coming.

//

While the argument downstairs boiled over, Peggy's room on the second floor was locked tight as usual, with client. Campbell rattled her knob first, just in case, then he moved on, not daring to even touch the door to the room occupied by The Whore Without A Face. RH Alexander didn't even hear him. He was lolling in his bath, kissing Peggy's salty arms when he got the chance as she scrubbed him down. The lace curtains were drawn across the window and secured with a clothespin. RH pinched its wood mouth open and slid the curtains apart to stare at the wet blur. She soaped him. Massaged him. Her thumbs worked out the knots between his shoulders. It was quiet enough in her room that he could hear the candle burn. He could hear the bubbles in his bath pop one by one. His eyes were shut, the lashes sticky.

Oh, he said, that's wonderful. Up a little.

Here?

Oh, that's—*Ow, ow,* ow. Oh, m*y*. Where did you learn this art?

Same place I learned who'd pay for it.

She held his face in her hands, twisted it towards her, smiled, and kissed him. He blinked, and smelled her on his lips. It was the first time she'd ever kissed him.

What was that for?

For all the hard work you do, honey, she said, and threw the sponge in the water, splashed the window.

What a you know aboot it? RH thought to ask her.

I read the papers. I see your name and make sure to read the story. You don't think I'm interested in my man, but I am.

I don't know what you like, said RH. Well, this city is still so young. There are men with a superior vision for the future and those who see only today's dinner plate.

And what do you picture these future superiors will do for relaxation? Same as always?

Indeed, said RH, as it always has been, and nothing new. In terms a relaxation, a madam for a mistress, a ball a opium in a pipe, and a bubble bath, I don't see any reason to change a thing. Some economic spheres are perfect globes while others are lopsided, oblong, or completely flat. The issue a labour and capital in my field is still lumped and jagged, not at all in sustainable shape, for it continues to be moulded by innovation. Your home is a perfect sphere. It has been for millennia. No intelligent man would damage your world.

Good, she said, suppressing a yawn, because believe me, darling, I surely hope you're finished stepping on the nice mayor's toes.

What aboot him? RH splashed around in the tub to look her in the painted face. *Nice* mayor's toes? Don't tell me—we had a *pro*mise.

She rolled her eyes. No, I'm not talking aboot that. *Men,* she said, groping down under the suds to jerk him a little, it all comes down to what your prick wants, eh?

To what are you referring then, *Stepping on his toes*? I don't follow.

Alls I see is one thing leading to another. It happens like dominoes. First you cry obscenity, then your morals catch up, and soon enough the po-lice are knocking on my—

This city lacks discipline. Its men are vagrants. You don't know the work I do trying to keep them in line. You don't know. And you see this and wonder why I require Chinamen.

You old fogey, she kidded, slapping his white-haired chest, come now, it's the generations, darling. It's entirely harmless. You mustn't become so upset over things that don't interest you.

Yes, a course, he said, you must a heard quite a bit aboot the man game.

Her massage showed no hesitation. I only meant to warn you that if you get a reputation for puritanism, you risk separating us.

Don't be sentimental, dear. Nothing is going to happen to us. Be sure a that. Now tell me, I'm very curious to know what you've heard. Have you seen one?

Me, no. Far too much distraction from the main attraction, hm.

Indeed. I'm glad to hear it. Well, who made this up? What dipsomaniac invented this? Is it Clough? I heard it was.

Bah, certainly not Clough, although … well, never mind.

So, you know more than you say. Hm, well, I'm surprised we haven't talked aboot this before. You kept this from me because you knew I'd be offended, didn't you?

Yes, she said.

Well, look, do I seem offended to you? Tell me what else you know. What was that noise?

W-what noise?

Did it come from … the room connected to yours?

Darling, said Peggy, climbing aboard his pelvis. She spends her days in complete solitude. Won't you allow her to conversate with her own self if no one else?

Why'm I not allowed a look, a quick peek …, said RH.

I already explained all the reasons, said Peggy, her lips brushing against his.

More, he said, tell me more aboot the man game.

Really, darling, not much. Nothing more than I've told you. I stay *away* from that element.

Don't be facetious. It hardens my sympathies for you. You must know a great deal. You've already shown me that you do.

She stopped massaging his chest. She raised a hand out of the tub and rubbed her forehead with the flat of her arm, dripping suds on the Persian rug. Darling, she said. Sometimes, let me tell you, you can be such a bore. Do I look like I care aboot what goes on outside my doors? Alls I hear is what the men come in talking aboot, and yes, lately, it's been nothing but.

How long?

I forget, maybe the last few months. That's the only reason why I got concerned. Seems to me the men in this city enjoy the game. Men in this city like Wood's and some a those same men won't admit it in public. You seem to see a difference between what I do, but … You begin to see how I get concerned.

Bah, said RH, imitating her. You're being unreasonable,

you gorgeous thing. I see no cause for concern. There's not a man in this city who would vote to see you gone, least a all me.

Wives. When the wives start coming.

Wives can't vote, Peggy. He was going to continue his harangue, but something in the way she held herself at that moment gave him pause. He realized at once that she knew far more than he, and that probing her for answers was merely providing her with more ammunition. Peggy wasn't a young woman. She was twice his age and then some. She was older than everyone combined.

Suddenly, RH heard at least five wooden clotheshangers in her giant mahogany wardrobe fall to the floor. An avalanche of rumpled dresses pushed open one wing.

What the—arrgh, said RH, splashing her off him to get a better look.

And then just as suddenly—RH wasn't sure where to look, it all happened so fast—the front door of Wood's slammed shut and rattled all the walls, tinkling a whisky-soaked tumbler on a silverware tray next to Peggy's bed, and it might have been the cause of the wardrobe popping open if it weren't for Litz on his hands and knees in among the shifts and gowns, whom RH didn't see, because he turned in the other direction to spy through the window lace where he witnessed Campbell storm out to the end of the yard and stop there, looking back up.

What's all this, Peggy? he said. Who is that there, why, it's Campbell, that fool.

Worried that he'd be seen, RH ducked low at the window when Campbell yelled up: Hey, you, Moe Dee? Hey, how's aboot you get off your whore. I know you're in there. Get off your mink and come outside.

Under pretense of addressing the fallen clothes, Peggy ran to the armoire, closed one door to quickly conceal Litz, then gathered the dresses and hung them again. RH remained preoccupied with the scene outside while Litz was in plain view, scrabbling to hide himself with any garment he could find while the doors gaped open. Peggy shut the second door panel.

There was a satisfying noise when the oakley's two doors connected at their brass clasp and Litz was once again out of sight.

Peggy, said RH, finally turning to see what she was doing. You should really come see.

What is it, dear?

He looked down once more. On the path to the gate, Campbell stood and unbuttoned his collar, undid his tie, took them off, and hung them on a fence peg along with his hat. Piece by piece the clothing came off until he was naked.

Through the wainscotting RH heard the crunk of feet in the room next door, the murmur of a man's voice saying: 'The fuck? The next-door window's hinge squeaked and a flustered head poked out and looked in all directions. 'The fuck? said Moe Dee.

RH splashed down in his tub to get completely out of view when Peggy opened the window and, wearing only her black gauze, remained standing there, smoking a cigarette, watching Campbell in her yard.

What's going on, Peggy? said Moe Dee from the next window.

Hell's bells, said Peggy. Campbell, what a you think you're doing in my front lawn?

Campbell said: Get down here, you bohunk. I heard you're speaking lies saying I can't play the man game, is that right?

Yeah, that's right. And I never seen you prove me wrong.

You cheat, you liar, you poltroon, said Campbell, fists clenched. Get the fuck down here and say that. Let's see if you got anything to back up your words. Play me or get the fuck out a town, because you ain't got a friend around here otherwise.

You're on.

The red lantern hanging from the front door swayed as the crowd ran out and others huddled at the windows and on the porch. The sign NO MINERS ALLOWED fell off the gate and was crumpled under boots. If you were a young peeler who wanted to gain respect from your fellows, you got as close to the action as possible to see Campbell versus Moe Dee. It was early enough in history that every sighting was worth seven stories.

Moe Dee didn't even dress to go downstairs. His only comforts in life followed him to the banister and, holding her towel against her with one hand, cheered him on with the other.

Swing low, she cried, Remember he a shorty.

He ran out the door straight at Campbell. Campbell fisted both hands in defence, and when he chucked a punch Moe Dee snatched it at the wrist and dragged him two-three-four steps through the mud and shoved him through a pirouette down one arm, catching him, then spun him across his body and pirouetted him down the other arm, this time not catching his fall *{see fig. 13.1}*.

That's my *first* point, said Moe Dee very loudly. I'm in the man game, he hollered. A lot of noise was made to celebrate this, most of it made by Moe Dee.

Nice addition to the Pisk, said a connoisseur, the clean white sling on his arm explaining to one and all why he, brave though he was, and so expert in the qualities and nuances of the man game, could not himself partake.

Trying to deke Dee out, Campbell lurched around and swooped in to take him. In Moe Dee's peripheral he saw Campbell start to drop, gently, like a maiden in front of him. He raised his arms above his head to exculpate himself from the obvious fainting spell that landed Campbell flat on his back in the mud again.

FIGURE 13.1
The Pisk, alternative sketch, moment of release

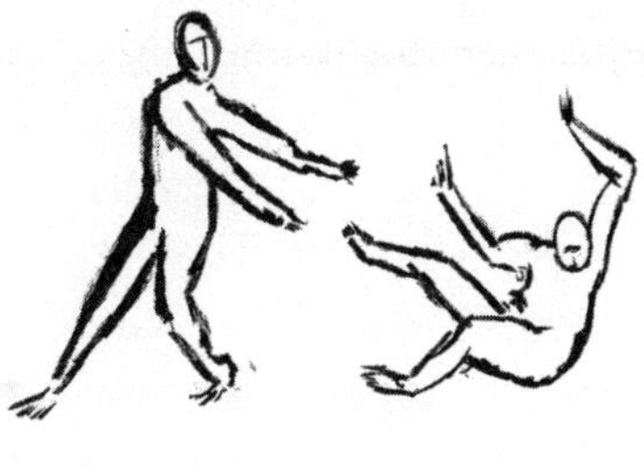

The Campbell, cried those who recognized the flop *{see fig. 13.2}*.

I told your owners you were no good, said Moe Dee while everyone else laughed.

A different cloud's rain fell on their heads. It was a new day according to the lean moon's place in the sky, past midnight with cumulonimbus on the run. Campbell smashed his fists into the black muck. It's going to work, he said.

Who the fuck invited the po'? said one fellow shouldering his way quickly through the crowd, looking over his back as he ran.

Before anyone had a chance to react, the po-lice came a-running behind him with billy clubs and whistles.

Ah, shit-fuck, said Campbell.

The po-lice tied three spectators to the fence and chased Moe Dee and Campbell through the house to the top floor of Wood's where they lost both. Opening door after door, all they found were shocked johns and yawning whores, but no sign of Moe Dee or Campbell. When they got to Peggy's room, she was sitting in the bath. Problem, sirs? she asked the po-lice, while she lathered her slim arms.

Smells like pipe smoke, said the po-lice.

Who are you hiding? said the po-lice, crumpling up the covers and looking under the bed.

I'm right over here, baby, she said, nearly shrieking. Are you here to arrest me, or just to look through my delicates?

FIGURE 13.2
The Campbell, alternative sketch

There ain't no buddies here, said the po-lice, opening the wardrobe and fingering her clothes indelicately.

Madam, said the po-lice—she knew them well—tipping their hats, shutting the door, and running back into the hall looking for Moe Dee and Campbell.

When Peggy bent to raise herself from the tub she pressed her buttocks right on Litz's chest, and he couldn't hold his breath any longer. Flailing his limbs in desperation, he sucked in full lungs' worth of RH Alexander's bathwater. He threw her off him and leaped up, collapsed over the tub, splashing all over her valuable rugs as he fell to the floor and gagged and vomited and convulsed in all directions, unable to breathe, suds oozing from his mouth, nose, and eyes. Peggy watched him, laughing.

Thanks to Peggy's good thinking, RH was long gone through the secret staircase before the po-lice even got in the house. It took him from the second floor of Wood's straight to the coach house in back. There, he went behind the gambling room and found the hidden switch that opened a door to the narrow corridor leading to the ladder that took him down into the tunnels under the city. Knowing this maze better than his own convictions, RH was at ease down here in the candlelit tunnels and, before he knew it, he surfaced again behind the wall of his private bathroom in Hastings Mill, and after a cursory look through the papers on his desk, proceeded home to his wife in a foul mood.

Moe Dee and Campbell weren't far behind him. When Campbell reached the entrance to the corridor in the coach house he turned to Moe Dee, out of breath, and said: You're part a the man game now, so I got to show you this, too.

Just hurry up, said Moe Dee. They were both naked, and Campbell was dirtier than a river rat. The po-lice were still on their tail.

In the liveliness of the moment Moe Dee had mistaken the secret staircase in Wood's for a normal architectural feature, so when he found himself in the coach house he was confused, he was alert, he realized that the entrance to the tunnel was a secret. A secret lever opened the panel in the wall to a crevice that he was expected to enter, very narrow, as narrow as the space between Peggy's bosoms. For Moe Dee to even get in there he would have to take a deep breath and put his hands above his head. It was a completely unlit narrow hallway that led straight into the wall, and, if he could trust Campbell, to a ladder that went straight down into more dark.

You ever been in the mines? asked Campbell.

Hells, yeah, said Moe Dee.

Shh, keep your voice down, for Christ—

I'm twice your age, you little—

Quit breathing over me, said Campbell. Goddamn. We're safe, man. Don't worry, loosen the reins a little.

'The fuck's that supposed to—

Shh. We wait down here till the coast is clear. This is a secret a the man game, kumtuks? You don't tell nobody aboot this.

Moe Dee was uncharacteristically silent.

Campbell guided him to the first lantern in the tunnel where they talked as it flickered against the hard earth. The cavernous, dripping earth was supported by massive lumber beams. A trickle of metallic water fell off the ceiling straight into a puddle and was absorbed just as monotonously. A white worm seethed out of the wall and necked its way into the cold emptiness.

Campbell said: You're good, Moe Dee. Where'd you learn to do that? You want to practise with us? We're looking for more players.

Is that right? You and your owners?

Yeah, you heard me, eh, said Moe Dee. I beat you fair and square. One-nothing.

You don't kumtuks the ins and outs, do you? Bah, he said. Campbell washed his hands of this guy. He added: Do you even know what you're doing? Who's your coach? Ha ha. Furry and Daggett told me you called me out at the Sunnyside Hotel. I thought you might know the man game, but you were just being your same-old loudmouth self, eh? Ha ha.

I *beat* you.

I can't bel*ie*ve I lost to an amateur. Goddammit, my luck.

I got to forget aboot this damn move, because I know I can beat you. I know I can.

//

Toronto brought Sammy a telegram in an envelope. Sammy asked him to open it and show him. After he read the telegram from his father, he had Toronto throw it straight into the stove. It said: BROTHER DEAD STOP MA DETERIORATES STOP.

His father was always so parsimonious, Sammy thought, even when doling out tragedy. Ever since Toronto mentioned that his brother had stayed at Wood's, he couldn't get the scene out of his mind. When his mind should've been on accounting, it was instead on salacious details. Scandalous venereal possibilities. The Whore Without A Face. The egg-white sky lacked its yolk, as if this clouded gesso had swept clean the canvas of all previous solar and lunar mistakes and started the atmosphere over. Nowhere did it look like weather. Preweather. People's moods could be equally indiscernible.

Upon Molly's arrival home, Sammy confessed: I heard from my father.

Molly said: What did he demand you do this time? Divorce me? She took off her shoes, unleashed her scarves, and came with a flourish into the living room, kissed her husband lovingly and went and slumped on her stomach across the sofa, with paper spread in front of her, illustrated with figures.

Who drew those? he asked, distracted enough by her activities to forget to answer her question.

Her eyes lit up. Calabi, she said. I never even asked. Can you imagine?

Toronto went to the hearth and balanced a log on the ashing fire.

Yes, I suppose I can.

She said: It's such a kind gesture. Both he and Yau are the string that binds us all, they're connected to everyone in town, aren't they?

In a manner a speaking, said Sammy cautiously.

Those beautiful pastries. Pure inspiration. Just a girl on a sofa, she kicked her legs in the air behind her as she leafed through the illustrations made for her by the ever-dextrous Calabi. She arched an eyebrow at her husband, said: … What was it you said aboot your father?

Yes, ah, more news aboot Dunbar. Apparently, he became deathly ill almost immediately after leaving Vancouver, said Sammy, drawing conclusions.

A single eyebrow ticked in her expression. He watched carefully, studying her for the blush of deceit. She said: With what?

Rampant venereal disease, he said flatly, waiting for her reaction to his conjecture. Sammy looked at his wife with an expectant glare.

Is that so? she said, unsurprised. Hm …, serves the philanderer right, then, one might argue.

You would?

Darling, death's a pity. You have my sympathies.

You pretend to be upset. Why? Why even pretend? Did you—did you send him to his death? he blurted.

Me? Why, whatever do you mean?

Sammy wept. After nearly a year as a man without power over his body, it was as if he'd finally lost control of his head as well. He was helpless to contain his blubbering lips and streaming tears. In a single movement she was beside him, kissing his neck.

I didn't know your brother, Sammy, but it still affects me, Molly said. It's my loyalty to *you* why I fail to muster your deep sorrow. You were his brother. He did not even attend our wedding. What I know a him is only that he tortured you. I see he tortures you even in death.

Alas, said Sammy after she daubed off his tears with a kerchief, you're right. I don't feel any sorrow, either. Oh, I'm sorry. I only thought that—well, perhaps if I could draw you a fine picture, or make you a delicious pastry, or dance in the street for you … never mind.

Oh, these are trifles compared to thee, she sang. My hard work is all for you.

Likewise, he said. Sammy decided not to pursue her strategies any further, for now. If he was going to find out, he realized he would have to investigate this from other angles. The only way to understand Molly's motives was to approach them slantwise. Pick up the trail left behind the wheels of her machinations, and draw conclusions based on the circularity of the path. He calmed himself and said: Perhaps I even feel like a knot a anger has disentangled. Yet. While he was in town, I wrote in my journal that I wished him dead. And today it's so. What do you think?

Oh, my dear, warm-hearted Chinook, she said and petted his hair, kissed his face, landing her warm, swollen bottom lip over his, the telltale sugar on her breath. My love, she said.

Her pink cheeks brought out the epic in her eyes. The blue-flecked green of islands, earths. Sweet Sammy, she said, and nested her head under his chin. He was stranded on her, and content, though certain he'd just been deceived.

The night came fast. He slept in fitful purges. In another life he did not dodge the things he feared.

When he awoke she was still beside him in bed. She smiled and stretched her fine arms. Her arms reminded him at that moment of the shape and colours of the arbutus tree, chocolate-blond with a fiery streak; and the arbutus, the dancer of the trees, reminded him of her preoccupations, her history, the man game, the theatre. Oh, I had the best sleep ever, she said.

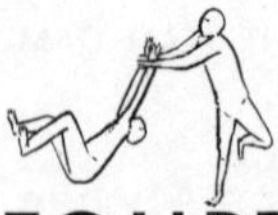

FOURTEEN

> ... a trade language of some kind probably existed prior to European contact, which began "morphing" into the more familiar Chinook Jargon in the late 1790s, notably at a dinner party at Nootka Sound where Capts Vancouver and Bodega y Quadra were entertained by Chief Maquinna and his brother Callicum performing a theatrical using mock-English and mock-Spanish words and mimickry[sic]of European dress and mannerisms.
>
> — WIKIPEDIA

At the bottom of high tide, sole, flounder, cod, and crabs drove in to eat from southern shores of the inlet, below Sammy's office. Sometimes when the tide sucked back out there remained fish trapped in rock ponds. The smell around Vancouver was sometimes poisonous from the schools of dying fish. If the wind blew south off the water, nausea crashed over the whole township.

The office doorhandle wobbled around and a Hastings Mill messageboy slid in and noiselessly delivered a telegram folded in half. Toronto opened the paper, dented with type, and showed it to Sammy, who read: YOUR MOTHER DIED STOP FUNERAL SUNDAY STOP ...

Sunday stop. Your Mother. He stared at the telegram for some time. In the weeks since his brother had left town, he'd been thinking about him. Dunbar. Again The Whore Without A Face. His brother and mother were dead. And the two telegrams were the most he'd heard from his father since his decision to move to Vancouver. There were more words in the telegram but they didn't appear on the paper, they just appeared, as if transcribed from the cold heart of reckoning.

His wife was a destroyer. He blamed her. Slowly but surely she was bringing his whole family crumbling in on him.

His heart, a little bruised, compelled him to speak, and Toronto listened to him talk about his mother: During my boyhood I saw Mother as no different from a toy. She was a top that I let spin around the kitchen, preparing meals—a *joy*, she said—bouncing her off the walls a the living room with a duster in her hand while I followed, laughing at the brink a tears, spinning her further and further away from herself until my brother caught her, scolded me, and sequestered her in the library where she quietly, assiduously helped him study agriculture. Pardon me my reveries, Toronto. How are you? Sammy asked.

Better, said Toronto. Much better, thanks, sir.

Sammy had a peregrine falcon inside the bookshelf, on the topmost shelf, perched on a block of wood in its aerie between leatherbound journals of advanced teleological accounting, staring perpetually over its wing down at the two men seated in the office. There was the slope-shouldered redskin dripping India ink on a rulered page. And there was the immobilized one who looked back at the falcon with complicated envy.

I trust you with my innermost thoughts, said Sammy. I trust you with my deepest fears. My cruellest imaginings. My worst prejudices. I trust you without judgment or protest. And I trust you to keep it all a secret, as if from your own mind. And you have done so without fail.

Toronto nodded.

And I need that more than ever now. I have no defences against you or the world, Sammy said. I haven't a single means a defence. I could die by your hands this very moment. Every word, I trust you not to strangle me with. These words are all I have. I don't know how else to explain it. I barely enjoy life. I tell *you*. These journals feel like my only freedom from the prison a my blasted head. May I ask you a question?

Toronto nodded.

Are you telling me the truth? Are you feeling better?

Toronto tried but failed to convincingly nod.

I know you don't want to, said Sammy. We must. We must see your father, your mother, your chief.

Yessir, said Toronto, but Indians might kill me.

You might still die if we don't.

He didn't tell his ward about the death of his own mother, to keep Toronto's feelings uncomplicated. Still the Indian wept. He said: No one ever help me before.

Let's find Molly and take you to see your peoples.

//

Little August Jack Khatsahlahno, not ten years old, stood under the Burrard Bridge and watched the waters of False Creek break along the pebbles and bleached shells with a sound not unlike footsteps. Jack did not know to whom the ocean walked, or for how many eons the ocean's search had continued, but nevertheless the child was reckoned a genius by the members of the Snauq Indian reserve who had lived under this bridge since before there was a bridge, a Vancouver, a Whitemans. The Snauq had been living in this area so long, in fact, that their oldest ancestors had turned into stones, and so had their dogs. So no one thought he was being foolish, standing on the beach dreaming up ways to get attention, when this child skidded to a stop by the firepit in the middle of the longhouse to say there was a ghost on False Creek. And indeed, when Chief Chip-kaay-am and the others made their way down to the beach there was, as Jack had said, a ghost travelling towards them across the water. He paddled a cedar canoe, accompanied by two Whitemans, a man and a lady, as well as some cargo, namely a large wheeled chair.

When the canoe rubbed ashore, Chip-kaay-am held up his palm, made it clear he'd talk only to Sammy, and refused to allow any of them to disembark. He warned Sammy that if Toronto stepped foot on Snauq ground they'd instantly kill him. There were weapons among them. No one in the canoe was surprised to hear it. Toronto lowered his eyes. The three of them sat in the canoe, one behind the other with Toronto at the back and Sammy at the front and Molly in the middle, moving only their heads in the cradle of the waves, as Sammy reasoned with the Chief. English was not easy, so they talked partly in Chinook, and had to make do even as Chip-kaay-am grew more and more impatient at being misunderstood. There was no need for him to feel much afraid confronting these unarmed guests with two hundred armed Indians around him. He could have spoken Sto:lo with Toronto, but even the Chief was forbidden to speak to a ghost. Chip-kaay-am was flanked by two elders with stooped backs and forlorn eyes, each with a blouse made of woven cedar bark, one hooded, the other carrying an adze. The hooded old lady had both her legs slathered with black molasses. And even in the hands of an old woman that adze looked like a threatening tool, the way she clasped it to her breast so the stone blade glinted.

Sammy, meanwhile, continued to reason with the Chief. There seemed to be no reasoning with him. He was unflinchingly cross-armed. A Hudson's Bay blanket was draped across his shoulder and over his hands. But unlike most of his peoples, who wore cedar, the Chief was dressed in a brown wool suit that fit him well considering his full belly. He was shoeless. The feet had blackened soles. He was packed solid from the toeknuckles on up. Seven feet above, the ridge on the top of his skull was pronounced even through his full head of white hair.

Sick, said Sammy in Chinook. Hyas sick. Wagh, he said in Chinook. Piu piu, he added for emphasis.

Shem, said the Chief. Mamook isick home, he said, pointing to the waters they'd just crossed, meaning to suggest they do the trip again posthaste.

No, not, wake, said Sammy, repeating himself. Snauq kumtuks la mestin. Snauq tamahnous mamook elann Toronto.

Kowkwutl mamook elann memaloost.

Not memaloost, argued Sammy, Toronto is alive. Moosum, Sammy said, koko moosum.

Cultus wauwau, said Chip, brushing him off.

Cultus wauwau is right, said Molly, balancing herself in the canoe rim as she started to climb off the boat. I'm bored a listening to you boys talk and talk. You're never going to get anywhere with this man, Sammy. Chip-kaay-am, she said to the Chief, I'm getting off this canoe and don't get tied in a knot over it.

Wa wa, said all the Indians when they saw her begin to move.

Enough cultus wauwau, said Molly, splashing up the beach to meet the Snauq, who retreated in a kind of fear, raising their arms and trying to intimidate her even as they backed away. She turned and waved for Toronto, as if he should follow her to the shore. Toronto was not given the chance to so much as swallow before the weapons started coming out in plain sight. The Indians positioned themselves like that, ready for anything, and Molly made it obvious the performance left her unimpressed.

Molly, said her husband, I believe it's time you returned to the canoe before—

Oh, come now, Chinooky, she said.

Arrows pointed at you, said Sammy. Arrows, Chinook.

Pshaw, she said, arrows in the hands a sweethearts who never pierced more than fishscale. Toronto, will you assist me in taking Sammy's chair to the shore?

You be careful, said Sammy to his wife as she splashed back into the water, leaned over the canoe, and tried to lift up Sammy's chair. Help me, will you? she said to Toronto, and dutiful to the death, he obeyed her. He climbed off the boat, up to his knees in slippery green ribbons of seaweed. The Snauq hissed upon seeing him move, but what other choice did he have? Without the Erwagens what other life did he have? Exile. He heard the bows stretch back with arrows tracing him as he helped her lift the chair above the water and walk it onto the pebble beach. The ghost stood on the beach dripping.

Molly smoothed her half-soaked skirts and shook the water off her boots, arched her back, inhaled deeply and, making a clownish sort of walrus mouth, blew a ringlet of damp black hair away from one of her eyes. She was right. No one took a shot at her. She took out her change purse—they flinched as if she might have a pistol—squeezed apart its brass clasp, picked through the money, and asked for a third person to help carry Sammy off the canoe. Her nerve caused a minor furor among the Snauq, and at any moment a stray arrow was going to get shot off, so before things got retributional Chip-kaay-am quieted his peoples down again. Little young genius Jack was by this point at his Chief's side. They conferred.

What is the child whispering to the Chief? asked Sammy.

Shh, said Toronto.

Whatever the child genius Jack Khatsahlahno and the Chief had conversated about, Sammy was lifted from the canoe by silent Indian men and chaperoned to the safe land of the Snauq reserve in his wheeled chair. Chief Chip-kaay-am was leading the way up the beach to the longhouse. Most of the Indians who walked beside him were unusually silent. When the road became too rutted for his wheeled chair, they carried him again. An old woman with blistered skin wobbled alongside sucking on her lip and coughing until the amount of phlegm brought her to a stop and she leaned against the wall of a salmon-smoking hut to catch her breath. There was the ghost, named Toronto in his afterlife, here walking unaccompanied through the village of his childhood, among family, brothers, sisters, cousins, uncles, aunts, his own mother, and still he walked alone. He was, Sammy noted, the darkest Snauq among them. He saw that Toronto was unable to resist staring down into a cedar box filled with pungent oolichan fish grease. Little Jack ran up beside Sammy and put his hand on the armrest of his wheeled chair and followed along for a few footsteps, staring into Sammy's eyes until Sammy said: Klahowya, in the voice a man uses on a child, with discipline in mind. The very next instant, a score of bumbling children in woven clothing skipped around his chair in play circles as he rolled his way to the longhouse, all of them wanting to hear the crippled Whitemans say: Klahowya.

Molly rolled her husband past a Snauq crouched on the ground fanning a pile of white ashes that gave off a hot, clear, bread-scented smoke. Her hands were a hundred years older than the rest of her, but moved nimbly over the roaming heat. Molly leaned with her shoulder to get Sammy over a slow patch of mush, and whispered in his ear: Love you. She also kissed him half on his lips, half on his cheek, and he loved her. Such was his life, highs and lows and interminable anguish. The high cedar doors of the longhouse were carved with the design of a raven's head tilted up, set inside the shape of a coin or shield. Sammy said: I'm looking forward to seeing the inside of the longhouse.

Oh yes, said his wife, as am I.

And then at the doors, the Chief turned to the couple and asked that Toronto enter the longhouse unaccompanied. Molly's shoulders fell, and her chin stuck out. Girlish woman or womanly girl or performer, whatever it was made her say: No, we'll come. For his safety we should.

The Chief waved his hand, no. The Snauq wanted to speak to Toronto in private. It was time for the ghost of Snauq peoples to return home. But he must do so alone.

No, said Molly, we want to come, too.

Dear, said Sammy.

What? I think it's—

I go in alone, said Toronto. Is okay. Is okay.

The raven's head and beak split open, and the tranquil interior darkness of the Snauq longhouse—perforated by bands of linty sunlight—held the soul's own fragrance in its body. Not a house at all, but a creature, a sleeping beast. The great shadowy mysteries of the Snauq longhouse. And that brief encounter was all the Erwagens got before the doors shut again.

Those Indians who weren't included returned to their chores. A man added another bale to the stacks of dogbane tied up and piled against the longhouse's south wall. Beyond that, a long rope was tied between two trees where long fleshy sleeves of cedar bark hung to dry in the sunlight. A woman was lifting each tawny strip and rotating its position to give the other half some sun.

The Erwagens were left alone to wheel awkwardly around the Snauq reserve, first between the smaller log houses then finally making their way down to the beach, where the creek narrowed under the Burrard Street Bridge. They unnerved the ducks, who shattered the surface of the water as they took briefly to flight. A gull on a log raised its wings and jumped as the ducks passed, then resettled.

It's pretty here, said Molly.

You're pretty here, said Sammy.

I'm not pretty. I'm one a those ducks. I should flap over there with them and paddle along in the seaweed.

If those ducks looked like you, said her husband, the whole city would be swimming beside them.

Hm, said Molly.

Such as it was, the married couple were having trouble. It was at the beach, under the bridge, where they felt the need to reflect.

Molly said: There's a man game on Sunday, and I want you to see it. I believe it will be our first official performance.

What have you been doing till now?

Rehearsals, she said. Auditions, she said.

Rehearsals and auditions, said Sammy. Hm, that's not how I've heard it put before.

Sunday shall be altogether different. It's truly ready for you to see now.

You're certain?

Yes, I've decided.

It's all arranged then.

Yes, I'd say it's almost ready. I need only arrange for the competitors … but I need to know you'll be there, yes?

Let me take a look at the calendar, he said. Traditionally, Sunday has been the day I spend at rest, he added.

I swear, if you're not there to see it, I won't speak to you ever again. I might live with you, but you won't hear my voice.

Oh, come now. What if I have a crisis at the mill?

I *swear.* You don't come, I button down the lips.

The lips, he said. But I love the lips.

Then …

It was low tide, and they looked over the wide bar—fifteen-twenty acres of rocky, shell-crusted beach that Sammy yearned to walk over. How he missed the simple chore of walking on a rocky beach, turning over stones, watching the crabs scatter, prodding the starfish. The sea, cold as granite, and silent. The waves squeezed lightly on the beach like toes curling.

Sammy saw how they fished here. The top halves of a long set of fences were visible in the water. Made of maple vine and cedar stakes driven into the mud, they corralled the fish from the opening in the strait, and as the fish swam into the narrow, the fences tapered to a point in the waters entering False Creek, trapping the halibut, mackerel, and smelts together for easy netting. On the beach he could see the round nets, their fine thread of stinging nettle spread flat and laid to dry. He saw the mossed slab of island in the water, a sandclot in the tidal surge and suck, a few hibiscus growing in the gaps.

That must be where they put their dead, said Sammy. Toronto told me that when they thought he'd died, they wrapped him in blankets and put him on smam-chuze, the island a the dead. This must be it, eh.

You never told me he said that.

I didn't want to disturb you.

How well do you think you know me if you won't tell me a delicious story like *that*?

Nevertheless, this must be smam-chuze, the Snauq's island a the dead.

And he awoke …

Yes, said Sammy, and he awoke, almost suffocating inside the blankets, what he believes was the following night. He called across for help to return home, but no one answered him. It was as though he no longer existed. When he saw his mother at the beach, she fell to her knees and grieved to the island as if he had died, as if he wasn't calling to her. She disbelieved in him utterly.

How very sad.

It's become a sort a friendship between us, said Sammy. He was exiled from his family, and I exiled myself from mine.

He could see her thinking hard. Her eyes blinked especially hard. I like to know *everything*, she said.

Yes, I know, said Sammy.

She looked at the water. Oh, Chinook. You're so smart, she said, lifting herself onto the toes of her leather boots, twice, before settling down. I'm sorry. I know you'd never conceal something from me intentionally. You're much too good a man to do that.

Yes, he said, thinking of the telegrams he'd received and wondering why he couldn't tell her about his mother's death.

Behind them, they heard noises coming from the longhouse. As they listened closer, Sammy realized it was laughter. Peals of laughter.

Laughter? said Molly.

Sounds friendly enough, said Sammy.

I knew they would, said Molly. After all that holus-bolus, they welcomed him back in the end.

//

Greening treetops swayed in the breeze. The morning air was thickly fresh. The blowhards on the city's streets were huffing and puffing about the man game, imitating moves and guffawing. They gassed on about work, what little of it there was. A lot of guys were wasting their breath on next Sunday's meeting about the *pestilent wind from the Orient*, with speakers counting themselves among the Knights of Labour, according to the posters, which were everywhere.

With his head down, brushing dust from his whiskers, RH slinked in the door of the laundry, and with a less-than-respectable nod of his head to the Chinamen who struggled with irons over whole hampers' worth of Whitemans garments, each stack tagged with a card in Chinese, he proceeded past stacks of linens that waited to be spat upon and steamed of their wrinkles. With a shortage of labour, wait time for laundry in Vancouver, as RH well knew, was up to three days. His wife complained about this. Laundry was a concern. He knocked twice on a clapboard wall at the back of the store and no sooner had he rapped than a set of long-nailed fingers on the other side scrabbled and pried away a narrow splinter of wood at eye level to reveal the burning stare of a Chinaman guard, who let RH pass beyond into the realms of the unreal, the opium sellers' cave.

What you want today, Mr. Alexander? said the dealer in less than a whisper.

RH passed him the money and he handed RH two balls of mud for the dimes.

The dealer covered his mouth with one hand. He said: I hope you know how to fight for your life, sir.

What d'you mean by that? RH asked.

San Francisco know everyting happen here.

What does he know?

This meeting *Sun*day … said the dealer, shaking his head with disapproval.

The Knights *of* Labour, thought RH, are going to get me killed.

When the effects of the opium wore off and he was able to walk again RH returned to the tunnels, followed the wet dark underground route that took him to the Stag & Pheasant saloon, surfaced there in the ladies room, established his presence by ordering a whisky before saluting the patrons and rushing home. He credited the looks on everyone's faces as uncloseted patricidal envy. Once inside his home he shut the door, locked it, double-checked it, shut the drapes, took a breath. Without so much as removing his coat or galoshes, RH met his wife in the den, where she'd readied the trays and pipes and lit the paraffin so that the moment he arrived they could set down to smoke, relax the niggling intellect, and sink into calumny.

At the opium den he'd bought an ounce of Ta Sin, with its especially coca aftertaste. It said on the tin: *You will know no difference between day and night.*

Minutes later, the smoke lingered in the air. His wife sat. He laid his head in her lap, holding her at the waist. The Chinamen. They're going to kill me, he said.

I simply won't allow it.

If it's not the snakehead, it's my own *men.*

They'll have to come through me first.

Even this petty dealer. He knew I was marked.

Don't talk like this, Mrs. Alexander said. You scare me. He raised himself from her bosom and went to rest on the day bed. She followed behind him and knelt at his side, watching him explore the snug chasm between the upholstered backrest and seat. He found a dirty penny, pocketed it, and collapsed in fatigue.

Ah, God, he said, near to tears. I cherish the smallest compensations.

Darling, no, please, she said, kissing his knuckles. I've been waiting to share this moment a tranquility with you. I cherish this time, too. Let's think aboot your predicament after dinner. One must always make important decisions on a full stomach. For now, let us simply enjoy, as you say, our small compensations. I promise that no harm will … Her eyelashes fluttered and her neck bundled up as her jaw fell open with a dry smack. The cords of her neck blooded her mind. He knew where she was because he was there too. In too deep.

//

The sun was a vein of gold capping a lion's jaw of blue mountains. Great schooners sat anchored on their quiet reflections in the waters of English Bay. Up the beach, Toronto shook hands with Joe Fortes, who sat himself on a log overlooking the gentle crests falling on the sand. The Negro looked neither disturbed by the sunset nor at peace with it.

The two men talked briefly.

Fortes asked him: You wanna go for a swim with me?

Nah, said Toronto. Not today. Feel sick. Only stop to say klahowya.

Well, too bad. Even now?

Better.

What kind a sick you been?

Toronto pointed to his stomach and rear end.

They fixed you? Fortes asked.

Hoping so, said Toronto.

Damn, a swim do you good, no?

No, said Toronto.

I *love* a swim. Always have. Ever since I been a little boy it's been my belief that a swim in the ocean ever day is good for your health. Your lungs. Your muscles. Your joints. You feel good after a swim. Even your confidence is helped by learning to swim.

Toronto was looking southwest over the bay in the general direction of his Snauq Indian reserve, unseen behind a voluminous white mist. Where you come from, Joe? he asked.

Maybe this story's familiar to yours, said Fortes. Place called Barbados. Plenty far south from here. You in a boat for *months*. I learn to swim on my island.

You live on island?

Water not like here. Very warm, so warm. Beautiful island. You go around Vancouver in short pants you catch pneu*mon*ia. In Barbados, you swim all year round.

The waters of English Bay turned apricot as they rippled. Then plum. An evening wind picked up. A soaking wet Fortes was still seated on the log and Toronto remained standing beside him and they watched the sun go down. The blue herons returned to roost in the park's big-leaf maple trees, one after the other, shouting husbands returning with dust in their hair after a long day of neck-breaking labour. Then, as if experiencing a memory shared by every Vancouverite that ever was, Toronto watched Fortes bolt down the beach at a heavy clip, kicking sand, and dive headlong into the inky waters. He stood up from the first few strokes and hooted, wiped his face and scalp and turned to look back at Toronto. Come on in, Fortes said. Water's all warmed up.

No, Toronto shook his head, smiling. In fact, he had to be off, he had to go. He called out goodbye to Fortes, and Fortes stood with his fists on his hips, keeping his balance in the tide, and bid Toronto a perplexed goodbye.

You just gonna leave me out here alone? Come on, a swim be good for ever one.

Toronto was deep in the trees again. The jungle of Indian skookum. He knew it well. His path turned north at a mammoth red cyprus tree uprooted many years ago by shifting sand. From the darkened base where a cavernous muck formed inside the trunk and its tangled root system spoked out in every direction there were already two strong new saplings four feet high, green as can be and aimed for the sky. One of Toronto's relatives once told him that when an old tree falls, Salish go look for petrified elk dung underneath its tentaculate roots. This old tree's roots were cinder black, sashed with bright moss. The elk were no myth. No Whitemans ever saw elk, but Indians had lived here for three thousand years and still occasionally unearthed petrified elk antlers, even centuries after they'd been hunted to extinction.

He walked through the sloping dark trails towards the squatters town near Lost Lagoon where Clough lived. He'd never been to Clough's place before, so it was going to take him a moment to locate the right lean-to. He picked his way through, eyeing the driftwood abodes with sheet metal roofs and the great variety of indigent who pimpled this landscape. Sore faces, dug deep with scars and troubles, great sacks full of defeat slung below their eyes. Men sat on flipped-over buckets and smoked pipes and watched Toronto, slow-cooking skewers of grey squirrel over the smoking coals of a campfire. Hooch bottles were strewn everywhere.

Got any chickamin? begged one guy, too drowsy to even raise his hand.

Naw, sir, said Toronto. He knew he'd figure out where Clough lived if he followed the smell of all the animals.

Clough's makeshift poundkeep. The manure smell. Mildewed oat smell. The mutts barking. Clough's shack was the only one that had a fence around it. He slipped, muddied his hands, got up, studied and sniffed, wiped the mud-only grub on his legs, and when he came to knock on the door to Clough's shack, he cleaned them one last time.

//

Inside Clough's hut they heard Toronto's tentative rap and everyone turned their head to the door to look, except for Molly, who kept her eyes on Furry, and Furry, who kept his eyes on Molly.

Daggett, Clough, Campbell, Smith, Boyd, and Meier stared at the door until Daggett barked: Well, don't just stand agape—somebody answer it.

Too early? asked Toronto when he stepped inside.

No, right on time, Molly said, and rose from her seat. Furry and Daggett and then Clough rose from their seats, each following Furry's lead and putting on airs. Each and every man tipped his hat in respect for her. She was too pretty. None of them had spoken from their proper mouths. In the presence of a real lady, they'd been reduced to teary-eyed stupefied Duh.

She said: We have a deal?

Furry smiled. One brown tooth showed. He said: Yeah, I guess we do.

Why, just listen here, Mrs. Erwagen, said Clough. If nobody else's going to speak from the gut right now, then let me be the first to spleen a little. I got more than competition on the line here. All these men, their respectability among their fellows. You put it all in danger with your plans. You know that don't you? Comprehend one thing, Mrs. Erwagen. These men play along because we kumtuks what's to benefit. Long run, short run. We see opportunity. So don't expect we just lay down and let you rub our bellies like dogs. When it comes to the man game, we intend to never get beat. So this better not be some trick.

Isn't, said Molly. How could it be? We'll see you Sunday, then.

Sunday, said Furry.

//

Toronto was as keen to know what she'd said to Furry & Daggett as she was to know what happened to him in the longhouse. He tried with body language, but she remained stoic and introspective and didn't notice his head-bobbing, just as he had consciously ignored her head-bobbing after the longhouse. They retrieved the canoe and began the portage home along Coal Harbour. He was in the back using his paddle to steer while she thrust with great strength up at the front, cutting the waves and stirring up phosphorescent algae below. Three in the afternoon, the clouds so thick it was nighttime already. He faced her back, within the wind of her berry scent.

Soon she said: Sammy told me aboot your family problems. Aboot your death … had I known, Toronto … this, we could a solved this so simply and easily long ago. You see that I'm quite resourceful. I only wish you felt more trust. Toronto, there is so much a the world, a huge incalculably vast world, and yet this Earth is nothing but a speck in the infinite. You're reunited with your family. In the eyes a your people, you are reborn.

Yes, ma'am, said Toronto as he paddled.

Does it feel like so, like a rebirth?

Mrs. Erwagen, yes, ma'am.

Yes, I can feel you have a much stronger presence behind me right now even as I paddle. Yes, I almost don't need to turn around to see you. I *can* see you. Look, your face is the reflection a the moon on the water. Toronto, it may not seem as though I think aboot you, but I am beside myself to know how much you suffered in my presence. And without my full knowledge. And to deliver you back to your world, your soul. Oh, Toronto. How does it feel?

No way I can explain how.

Toronto, I simply must know, you simply must tell me what made you all laugh so much in the longhouse.

She approached the question with her usual grace and sensitivity. The waves lapping at the birchbark sides, the masculine freshness of the night air, the shattered clusters of stars above them, and her back to him. She was right to say she didn't need to face him to see him. His soul *was* back. The ache and wonder and colour of a soul in all its moods. In the rhythm they shared paddling the canoe he felt comfortable enough to explain one final humiliation on his path to recovery, on his path to what amounted to a Snauq's rebirth.

Toronto explained to her with his halting tongue how inside the longhouse Chief Chip had recited an old ghost story aboot the Snauq. The story was about how a Snauq boy who lived many generations ago died tragically. When the men went to hunt one morning at dawn for rabbits, the boy followed his father and his uncles into the woods, hoping to prove that he was as good a hunter as his father. The young boy crept soundlessly under the arms of the slouching ferns to wait for his prey. His father crouched with a spear in a similar position hidden in a great thicket of moist foliage. In the same instant his father heard a rabbit leap into the green grass clearing, his son was just pouncing to surprise the soft light creature as well, and as the rabbit's ears pricked up and the frightened thing scuttled off, his father stabbed the boy clear through his ribs, fixing his chest to the ground. Father and son looked at each other with terrible shock and remorse. He held on to his father's spear bored through him with bloodied hands. Everything in his heart quickly soaked the earth under his father's feet. Later, the son's body was wrapped in ten of his father's blankets and laid on the island of smam-chuze out of reach of night's wolves. At the first break of dawn after the boy was laid to rest, the father was awoken from a fitful, grieving sleep by a noise he recognized only too well. He was in his bed along with the others in the longhouse, and there was the sound of the embers crackling in the firepit, but this was different, this sound was much closer to his bed. And he distinctly heard what sounded like the breaking of plant stems and kindling. The exact noises he heard before he drove the spear into his son's back. And then, before his eyes, he saw his son. His son was standing in front of him. My son, he cried. You've come back. He reached out his arm to touch his son's chest, which had begun to bleed. My son, he said, and there no was time for the man to react except in horror, as he saw his touch once again transform his son into a gruesome, bruised shadow. Its formless shape dropped over him, baring its slobbering yellow teeth, and strangled the father to death in his bed.

Then, said Toronto, Indian man behind me grip his fingers around my neck. Strangle me.

Strangle *you*? said Molly.

I tried scream, said Toronto, but, Chief said, man's grip impossible. Ghost who talk to Snauq, we kill one more time.

Toronto's face had turned purple then green, his toes had started to twitch. His eyes gushed tears. His gums bled. His tongue fattened and dried. When finally the fingers let go of his neck, Toronto fell to the ground gasping and huffing dust. Then the Chief asked Toronto to show him the problem, and in a daze he proceeded to lower his britches and show the Chief the danglers in front of the community. At first only the Chief laughed, then everyone joined in. Toronto was lying on his stomach on the dirt floor of the longhouse with his pants around his ankles.

Is that how you died, too? said Molly. Were you killed by a hunter?

No, said Toronto. I killed by coho.

A salmon?

Brother schwack me over face with dead coho. Fall my head on rock, eh. Died that way. Waked up later in blankets up a tree, way out on island. I climbed down. When family sees me, Snauqs shrink away. Call me ghost. To Snauq, I was ghost. A ghost talks to Snauq must be killed one more time.

We three are all secretly ghosts, said Molly. Me, you, and Sammy. Perhaps Sammy most a all, eh, wouldn't you agree.

Yes, ma'am, said Toronto.

They were almost home. They docked the canoe and came up the shore, walking down the street towards their house, their footfalls illuminated by flickering gaslamps all along the way.

Exiled, said Molly, and especially my husband. As they took the steps to the verandah, she reached over to touch Toronto.

He still felt her hand on his forehead, where she petted him with great sympathy there on the verandah. And as he instinctively leaned towards her, she embraced him, smoothed his hair, and whispered: Oh, I love you so, Toronto. I trust you'll continue to stay with us? We'd be heartbroken if you left us now.

And he said this was where he belonged.

//

You're too late, said Daggett. He hadn't even changed positions. He was still seated in the same chair as when Molly had come to visit an hour ago. Most of his crew were outside smoking and practising with Clough. Daggett didn't even properly look at RD Pitt; he was the kind of guy who was hard to look at. The way the cowboy dressed, talked, walked, and thought was all wrong, and to look at it straight would be like a concession. We just set up a man game for that very day, Daggett said, and thumped his fist gently on the table like a gavel.

A man game? Why mess with that? I thought you *hated* Litz and Pisk.

We sure as hell do.

Then why have truck for their fools' parade? It's a damn shame, too. We could use your strength to rid this city a the Yellow Peril. Besides, you owe me a favour.

What's that?

Alls I done for the labour movement in this town? You'd be out a job if t'weren't for me. I expected you all at this meeting, goddammit, show this town is *unified* behind the goal.

What goal's that?

To rid this fucking town a the Chinamen.

Bah, I'm done with that route. A man grows up sometime around thirty and starts worrying aboot himself and not the other guy. I don't need to be an injury to others no more, said Daggett.

Horseshit, said Pitt.

We'll not squander our talents on you, said Furry.

On me? What talents on me? Brawn? Mettle?

Listen, Pitt, Daggett said. See, the way I grew up, I'm trained for pain. First thing I thought to do when you stepped in: kill him. Same thing I always think. That's one way to go through life. But me and Furry are devious motherfuckers. We're after one thing, and that's chickamin. Knocking his granite knuckles against each other, he added: Even when I lose everything, still I gain.

That's not the voice a no killer, said RD Pitt, sitting back in his chair and crossing his arms.

'The fuck you know aboot a killer's voice?

You ask me square, I tell you square, said Furry. Kumtuks?

Pitt looked at the dirt on his work-beaten hands, the calluses and scars, the long brown nails, and had nothing to say.

Yeah, I kumtuks, said Pitt, leaning forward on to the table and using his thumbnail to pry moose-jerky loose from his buckteeth. The gristle hit the table.

Ask me what you want to know, said Furry. Ask me.

RD Pitt looked up again from under his Stetson. He mulled for a while, then finally asked: Did you kill that snakehead?

Yeah, ha ha. That's what I thought, cowboy. Can't even look me in the eye. I took some men off the shelf. God forgive me. You want me to start listing. Yeah, I cut the snake to pieces like firewood and burned him the same. Daggett was there, he can tell you.

I accompliced that crime, said Daggett.

But that's not why I'm sitting here listening to you bark like a seal pup, said Furry, and you're the one asking *me* the fucking favour.

What a you mean?

No, no. Learn your manners, cowboy. Now I get to ask a question, eh.

O-kay.

You ever paid back any favours?

Hell's bells, yeah, Pitt said. Who do I look like? Alls I got is my balls and my word.

Furry grabbed Pitt's right wrist and pinned it to the table. Everyone backed off. Pitt shrieked. Furry untucked a handaxe from his belt loop and Pitt started to cry and his knees buckled so that his eyes were level with the table. Please please, no, cried Pitt.

Spread your fucking fingers before I take off the whole goddamn hand, you worthless mule.

Trembling, the fingers eventually did as told.

For what seemed like forever Furry held his axe above his head, waiting, his eyes on Pitt's hand until with vicious speed the axe came down hard on the table, clipping the long grubby moon of Pitt's index fingernail. Furry wrenched the axe out of the table but didn't let go of Pitt's hand just yet.

The fingernail lay there on the table like a dumb smile. It took Pitt awhile to accept the fact that his hand was still in one piece, and he stood on his knees weeping over the lost nail.

Nine more, said Furry.

Nine more? cried Pitt.

I cut you, then we go to the fucking Knights a Labour meeting. I trim your nails, I go to the man game, and you owe *me* a *very big* favour.

//

The homes on Dupont Street were supposed to remind Sammy of Victorian mansions, but with the expensive finials and other artisanal touches at best imitated here and at worst replaced by mildewy walls and tarpaper rooftops and all the cookstoves burning away. The homes on Dupont Street were to him like pretty faces on rotting decapitations. Sammy was upset to find that Wood's' front door resembled his own in all respects, right down to the knocker. Same exact door. He looked up at the windows and then down the street, and saw that candles were lit in all the windows on all the floors of all the houses, and that at every entrance a glowing red paper lantern swayed in the breeze. A girl on the second floor of Wood's leaned her elbows on the windowsill, purple shutters open, smoking a cigarette, swaying her rump. It was quite cold out for a lady to be seen smoking. At the thump of interior noise, she pushed herself off the sill and turned to look into her room and said: Yeah?, folded the shutters closed like a wink, gone.

I've never visited a bordello, he said; and was silently wheeled to the door by his ward, where he waited below the red paper lantern that in the breeze flickered its candleflame.

Klahowya, darling, said Madam Peggy, bending to put her hands on her knees to speak with him, exposing her cleavage to his eyes. You must be Mr. Samuel Erwagen. Her pearl and silver necklaces swayed in his face; *Father's cane* reared itself in his mind. Welcome, sir, to Wood's. I don't believe we've ever had the pleasur*e*. You must come in, dear. Make yourself *com*fortable. Or I mean—. Have a place for you right here. Does Toronto need to—I'm not supposed to have Indians in here is all. If you can wait outside, sweetheart. I know how to wheel a chair. I'm stronger than I look. Oh, she said, and put her fingers on Sammy's shoulder, touching his cheek, alerting his ears. It was all happening so quickly. Let me introduce you to a few a my little angels, she hushed into his ear, tickling it something fierce.

The girls in the parlour were all half-dressed together on a long sofa with clawfeet and purple cushions. Rose, Lily, Mary, Sable, and Dixie. She chided them for not sitting upright in front of a gentleman, and with a narcotic, shouldery squirm they made a big deal of yawning and folding over one another, and seemed to one by one fall asleep on one another's thighs again. He was alarmed by their naked legs, the first he'd seen after his wife's.

She wheeled him down a narrow hallway and through a second room much like the parlour, though its benches made no sense with the round tables. The air proved rank with tobacco. Was this a second sitting room for men with appointments; he wasn't sure. He had only a moment to look before she fit him into her office, weaved around and sat on the table edge in front of him, eased her hair behind her shoulder with a swivel of her neck, crossed her arms among her pearls and smiled warmly. What can I do you for, Mr. Erwagen? Any flowers in my bouquet interest you?

No, I assure you, that's not why I'm here.

Sure aboot that?

Fair madam, I find your line a business quite foreign to my needs.

I see. Yes, well, I shouldn't try to fool around with *you.*

I don't expect you to think beyond your own enterprises.

She looked at her slippers, thinking. Finally she said: I don't think nothing till I see money. And turning once again to face him, he saw that her face had completely transformed. The sweetness was drained away. So what can I do you for, then? she said with this new face.

You're acquainted with my wife, correct?

I know a her.

How well? You know her personally?

Can't imagine how the two, her and myself, could ever know each other personally, Mr. Erwagen. Alls I said was …

She told me you helped her with the man game, said Sammy, boldly. It was a ghastly hunch, but he'd carried it around in his mind for some time now and was grateful to at least summon the courage to start asking what he most wanted to know from this cunning woman.

Peggy's office was strewn with pillows. What wasn't threadbare was stained. A single painting on the wall, small enough to put under your coat and featuring a long narrow dirt road curving into a dark forest like a question mark, was not what Sammy had expected for decoration. There seemed to him great exhaustion of sin upon this entire place.

Ms. Erwagen's mind can be a geyser, said Sammy.

That's what this town needs, Peggy said, checking her vanity for dust with a long index finger, finding none and so continuing her speech. More influence upon the masculine side, more pursuasion by the feminine side, to get this town on balance. I must say that I admire a lady who's not afraid to get involved with these men. Before your wife Molly? These men never talked to no lady such as your wife. Not the way she comm*a*nds. Otherwise, they don't know nothing else but how to dominate. My girls? Imagine if they were out in the str*ee*t the way it is in cities. My little flowers are t*oo* fragile for street corners. Without my protection? Oh, this place'd be some kind a Hell without Dupont Street and us madams, that I can promise.

She dropped her arms, stared at him as her mood blackened. Taking a deep breath, she seemed to challenge herself to recover from the spell, and he watched her turn to face the cabinets and begin rubbing the edges of each polished shelf for motes of dust.

You tricked me, didn't you? she said. Your wife never told you anything aboot me, did she? No, I fell right into that. Fool. What's made you go prowling around like some dog sniffing for scraps?

Listen, I trust my wife more than I trust you. She obviously tells me more than you. I am asking you to disclose what you know.

What do you hope to gain from all this?

A more accurate sense a history.

Spit on it. Your wife she's a unique girl, eh? If there's ever a lady to care for you, she's the one. I liked her the minute I met her. Might be the one and only time I ever was surprised to see a stranger in my bedroom. My door is always locked. But there she was. How she got in, no idea.

Molly is very resourceful, said Sammy.

I open the door and damn, there she is. She was standing there in the middle a the room. I mistook her for a ghost. All in white linens, very flattering, shapely clothes. Her green eyes there shining out from that perfect face and great mane a black hair. Oh, she is too lovely for earth. At first glance, well, she frightened me more than any po-lice bust.

When was this, that you first met?

I'll tell you something you should know, Mr. Erwagen … We only met that once. I never saw her again.

When exactly?

After that first meeting, said Peggy, standing and turning away from his eyes so as to better conceal her mendacity. After that, she always got her men to carry messages to me. Not even messages on paper, mind you. Just *words* she wanted to relay. I knew my responsibility. I distributed gossip and turned the rumour mills. And kept her secret. Gossip. I knew and I agreed to *play my part.* To help her, your Molly. How could I not? You see, for a lady to approach me. It's been an honour, Mr. Erwagen. That's alls I can say. It's been a true honour to help your wife.

When she was done prattling on, Peggy continued to nervously comb her hair through her hands.

When did you first meet then? Sammy asked.

Oh, well, *inspector,* when was it, last fall? I believe, yes. Yes, she said she'd begun a new project. Rehearsals, was how she put it.

Yes.

And that's the only time I ever recall conversating with her, that I can remember. I never saw her again. Well, that's it, really. As I recall, she asked if I would agree to help.

Help how?

Encourage the men, like I says. Encourage them to gamble. Encourage them to gamble on the man game instead a all the other ways the men around here wile away the hours. I gather she understood we were in competition for the dollars in these men's pockets, see. She respected my business sense. I'm a capitalist, Mr. Erwagen. Same's your boss at Hastings Mill. No different at all. I respect leadership. Talk to me aboot love, I can tell you I don't know the first. But when it comes to money, power …

Molly is very skilled at seeing the world from another's point a view. It's much more difficult to see the world through her eyes.

Always the case with true beauty, said Peggy. No point even trying. You might as well try to lay an egg. When did you first meet her?

Peggy was acting naive for Sammy, but he was already too suspicious to be convinced by her shy manners. Instead he noticed that her hands were like a man's, two bony insects with leathery legs. A farmer's hands with the long painted fingernails of a delicate concubine.

You know why else I came here, said Sammy. Don't try to fool me. I see what you've accomplished.

Darling, I'm clueless. Tell me.

Don't play the peon. Dunbar.

A who?

Dunbar, my brother. There's no use denying it. He spent some time here. My brother's last days on earth were in the clutches a one a your notorious whores. Now out with it, woman.

Dunbar? Peggy said, as if relieved the subject was finally broached. Was that his name? What a tragic face. Worse than yours. Oh, you think *she* had something to do with that as well.

Excuse me, said Sammy, sputtering at Peggy's unexpected accuracy.

Darling, she had as much to do with that as me and *you*. Why did Dunbar come to me, if I may ask, when your own homestead ... only minutes away?

Well, I ...

No. Dunbar came to me because a the tar-black, sick, degenerate lowliness in his soul. I seen a lot a heavy-headed men. I seen a lot a lost souls, dead souls, rotting souls, raped souls, you name it. But for a man who could walk and talk, he was the most truly dead-looking I ever seen. You must a saw that yourself.

I never characterized him quite that way before, but, yes.

The orphanage nuns taught me at least one good thing, she said. A man who got no soul, you do what he says or it's trouble, and you get him out your door soon as you can.

Yes, he said, thinking of how quickly he'd rooted Dunbar out of his own house not so long ago. Sammy's gaze fell downward to the Persian rug on the floor of Peggy's room, covered in dirt and hair.

And anyways, if we're being on the level, wasn't your wife preoccupied that night with a game? said Peggy. She had regained her full voice, that low-swinging criminal burr he was frightened of and beginning to enjoy. She almost laughed, but her smoking habit turned the laugh into a cough. Don't you know your own wife? Would the Molly you know—.

As I said before, it was you I suspected ...

Peggy found her way back to the table edge in front of him as she spoke. No, that's what you're telling yourself maybe, but that's not why you're here. I'm no murderer, Mr. Erwagen. Your brother chose her k*no*wing well. I told him myself who she was. He went in to her *room* k*no*wing. I'm not peddling in violence here. That's not my business. I don't let my girls be flogged or birched and I don't murder customers. There's none a that here. You want to meet her, I can tell.

May I?

She's far too delicate. The *most* delicate.

Why did you let my brother?

Came in here all hunched over from the cold and tears in his hollow eyes. He told me he'd left his wife in Wyoming and had got no relations from her in so many years anyways. It was a pitiable story.

I insist I be allowed to meet her.

Nothing doing.

I insist. There's ten dollars in my pocket.

Damn you men. You're all the same. Your wife, she pays me nothing for the honour. I respected you, Mr. Erwagen, until you offered me the money.

She took the ten-dollar bill from his pants, went to unlock the door that connected her suite to the one beside it, and got set to roll Sammy into the blight.

Through the doorway, he saw into the room where The Whore Without A Face lived. At the far end of the room he saw a stained-glass window, and through it light bled across all the surfaces. She lay in her bed, facing the window, just beginning to realize that it was not only Peggy who was entering. She began to turn, the black hood locked to her neck by its leather collar, a cigarette pressed to the fabric at her mouth. She paused, took the cigarette in her fingers, and a bud of smoke appeared to leak from her hood into the atmosphere, where he saw every carbon mote in the light streams. As The Whore With No Face began to speak so did Peggy, and Sammy interrupted them both.

Peggy, would you mind leaving us for a moment? I have words I'd like to speak to her in private.

Yes, I must—

I'll call for you, thanks, said Sammy, and watched to make sure she shut the door properly before he returned his attention to the girl on the bed.

Dun-bar, she whispered. Her arms covered her bare chest as if to show modesty in the presence of a lover.

She said his brother's name once more and he answered this time: Yes, he was my brother.

Why you—, she said. Her voice was gentle as tissue paper. You did. You *promise* you return to me.

He did, said Sammy. She did not understand yet that he and Dunbar were different people.

Yes, she exclaimed, nearly in tears. First love I ever see again.

But, no, it wasn't *me*, said Sammy. It was my brother. Why did you …

She flinched. He expected her to. As she twisted her legs to one side on the bed and sat in that position, the sun shone through the side of her hood. The fabric was veil enough to see at best a shadow of her features underneath. What he saw conformed with no shape he knew for profile or portrait;

rather, he saw another mask, this one carved from solid wood, exaggerated to barbaric proportions, with a screaming mouth, flared nostrils, and ridged cheeks. She caught sight of her shadow on the bed, the silhouette and the cloth, and she moved; the view was gone as quickly as it had come.

He understood his brother. The repellent features were concealed and, after a fashion, morbidly desirable, censured as they were by the glossy, almost perspirant finish of her black hood.

Why you no move? she said.

I almost died.

Wa, she said, upset at once and on her feet, now in front of him.

This was his opportunity. He was alone with her. There might not ever be another moment like this in his life when suicide was within reach. Why he didn't choose suicide, as his brother had, was what shocked him.

FIFTEEN

> Attention, Taliban, you are all cowardly dogs. You allowed your fighters to be laid down facing west and burned. You are too scared to retrieve their bodies. This just proves you are the lady boys we always believed you to be.
>
> – SGT. JIM BAKER'S RECORDED MESSAGE TO THE TALIBAN, 2007

On Sunday, as expected, twenty-four Chinese arrived from Victoria to clear the Brighouse Estate. News travelled fast. Toronto held a poster made fresh on Saturday that exclaimed in bold sho' card typeface:

> KEEP VANCOUVER WHITE; A Public Metting [sic] of the Citizens of Vancouver will be Held In CITY HALL On Sunday Afternoon, FEB. 20 at 2 O'Clock; To Appreciate Freedom We Must Prohibit Slave Labour; Turn Back The Repulsive Chinamans; We'll Hold By Right & Maintain By Might; Till The Foe Is Backward Driven; We Welcome As Brothers All Whitemen Still; But The Shifty Yellow Race; Whose Word Is Vain; Who Oppress The Weak; Must Find Another Place.

It also detailed the list of speakers and finished tritely with: God Save The King.

A skimpy illustration of a buck-toothed face with slitted eyes accompanied the text.

The po-lice were on patrol.

Pantcuffs cuffed up, hats tugged on tight, milkcurds stuck in their moustaches, the crowd waited in anticipation on the steps and on the street outside City Hall where they joined the men waving placards and added their own curses to the hated *Chinee.*

Toronto overheard Terry Berry say to a navvy: You going to the man game after this?

Yeah, said his friend.

The return a Litz and Pisk, said Terry Berry, whistling and nudging his pal Vicars in the belly. Won't miss this for nothing.

And I hear Furry and Daggett're playing, too, said the navvy.

Waited a long time for this, eh. *Big* night. Return a Litz and Pisk. Wa.

Wouldn't miss it myself neither. After hearing them jaw on aboot how good they are ...

Who're you going to bet on? said Terry Berry.

Well, listen. I've seen Litz and Pisk, and I know what I'm getting there. And remember it all began when Pisk took Daggett down in the street, eh?

I was there, I saw it, lied Terry Berry.

Yeah, and, even if Daggett and Furry *are* good players, well, I just don't bet on a speculation. Too risky.

Me and a couple other guys been practising a bit ourselves, piped in Vicars.

That right? Where?

Over by the oilery. Nothing too complicated. Just some moves and the basic idea.

Toronto squeezed his way through the crowd to find a free seat on the benches inside. By one o'clock there was already a strong smell of old boots and wet socks. City Hall was two hundred men heavy already, and nothing had yet been said. They were mutton-chopped and of sturdy mien, wearing stiff collars up against their chins, their fists in their laps. Shirtsleeves were generally frayed at the cuffs. Hats were brown or grey manhandled rabbitskin. Toronto wasn't here for the same reason as everyone else. He was here because Molly had asked him to be. You are my eyes on the city, she'd told him before they all left the house that afternoon. She and

Sammy went to Hastings Mill, and Toronto was asked to go to City Hall. She kissed him on the cheek.

Don't do anything, she'd said. Don't talk to anyone. Just watch. Watch for me.

It was still tingly there where she'd kissed him. So he kept his eyes open to everything.

I can help you with that dike, said a man leaning on his elbows, but I can't do it for less than seventy-five cents an hour, eh.

His partner shook his head. Let's work out a deal that's best for both of us, because I cannot afford that.

I thought we're here because we respect each other.

I do, said the employer, grinding his jaw.

They set to talking prices.

Seated beside the colonial flags there was some long-bearded old man with soot in his ears and no front teeth who said a lot of foul things and got laughs for it. There was the longshoreman with a pair of green heels on his wrist and a set of green legs going all the way up to his elbow, a big green bosom on his bicep and a flowing head of green hair over his shoulder.

Toronto remained silent among the men.

On either side of him on his pew were teams of loggers whose rowdiness and surly mien Toronto avoided. On his left, the subject was mink. On his right, it was chickamin. These were men who harpooned whale and shimmied two hundred feet into the air and ate nothing but stale biscuit for weeks without complaining more than every fucking minute about it. Moustaches outnumbered beards. Clean faces were not invited. Even Toronto had a sparse moustache these days. The idea of being seated for a couple hours no longer disturbed him as it had before the visit to the longhouse.

//

First off the cowboy came on stage and quieted them down, greeted them, and said: Some a you might know me, my name's RD Pitt and I'm a member a the Knights a Labour.

He removed his hat and let it dangle behind his neck on its chin strap. He placed his hands on the podium and every nail was trimmed and every finger intact.

We're here today speaking on the Yellow Peril facing us. You already know this is serious business, otherwise you wouldn't be here, eh? As you all know twenty-four Chinese arrived from Victoria today for clearing the Brighouse Estate. Yes, I agree, this is a terrible situation for the noble white labourer. So let me start with a little aboot the Knights a Labour if you don't already know. We're founded in 1869 by a guy, Uriah Stephens. Him and five others left the Garment Cutters' Association a Philadelphia to start the Knights a Labour. Back in those days it was open to all good Christian working people, except for bankers, lawyers, stockbrokers, doctors, and liquor manufacturers. Knights a Labour was a secret organization to begin, but since Terence Powderly has took over, it's open to your public at large. A lot a the old traditions are still with us in the Knights a Labour, and to learn the meanings behind ah, our insignia, our secrets a life, and secret handshake, you got to join up, eh. But the fraternity of Christian labourers has got to be together united, you understand, and the Knights a Labour support that position across the board. We invite both sexes to the fraternity. Aye, it's true. Wait and listen, because the female labourers are as much in the industrialists' plan for society. It's true that our capitalist bosses intend for our very wives to work alongside us. And we must be organized before they turn women into slaves no better treated than Orientals. You see? Look at us. We got all this forest, fish, and we're all starving. Why's that you think? Because the chickamin all goes back to Toronto. And we're left with what? How you say it in your Chinook? *Cultus: nothing.* I been running around Canada for work. I come here, figure there's got to be a strong labour force and a lot a work going around. What do I find? I see men in shacks in the jungle living off mulligan, eh? You think this'd be the case if it weren't for the Chinaman? A panner can't live off gold dust. Lumberjack can't live off wood chips neither. And this railroad? I suspect it carries us more heathen than Christians. This rotten country and this rotten province and this rotten city is all the fault a the Chinaman, thank you very much.

A few rowdies clapped for this, and one of them shouted: No more Chinamen. Pitt touched his belt buckle, hoisted his pants, continued: After the speeches if you're interested in joining our cause to unionize the workers a Vancouver, come talk to me. You sick a asking for the ten-hour workday and not getting it? You interested in some kind a job security? You started to get sick a seeing the little Chinaman across the street from you get a job in the morning before you, well, I'm also heading up another organization I'm sure you'll all want to join. It's called the Anti-Asiatic League. Talk to me aboot that and I'll sign you up. All right, thank you for your applause. Listen, our first speaker for the night is GM Sproat, you all surely know him. He's a prominent figure aboot Gastown, has been for a lot longer than them Chinamen down on Coal Harbour, that's for damn sure. And if you know him you know his opinions carry weight around here, as I'm sure you're aboot to hear for yourself.

GM Sproat rose from his chair on stage and bowed and shook Pitt's hand with enthusiasm. The clapping was sustained, and Sproat used the time to talk into Pitt's ear.

I can't hear you, said Pitt.

No, you shithead, said Sproat, I'm just killing time. Now shove off, you fucking cowboy. Sproat swooped in on the podium as if it were a rabbit and began to speak to his audience in a low growl that grew to a hyperventilating rage that could be heard down on New Westminster Street and that rained down heavily on the first row inside.

John Chinaman. The heathen Chinee. Who'm I talking aboot? Your neighbour? I don't think you want him as *your* neighbour. Oh, but these are such fine-featured folk. These almond-eyed sons a the flowery kingdom. Yes, they almost look like women, don't they? Ha ha, that's right. Show a hands who agrees with me. Okay, I see I'm talking your language. You agree them Mongols aren't built to withstand the brutality a this land? No. No. For as long as they been a race, the

Chinaman has got to compensate for his physical inferiority with cunning and deceit. Thank you. Underhandedness, my brothers. Yes. Simple as that. Give that man in the back another drink, ha ha. The heathen Chinee has no morality. That's right. They come from a garbage society. You heard me. A garbage society. Greed outstrips fraternity where they're from. Am I right or am I right? I'm right. Yes. Fucking right I'm right. They been known to commit *infanticide* in the Orient. That means murdering their own childs. Insanity, absolute barbaric insanity. Their intellects are perverse. That's right. They don't care aboot education or unionization. They work so bleakly. Little flesh drones. Thank you. I tell you, I know from personal experience, the Chinaman is an alien creature, beyond our capacity to control or change them to the image a God. Their lowliness prevents them ever becoming Canadian. For us to allow them *more* entry into Canada, well, means we risk getting overrun with the Orientals and *their* way a life, which is crude, filthy, and irrational. China's just a vast reservoir a helotry. They developed as a race a slaves, or at any rate, a lowly animal existence. Thank you, and God Bless.

During the roaring, seething applause that followed Sproat's soliloquy, he stepped back from the podium thrusting his fists in the air while another man ran out from backstage and shook Sproat's hand as they passed.

The new speaker saluted the crowd of men, took the lectern and waved down the noise and said: Hey, hey, Sproat's right. The Orientals are inherently leprous people. Hi, I'm BJ Cockburn. I'm a member a the Knights a Labour. I been with them from way back. That's right, folks. The Chinaman are a bacterial race. Innately unhygienic. Are you wanting your linens spit upon by leprous mouths? No, sir, I for one do not, said the *wise* man. Ha ha. And then you touch it? Hell, no. And that story's true Sproat told. All your guys' dreams a someday starting a life here? Forget it. You count fourscore Chinamen sleeping in a *single* room, what're you supposed to think, eh? This the way you want to live? They got a few coarse enjoyments like gambling and whoring. That's right. They're obdurate.

Thank you. They all got fixed persistent staring little eyes and rot gut. You heard me. Who hasn't shrank from the Chinaman's foul breath? He stinks a a gull's regurgitations. He brings with him pestilences. Thank you, yes. He got smallpox to cholera and leprosy. Crabs. That's right. Thank you. Woo. That's right. Yeehaw. I seen the lepers among them. Syphilis, you know it. Are we afraid a them sleeping in our laundry? We should be. My brothers, join me in a crusade to rid our society a this threat to public *health*. Fuck the Chinaman, thank you.

There was dry-mouthed silence at the end of Cockburn's speech, and RD Pitt came running back on stage and yelled out: Who's taking all our jobs?

The Chinamen, replied the crowd, a few swinging their fists to regain momentum.

He cupped a hand to his ear. What's that?

The Chinamen, they hollered louder.

Are we going to disinfect ourselves a this pestilence once and for all?

Aye, we are, said a man, standing.

All in favour a rounding up the Chinamen tonight say Aye.

Aye, said all, and with unruly applause they rose off the benches to their feet and waited impatiently in line to storm out the double doors and congregate on Westminster Street with the rest.

To Chinatown, exclaimed Pitt from atop a milk crate on the curb. The men on the street broke out into a great swelling cheer, three for Pitt and three against the Chinaman. The more men who gathered, the more there seemed to be no turning back. Tonight they would do it. With the speeches over, Toronto briefly spotted HO Alexander and his younger brother TK as they ran north up the sidewalk, surely towards Hastings Mill where they would tell their father that men in town were setting to riot.

//

RH took the news with a blankening of expression, as though the thoughts on his table had been swept to the floor.

Mrs. Alexander was holding a saucer in her lap and a teacup in her fingers. She laid down both on the desk, trying not to upset the tea, and said: W-we must stop them at once. We must put an end. Dear—, she said. She put a hand to her chest and took a deep breath. She stood up. Dear, she said, the Chinaman from San Francisco ... whatever shall we do?

His sons watched their father. HO, behind a history book. TK, mouth-breathing as usual.

The veins in RH's nose and cheeks faded and his neck slackened. He slumped back in his leather chair and dropped his arms. He gurgled. His sons regarded him wasting away with excited disillusionment. They were still young and stupid enough to feel powerful at the sight of a God turning into a mortal.

Leave the room, boys, he said.

But, Da—

Leave the room, he barked.

After they were gone, his wife whispered: If you don't stop the men, he'll kill you.

He said: If I try to stop them, my *own* men kill me. My own men. They despise me. When I hired the Indians, they said nothing. When I hired Kanakas, they stirred. When I hired Chinamen, they revolt. It's too late. I misread them. My fate is to be the interloper, sigh, not the boss.

Don't lose your resolve, dear. Need I remind you that we are *all* Chinamen in Vancouver?

Please, he wept, covering his eyes, don't remind me.

She grabbed the cowardly hand and shook it furiously. You poor old man, she said. The bones beneath the slackened glove of his skin rattled in her grip. I may've taken you for granted at times, but not now. Now I want you to *spring* to life, show courage—

He said: You don't understand what it is like to be a man. If what a man wants is revenge, then it shall be so. One requires force to subdue a mob; nothing else works. And I am not a violent man. When a war erupts in my life, it's over a table, over a piece a paper. I am inclined to debate, politic, manoeuvre, and backstab. I am a tactician, not a field commander. And today, said RH, I'm a fallen general.

Enough a your grandiloquence. This is not the time. What are you to *do*? Our lives are at stake.

Nothing, he screamed. Absolute nothing left. My fate has been ransacked. I'm doomed.

You've gone mad. You're a mad dope fiend. That's what it is, isn't it? Oh, it's true. She stepped back and rested a hand on the desk while she caught her breath. You're not my husband anymore, she said. Where's your strength? Where have you gone? She began to cry. I thought you were made a stronger stuff. Apparently not, eh. It's sapped you a your will to live. I slept to ignore it. Oh, RH, this is a terrible city. Look what it has done to our souls. Wake up. Wake up to that fact and we might be saved yet. Yes, that's what we'll do, we'll leave tonight. We'll never come back. It won't be so hard. Quickly, let's run and pack.

The mill …

The mill is being pulled out from underneath your feet as we speak. We've nary a moment to waste. Come, we must go now.

I can't, he said, resisting her embrace, paler and paler, and that, inexplicable to her, was final.

//

The men back at City Hall didn't have far to walk. A block away was Pender Street, Chinatown. Trundling down the sidewalk two or three men deep, rolling up their sleeves and *whourking* as they went, it wasn't like a parade. Toronto glided among the agitators without expression, dodging expectoration and ducking confrontation. He responded to any question with: Yes, sir—; shook hands, and though he found it hard to look Whitemans in the eye, he tried to do so today in hopes of better fitting in. He hid under a sho' card for a chop suey house and waited there as a group of three grunting sulphur miners with exceptionally gold-toothed underbites ran by kicking sticks out of their way on the packed-dirt road, nudging out stones and booting them against the walls of the Guan Wong laundry, the last building on the street built over dry land. They continued west followed by the mob, but no Chinaman was around.

A man said: Where's the Chinamen?

Round up every one you find, said Pitt.

Yeah, but where are they?

Clicking their eyes along the woodslat buildings on stilts over False Creek's high tide, they spotted no signs of the *despicable* race. Not in any window or doorway, not on the boardwalk or anywhere else. Aside from a lone vegetable cart covered by a deerhide tarp, the street ahead lay empty in the night haze. It felt like a trick, a case of Indian skookum. The Chinese silk merchants weren't in their shop, nor were the lottery boys of the Chee Kung tong making their usual frenzied rounds on the sidewalk. The Wah Chong laundry, whose heavy-set old owner invariably sat on a wood crate at the steaming entrance, was closed tight. Across every bay window in every apartment above the street the shades were drawn and the lights out. There wasn't a Chinaman anywhere to be seen. Water was the only sound, splashing against the dike.

They must all be at the fucking man game, said BJ Cockburn under his breath to Pitt.

How could all a them be? said Pitt, looking around in vain through the inky, vacant road, seeing only the red lanterns of the Dupont Street bordellos pulsing red and swaying back and forth in the slight breeze. Another distraction Pitt had to be sure his supporters avoided.

What are we going to do? Should we go over to Hastings Mill, round them up from the man game? We can still take them to the docks.

We can't do that, said Pitt. How can we do that? Propose we pick them out one by one from the crowd?

'Sides, said Sproat, I saw men leave for the man game straight after the speeches. How many more'd we lose if we collided?

We did this all for shit?

Not so long's we can find some here, said Pitt, rubbing the residual tingle off his squared fingernails. He said: Tomorrow we'll come back early and get the rest. This'll be enough proof to the men we can make it happen. Tonight we leave an impression.

Pitt weighed a rock and handed it to a young boy, no older than nine, who'd followed along in search of adventure. He told the child to throw the rock as hard as he could at the windows of Ho Ho Curios. Make it break real loud, Pitt said.

After the last shard dropped off its frame and sprinkled itself in the moonlight, the men inhaled one final moment of silence and then turned rowdy. Glass instantly looked scarce. Everyone wanted a shot. Fuck you, Chinaman. Where are you? Come oot a there, come oot a there, you yellow cowards. Ha ha. Singing: Chin-a-men, China-men. They paired off and made bets who'd hit a pane first. Grids were emptied one by one almost as fast as they could throw. Over here. Pass me that there. Follow me now, boys. They crossed the planks over the dike and spread out on the sidewalk, their footfalls spitting water through the slats as the sea lapped under their soles. Heave-ho, they sent lumber through the main-floor windows of a laundry and broke everything at once … and:

> Ching Chong Chinaman
> Washed his face in a frying pan
> Combed his hair with the leg a his chair
> Ching chong Chinaman
> Miss-ee Lee want-ee pee
> Turn-ee up and let-ee see
> Loong callot
> Willa wallla willa walla
> Knights a Labour yah yah yah
> Who are we? You may guess
> We are the boys a the KOL …

The squaws in the whorehouses across the street peeped through curtains as the men dispersed and started causing havoc up and down Pender. The po-lice stood at the end of the block, unable to muster will to quell the mob. Kicking the door open on Chow's boarding house, three square men stormed in hollering at the top of their lungs: Every last one a you canaries oot on the street before we crack your fucking beaks.

Toronto witnessed these odd-jobbers muscle through Chinatown, and his unease grew. How long, he wondered in his own language, should he remain here? A set of tetchy men unveiled the vegetable cart, threw the deerhide tarp in the dust, and proceeded to tip the cart on its side, strewing potatoes and leeks and cabbage across the ground. They doused it in kerosene from a lamp and waited for approval to bonfire it.

At last on the upper floors came the sight of worried young Chinamen skipping back and forth in and out from the balconies trying to solve their dilemma. Many were barely men at all. They were adolescents, uneducated and malnourished sons of farmers. A man smoking a cigarette walked quietly out onto the second-floor balcony at the Chow building, cautiously overlooked the parade. The tattoo on his wrist continued under his coatsleeve.

Get the fuck down from there.

The Chinaman shook his head no, and dodged the rocks that bounced off the walls and crashed through the window behind him. He stood up again, gleaned them as they gleaned him, then quickly stepped back into the confusion.

The men poured into the unlit building but were held up at the door when the first of them reeled back at the odour, pungent like spoiled lemonade and fish intestine. As they searched the darkened interiors, a man called out: Look at the Chinee run. A rumble of heavy boots came from every direction, crunching over broken glass, one pair destroying a tea set laid on a floor mat as other Whitemen shoved aside wicker furniture and elbowed over kerosene lamps and toppled screens made of walnut veneer with lithographs of swans and waterfalls. The Chinamen were running through a back door. Over there. Get them. I'm going to fucking—. They hunted them to a short dock posted over False Creek, saw three men dive straight into the chilly water. Another couple men were already wading. A fatty was stuck on the dock reluctant to make the jump: the men caught and shackled him up.

We got one.

Take him out to the road.

I'm going to survey these ones, wait till they come ashore and get them.

There's more upstairs.

Men stormed back inside roaring with beery gusto, listening to the boots of their colleagues on the dusty wood floor above their heads.

The Chinaman they'd caught on the dock was thick and strong but overweight, and he was pushed along fiercely. A factory worker sneered and sniffed as he escorted the big man through the house and out onto the street, gripping his arm the whole time. I never touched no Chinaman before, he said, feels like I'm holding on to a goddamn plucked chicken. His face expresses nothing to me. Go on, you sheep-witted Chinee. Move it.

This sloe-eyed bachelor forced the Chinaman onto the sidewalk and down the plank to dry land where he met with a couple other young men they'd already rounded up, tied together by their pigtails. Want me to do the same to this one? His pigtails are all the way to his shoulders.

The Chinamen didn't speak as they pulled his hair. They huddled skull to skull wondering what next.

Upstairs it was the same. They chased a few Chinamen down the hall and onto the balcony over False Creek and watched them dive off into the black water.

Get back here, Pat Pongs.

I won't let them get away. I'm following them, see where they come ashore.

Heard you the first time.

I'm on their tail.

Fucking go do it then. What're you up *here* for?

Taking the stairs two at a time they were back on the street in a second, in time to hear Sproat order: Tie them together like the rest. They regarded four sopping wet Chinamen slouching their way past them through the crowd to meet the other prisoners.

Where's the rest?

I don't know. Drowned.

Drowned?

I said I don't know.

He and the curly-haired fellow took off to look for stragglers.

I'm going to catch me a Chinaman or my name ain't—

Someone found a spool of rope and a young man knotted the new prisoners at the ankles until they ran out and decided to go back to tying them up by the pigtails again. There, that'll teach you, damn it.

Another window shattered and the Whitemans cheered.

Peggy slammed the door at Wood's, slipped down the staircase in her long pearlescent gown, and came onto the street hectoring: Tell me what the hell you boys think you're up to? I'm not talking to you, Pitt, she said waving a painted finger at him, I know you're not no *boss*. Oh, big man, you can put together a posse and shove oot the Chinamen. Good for you, big boy. Come on, fellahs, there's plenty more a interest to you inside my domicile. Ee-na half-price this next whole hour.

Don't listen to her, men, cried Pitt. She's a temptress from the exact same pool a sin as the damned Asiatic. Look away, avert your eyes, focus instead to a vision a Vancouver with no Chinamen in the twentieth century.

And you know what *I'm* talking aboot, barked Peggy to the crowd, not for anything impressed by Pitt's rhetoric. Name a man among all your guys' numbers who hasn't tried a Ming Ling girl, eh? Don't you like them concubines? I'm talking aboot a velvet mouth easing herself down your spike for a *ni*ckel. You hear that, boys? A nickel. Untie them poor Chinamen and I'll suck you myself. She turned her head to the girls on the verandah and said: These Knights a Labour are bad for fucking business.

Enough men saw the value in Peggy's offer that Pitt doffed his hat, slapped it on the ground, and whined: Aw, come on guys. Don't go chasing mink *now.* This is important.

Never you mind, Pitt, said one, I was going to see a man game, anyhow.

What's a man game? asked a slimly built, rotting toothed dotard with an anomalously clean-shaven face and bright black leather suspenders.

'The fuck? You haven't heard a the man game? Where you from, New Westminster?

... And despite the many appeals by the cowboy RD Pitt on behalf of his Knights of Labour, the bedrooms at Wood's soon filled again with customers.

In response to the defections, the remaining rioters defaced all the sho' cards with Chinese characters painted on them, flipped them in the air, tossed them onto the vegetable cart with the other debris awaiting bonfire. Toronto saw one man whip a galvanized steel bucket overhand at a thin Chinaman holding out a broomstick to protect himself. Broke his nose. Tied him up with the rest.

Toronto stood quietly, obscurely, nonviolently next to the unvarnished fence of a Chinaman fruit farmer named Taisan. Plums, peaches, blackberries, apricots, kiwi, he had a fine orchard all things considered. Toronto stood there until he was compelled to leap aside when a couple navvies with hopheaded ideas decided to shake apart the fence and push half of it to the ground. They didn't notice Toronto, such were his skills of bearing witness. As they tore out fenceposts and cursed, Toronto resisted the urge to raise a hand and interrupt them. He might stop them for a moment, but only for a moment.

That's it, good good, keep shaking it—, hopheaded sweat on their faces, their few teeth shone in their beards as they tore down and flattened the fence.

Toronto could hardly fathom these Whitemen whose souls had turned to chalk. With the fence broken, a dirty goose, chickens, and a giant purple sow all ran to incomprehensible freedom. The purple sow squealed down the street ... that tortured laughter, as if a pig were once human but long ago cursed by vanity to live for slop ... Toronto was deeply troubled by the sound. He saw the Whitemans run the other way, into the orchard towards Taisan's frail shingled house. They brought the old farmer out by the arm. He was older than the rest of the Chinamans, and wore his short hair inside a black Mandarin toque. Raising his arms against the Whitemans' swats and punches, he prattled on in his language. One heavyset Chinaman among the prisoners protested, and the Knights were forced to subdue him with blows to the stomach. And when they brought the old farmer closer to the group, they realized that it wasn't the orchard keeper Taisan, it was the baker Yau.

Yau, said Toronto with a dry mouth.

RD Pitt laughed at the baker, seeming not to recognize him. He slapped Yau up and down, said: You don't like it? What wong, Chinee? How do this feely, eh? At that, he doubled Yau over his fist. The baker crumpled sideways to the ground coughing, vomiting, gagging.

Pitt's friend Sproat watched for a while before turning his attention back to the heavyset prisoner who'd been the first to protest. Sproat eyed him. He leaned in and said: Scared a me, eh? Scared a me? Scared a me?

The Chinaman, despite being tied to another fellow, had stayed calm whenever Sproat tricked him with a fist, just short of hitting him in the face, amusing himself every time one of the smaller Chinamen flinched when he raised a hand. You all smell like blubber, you know that, eh? Eh? EH?

Pitt now chose to single Yau out for special attention, pinching the baker's arm in his grip and dragging him back a few steps towards the shoreline. The other Chinamen shielded him while they could, but the new immigrants' instinct to protect a respected local only sparked Pitt's cruel streak, for now he was determined to get his man. He shouldered his way through the Chinamen unafraid and slapped the baker across the face with the back of his hand. He took the baker by the arm and led him across the dirt-packed road all the way to the edge by the water and pushed him down onto his knees. He was standing above him in the mud. Across the street Toronto heard everything, every profane word Pitt barked at Yau, on his knees with his head down, waiting. Pitt slapped him again. I asked you a question, he said. Toronto couldn't hear Yau's answer, but it was short, like a yes or a no. It infuriated Pitt. He took Yau's neck in his hands and pushed his head into the water. Yau's arms flailed, trying to box Pitt, who redoubled his pressure the harder Yau fought. The water frothed as Pitt tried to drown him.

Agitated protests began to rise up from among the outraged rounded-up prisoners, who flailed their arms and spat at their captors as they watched Pitt throttle the baker on the beach. The protests only frightened the other White rioters, who turned their backs on the scene and muscled in on the group, skulling the most aggressive ones, pushing them all hard on the sides, herding them like heifers towards the loud barn. As if in conspiracy with Pitt. Let the baker die without a witness.

When you are down on your knees about to die you know what it really means to pray to God. You pray with every bone in your body, from the heels of your feet on up, you pray so hard you can levitate.

In two steps, it felt like two steps, Toronto was across the street, and holding a downy white chicken he picked up along the way—how, he can't remember—he raised his sacrifice, took aim, and swung the bird by its legs and hit Pitt across the face. Impact sent a burst of feathers in every direction. Pitt flopped to the ground. Swearing the almighty, Pitt grabbed for the chicken with all that anger meant for Yau and viced the bird between his knees. Screaming, screaming, he gripped the neck waddle and tore the fowl apart, head first, then limb from limb, red viscous entrails spilling out down his denims and soaking the insides of his boots. His fist was still clenched around the chicken head.

Toronto fished Yau out of False Creek gasping and incredulous. The two men lay on the ground to catch their breath as they watched Pitt scrabble around on the dirt like a broken wasp, trying to regain his anger if not his consciousness. For Toronto, the greatest urgency remained to protect and assist Yau in escaping the chaos of the riot. Find safer ground. He lifted Yau to his feet and booted it down the block to Main Street, where it would be easier for Yau to disappear.

Thank you, thank you, said Yau, weeping, and embraced Toronto. Thank you so much.

No, see, no, love your pastry, I love Calabi&Yaus … When the two men separated Toronto realized that no, it wasn't Yau after all. It was and always had been Taisan, the orchard keeper. Of course Toronto knew that Calabi and Yau frequently bought their fruit from Taisan, and that must have been why he'd so persistently seen the face of the man he most feared would die. Yau and Taisan and Calabi and the pastries, it was all one. Run, said Toronto to the orchard keeper. Run.

Toronto watched him escape down the street and around a corner then he went back to the riot.

Come on, no time for delay, said Cockburn, there's still these coolies to take care a.

The Chinamen cowed and pleaded, cried out in hopes of being heard beyond the bordellos to civil society. The Vancouver po-lice stood in the darkness out of sight and didn't budge. As more coolies were found they were collected like the others, knotted together and forced to walk among the rioters as they moved through the shantytown in the mudflats looking for more. The homes erected over the salty spongeland of the maremma came down quickly; the men had only to rattle their walls for the whole community to fall in among the salty reeds and bristle. As the Knights patrolled the street a set of rowdies made swift work of flattening every shack, scrapping every cobbled-together abode, the wood thrown in a heap intended to be set ablaze.

Toronto tried to catch his breath. He saw the po-lice but didn't think they'd seen him. He was perhaps better set up for invisibility, not as difficult a trick to execute as one might believe. Toronto vividly remembered his father's stories about entire tribes walking together unseen into a warring neighbour, surprising them by slitting their throats on a sunny afternoon. Witness the event. Molly's words. After freeing the farmer Toronto's whole body felt weak, especially his ankles; his stomach was upset, his throat was raw, and he couldn't shed the feeling of wet terror from his cold skin. It took all his concentration not to faint straight away. A fence or a home can always be rebuilt. But if Yau was Taisan and Taisan was one of the prisoners and the prisoners were in danger, then if it came to it again, Toronto knew he must no longer play invisible.

//

Mrs. Alexander held up her wool skirts as she ran through the streets to catch up with the men. She didn't know what she thought she was doing. There was a cool fog in the air and her grey hairs kept blowing in her eyes. She ignored it and held tight to her skirts, watching the sidewalk for loose boards or a slippery patch of moss that might take out her footing. She cursed her husband. She cursed him loudly and prayed under her breath. Turned the corner, saw the men swarming around the bound prisoners, reared up on her heels and paused to build up her druthers. Throwing her back into it as she rushed them, screaming at her most authoritative: Stay away from those Chinese.

If her husband couldn't muster the courage, she would stand in his place and put an end to this folly once and for all. She forced her way through the men, kicked their legs, yoinked them back by their collars if she had to. Young belligerent woodsmen shook her off, saying: 'The fuck—, and got a slap across the face for using profanity in her presence as she chirped at them like the fiercest mother Heaven ever sent. The waddles of her neck trembled as she screamed. Inside her navy-blue Anglican wool dress her big motherly rump started behind her breasts and went halfway down her legs. She waddled in front of it, slashing her hands in the air, talking crimes and punishments.

Move aside, young man. Where's your head? I don't want to hear none a your back talk; why, you're old enough to know never to talk that way to a lady thrice your age. I'll have you all thrown in the mews if you don't watch yourselves. I'll drag you in one by one by the ears, and just watch me.

Her hair was pulled into a solid sphere at the back of her skull, the white moon of her scalp making the dark craters around her eyes all the more unsettling. Her eyes were wet ponds inside those depressions. She had their attention but they didn't know what to do with her. She understood immediately that the Chinamen's predicament was serious, and asked the crowd what they intended to do with their prisoners now that they had them. Quickly enough she'd separated them all from the Chinamen, who had nowhere left to go.

None of the faces showed any ideas, and naturally the cowboy RD Pitt spoke up and said: We're shipping them off to Victoria tomorrow on the next ferry, back where they came from.

You aren't going to lay a hand on these men, she said.

No, ma'am, Pitt said. We aimed to ship them back whence they lived before they got hired to come here, is all.

Where's the po-lice?

Pitt shook his head subtly to the left, where in the darkening distance the po-lice stood, mute statues.

Why haven't they arrested you all? Shall I go call them over and see to it myself?

Everything's under control, Mrs. Alexander, said Pitt. Look around. No one's harmed.

Don't think I'm budging till someone lugs the po-lice over here to arrest you all. If you so much as *touch* these men. Absolutely unacceptable behaviour from supposedly civilized gentlemen—one would hope you'd want to set an example. Show some manners for our Chinese visitors. No, instead look at you. Are you all Darwinists? Am I among animals and atheists? Are you God-fearing men or has Indian skookum got hold a you completely?

She bawled them out for what seemed the first time since they were children. She knew just the words to strike deep. Some of them had never had a mother to speak of. And some of them didn't know what to do but huff sadly under their breath, under their hats, under the cover of dark, under the wishing stars, under the ceiling of God's business. It was only smoke, it was a flick of dirt. It was anything but sorrow.

When the po-lice finally arrived she bawled them out too, and there was nothing to do but apologize.

We're sorry, the po-lice said.

Where were you all this time? Look what these men have done. What is your excuse? They met in City Hall, for the love a—

W-we were protecting the mob from getting too frisky, said Constable Miller, tipping his hat.

What are you trying to say, sir? Are you all nothing but cowards? Didn't want to confront this mob, eh? Really. I'm deeply troubled by this lack a perspective. Look at me, a simple old dame. What, now society requires its elderly to end disputes? Must I stand up and take action? Do you see a badge on *my* chest? If I were you, I'd watch over these men and see no harm comes to them. If I hear any a you leave your post and these Chinamen go missing, boots start showing up like last year? I'll see to it that every one a you gets a black mark and never works in Vancouver again, understand me? She turned her attention back to the cowboy Pitt. Am I making myself clear, young man? she said. There's going to be no more cowboy tactics. This is Vancouver, sir, not Calgary. We are the Queen's rarest jewel. Treat your fellow men as you would Lady Victoria herself, and make Britain proud a her Columbia.

Yes, ma'am. We're sending them on the boat for Victoria, said Pitt, trying to regain his stones after the squashing her matriarchal presence had inflicted on the men. They came here from Victoria, and alls we want is for them to deal with their own problem. We don't want their Chinamen. They go back to their homes to-morrow morning.

I don't see what good it does you. The boats return as frequently as they go.

The rioters stood there. A whiff of Mrs. Alexander's civet remained even after the lady left. Scoldings upon scoldings. The words burned. Was it her lingering perfume or her acid condemnations that stung their eyes? Some of them were too wild to know better.

What're you got planned for us to do now? said Sproat.

To-morrow we come back here, said Pitt, and make sure they're deported one and all. For now, let us get down to the business—who's with me for taking down this undeserving village a illegal squatters, say Aye.

Aye, said the men.

The whores looked more upset than the po-lice. No one was sure how to stop it from happening. It was as if they'd all forgotten about Mrs. Alexander, who was barely out of earshot. The po-lice saw the men proceed down the street and quickly take to dismantling the shantytown, lighting fires, wrecking the haystacked yurts, the shakewood teepees, the log cabins. The po-lice just stood there while dozens of men descended into the mudflats where homes had been erected even on the skewback. The tide was a dark creeping gloom of ink. It was late February, and although unusually warm, snow still lay on the ground in places. Here, beside Toronto's foot, was a clump of it stuck to the northern peak of a cutbank. It melted quickly as the bonfire caught its wind.

SIXTEEN

It is hard for thee to kick against the pricks.
— ACTS IX. 5.

'The fuck is Pisk? bellowed Daggett, wiping his mouth after saying the cursed name.

As many as a hundred of the Chinamen in the audience at the man game this evening lived on the mudflats where RD Pitt and his gang were presently rocking and axing their shanties apart, dousing sackcloth in alcohol to speed the burning of the pyre. Another three hundred from the established part of Chinatown were at the man game as well. Only thirty-forty Whitemen were on Dupont Street causing all the trouble while just north, across Hastings Street, Whitemen at the man game already numbered in the thousands. Included among the melee were plenty of RD Pitt's early supporters, more interested in seeing the game than causing a ruckus. That was all. They wore shabby leather suspenders and dungarees with steel-riveted seams because that's what Furry and Daggett wore. They were the dogs of men, not the wolves.

You think I came here to be stood up by this bastard? said Daggett. I'm talking to you, Litz. Where is he? Or maybe it's true what we hear, that he's dead.

Unless your plan's to disrobe, there's no point conversating, said Litz. His arms were crossed over his bare chest. His eyelids were coolly sluggish, the thick lashes and thicker brow concealing the intensity of his focus. He stood at the foot of the steps to the Hastings Mill store with a silent band of loyal supporters.

If there's no Pisk, we'll tear an extra strip off you, how's aboot that?

Calm your heart, bellowed a familiar voice, I'm right here.

It was Pisk's voice, heard by unshaven men in the audience who could not locate his whereabouts, looking this and that a-way, looking for where, where. He came from inside the mill's store, swinging himself towards his rivals on a set of handmade maplewood crutches. Litz kept his eyes on the crowd, which he estimated to be huger than any previous man game. As Pisk eased himself down the stairs to the street the audience collectively gasped to see his feet wrapped in thick hives of white bandage. That's right, take a gander, you bohunks. Never seen a fucking injury before?

This doesn't satisfy no contract we had to be here.

I'm here, said Pisk, leaning heavily on his crutches.

No way you can play like that.

Our deal was if you win at the man game we leave town, said Pisk. But you know how we play. Each crew picks a first. Your first is Campbell, right?

That's right.

And I'm our first, said Litz. If any one a you *poltroons* can beat me, go right ahead and battle Pisk. Be my guest.

But no one here, said Pisk, expects any a you dick-biters is going to beat Litz. And if by chance or cheat you do, I can whip every one a you five-nothing standing on my hands the whole fucking time, and you know it, so don't pretend you're balls-out swaggering today.

You're saying if any one a us beats Litz, you'll play? said Campbell.

'The fuck, you deaf?

The audience erupted into debate. Furry & Daggett's crew tossed their hands in the air and threatened to leave that very minute, but Clough calmed them down using grandiloquent gestures, slashing his one arm back and forth as he spat out reasons to stay put. It was theatrical; there didn't seem to be any chance of anyone going anywhere. Whitemen were still laughing and making jokes at Furry and Daggett's expense, but nothing so disrespectful as to warrant a belt-whipping, more as cajoles and pleas for them to stay, stay and play. The Chinamen laughed and hugged each other, shook little fists at the competitors and made noise in their language. They all kept one eye on the bets.

Pisk's beard was longer, thicker, and much greyer. It was trouble for him getting down the stairs, hobbling on no toes, and his clothes hung off a thinner body, a shallower chest, no bulging gut, dehydrated musculature. The feet were serious. He was on crutches. He couldn't play. No one in the crowd today was going to bet Pisk could play. Calabi was surrounded by Chinamen with questions. Hoss was surrounded by Whitemen with demands.

Clough separated himself from Furry & Daggett's crew, stood in the empty space awaiting two players, and addressed the audience: What fool believes Litz can beat all a Furry & Daggett's crew single-handedly?

If I can't get a rematch with Pisk, then I definitely want a piece a Litz to take home with me today, Campbell said, unjacketing. He shucked off his clothes with practised quickness, seeming to wave his hand across his body and be undressed. He threw them to Clough who folded them casually and rested them on the stump of a thousand-year-old cedar.

You seen me play, said Litz, but you never played me.

Who's your coach, Litz? bellowed Vicars, a character Litz was only beginning to recognize, a late-coming popularist of the man game, along with his friend Terry Berry.

I thought you were, Litz said, pushing his jaw to the side with the palm of his hand and cracking his neck.

Better not be me, said Terry Berry, cannily, or I'm betting on Campbell.

Campbell showed more professional demeanour this time around, or was terribly nervous, partaking in none of the ribaldry. Stepping away from the pile of his woollen calicos, there was none of the self-consciousness that had lost him his match back in January. He walked with a different strut, and different still when he was undressed. It was as if in disrobing he'd chosen to speak a foreign language, one that gave him a greater versatility of expression than his workaday vocabulary. His arms no longer swung rigidly at his sides. They hung rather more loosely now, along with a newly trained footstep that was as sure as it was elastic and racy. He had more sinew where there had been cumbersome bulk, and his skin had a gingery burnish from exposure. His breath steamed in dragon gusts.

Gamblers had good reason to rethink their biases. Like horses before the race, the men were eyed for their gait, physique, temperament, and breeding. Beasts. Bloodsucking. A spider's nest of tired, greedy eyes dilated black with high hopes for blood and sweat and a life-changing win. Sweet chickamin. In 1887 there was even a saying in Vancouver's Chinatown: Every win is as enlightening as a shot of moonshine, every loss is as cruel as a dawn of sobering sunshine.

Litz took a couple of quick jumps, closer then closer to hovering, until he felt satisfied with his float and pointed a long index at Campbell and said: You got no idea what you're in for, eh?

I got a couple moves I want to show *you*, said Campbell.

You'll have to show me first, said Bud Hoss, who appeared from behind a fence wearing only his histrionics, ready to play the man game. Naked and stocky as a tankard, he said: You'll have to get through me if you want to try Litz.

'The fuck are you talking aboot?

I'm playing today.

That so?

Right it is, said Hoss.

What absurdity is this? said Vicars, loudly echoing the many voices asking the same question in simpler terms.

Who'm I betting on here? Is this man game cancelled?

No, it's not fucking cancelled, spat Litz. I'm still here, and if I must, I'll see to it each and every one a you sees your ends. But this is an official announcement that Hoss here's part a mine and Pisk's crew.

He is, eh? said Clough, who hugged himself roughly, a substitute for crossing his arms. What, thought you said you could do this all yourself?

Why should I waste my energy on so many a your bohunks? said Litz.

And Hoss here is our first, said Pisk. Then we'll take it from there.

What makes the cripple *third* on a team? said a gold panner in tar-smeared overalls with a broken nose, burnt chin, and a full mouth of gold teeth.

Pisk's been the last to play right from the start, explained Moe Dee in that voice of his, audible across rivers. Ever since the man game started. You protect your player under attack, who is Pisk, so that makes Litz first. If not Litz, then this dude. Last player can start a match whenever he wants. Last player can hold back to wait, see what happens.

Furry's trying to get to Pisk, said the panner.

Daggett's trying to get Pisk out a the city once and for all.

Nothing I hate worse than to see Whitemen taking out their conflicts on Whitemen, said a dissenter, a specialist, a saddlemaker. Didn't none a you know there's a band a men going down to Chinatown right now to take care a the real problem in your lives?

//

See, said Molly, sweeping her wedding ring against his cheek, I made it easy for you to spectate. You don't have to be on the street with the rabble.

Thank you, yes, I appreciate that.

I'm very excited. To think all this was scorched earth not even a year ago.

The ground is still black, he said.

How much the city has changed since we arrived.

Do you plan to claim responsibility any time soon?

How unfair a you, darling Chinook. You love me, though, don't you? she asked.

Oh, yes, look, it says so on my sleeve, he said.

Shh, watch the man game, she said.

He frowned. Did you plan for all this to transpire?

Oh, naturally, said Molly, holding her Stars & Stripes at a pause from her mouth. A course I did.

There was a noncommittal rap on the door to the office and Molly shrugged when Sammy looked at her to see if she had anything to do with this as well.

Yes, enter, said Sammy, assuming it to be Toronto.

RH Afterlife inched through the door to his accountant's office and crept along the wall like a wet insect, a millipede man sneaking along the wallpaper, afraid of the exposure, looking like a prisoner in his own mill, jailed for what? For falling for the perfumes of the Orient, and now he was shackled to his heavy fate. Mr. Erwagen, I have terrible ..., and seeing his accountant seated at the open window beside his wife, the beautiful Mrs. Erwagen, he began to hear it all again: the riot on the front steps of Hastings Mill. He was sure that if he so much as poked his head up to the window a sharpshooter would split his scalp open. And here the Erwagens were watching in plain view. Anguish had kept him locked in his own office, doubling his dosage, hoping that by the time they torched the mill he'd be dead. He staggered thus towards the window and the Erwagens, who regarded him with what must have been great pity. But when he finally took his first look and saw the mob in front of the mill, all he said was: Oh, lord. Then he backed away and pressed himself flat against the wall. He could feel his cold flesh tight against his skeleton. The

Erwagens showed more pity. The rioters, the Knights of Labour, the Anti-Asiatics, the Whitemens were on his doorstep, here to exact revenge. His blood would merrily be spilled. His heart would be stolen and played with on the streets like a kickball until they lost interest and a dog sat down to gnaw on it. The riot was his end, he was sure of it now. It did not matter he was an old man. He still was not ready to die. Never. His vision blurred and started to go black at the edges, as if on the brink of a faint. He said: Are they here for … me?

It's a man game, said Erwagen.

A man game? said Alexander, regaining a little. At a time … like this? Who?

Looks mostly like our own men, said Erwagen. I see a lot a Chinamen and lumberjacks and millhands and such and such. The game's not begun yet, but the crowd seems in good spirits.

You don't say? said Alexander, becalmed. His writing hand fixated on his beard as he felt the first few twists of a strategy forming in his mind. The other hand was still unconsciously gripped to the curtain, but beginning to relax of its own accord. He mumbled something and then articulated: I thought it was only just outlawed.

Perhaps the po-lice are attending to the rally down at the City Hall, offered Molly in her musical voice.

Y-yes, said Alexander, remembering, but not really, something about his wife dashing out the door not long ago to put a stop to it all. I suppose those KOL rabblerousers are …

I'd rather my wife see *this* than that, said Sammy.

Well, said RH Alexander with a forced-sounding, war-weary laugh, ha ha, we should shut the mill down early today then, eh? What time is it? Six P.M. already, eh? Shall we allow the rest a our men to enjoy this beautiful evening? Yes, let's give them a break to watch the man game.

A wise and charitable gesture, sir, said Sammy Erwagen. Your men will surely enjoy the spectacle … Why, quickly then. Call off the work. Look at them now. Two a them are ready.

Unable to resist a giant grin, RH took a place at the windowsill and leaned a hand against the shutter as the wintry warm evening air fanned him. Ah, yes, I recognize … that's Mr. Litz, a former employee a ours. A good man. I'd put my money on him if I were down there. And look at all the Chinamen. I never realized. Yes, I simply must close the mill so our employees can enjoy this game.

You got some tricks up your sleeve, eh? they heard Clough say. Hoss is going to play for you? Fine then. It's Campbell versus Hoss rematch. Get your wagers in.

//

The whores were out on the porch and up by the fence to watch the fire burn across the street in the shantytown. They teethed on their fingernails and glanced worriedly at the rioters. The fire kicked up a lot of smoke, blowing its ash right at them. Thankfully the flames weren't strong enough to climb the dike; Dupont Street homes weren't in immediate danger. Still, they could see orange and red globules of flaming char drip and hiss and land on their reflections in the dark waves.

The mob arrived once again at the flipped-over vegetable cart. All it took was one timberstick to light the whole thing. They'd been throwing cottonwaste on it all night to fuel a quick blaze. It was this second giant bonfire that finally drove the girls back inside. Peggy dashed to her back office where she rang her special *direct line* to the fire brigade. The line had been put in by the kind old captain and his men; courtesy, they told her, of the mayor himself. When the bell rang at the station the firemen ran from where they'd been watching the man game back down Dunlevy to get the fire truck. Harnessing it to the horses, they were on their way. As they rounded a corner on their way to Dupont the horses trampled an American tourist to death.

//

Sammy heard RH Alexander below him on the porch, telling his men to back away from the potted plants, laughing and berating them and saying: Come on, let's hear it for the man game. Raving applause every time he said it.

Sammy said: What do you think RH has in mind, inciting the men like that?

Molly batted her eyelashes as if to shoo away a mite. That's none a my business, she said. I've no idea what prompts that man's actions. She pressed the cigarette to her lips, inhaled, and said with a drifting smoke: A wonder he's able to manage this mill. If it weren't for your system, he'd likely sink. Man can't make a decision unless it gets him money, mink, or muscle.

Money, mink, or ... well, I had no idea you harboured such strong feelings towards Alexander.

He is a tool. A magic wand. You can snap him. Compared to him, I am a hat full a tricks. Without him, I'm very normal. With him, I am the whole show, you see? I need him, but I don't have to like him for it.

Yes, said Sammy, comprehending a little more the lawlessness of his wife's soul.

Sunday, February 20, 1887. Some kind of day. Sammy watched over thousands of men gathered to watch the game. There were men on the peaked rooftops seated with their knees up, men crowded along the balconies of the Stanley Hotel to catch a view all the way from Powell Street. There were close to fifteen hundred Chinamen. Felt like more. There were droves of lumberjacks and throngs of fishermen. There were heathens and providers. Coal miners and farmers and stevedores, and none of them with perfect eyesight. Not a bank in the world knew any of their names. They lived one suit at a time. Today's jacket was faded and frayed at the cuffs and two buttons had been replaced and both armpits had been mended and the pockets were in different places than when it was bought. Chapped lips, gold teeth, moustache: a portrait of a man in 1887.

The first match of the afternoon, a rematch no less, was about to take place: Hoss versus Campbell. Over at Furry & Daggett's side of things, Campbell got some final punches and pushes of moral support before he walked to the centre of the open space. He'd beat this guy before, and not too long ago at that. Campbell looked at all the new faces in the crowd. Most had never seen a man game before, and they stared and jostled and called out fiercely to Campbell, who found himself, though unable to admit it, growing ever more disgusted with his own audience.

The men scuffled to the centre of the pitch, shook hands quickly and split apart again, signalling the game was on. Campbell went up to individuals and pushed them back. Give us some fucking room, eh, before I strip you down and man game you in front a all your buddies. Campbell was raw as a burnt board, his each and every muscle extruding from his bones as if peeling apart the skin from the strain. His face was abandoned to bearded squalor. His eyes were the whitest thing about him. The rest was hair and filth. You think you know pain? he said. You think you know pain, Hoss? I'll show you pain. A bet on me is a bet on Satan himself, believe I'm that dangerous.

You got him, Campbell, said a supporter. Filet him like a bloody steak, Campbell.

Don't worry, he said. I named this the Cerebus.

What're you kykying aboot now, Campbell? said Hoss. And then he said: Weeaargh, and staggered backwards as Campbell was on him like a vampire's mandible, faster than poison, knees clenched against his ears, fingers in his nose, headbutting him. Six-seven-eight headbutts until Hoss collapsed on the ground, Campbell doing a three-sixty handstand on his chest before dismounting and immediately retreating four-legged as a canine to his post guarding Furry and Daggett, unmoved but alert to the tremendous and sustained applause, the likes of which the man game had yet to hear.

That was a decent enough move, said Pisk. The Cerebus, eh. I don't think so. Wishful Thinking more like.

And Wishful Thinking it was to be; a point for Campbell no less *{see fig. 16.1}*. Hoss was totally brained. Felt like he was rolling the losing numbers to the lottery around inside his head. Campbell skulled him eight times. After that hammering, all that was left for him to gaze at was glittering snowflakes swimming left and right. He didn't even remember to breathe.

Campbell looked a little muted himself. A purple veiny welt started to show up in the middle of his brow and his eyes kept fixating on the bridge of his nose until he squinted to unstick them. If Pisk had been a little closer he would have seen that Campbell wasn't humble so much as completely rocked. His eyeballs wouldn't steady inside their sockets. He'd headbutted Hoss eight times on the brain. He felt a ringing in his ears like he was standing inside a church bell at dusk. His head was making concentric circles around a queasy pivot in his lower gut. The knobby knees were wobbling and so were the bumpy ankles. Pretty soon he'd make two regurgitative belches, and soon after that regain his bearings, satisfied he'd won his first point.

How'd you like the Cerebus? he said out one side of his mouth to Litz once his mind had resettled.

Wishful Thinking.

FIGURE 16.1
Wishful Thinking

Calabi's commentary: You cannot allow your opponent to anticipate what a bloodthirsty parasite you really are, and however painful it might feel as you feed on his skull, keep in mind that you will be awarded the point.

Silas's commentary: Both feet must be above your opponent's waistline before you may begin the headbutts.

'The fuck?

Amateur move, said Pisk.

Unfazed by the patronizing way he'd been given the point, Campbell won his second with an impressive start, an extremely fast and concentratedly difficult solo dance routine that saw him cross-stepping through a heel toe heel toe hip knee hip chest hip chest shoulder shoulder neck spring arm swing, double jeté, head-first divebomb, and barrel roll, up into first position exactly in front of Hoss, grabbing his arms in falling balletic momentum, swooping like the weight on a metronome and dragging Hoss through what was suddenly the original move, the Pisk. Hoss ran with it until Campbell released him out of a pirouette and he toppled to an unspun halt against the shins of laundry-house Chinamen.

Dammit, said Hoss. He brushed the clods of street dirt from his back, thighs, and nostrils. Spat. From these brushing motions he began a subtle, musical shimmy, appreciated by man game veterans and unnoticed by newcomers. The transition then was quick but organic. His hands swept in front of his body as he sidestepped the circumference, backing everyone up a step or two, the dance getting quicker and quicker as he approached Campbell. By this time everyone had cottoned on. This was all of seven steps. Campbell didn't know where to move: back, to the side, or take Hoss face-to-face. On the strength of his two-point lead he decided to meet him head-on, and poised himself thus for a direct blow. Hoss anticipated it and darted left, body-checked Campbell into the audience who caught him and threw him back into the ring where Hoss took him out of his running stumble, clasped him hand-to-hand, the pink clap of their cold chests colliding heard by one and all—; Hoss bent his knees and leaned back, leveraged Campbell up and over, tossing him into another sea of men who caught him on their hands and fell to the ground in excitement, wailing like children at the edge of a river. Campbell righted himself and strode nonchalantly back to his team while the applause achieved high decibels.

One for Hoss, snarled a gambler.

That's no move, said Campbell. I'm the one who did the mid-air somersault I didn't have to do.

Hoss spat. There was no way of knowing if the move could be duplicated, but no one argued when Hoss was given a point for what he'd done, sending Campbell into the crowd twice like that *{see fig. 16.2}*. So it was two-one for Campbell.

The gamblers way down Powell Street at the very back of the crowd only now got word that Campbell had scored his second point.

Meanwhile Hoss tried to duck and dodge Campbell's new tactic, high kicks. He could extend his leg straight out in front of him and put a heel in Hoss's eye if he got the chance. Kept kicking the left leg at him, and Hoss kept avoiding it by rotating up and down through a low crouch and trying to sweep in an ankle kick to get him off his feet. All the while Hoss was keeping his fists at eye level, looking for a strikepath to Campbell's weak jaw, missing each time they'd been fired so far. Eventually the sparring turned into an open telemark, Campbell leading in a foxtrot's natural turn, Hoss taking an outside swivel to a feather end, and Campbell doing a planche freeze and bouche fallaway with a weave ending. Where and how the transition occurred from dance to game point no man could say, but it did, and Campbell was up two. Three-one for Campbell.

An unsettled fever coursed through men in the crowd, a mob who felt alternately discouraged by the lack of blood and

---

FIGURE 16.2

Flippin the Bird, aka the Hoss

Calabi's commentary: The Hoss is an excellent beginner's move, for it requires only that you properly time your positioning so that you're ready to send your opponent into the crowd.

elated by a brand-new move—some of the more ardent followers of the game even took to circling their hats above their heads—a halo spinning on its stick—as an additional way to applaud.

What was that *a*mazing move? squealed one adolescent boy with smelting smoke on his neck and hands and a spar in his mouth that smelled of red-haired hemp.

That's the Litz, eh, said the man next to him, a *foundational* move, eh. Pass that here.

That's a nice move, too *{see fig. 16.3}*, said the boy.

Hoss finally lost the match to another of Campbell's brand-new moves, a modern galliard in reverse and so even more baroque, even more abstract, the two men stepping in queue, Hoss behind Campbell, wrists bound in Campbell's grip. It looked as if any moment Hoss could undermine everything Campbell had planned. And each time the audience sensed Hoss had a window of opportunity, Campbell sensed it too, and the rhythm increased. It didn't allow either player much room for error, but still it was Hoss who stumbled to keep up. Campbell suddenly torqued Hoss over his back. With his arm behind his back, Campbell had Hoss in an upside-down headlock. Then he let go. It looked like Campbell just let Hoss fall on his ass. Hoss flailed and rolled until he was flat on his back, heezing and wheezing to catch his breath as a paff of dirt resettled around him, on him, in his eyes. He cried and spat and rubbed his chest and lay fetally squirming on the ground while

---

FIGURE 16.3
The Litz, alternative sketch

thousands of men cheered his defeat *{see fig. 16.4}*.

Your turn, said Campbell and pointed to Litz.

You'll get yours, said Litz as he came and dragged Hoss back to his side of the ring, and that was also humiliating on top of everything else. But the people loved it.

I'm sorry, Hoss said, finally able to sit up straight. He rubbed away the dirt stuck on his face by spit. There were skids down his chest, bulbs of blood on his elbows. Shit, I'm really fucking sorry.

Not a worry, said Litz. Major move he pulled on you. You played well.

Think so? I listened to what Molly said aboot the fact's not always aboot the fight, it's aboot the show. Guess I didn't learn how to—

Pisk was next to him as well now, and leaning down on his crutches, he said: You lost because you wanted to see what he was doing as much as the rest a us. Don't worry aboot it. Took me and Litz better part a four months to figure out how to do a Hatched Back. If Campbell's learning moves like that, he's practising every day. Who cares? Crowd was entertained, the chickamin is bagged up. Just wait and see how Moe Dee wins it back for us.

I walked out there feeling like I could flip a ship, said Hoss. Dejected and exhausted, he slouched low, and dragging

---

FIGURE 16.4
The Hatched Back

Calabi's commentary: The reverse galliard is as difficult as scaling a mountain backwards, and the back-to-front under-arm headlock toss-around should make this move count for two points.

his knuckles between his legs, said: I did it for the looks in the audience.

Yeah, said Litz. It's no problem for us. Moe Dee'll take him down.

Moe Dee was already naked. He smelled sourly of something no one could put their finger on, an odious smell, a skookum smell. His socks and drawers lay in a steaming apotropaic bundle next to the stable doors, a space unpopulated by mankind within a ten-foot radius; even the horses cowered at the back of their shelters. Dee clapped his hands together, licked his lips, was on his way. He shouldered to the front of the crowd and did not even bother to ask for pardon, whiplashing bohunks, startling dotards, smacking upside the heads of poltroons, salty dogs, navvies crying back: 'The heck are you—oh … Hey, watch yourself, buddy, eh, ah, oh … What the—, *ohhhh* … Someone's eyes drifted below the *belt* got Dee's elbow in the face. He made a swath through the crowd one elbow at a time. Campbell should have paid attention to those arms. They were the tablets of Moses. Dee fixed himself in the middle of the ring, only five-six feet away from Campbell. He stood with his legs far apart and his hands crossed in front of his chest above that huge waistline, his chin cocked high so that the flaring and dilating of his nostrils was appreciated by all. He said no words, didn't have to. He was here for one reason. Play the man game and win this time.

Now you're with Litz and Pisk, too, is that it? said Campbell.

Corr-ect, said Moe Dee.

Well, fuck a duck, said Daggett. You cheats.

You really this afraid a me, Litz? said Campbell.

If you're so keen to play Litz, said Moe Dee, why you so afraid to play me?

Didn't say that, said Campbell. Did I look fearful a your useless knees when I gave you that lesson a week ago?

No need for me to introduce Moe Dee, said Litz to the crowd, you already know he plays the man game for us. He's our second.

A real man don't fake his injury so as to make a guy compete versus a bohunk, said Campbell, referring to Pisk.

I could beat you if I were legless, said Pisk in his formidable voice, king of the bohunks. A great rallying cheer proved he was still known as the first man of the man game.

Don't want to waste my talents on this bohunk, said Campbell.

I'm no bohunk, said Moe Dee. Enough talk, let's settle a score.

Make your bets, cried Clough.

The neurotic surds of wagering began, grew fierce, as passionate as first love, then more tense as time elapsed, the rush of last-moment bets skewing everything until the bookies closed the tables with the most odds on Campbell for a change. Doubtless the results shocked and pleased those men who believed they knew better than to bet on Campbell. In their minds what the results really showed was how many here today had never seen a game.

The competitors shook hands.

Let's settle this, shouted Campbell, who darted in a left-right zigzag meant to confuse Dee. His flesh remained taut at all angles. Not a ripple of flab on his entire body when he ran. Within spitting distance, he assumed the gestures to begin a private milonga, and that's when Dee clipped him in the mouth with his elbow. One of those famous slabs. Came out of nowhere and knocked him off his feet. Campbell wailed and threw his hands up in the air, lost his balance, and slammed to the ground, nursing his face *{see fig. 16.5}*.

FIGURE 16.5
The Bookend

Calabi's commentary: Interrupts any thought, kills any plans. Your opponent expects more from you but reaches a dead stop.

Do that again, Moe Dee said as he brushed his elbow off.

Ten Commandments, someone in the crowd yalped, sounding well and sloshed.

From then on Campbell got nowhere with acrobatics. The flexible impressiveness of his style had the audience on his side, at least in their sympathy if not their bets. He was putting so much into every single gesture he made. Whatever was said about the man, it's agreed among Ken, Silas, and Cedric that Campbell introduced big style to the game. The philosophy behind Campbell's approach was that the man game, at its root, was a solo sport; that sparring was pretext and individual style was its most important element. Even within Furry & Daggett's crew, his ostentation was not always tolerated. Eventually though, swagger would become the norm. Men who favoured Campbell in every match, who were loyal to his style, believed he was directly responsible for the separate strain of man game that appeared around the turn of the twentieth century. In this form, a player did not score a point by forcing his opponent through a move. Instead, a series of face-offs, solo moves where players repeat and advance each other's tricks, moves, styles, and intimidations, constituted the basis of competition. This Campbellian form was derided by traditionalists, but most players around that time were capable of both. Meanwhile, on that day back in February 1887, Dee just elbowed Campbell in the face or straight cold-cocked him every time he built up some momentum. The audience was easily seduced by Campbell's baroque movements and sheer flexibility, but Dee was nonplussed. His idea of a man game was a lot closer to the brawls he got into on a regular basis but with a stronger veneer of respectability, the chance for quick money, and a definite sense of personal glory that he never experienced after a night of brawls. If there'd been a rule against shit-kicking Campbell he probably wouldn't have been naked there on that day in front of so many fools. He liked the man game because it forced him to invent new ways to hurt someone. So when Campbell thought he'd finally succeeded in pulling Dee through a running finish on a double-fast Spanish Layover but ended up losing his footing and going assback on the ground instead, Dee stood up and stepped on his belly, heel first, to grind in the fact that Moe Dee was a serious contender *{see fig. 16.6}*.

Oof, said Campbell, losing five-one in as many minutes. Easy come, easy go.

The audience was so big and so loud that RH was by this point satisfied that he'd properly fomented the makings of a riot that required serious help—unaware still of the real threat a few blocks south—, so he took his leave of the mill store's front porch, where he stood side by side with his nearly deported ex-employee Pisk, and proceeded back into his office where he wired the po-lice in Victoria.

An anarchist uprising? cabled back the Victoria po-lice.

Correct, cabled RH.

Reckon?

Thousands.

Minutes later, RH received a cable that the Victoria po-lice would arrive on the next ferry.

So it was arranged. RH checked his visage in the mirror, a grand, fulminating white brow over glacially blue eyes, omnipotent moustache, stone for a jaw, corded neck. Age had not been kind. His deportment in check, he returned to the street and watched the man games awhile longer before heading to the Carter House to reserve enough rooms for Victoria's entire force.

Now where's Alexander off to? said Sammy, still watching from above.

Drum up more publicity for my work, assuredly, said his wife, dragging on her third Stars & Stripes of the hour.

He laughed; she was probably right. But was she on edge?

FIGURE 16.6

The Point and Click, early sketch

What rattling was she hoping to quell by her many cigarettes? He did not ask, regretting it later. For isn't acknowledgment half the solution?

//

Moe Dee took Campbell five-one, a huge turnaround from his spectacular loss a week ago. Then he moved on to Boyd. Boyd got two points on him early and then Dee took the next three. In his second point, part stranglehold, Moe Dee made Boyd faint straight away. When Boyd awoke, his skin was lavender. There was blood in his nose. He lost five-two. Then Dee took down Smith five-three. Moe Dee was flabbergasting everyone.

How's he learned to do all this? said a fellow at the Bar Rústico.

Must be a natural, said Miguel, with a crick in his neck that made washing cups a chore, still smarting from the memory of his turn as executioner.

Dee's final move of the night was to grab and twist one of Smith's pectorals with enough strength to actually flip his opponent off his feet, send him spinning through the air to land doubled over in pain. Moves like these were quickly making Dee the most loved and feared character in the man game *{see fig. 16.7}*.

FIGURE 16.7
The Totoosh Twister

Calabi's commentary: A variation on the Point and Click that prefers a clench to a punch. A move like this turns opponents into enemies.

A lot of bettors made their disappointment in Furry & Daggett's team known. That's what you get, believed Vancouver men, when you trust a one-armed coach. One after the other Dee felled their crew. Daggett cursed every chance he got. His partner Furry punched a horse to the ground when he saw Boyd lose.

What's the holdup, Clough? cried those among the crowd who felt swindled and snookered. Whatever the final result, Dee was the big winner of the night. Having dealt with three men, he stood to pocket in the neighbourhood of a hundred dollars.

By the time Meier came out of his clothes and onto the pitch, Dee must have been tired. A ghastly sight was Meier, whose loyalty to his fellows at this moment was truly murderous. With teeth and fists held tight as caskets he seethed and hissed at Dee in his fury, standing in his own shadow, ominously, as if he carried a pestilent aura.

Dee swallowed his acid reflux.

Shaking hands, Dee got his start the old-fashioned way, turning his body right around and backflipping onto Meier's shoulders, taking the initiative for a Gone Fishin *{see fig. 16.8}*, at which point, contrary to tendency, Meier ran straight forward (not falling back) and tossed Dee into the crowd, who launched him back into the circle where Meier decked him so hard across the face that Dee completed a three-sixty whirling through the air, his fall broken by Meier's knee catching him on his stomach,

---

FIGURE 16.8
Gone Fishin, alternative sketch; the ascent before the leap

winding him so completely that his grovelling around on the dirt looked like death throes.

Meier received the point, and the move was later named Knuckles on the Bar {no illustration yet found}.

At the time, Dee argued that because no one had ever done it before it couldn't be a move, but Pisk said it was good, awarded Meier the point, and aimed to try that one himself sometime.

Meier was unlikely to be in good shape for his next fight, against Litz. Dee and Meier were two serious bruisers, and both were whipped top to bottom by the time it was over. Even still, Meier beat Dee by only one point using a Somersaulting Carpenter.

I crapped out at the end there, said Dee to Litz and Pisk afterwards.

No, for Christ—you were slaughtering out there, said Litz. Where'd you learn to—

You fishing for compliments or points or what? said Pisk.

No, I—

You beat *three* a those dudes, said Pisk. Be happy for yourself, eh. Meanwhile two a those dudes should a been for Litz. Who do you think you are?

I just meant—

//

What do you think so far? said Molly, looking down at her men.

Call down to Langis. I want to put ten dollars on Meier to take Litz.

Ten dollars?

I feel lucky.

Are you s-sure?

Are you really behind all this? Every detail? Was Smith to go out when he did? Is Litz sure to win the next game? These are my questions, Chinook.

Oh, Chinooky, she said, and swatted him. You tease me. Do you really care to know? Don't you like it?

I do, I really do.

It's funny, isn't it?

It is, yes. I may not have laughed aloud when Dee stopped to pick Boyd's tooth out of his kneecap, but I saw the humour regardless.

Would I marry a man who didn't love theatre?

He gazed at her, gazed at her soul all the way to the other side of this very weakness that pinned him down, and saw his solution in the watery green lakes of her gorgeous, maieutic eyes. This was one of the not infrequent occasions when his love was acutely defined by the panic he felt at the possibility of losing her.

//

Litz and Meier shook hands and Litz didn't let go. It was exactly what Clough had cautioned would happen. Meier tried the swift body flinch Clough had taught him, but it didn't work and soon they were in a tug-of-war over Meier's fingers inside Litz's ever more pinching claw.

Ow ow ow ow ow, said Meier. Litz had him in a brutal handshake, to the point that Meier sank to his knees in tears. His tears soaked his beard.

Clough shouted: Get the fuck back on your feet.

Meier was clenching his teeth and screaming: Oh, please somebody make him stop. He flipped flat on his back when Litz rotated the handshake a little so that if Meier didn't lie down it felt like his arm was going to pop out of its shoulder, elbow, and wrist sockets and all the tendons were going to rip apart like splintered trees. He begged Litz to stop, at which point Litz did a one-handed cartwheel and whiplashed Meier back on his feet. Still in his grip, Litz used the momentum to send himself flying over Meier's head, rotating their locked arms in space. When he landed he was still attached to Meier. He dug his heels in the dirt and chucked Meier over his head one more time. He let go and Meier sailed into the crowd *{see fig. 16.9}*.

The critics responded:

What—

'The fuck—

Did you see that? Did you see that? Mother—

—'Fucker.

That was some fancy footwork.

First point to Litz, said Calabi, putting nib to pad.

For fuck's sake—, screamed Daggett. 'The hell was that? Don't tell me he meant that. No one means to do that. It don't make sense to look at.

That's the Flipping Handshake, said Vicars, hopefully.

'The fuck asked you?

No answer from Vicars.

That's no move, said Clough. That's purely accidental. The wind helped.

You saw as clear as anybody here, said Litz. It's my point. Call it whatever name you want, I'll show you the same handshake right now if you want, he said to Clough, reaching for his one hand. I'm a ballpeen hammer nailing you. I'm going to put each a you in the earth like a railroad spike. You see what I did to your poor friend Meier? The same for you two.

Not so much as a bead of perspiration lay on Litz's body. The audience was a little slow to comprehend the difficulty of

---

FIGURE 16.9
The Somersaulting Carpenter, aka the Flipping Handshake

Calabi's commentary: This move requires plenty a space and a limber opponent.

the move. Litz made it look like no more of a challenge than handwriting, something for experts, not masters. But then it became clear, in reviewing the move in their minds, that it was physically impossible, and that Litz was a god. Flick you off the ends a my fingers, he said to Meier, dancing riotously in the sudden applause. Litz was flexed at every step. Top condition. His skin looked thicker than cured meat.

Happened so quickly, said Sammy, upstairs. I hardly had time to focus. How did he do that?

Litz has such long arms, said Molly, and he's firmly planted on the ground. It took us a few weeks to perfect it.

Only has a few moves, then?

When I was in Moscow, in three days an old master taught me, oh, it must be hundreds a dances. I learned how the b*od*y remembers. I can teach this way, so that the body remembers very easily. And now you see, it's been how long? six months we practise the man game?

Has it been so long? I see. The moves they must know …

Shh, she said, catching the insinuation in his voice. Oh, Sammy. Come to your senses. I would not betray you even in death. These are sportsmen. I love them as a prayer loves God, unrequited. Laughing at herself, she said: Quite unrequited. When will you trust me? When will you end your jealousies?

When we send our first child to war.

Our first child …, she said. Would you like to give me a child?

I'm not so foolish as to try to contain you with motherhood.

Motherhood would not contain me. Oh, try being kind to me for once. I'm so upset that you don't enjoy the man game.

I do, darling, I really do.

//

And so it was that the dodges and parries of love continued on upstairs while down below, surrounded by hate, Litz taught Meier how to do the Hudson's Bay Blankets, bearing down on him with all his weight.

I'm going to put you in figure-four leglocks, Litz said, walking past the audience, shaking hands with the hoi polloi, talking to Meier in high swagger. He took big tramping steps around the circle and snuck up behind and baited and swiped at Meier, just out of pleasure, then swooped in and connected, startling his opponent with the swiftness of ice water. He jammed Meier up at the knees in a rugged mazurka and broke him down, merciless. It wasn't even a move. He bragged about what he was going to do to Meier in very specific terms and then spooked him out completely by doing it, half-finished moves, crabbing up him and readying his forehead for a headbutt just to prove he could do the Wishful Thinking at any moment and finish him off. Litz did half a move, and then did the same half backwards. He made Meier look like a raggedy doll with no control over his own body. He was humiliating Furry & Daggett and they sure knew it. Clough was shaking his fist at him. Men in the crowd routinely took their hats off their heads, slapped themselves in the face with them, and said: How the fuck—? Tongues lolled below moustaches. Moustaches yellow-brown from smoking tobacco. Tongues grey-black from chewing tobacco. Jesus fuck—, they said. Motherfuck—, they said. Holy shi—, they said. He came in from above, moving with airy swiftness, and did his moves inside a blink.

I'm going to lean you over my shoulder like a blanket, fold you in four directions, throw you in the corner and get a dog to fall asleep on you *{see fig. 16.10}*.

FIGURE 16.10
Hudson's Bay Blankets

Calabi's commentary: Convince your opponent to flop across your back and carry him for twenty paces before dumping him.

Again, the entire crowd gasped.

Watch these murderous acrobatics, said Litz. Watch me paint you like a sign and nail you to the wall. I'm the ballpeen hammer, he repeated.

The next move ended with an unneccessary but instantly popular swooping gutkick that sent Meier into the crowd so hard that whole sections collapsed on top of each other like a pile of kindling sticks, Chinaman upon Chinaman, laughing with pigtailed glee. Hoisting Meier to his feet, they tossed him back into the ring for game point, limping to his fate, even dropping to a knee, head doozy, looking airless. Litz put his hands on Meier's chest and held him standing. One of Meier's eyes was bruised shut, the other wasn't focusing more than a bit.

You're making it look too easy, Litz said under his breath.

I'm fucked, said Meier.

Bullshit, said Litz, you're lazy. He grabbed his partner's wrists and took Meier through a fast waltz, dipped him once, waltzed back again even faster, dipped him again, then, after an enchanted pause, let him drop. It was standard vaudeville, but it was enough to win Litz the match. Five-zero. Shut out. Meier lay there, mouth ajar, his one decent eye looking stunned.

Cheering reached insurrectionary levels.

Litz stared down his challengers. Furry and Daggett alone remained. They seemed decently impressed with how speedily Litz had mopped up their best crewmate. Despite the unwavering poker faces, their respect was still visible in their shifting feet and hip swivels, plenty enough exposed weakness for the audience to see they'd taken a personal blow. True that Litz was a stark figure there in the chill, steaming. Undressed and unbeaten, inarguably the best player on toed feet. Anyone in his right mind would be intimidated.

Vicars was talking his mouth off.

Pisk, the crippled eidolon, prime number among the real fractions, leaned down and said to Vicars: Listen, brother, I never seen you before in my life, but let me put a bug in your ear, eh. Listen, I know you like what you see. But there's things you missed in those moves. You didn't see it all. It happens too fast. That's Litz's style. He's the fastest man game player you'll ever see. If you saw all he did you wouldn't be talking right now, you'd be shut the fuck up.

When Furry motioned that he'd play next, the gamblers started their exchanges. Litz's preference would have been Daggett, but it wasn't his decision. Daggett, like Pisk, was their first. Furry cracked his knuckles and shadowboxed while Clough and Daggett remained in a tight huddle speaking in fast suggestions. Furry came over to them now and again and agreed with everything they said, then went back to his preparations.

Clough said: Don't even think a yourself as a man when you're oot there, eh. Think a yourself as a predator. You're a fucking bear. You're a grizzly bear.

I'm a grizzly bear, said Furry.

You're no human. You're the fiercest maddest most dangerous beast around. You're Furry. You know who you are?

I'm Furry.

You remember when we just started out in this forest, and we ran upon a lone wolf, half-starved, wanting us for a meal?

Yeah, I remember.

Remember how when he lunged at you, you hacked that wolf's head right off his neck?

Yeah.

With your bare hands, man?

Yeah.

Well, that's what you're going to do to Litz *right now.*

Yeah.

Where're the Chinamen getting all their money for betting on? said a dusty gambler in the line to make a bet. The men around him turned their attention to the Chinamen and their money piling up in Calabi's leather bellysack. The Chinamen bet with a kind of melancholic addiction to the act itself, the transaction. Addicted to the point of purchase. They revered the moment of delivering their money into the hands of Fate. They did so quietly, with unequivocal manners and inordinate subservience. I'm not letting some Chinee outbet me, the dusty guy said, shaking his changepocket. When he got to Langis and asked how much the Chinamen had bet, Langis told him they usually started at a dollar. A dollar, eh, said the bohunk, fidgeting his money. Well, gully-gee, where the fuck they getting all their blankets from, eh? That's a lot a chickamin.

Are you making a bet or what? I got a line goes twenty deep behind you, sonny, said Dr. Langis.

Yeah, yeah, okay, sorry, he said. Fuck, make it a dollar and a nickel on Litz.

Show it. The kid gave Langis his money and Langis wrote it up in his book. All right, next, said Langis.

Litz didn't acknowledge he even had a competitor until Furry was out of his clothes. This was Vancouver's first chance to evaluate Furry's physique. Litz's gaze was especially prudent. He looked Furry over bottom to top. The man was seven-eight feet tall by all accounts. His shoulders fit an ox's yoke. He was an even huger version of Litz, also long-armed. His knuckles were freshly scabbed. The mouth on his face was turned down with an almost sickened expression, as if he'd just swallowed all the blood from a fat mosquito in his mouth, and he regarded Litz with genuine unhappiness in his eyes. A man born for disobedience, for the woods of British Columbia. The look in his eyes had that hideous directness, like a bear's eyes, of pure intelligent blood instinct.

Ever heard a bear-baiting? Litz asked. Ever heard a when they stick a bear until the old boy bleeds to death? That's what I'm going to do to you, you fat *Furry* bear. I'm going to bleed you dry, you bear-faced bohunk.

Furry said nothing. Furry was staring down his nose at him.

Forget your talk, Litz, said Daggett from the sidelines. We're not afraid a you. Furry's up there at Wood's knocking on your wife the day you married her, and what a you do aboot it, cry? Sure, and then you *get*. Go hide out in the skookum and keep your wife locked up to keep her away from our door.

That so?

True, I remember Litz's wife, said Furry in his dry dog voice, I went at her for aboot a week there just before she left Wood's. Yeah, we got something in common, me and you, Litz.

Your wife. Guh, I thought there was *some*thing, but then next week … naw, it was nothing.

You cross a line here, said Litz. Don't cross that line.

Already did, said Furry. I left it wet for you.

The crowd's mouths were open. No one spoke. It was Sunday. It felt like Sunday in the silence, like just before the Messiah comes to strike them all down. The silence even grander with the mill shut down. Indian silence. Litz's reaction: He didn't have a word of comeback, didn't even curse. All his swaggering talk ended there. This man game was going to be on different grounds, and Litz was already feeling it. Eventually his eyes cooled. He walked to the centre of the pitch and they shook hands, two shakes, and began to make their cautious circles. Furry stood bent at the knees, crabbing to the side as Litz repositioned himself step by step, breathing through his teeth, his hands clenching and splaying. Then he was on Furry with knees and knuckles. He could move at windspeed, a sensation that got Furry ducking in an uncontrolled and precarious way, like a man at the barrel end of a pistol, giving Litz the opportunity to switch it up, change tacks, deke him out, and land beside him. To save his landing he took Furry's wrists and yanked him into a series of bouncing twists like a jig, put him in a headlock, and drove his face into the ground. The first point went to Litz *{see fig. 16.11}*. Clough was outraged. He shook his fist and spat

---

FIGURE 16.11
The Corker

Calabi's commentary: If your opponent isn't perceptive enough to stall you with a Bookend, this move transfers all your travel speed onto the unmoving target, whose entire body screws around to compensate, and all you must do is guide the head towards the ground to score.

and swore to God. It happened too quickly. No one was sure but Furry, who respectfully conceded it.

Over the woodsmen's pandemonium, their gobsmacked shouting, Sammy realized he could account for it all. He saw these naked men in a new light. Instead of brutes, suddenly they were professionals, accountants of their own charts, artists without canvas, just as the lion tamer is an artist, the strongman, or the singing Jew in greasepaint and straw hat—all artists, or at least, entertainers.

At last he saw the man game as she meant for him to see it. Instead of competing with it for her affections, he realized he was somehow at the centre of the game, a missing centre. The man game had been created for his amusement, all for him. A gift from his wife. Could it be true, he wondered, that all this time I've misunderstood?

I really am enjoying myself. Immensely, said Sammy. Why, I can even feel a smile appearing on my face.

Oh, how wonderful, said Molly. Do you really mean it?

Yes, I do. I think I may smile.

I don't see it yet.

It's coming. Be patient. I might need to watch another few moves.

It's been so long since I've seen you smile, said Molly. If you do, I think I'll cry.

Can't promise anything, but I do feel more joy today than ever since the accident.

I love you so dearly, said Molly, kissing him. I only ever want to entertain you, Chinook.

You have, he said.

No one but you can understand the man game properly, she said. I made it for you. Whatever you kumtuks now, then that's the truth.

//

Campbell said: It were the hugest upset in the history a the man game so far. Never seen nothing like it. A spectacle unparalleled. There might a been a good many men who put his money on Furry but he hardly could expect to see his gamble's fruits. No one seen Furry play before. I mean, I saw him learn these moves, but. I mean, and everybody knows how I play the man game. It's a matter a education to bet on me. But Furry? Furry, he's my boss, but he was an unknown integer to the town. And here's Litz, you should a seen him. Lean. Leaner than a creek in the heat a summer. Nothing but stones. Is that my beer or your beer?

The bar was filled past capacity with keg drinkers. The siphon tubes streamed and foamed endlessly into mug after greasy mug as the night wore on. Fortes collected on old tabs and totted up new ones. The player piano went *a-rinky-da-dinky-dink-dink-da-rink,* and the Irish sang along. Beer dripped off beards. The only women in the crowd were tattoos, excepting Molly of course (muse of all tattoos), who accompanied her crippled husband Mr. Erwagen, feeding him beer. They sat happily in the corner, laughing along with the stories, lies, and gaffs of the night's scandal. She had an erotic way of tipping the mug to Sammy's mouth then turning her bamboo wrist to daub the foam off his lip. Her ministrations were nurselike, and her remedy was the best beer in the world. Sunnyside delight.

At another table near where Campbell was grousing on to almost anyone who'd listen with stories of that Sunday a week ago when Litz beat Furry, other men argued over details of the day.

I'm *Meier,* said Meier, stressing not the pronunciation but the importance of his name. 'The fuck you know aboot me? Matter fact don't say shit. Tired a hearing bohunks talking not make sense. Fucking tell you how it went, eh. I was robbed, and Furry was robbed. That's how it went. Pure robbery. Litz, he's no better than that damn Indian we strung up. If Litz played straight? That match would a been ours for the taking. He used the hovering technique and *that* is illegal. Starts off they meet, shake hands, and Litz is instantly trying to box him, shooting left jabs and hooks, and Furry's putting up with it somewhat. Takes one swipe and you can tell Litz is trying to get him to do the Daggett, eh. He's frustrated Furry's not going for it. 'Course Furry knows Litz is trying to insult him. Trying to act tough swiping fists a hair from Furry's nose. He's trying to make *Furry* do the Daggett, eh. Not funny. Well, he dodged low and went in for the Hatched Back, scooping Furry up onto his back, spinning him around … and besides Campbell already did a Hatched Back, and *better.*

I declare a rematch in order, said Terry Berry.

And I second that, said Vicars.

Wa, said all.

Meanwhile, over near the back of the bar, a black shade partly lifted in Sammy's world. Though he was still as ever trapped in his wheeled chair and unable to move below the neck, Sammy sat in the bar with a different face. It was as if in the space of a week—a week since seeing the man game dedicated to him, from his wife—the spectrum of his identity had grown dramatically more arrayed.

Shall there be more discoveries, he asked aloud, his wife listening with affection. Shall I ever walk again? Or will I live out my days as a mind poised against the physical dimension? Or will this enlightenment bode well for my impediments? God has taken care a me thus far, Molly, despite my own worst intentions. I should like to imagine that if I am given the right motivation, He would send me to my feet again.

Sammy was an old man. He was another generation older than everyone around him. The men in the Sunnyside saloon were seventeen, eighteen. Bright faces, tanned by labour. They had fisherman's hands, pink and big enough to touch thumb to fingers when fisting a beer pitcher. A trapper's education, on their knees in the forest smelling yesterday's turd. Portaging across Manitoba at the age of fifteen, weighted down by rabbit pelts, dreaming of mother's milk. Scared and alone, far from their families, they became dangerous men. Half-wild from a lack of civilization, they looked upon the streets with a cougar's suspicion. They had a cougar's smarts. They had bear's eyes, bear's claws, bear's hair.

If there's any one event that Ken, Silas, and Cedric all agree was a catalyst for the man game to proceed from its original players of 1887 to a citywide phenomenon by 1900, with teams, leagues, divisions, and an economy, it was taking place this very moment, as the next generation of players listened to Furry & Daggett's crew tell their official histories. The men not only listened, they planned their own comeups. Their own secret plans were already starting to hatch. To prove themselves, these men would go out and create their own moves, and strip to challenge the very men they once hoped to befriend.

Where are Furry and Daggett? Why aren't they here?

Boyd said: Forget that. Any time you see Furry or Daggett you got to be prepared to play them the man game, eh.

I heard they challenged George Black.

Yeah, said Campbell, and the butcher declined like a mink. That going to be you?

Twenty-seven years old and two hundred seventy pounds, Smith had the wisdom of a dog. If you tested his loyalty to Furry and Daggett his revenge knew no boundaries; the man was known to kick down homesteads. His audience of intent young men had everything to prove. Okay, he said slowly, Litz did a Corker. Furry did a Hatched Back. Then he did a Rook Takes Pawn, that was his second point. The Litz was Furry's fourth move, I'm sure a that, because I remember it caused a big uproar. Just before Litz did the Medical Breakthrough, and that's what won him the game. A Medical Breakthrough won him it, because there was no denying he meant to do that. That was his plan all along, to finish him off with the Medical. Damn. Litz, ah, let's see, his third point was a Point and Click. I remember now. That's where instead a landing flat on top a Furry, he flipped it wrong so he was landing on his belly, eh. You can call that an easy point but you see how fast Litz moves; for Furry to get in there and gutpunch him like he did, *that's* what deserves the point. I don't care what you say.

But man, that was some Totoosh Twister Moe Dee pulled earlier, eh? said a fan. Woo, can't wait to see that again.

And Campbell, directing his stern glare to the corner table by the bronze bust of the Queen where the cowboy RD Pitt and the Knights of Labour sat in the seventh moon of a crapulent bender, said: And *then,* because a some stupid shit aboot a riot, someone called in the Victoria po-lice. All the way over on the ferry just to put an end to our game. Fucking swear to you, just when you think we get the po-lice back on our side, some dry turd from Alberta's got to roll in and ruin everything for everyone.

Nothing changes, said Pitt, recognizing that Campbell put all the blame on him. You're all still in his pocket as usual.

No, we're not.

Look, all your guys's playing your fucking man game *right there* on the man's goddamn porch, for Chrissakes. Hassings Mill, fuck, eh. You think this is rebellion. I'm rebellion. You're all vaudeville, thassall.

Your fault the whole thing—

Don't go blaming me for changing things, said Pitt. If you weren't around I'd a had *thousands* a men down there to really change some fucking things. You do your fellow men a disservice not joining the labour movement. You do yourself a disservice. Who you think's going to take care a you when industry hits hard? You think RH's going to have a sudden change a heart? Fuck, eh, you can't be indolent aboot this. Alls you guys, said Pitt, sweeping his hands across the room, do a disservice to yourselfs.

You do a disservice to the labour movement, said Meier.

Why I oughtta … said Pitt, trying ingloriously to stand.

Pisk would a taken Daggett, said Vicars to Campbell. Would a beat him something stealthy.

That's yet to be decided, said Meier, eager to change the subject.

Campbell took the deep breath that Clough advised for situations such as this (Take a deep breath and go privately punch the ground as soon as you can, was his precise advice), when he wanted to crack someone's head in.

Pisk would've taken both him and Furry. No doubt. Maybe Furry gets two points on him. After what I saw. Even with no toes, Pisk would a taken him. Daggett the same treatment only worse.

Get the fuck out a this bar, said Meier. I never want to see your face in here again.

What, I—

//

The losers drank in private with their coach, Clough, who knew where to get the best bootleg. They sat around the light of a single candle, gripping their tumblers and repouring skinfuls. The wax melted down one side of the stick and solidified again as layers of dribble and a smooth elliptical gobbet on the tin plate. They drank ruminatively. The loss at the man game the other week had not dampened their rage. Their breath provoked the candle's flame, and shadows palpitated on their faces.

Calling out Pisk is a good plan, said Clough. Pisk might accept the wager as meaning you and all your men will leave town if you—

Who said anything aboot losing? said Daggett. Not going to lose. And I know Pisk. Guy, he'll take the bet. I'm not worried aboot that cripple.

If there's chickamin to be made in this game, said Furry, then I want it in our pockets. We got to take out the competition, and rule this city.

Then we better practise our hearts oot, said Clough. You got to be top shape if you're going to win this for sure. Daggett, are you listening to me, man? I want to be coaching you every day, morning, noon, and night. Are you with me?

Furry raised an eyebrow to his partner, and they nodded to each other. I'm with you, said Daggett. They clinked glasses and swigged back.

When Clough left Furry & Daggett's logging camp, heading home to his shack, he was stopped at knifepoint by a figure draped in black. A great steel blade flickered at him. Black hood, black jacket, black pants, like an adder with a steel tongue, leaping from the grey ferns.

The mugger.

Well, I'll be, you're real after all, said Clough. Can't believe I didn't sight you sooner.

Shh, said the mugger.

The blade cut through the moonlight. Clough raised his arm. He couldn't take his eyes off the blade.

Okay, my arms are up, he said. How did you elude me so long?

The mugger backed him against the wall of Red & Rosy's and frisked him. Clough held still. The knife came close enough. Took his fob watch and moneypurse before he even noticed. Waiting for his moment. In order to check his jacket pockets, the mugger had to very slightly adjust his balance, and that's when Clough saw his chance and socked the mugger on the top of his head with an elbow, stepped on his hand and retrieved the blade, pulled off the mugger's headscarf to reveal the face of a Chinaman.

And me with one arm, said Clough. You rat … Pulling the mugger by the collar back into the street. Come on now. Now what have we here … what's that, eh?

When he saw the mugger in better light, he realized that his prisoner was only a boy. Nine years old, according to his uncle, who came to see him in the prison mews. He regarded the boy sullenly, as if only annoyed by something that should be more horrible. The mayor himself visited Clough to thank him for capturing the mugger.

You're welcome, Mister Mayor, said Clough.

Shaking his hand, Mayor McLean whispered in Clough's ear: Shut the fuck up, you lying no good … make a big deal out a this and you and all your kind are through, you hear?

The following day the *Daily Advertiser*'s headline read: A DEMENTED CHINAMAN; LOCAL HERO CAPTURES WANTED MAN; ACCEPTS NO REWARD IN RETURN FOR VANCOUVER'S NOTORIOUS MUGGER; WISHES NAME BE WITHHELD FROM PRINT … What is yet another example of the scourge of the Orient upon our civilized society, or what we nobly attempt to be civilized … it was confirmed that the mugger who has been terrorizing our streets was indeed, as long suspected, a Chinaman … The mugger, when apprehended, turned out to be nothing more than a greedy Chinaman, his face well-known among the denizens of the many disreputable businesses whose entrances are found in Chinatown's many sulphuric and unGodly alleyways … The mugger is but a symptom of what ails our city. The increase in Asiatics has seen an increase in crime, disease, and poverty. He will be hanged to the death next Sunday at the first strike of noon.

//

The first strike of noon. I read that scrap back to everyone in the basement. What ails our city, I quoted. Asiatics.

We have information here, said Ken. We have a serious amount of bookkeeping and news clippings and illegible scraps. And there's also my great-great grandfather's diaries. Samuel Erwagen. Nothing after summer 1907, Vancouver's second riot.

That's when you think the man game ended?

The man game never ended, said Cedric, using his gross fingers to ramp up the crooked stairs and climb perilously hand over foot to the landing. At the kitchen he called for me to start my ascent.

Due to my gangliness, I found the hoist from the basement sofa to the staircase undemanding, and my long legs and enviable reach propelled me up to the landing in what felt like no more than two steps. I met Cedric at the top and called down to Minna that I could help her if she needed a hand. I kept my arm outstretched for her, kind of spotting her. But she didn't need any help. Ken and Silas followed her with ease. After years of living here, it wasn't surprising they got up the staircase so quickly, but I wondered how long it had taken them to master it. To keep themselves busy while we talked, Ken and Silas tried to see which of them could jump to a seated position on top of the fridge first, no-handed. From Ken's first leap it was obvious this wasn't going to take up much time. He wasn't tall, and the game hadn't occurred to them before now, but after Silas managed to get the exact right height on his first jump, Ken's second attempt got him sitting on the fridge, but just barely, shaking the appliance as he landed. It finally tossed him off, unpuckering the door and rattling the condiments, leaving it to Silas to make the win.

Damn, said Ken.

Yeah, that's aboot what we figure, Cedric was saying to me and Minna. Looking through these records downstairs? What we can tell is that nothing has happened with the man game since the summer a 1907 till now. When we started playing it last fall. That was probably the first time it'd been played since.

Cool, I said, noncommittally.

The day a the riot in '87 there was a major game. There was a few major games that were documented. That one, and the one on Dominion Day in 1887, too.

What happened at the riot? I asked.

Guess we should be going, said Minna.

Say what? I said. I'm just starting to admit I'm interested in this.

Look at him, said Cedric to Minna, pointing to me. He's all ears. He wants to know if he can join up.

Squeaking and stretching out her arms, baring her midriff. All us men peeked. Smiles on, hoping to be the first face to meet her eyes when they opened again. The other boys were unlucky, but not me.

P'raps you're right, I said. It's almost three o'clock.

Okay, said Silas, kind of drooping his head to talk to us on the landing, where I already had our coats on.

Sounds good, said Ken. Yeah, you should definitely come back and check it oot again.

You should practise sometime, Cedric said and pointed at me. We could use a fourth to really get this going.

I laughed along with Minna and waved goodbye. I said: It was really cool to meet you guys, thanks.

Yeah, let me give you my email, said Silas who got a pen and paper.

//

When we got back to the car, I saw there was a strandy tangle of what I thought was torn stocking but turned out to be human hair wrapped around the muffler pipe and the rear axle of my Dynasty. I walked up and bent down on my knees and inspected.

I'm beside myself, I said.

Don't touch, don't touch, ew, ew.

I tried to pull the hair away but when I touched it, I was repulsed. The instant my fingertips were on the black hair I could tell she had used a quality shampoo. I backed away. It's silky smooth, I said, wincing and rubbing my fingers together to rid them of the horror.

Why?

I did not know.

Do you remember running over someone?

I said: I'd remember running over a woman with silky smooth hair. I'd remember. Someone must have put it there.

Hearing no more objections from Minna, I got into the driver's seat and keyed the ignition. She slid into the passenger side and did up her seatbelt. Those were nice guys, she said, putting her feet on the dashboard and unlacing her shoes. She started to say more but I interrupted.

Nice, I said, hitting the signal as I turned left at a corner. Nice. Yes, I said. They were very nice.

Well, I don't know. I thought they were nice enough to show us around the house. And explain what the hell they were doing. Showed us the archives.

The archives. Those archives were designed to suffocate. Those were the archives a some troubled incoherent person's whatever. No one could ever form that.

I bet you could, she said.

Who me?

Yes, you. Who else? Come on, admit you loved that.

I continued to drive. I drove past who cares. I drove past never mind. I drove past forget it. Even as I drove my disapproval faltered.

I thought you loved that kind a stuff, she said, all that unknown weird.

I do.

We argued for another few minutes while I tried to concentrate on the road. The pace of traffic this far east and south of my own neighbourhood was completely different, and I was having trouble adapting. Because of a strange congestion of right-lane traffic all wanting to get back into my lane from a dead stop I was a little tense. The lane was edged by leafless cherry trees. We passed a family of condos, the last of which was wrapped in tarp and scaffold while a construction team replaced all the rain-damaged cladding and fixed the many many leaks. I was in an unfamiliar part of town, but the problems were the same.

She grilled me on the man game but spared me the embarrassment of acknowledging that I was completely lost. My sense of direction was mucked with by the crescents and cul-de-sacs and the plenty of very similar truffle-brown townhouses with matching gateways. Then I saw the WALLY'S BURGERS sign in the middle distance and I felt my inner compass wheel violently back to north as I aimed us for Kingsway. At last, a street I knew. It was three in the afternoon. Blue sky had been replaced by shades of dishwater pink that moved smoothly over town. In an hour it would be night. Now the coverlet was approaching us all. Beyond its pale inestimable surface glowed an administrative light. It was an office ceiling, an indoor fluorescence that reminded me it was back to work tomorrow, and that we were driving to Knight Street to buy me a bed for tonight's sleep. My new roommate said he wasn't going to get a bed, choosing instead to sleep on a blanket on top of a couple layers of bifurcated foam that my parents bought me at the Hudson's Bay downtown and which I offered him when we decided to move in together. He started to refer to himself as a prisoner of conscience, which perhaps left me in the position of warden. Why did it seem so perplexing to us that we were single? I was about to buy a bed out of an aluminum shed in the backyard of Minna's Chinese connection.

As we snaked down Kingsway and turned on to Knight Street, I kept one eye on the street numbers and another on Minna's thighs, pinched together on the blue velour car seat, jiggling to the rap music. I suppressed the violent urge to put my hand between her legs and rub the seam of her jeans with my middle finger. The urge was serious enough to consider—for only a moment—the idea of begging. The sky was a peptic colour, a cherry milk coating over the entire atmosphere. From a romantic context, I can see how this sky might have aphrodisiacal properties. But this was not a romance. I was not in a world where pink skies meant pink thighs, and every lonely man goes home with that which he desires most. I lived in a quieter world. I didn't want to live in this world any longer.

She said: That's the most beautiful sky I've ever seen. Oh, she squealed, and grabbed my knee and held it, rubbing and scolding (smak-smak-smak); she said: What a perfect day. I can't believe it. We have such fun together, don't we?

Hey, Minna, I said, steering this way and that. You know, I know we've gone over this before. When I kissed you that time last February, but anyway ha ha … And I realize we agreed to just be friends. But heck, I don't know. I tried to see if I could be your friend, but actually I still am very hot for you.

Ha ha, she laughed, and tossed her head back, her feet going up on the dashboard again. Oh, Kat. That's so sweet. I had no idea. Oh my god, that's so sweet. Are you serious?

You're impossible. You really couldn't tell? All this time? What should we do? Marriage? Do you feel the same way? Are you hot for me, or what?

How many times a day do we have to have this conversation?

Look, I said, turning a corner, we've arrived.

Yes, she said, this is it.

We parked. The house across the street was about what I expected: painted a mud-brown that was old and cracked, shades pulled over all the windows, a marginally taller than average fence. Not enough to draw attention, but enough to keep away prying eyes. There was a sign on the wire gate that said: BEWARE OF DOGS. *Dog* had been pluralized by Jiffy marker. I made note of that. I was about to buy a bed from this place. And indeed I saw the storage unit at the back of the yard where he kept them. It was made of large sheets of corrugated plastic and aluminum, very filthy in the gutters, connected using ashy two by fours crawling with pumice-green lichen. This was where he kept the mattresses apparently.

Maybe he's not home and we should not come back, I said.

She walked up to the gate and looped her fingers through the wire. Immediately the house was alive with the sounds of the two beasts, barking loud enough behind insulated walls to pose a realistic threat.

Beware a dogs, I said.

Relax, she said.

No, I distinctly read the word *beware*. It doesn't say, Relax, There's Dogs. It says—

Okay, enough out a you.

He was a short, stout, middle-aged east-side Asian with a bowl cut, a strip-mall sweater, and denims. And sure enough, pit bulls. He held them on a short leash at the top of the staircase using his back to hold the screen door open. The pit bulls were scowling and slobber dangled off their teeth in ropes. Whenever they barked the saliva flew into the air, and he shortened the leash and told them to be quiet. With pit bulls it doesn't even look like rage, I thought to myself, it looks like blind pain. I was standing beside my Dynasty while Minna stood with her fingers through the gate, explaining we were here to buy a bed, dogs howling at her.

What's the name a your dogs? Minna asked.

King and Kong, the man said.

Remember me? Minna called out to him. I came here and bought a bed from you last year?

Looking her over, he shooed the two dogs back through the screen door, throwing their leashes along with them, and shut it firmly. Wiping his hands on his pale jeans, he walked down the stairs to meet us at the gate. Very protective, he said, and unlatched the gate to let us enter his backyard. What you looking for? Bed? he asked, and led the way to the shed. The troughs were thick with leaves; you could see them in the light from inside the shed, which was indeed stocked with beds, ten in total, five queens and five doubles stacked side by side, with matching boxsprings and metal frames. The mattresses were in fairly good to spongy condition, with few if any seriously unacceptable stains. They were all of a brand, pale blue and slippery to touch, with typical white piping along the edges. A tarpaulin on the floor kept them from resting right on the wet concrete. They were used mattresses to be sure. They were essentially being stored outside. Too late to be squeamish about it. I waved my eyebrows at Minna and she nodded like get a move on. I took a look at the queens. I asked how much all included.

You good customer, he said to Minna. I remember you. He looked at me. I sell it for two hundred dollars, okay?

That sounded like a deal.

You deliver?

Where you live?

I told him I lived in Mount Pleasant and he said: No problem. You good kids, right? he asked us. I show you inside? More furniture inside. Yeah, yeah. More furniture?

Like what? I asked.

Minna put a hand on my shoulder and pushed me forward, saying to the man: Yes, let's see what you have.

He unlocked a door on ground level underneath the staircase and went in first then held the door open for us, smiling and waving for us to enter. He made it seem like now we were in a hurry so I rushed in and thanked him awkwardly for holding the door open as I passed, not certain what I was doing. I wondered if we should take our shoes off and he said: No no. As soon as we were inside, an unshaven man in a faded Mickey Mouse golf shirt slipped between us, excusing himself as he tiptoed in tubesocks from one room to another. I second-guessed our host about shoes, but already he was ushering us down the hall. As we followed him, I tried to get a look at where the other man had come from, saw a plywood door with a brass knob, the kind with a push lock, and a band of light along the carpet.

I followed behind Minna into a room where there was nothing but sidetables and lamps. The room smelled of cigarette smoke and old vinyl curtains, neither of which appeared anywhere among the piles of furniture. Most of the sidetables were in a dark wood veneer and octagonal, with the snapping doors that open the two front sides of the thing. Some other tables were of a paler grain. They were stacked on top of each other in no sort of organized way. The lamps were all of an identical design, this huge butternut squash-shape covered in a bubbly white skin. They were topped by the most nicotine-stained white lampshades, all more or less with the same amount of decorative trim, gold fabric braids with gold strands. I didn't want to buy any of these, but I realized that with this man's help I could decorate my apartment to look exactly like a room in a hotel off the main road.

Mirror? Dresser? Closet?

Oh, yes, said Minna, see there's mirrors along the back wall.

Yeah, mirrors, said the man, pointing to them. They were all that leaded kind in shapes that recalled chest armour. Very nice, very good.

I shook my head no thanks, smiling to show my appreciation for the offers. Our host was a perfectly nice gentleman, but we had to be on our way. I tried to express as much with my body language. While Minna opened and shut the drawers and seven-foot mahogany dressers I was facing the hallway, where I could see another spare bedroom on the other side where there were even more mattresses, and these ones had people on them.

People. These mattresses were *in use*. Startled by them—I hadn't seen them till now—I didn't know where to put my head. I wanted to stare at them, but I didn't want to look like I was. At least a dozen mattresses and probably three times that many people. If I had to count. I saw people sleeping on beds, and sitting on them, and some of them looking away from me, and others looking at me as directly as I looked at them. The fluorescent light in our room was on, and the one in theirs was not. The difference was staggering. Their room was grey dark. The white plaster on the walls looked smoke blue. At ceiling level there was a single window with a steel bar across it that poked in a little light. Other mattresses were stacked against the wall. People were sleeping against those ones, too. I didn't really have the time to study their ashen faces more than to nod hello, and all were weak or sick or starving-looking. One of them wore an extra large granite-coloured Mickey Mouse shirt with a soy sauce stain over Mickey's white glove. Of the dozen or so people, none had fresh haircuts. A woman in there shouldn't have been pregnant. They seemed equally curious to see us. They were only ten feet away, after all, but it felt like a world apart.

I was about to speak when our host caught me looking at them, and laughed. He said: Big family. We have family reunion, ha ha.

Oh, I said, that's great. Lucky you have all the extra beds.

Ha ha, he said. Yes, yes.

I said: I like all these sidetables, but I'll just go with the bed for now.

Okay, ha ha, that's okay. Good bed. Maybe later you want lamps or tables.

Yes, maybe later.

//

We drove to my apartment and waited for the guy to arrive in his half-ton with the bed. The whole way back we talked about who we thought all those people in the other room were. We drew many conclusions. I stopped my Chrysler on the one block in my neighbourhood that wasn't permit. There were already three cars parked on the same block of free parking. Minna called these kinds of parallel parking nightmares *tight pussy* spots. Nine points later, I jacked up the anti-theft bar, put my stereo's faceplate above the sun visor, power-locked the doors, and walked to my building where we stood in front and waited.

Minna yawned, squeaked, and stretched up her arms. Woo, she said. I'm going straight home after we set up the bed. I'm totally 'zosted.

Don't want to stick around and watch a depressing movie with me and my roommate?

Your roommate's always watching depressing movies.

He finds them inspiring.

I find them depressing.

He finds life depressing.

A person can be positive or negative. It's a choice.

It's true, I said. But I've met happy positive people who are depressed.

Like who?

I don't know. Like you?

Me? How do you see that?

Oh, Minna. You're lonely. You're lonely like me. Sure you are. If it wasn't for me …

I trailed off. I didn't have the heart to say more; I'd tried before and it never worked. I could tell she thought I was joking again. Rolling her eyes. Fair enough. I was being selfish. She was the one who had been honest while I was the one who'd deceived myself. She was the ghost of a lover. The ghost of yesteryear's love or future's perfect. She was not present. Minna was everywhere in my life but today's body.

SEVENTEEN

> You need to listen to your body because your body is listening to you.
>
> — PHILLIP CALVIN MCGRAW

Cane first, followed by the good leg, down on the riding heel of his leather boot, then, with cane and left leg, proceeding to stand upon the arrivals platform at the CPR train depot, greeted by celebrations beyond his reckoning. He brought the favoured leg down off the train as stiff as a rifle against his thigh. The crowds milled and dawdled through festoons of wild lily petals falling like snow, and shook their hats over their heads, hurrahs escalating all through the station. Refusing any assistance down the stairs from friendly porters and ticketers, the old man taxed everyone's time with his slow descent. A boy was paid to lug his bags, but no one would *ever* help Mr. Erwagen take a step. Sammy was familiar with this scene, or at least many just like it, in which his father's determination to do things himself wound up stalling everyone else around him. For as long as Sammy had known his father, he had been this old or older.

Sammy chewed his lip, absently reabsorbing his own salt.

She cooled herself with a paper fan. Man alive, she said, is it hot.

Indeed, said Sammy, seated still.

It was late May, and a taste of summer arrived with perfect timing to celebrate the first official passenger train to Vancouver's recently built CPR station on the False Creek flats. The moist wind off the water spiralled together with the engine's steam between the train and the station, coils of fog here and gone, upsetting his father's black suit. The man was unperturbed; hunched, but only to protect his beaver pelt hat as the gust lifted his clothes around his frame, and he remained as rigid as a tent peg. His father's patriarchal skull sat bobbling atop this rigid frame like Death's glowering lantern. Behind his stature, Engine 374 wore a handsome wreath draped down its black flanks, twelve-point antlers, and a floral replica of the Queen's own crown fitted over the lamp. The cars behind it were arrayed with streamers and people waved their white summer hats out the windows, flower petals everywhere. The train carried a special message written by the Queen, stating how proud she was of her colony's accomplishment, a landmark achievement in ingenuity for her to celebrate on her Jubilee, the transcontinental railway, some hundred thousand miles of hand-pounded iron trestle.

What are ye doing? said Father to his son. Stand up from your chair and show respect. Get up, say I. No more a this nonsense, eh. Who do ye think ye are? I put out my hand, ye simply—

Father, Sammy said, I've been crippled in a fall.

Eyeing Toronto for the first time, Father said: Who be the Indian with you?

My ward, Toronto, said Sammy.

Squinting in the sun, he swung out his hand to Molly. *Lady,* he said with unalloyed suspicion. You're a true *lady* to stand by my son through such catastrophe. You're a model a strength for the rest a your sex.

//

They brought Father home in silence. Sammy's frail tall father held firmly to the silver handle of his cane as he lowered himself onto the sofa. The hands were bony and long, white as deep-sea cretins, with veins blue and red that wormed with blood. Sammy was unable to help him sit, no matter how much of a show his father made at the difficulty.

I must speak unto my son in private, were his words to Toronto and Molly once he was down. Seated, his eight-hundred-year-old father's skull was still well above the wood-scalloped edging of the backrest, but somehow Mr. Erwagen was not the same giant he'd once been; even taller now in his thinness, somehow in his frailer state he'd reached a greater, grander, somehow taller majesty. In his scaffold-like rickety-ness, he towered higher in his decrepitude than he had in his middling robustness. All the nails showing in his construction, seated, his legs flung high and wide, with those terrible knees pointed like arrowheads under his wool slacks.

You may fool a lumbermill manager out in nowhere to adopt your profane techniques, his father said. Any professional in Toronto would surely balk at your imprudence.

Precisely why I moved, said Sammy.

After much direct and indirect conversation with the Lord, I came to realize what a victim a circumstance is thee. Born with your father's talents, and I did nurture them. I did try; try too hard, this I do not know. The Lord counsels a son to respect his father … But you never had my self-control. When your mother had the croup, I recall you so afraid, ha ha, afraid she would die that nay did you leave your room the entire time a her protracted illness. You never visited her. You surely recall this, eh.

That was a decade ago, Father. Yes, I remember.

How I de*man*ded. You, insisting not.

… In the study. I was in the study. You interrupted my studies. Twenty-two and in college. Studying for my exams.

Studies … She might well have died. Her last words were, Where is my baby?

Those weren't her dying words. She didn't die.

She *did* die, said his father, swishing his cane across the floor like a stiff probe. It suddenly fell out of his grasp and clattered on the ground in front of their feet.

Not then, said Sammy. She didn't die. That was thirteen years ago. Father, she was—. The doctor said she'd recover within the week. She did … the croup. Thirteen more years she lived. It's your own …

For you, excuses. Now look upon thee. Keep a secret from me, as usual, eh. I was the only healthy one in our family. Everyone was sick but me. Your brother was never long for … Oh, and for this I find myself alone, an old man asked to survive.

Listen to me, Father …

Why treachery? You must've cooked more deceits over this past year. What else must I get to learn? No. Wait until after I eat before you begin. Doubt I could endure it on an empty stomach.

The old creaking man stood up. He turned his back to Sammy, bent over slowly to pick up the cane, his bony ass in Sammy's face. And then, without thinking, Sammy gave him the boot.

//

What happened between us, said Sammy, as he explained it to Molly, was in its way as much a shock to my father as it was to me.

A shock indeed, said Molly, looking at her husband. I can hardly breathe. Since you can move again, make yourself useful and unbutton my dress.

Yes, it's true. My god, it feels so good to … feel. To feel you. It's as though I've drunk a hundred cups a coffee. Every sense is screaming, I can feel every thread of your slip, every pore on your body, every freckle.

Go on with the story …

Yes, I realized only after it happened. It was as incomprehensibly my own fault. Like the accident in the train tunnel a year ago. My first thought was you. Molly's got to know right away. Until Molly knows I can move, that my legs can move, that I've regained sensation throughout my body, then it isn't really true. He ran his thin, soft fingers through her black hair.

Well, like my brother, Father expected me to offer him a bed for the night, said Sammy. As he spoke, Molly listened with all her attention, no matter how often he became distracted by the feeling of his hands on her face. The pleasure of her nape was blurrily intoxicating. When he passed his hands over her breasts and nipples, he heard each fret of his fingerprints ring out in his ears.

He knew I'd sent my brother away. He didn't know if I'd do the same to him. I certainly could have. I'm done climbing mountains trying to talk with him eye to eye on things.

This time he came to you.

As Sammy talked, he conducted a full investigation with his hands across her body. She set to work on an investigation of her own with her lips all over his neck. She wanted to know if there was anywhere on his body where sensation had not returned. Each of her moist kisses, wherever placed, be it his chest or his stomach, his navel or his hipbone, no matter where she laid those lips, he felt it, they burst as if a ripe plum were split open at the moment of contact with his skin.

At the time it gave me great pleasure to throw Dunbar out. Fortunately for Pa, I am a different man today than in the days a our youth, said Sammy, pinched between her thighs, as she, braced there, listened to him.

Much stronger now, I'm sure, said Molly, running a finger across her plumlips then rubbing the finger against his stomach. She. Making her way up beside him again so that their stomachs touched, and he felt that warmth that emanates only from a woman's belly and he wanted very much to enter that warmth to be a part of that warmth and so he pressed his stomach to hers and he gripped his weak hands to her ribcage and marvelled at the living organ, her skin, in all its radiant topologies.

The Erwagens were upstairs in their bedroom lovemaking on the black fur rug on the floor beside the window while Mr. Erwagen Sr. was in the main-floor dining room going through intermittent coughing fits as he supped.

We continued to talk, said Sammy. When he saw getting angry at me had no effect, and even made him feel rather guilty, I suspect, his frustration began to show. He began to sweep his cane to and fro. How many times I must have seen him do this, and it never ceased to grate on my nerves. I was convinced that his cane sweeping betrayed his true feelings, unsympathetic, angry, urged to discipline me, punish me … an even deeper lack a respect. To see him absently staring at his cane, sweeping it to and fro across the rug. Looking at the arc he carved in the rug. It kept sweeping closer, and finally it tapped over a wheel on my chair and the handle fell out a his hand. He looked me in the eyes almost like a child. The expression faded quickly, but it was not his own childhood I saw there but my own. His face had accidentally mimicked my own, the face he saw so many times while he punished me. Just then, I relaxed. I felt it throughout my body, this sudden physical calm, but didn't immediately acknowledge it. That calmness was alive throughout my entire body. His features returned to their stern, frosty glare, which he pointed to his cane lying there on the floor.

The lovemaking approached a state of harmonious labour. Like the waterwheel, the couple moved in a perfect, constantly wet rhythm. He babbled on like the proverbial brook. She was swept up in it all.

So my father says, he looks me up and down one more time and says, When's dinner? he said. I had no answer. Is there a word for that, when you have no answer at the time and all the best retorts later on?

I'll remember in a minute.

Well, there I was with nothing to say. He growled at me, or what I thought was a growl which then became a hacking, webby cough. As he caught his breath, I could see his frustration again.

He said: Well, I shall not wait around here. You'll find me seated at the table, he said. Tell your Chinaboys I'm ready for my soup and bread.

Oh, that's fine, I thought to myself. As I watched him stand and right himself, I thought, He still looks imposing as all hell. For an old guy. Old as a damn cedar. I felt a strange sensation which I mistook for nausea. It came on with great urgency. It was a giddying in my spirits. At the very moment, I wondered for my safety. It was an involuntary fear with digestive reactions I felt. In a kind a brief fantasy, I feared I was aboot to regurgitate yellow foam. But yes, it was something like a giddying. My spirit was giddy. I know that now.

Whatever caused this giddying? Molly asked, kissing him frantically and huffing each word on her breath.

I don't know if seeing my father stand up was it. Yes, because it was also the fact that I was seated. I became infused with the memory a the night we met.

The night we met, she growled, clawing, biting, licking, and slapping him with her hair.

At the music hall, yes. I was filled with a great swelling yellow glow. Big bright and anxious happiness. Like none other I ever experienced outside the music hall. It was a delirium, sensual in the worst way, but without a thing wrong with me. In this case memory was my pathogen.

Yes, and, and, and …

He rubbed his hand across her neck, collarbone, and squeezed her bosoms together, and said: Ever present in my mind was a vaudeville routine. Looking at Father, I recalled at that very moment an old vaudeville routine. When Father bunched up his slacks so he could bend down to retrieve his cane, I saw my opportunity and kicked him.

Oh, yes.

Yes, and oh, he fell straight on his face and his arms splayed out in both directions, heels in the air. And let out a squeal the likes a which I'd not heard from this man *ever*.

Oh my, oh my oh my.

My belly was sore. That's when I realized, my limbs and organs. My father's eyes were wet and his body shook as he came to my side and we embraced. I told him he was welcome to stay in our house. He thanked me and we shook hands. He quickly left the room as both he and I were aboot to explode in tears. Oh, Molly, Sammy said and wept, it's taken me this long to see I've been such a burden on you. I am a different man today than I was before I saw the man game.

Oh, dear Chinooky, say it every day, she said, pulling his face to her to meet him at eye level and kiss the inside of his mouth. Say it every day.

I'm a different man.

Say it every day.

She rested her hands on his and he caressed the palms and followed the veins from her wrist up the graceful bend of her arm, marvelling with a new touch the wonders of her skin. Like a dog shaking the last water off his body, the last of Sammy's nerves tingled awake. He blurted out an involuntary yowl. Symbiosis. At climax, he lost all sensation above his neck. His face went totally numb. He went blind, as if he'd just walked into a cloud. His blind eyes glazed open, stopped moving, streaming with tears. He lost his hearing next. He couldn't see, he couldn't hear, and he couldn't feel his mouth hang open. He kept going in her. His big numb head slapped back and forth at the top of his neck as he pumped towards it. Drool fell from his lips splattering all over her back and rosy buttocks. He didn't know. He couldn't help the drool and he couldn't hear her giggle. Numb in the head. It lasted only a moment.

//

Western clouds at the horizon opened briefly, allowing the sun one last dusky look at Vancouver before it melted into the waters of the Georgia Strait. Above the yolky orange at the horizon, the sky turned a milky lavender. With the sun gone, the beaches, mountains, and trees all turned a denser shade of blue. The mountains wore a heavy aura against the burning-out sky. At dusk the forests came alive with nocturnals, and any man worth his stink could feel the animals begin to roam. Hear the bears yawn. The wolves sniffing on the cliffs. Raccoons in search of loot. A man could feel the animal eyes on him with their nocturnal hunger everywhere.

RH had heard head nor tail from the snakehead since the riots. By calling in the Victoria po-lice to beat some sense into the men, the story got play in newspapers across Canada and the States—savages in the West. Since then, there had been no word from San Francisco. No threats. Not another visit. Strange. Then one fine spring evening, RH Alexander received a knock on his door.

Who could that be at this hour? said his wife.

RH put down his pipe and strode to the door of the library, then promptly decided to sit down again and wait. His wife watched him.

Who do you think it is? she said.

How the hell should I know?

At last, a manservant asked to enter the library, and then announced that Molly Erwagen was here to see them.

The Alexanders looked at each other. Well, then, said RH, let her in.

Molly came into the library and greeted them both with a kiss. RH's cheek tickled with the opposite sting to a bug bite. She took a seat with them in the well-furnished den and supped quietly on her tea, using those very same purple cumin lips. RH became hypersensitive to how Molly suffused the room with a dazzling perfume of local berries, cosmopolitan spice, and rare pheromones. Youth in its elastic ripeness. She feigned interest in the weather when Mrs. Alexander brought up the subject of rain. RH's heart sank when she responded identically to the subject of horse races. Throughout the small talk, Mr. Alexander watched his wife's eyes recede further into deep craters of skin, the effect of skepticism on her flesh. In all, RH was disgusted to see a resemblance between his wife's face and a leather wallet spilling out with receipts. Any moment now she might burst out with an indiscretion. Remarkable virility for such an old hag, RH had to admit with some pride, considering they were such finely matched old lovers.

Tell us, please, said Mrs. Alexander, what's brought you here today?

Our dear Sammy has regained the use a his legs.

You jest, why that's simply m*ar*vell*ous*, cried RH.

I'm simply astonished, said Mrs. Alexander. A blessing. A miracle.

Why isn't the chap here right now so I may congratulate him in person? Tell me more. When?

Yes, this morning. Shortly after his reunion with his father, you'll be pleased to know. We picked up Sammy's father from the train station aboot nine this morning, and before noon Sammy was moving again. His hands, his legs. Everything. And he feels everything again, too.

Is that so, said Mrs. Alexander.

Yes, and so while he has the use a his limbs once again, his strength has greatly deteriorated.

Understandably. He'll regain it all, I'm sure. Well, I'll be.

He stayed at home to spend time with his father and asked that I come straight away to tell you while he rests. I'm sure he'll visit very soon.

It's wonderful news, said Mrs. Alexander, rocking in her seat on her big haunches. We simply must have you both over for a dinner as soon as possible. See? See, my dear? she said, addressing her husband. A whole new summer is here, she said. This is such good news. And we *do* need good news.

Yes, said RH, I know this city has its share a bumps, eh, but to know that your husband is back on his feet, well, that signals a boon. Mark my words. A boon.

Strangely, I have another reason to come visit you today, said Molly.

Oh, and what's that? I hope it's as good as the news aboot your husband?

To be perfectly honest, I don't know if it is or not. You see, when we arrived home from the train station, Sammy's father asked for some time to speak with his son in private, and I went to the kitchen. In the kitchen, I received a knock at the back door, and I opened it to find a young Indian boy. The Indian was doing the same thing our ward Toronto has done between here and New Westminster. He was delivering to me a telegram from the CPR station down the road. But when I took the telegram, the boy ran off before I had a chance to even look at it. The telegram was accidentally delivered to our address, Molly said. Naturally I didn't read it when I saw it was for you, Mr. Alexander. I quickly put it away until I had time to visit.

How long ago did you receive it? Alexander asked.

Just as I said, this morning. Molly produced the telegram, which she had folded in half and slipped into the cuff of her long-sleeved tunic.

Is that where you kept it? said RH. Marvellous. Here, let me read it.

The telegram from San Francisco said: A WISE GENERAL FORAGES ON ENEMY STOP ONE CARTLOAD ENEMY PROVISIONS EQUAL TWENTY YOUR OWN STOP CONTINUE BUSINESS WITH ME STOP CONTINUE MAN GAME STOP RECEIVE STRONGER MEN STOP

RH looked up from the telegram paper, a bit knocked out. His confused look, normally kept locked and hidden, was completely unveiled for Molly. It felt to him as if someone had just pulled the skin right off his skull. He was flabbergasted. He didn't know whether to be relieved or furious or frightened. RH was a strategist, indeed, but his plans never accounted for the strategies of his opponents, and inevitably he was carried along by the tide while thinking he controlled the current. His wife went a bit chalky to see her husband's expression. Knowing there was one or two things in RH's life that might cause such a face (the snakehead; the man game), she quickly looked at Molly, who was watching RH carefully but without any hint of the burning sense of victory that would belie ill intention.

Whatever is it? said his wife, to clear the silence.

It's from *San* Fran*cisco*, said RH, meaning to be euphemistic. As he said it, he grasped the sequence of the message.

From San Fran—, his wife paused, her voice gave out and she fell into a coughing fit. With Molly watching, she tried to take a sip of milk but most of it sputtered down her chin. Everyone was standing now. Mrs. Alexander was coughing badly. Her hands were flapping and Molly and RH went searching for a napkin or saucer for her to vomit into. Almost purple in the face with her wet and frightened eyes pushing out of their lids and her hands clawing the air trying to pull in more oxygen for her wheezing lungs, she still said, in the most horribly constricted, crocodilian voice: I'm fine, need a moment ... Mrs. Alexander finally excused herself from the library and, wheezing out of the room, sought help elsewhere. Outside, with the assistance of medicines provided by her Chinamanservants, she finally got in one great big gasp of air. They heard it in the library and looked at each other with relief. And then they heard a second deep breath. The coughing eventually subsided as well, but Mrs. Alexander didn't return to the library again.

Is everything all right? Molly asked.

RH looked at her without the faintest idea.

//

In the weeks after Father Erwagen arrived, Vancouver experienced an abundant thaw so that by Dominion Day, July 1, 1887, the annual eustasy that swelled the sea and soaked the land had filled the bogs and marshes and made the rivers run hard, everything that was once encased in ice spilling out everywhere in all directions. The parade down Hastings featured many local as well as imported traditions, all of them equally festive and exciting. Wild colours and feminine scent temporarily decorated the streets. Morning glory and daisies splashed their beauty over wreaths of magnificent size. Leafy vines wrapped and trussed up every light post and looped over the arch to Chinatown. Such aromatic decorations were not the work of lumberjacks or stevedores. A society group of wives from Vancouver and New Westminster, presided over by Mrs. Alexander, had been formed to encourage sobriety, diplomacy, virginity until marriage, and prayer, and they were awarded a float in the parade to help spread the message of abstinence and thanatos. Quilting, knitting, and home decor were three fundamentals the ladies preached. Called the Ladies Temperance League, their spring project was to beautify Vancouver's streets in time for the celebration. Everyone agreed they'd done an outstanding job. People waved at them and the ladies waved back.

The battery of Victoria po-lice on horseback was followed without much apparent irony by the Knights of

Labour marching band that played instrumental versions of sinophobic anthems like "John Brown's Body." Directly behind the Knights, the fire brigade wheeled their engine with Mayor McLean riding on top of it, circling his porkpie hat above his head, elated to see his people in such good spirits, not entirely ignorant of the fact that they were majority New Westminsterites. George Black had paid for a painter to do him up two classy Victorian sho' cards to hang on either side of a buggy advertising his butcher shop. He rode on the bench with his driver and waved to the people and tossed deer jerky to the children. Not to be outdone, the Oppenheimer brothers had hired an elephant that was led down the street wearing an Oppenheimer Dry Goods blanket draped across its back. The elephant later posed for daguerreotypes at the hollow tree. A horse was injured in the mud during a race on South Granville, and many men paid their respects when she was put down.

The mugger, good Christian women were pleased to know, had been hanged to the death on such and such a day, 1887. Such was life.

Ask me aboot the man game instead, said Clough when talk turned to the mugger.

I heard the mugger was just a *childs,* said one half of Berry & Vicars General Store.

I only know the same as you, eh, grumbled Clough, taking his business elsewhere.

//

The most notorious rematch in the early history of the sport began at sundown, Pisk versus Daggett. Night game. The ultimate battle, the men who started it all: the Dominion Day fight cinched a place in the annals of the game on that fact alone. The two crews met on the short grasses above the sandy embankment where the powdery beaches plunged into the moonlit tidepools of English Bay. The powdery sand was dashed with whitely dried logs that formed a broken line stretching all the way around the western curve of the government's land. In not long, they'd call it Stanley Park and dispossess its people. For now it was still a wild rainforest where skookum reigned, herons nested, deer and wild cattle grazed, where Clough and many others squatted for the time being, and where the Whoi-Whoi Indians had lived for millennia, and a day later were all dead.

July's temp was ideal for muscles. The crews appeared loose and limber and energetic. Furry & Daggett and their boys were on the beach, all of them standing cross-armed, from one side of the bed to the other, as it were: Campbell, Boyd, Smith, Meier, and out in front of them, coach Clough with his thumb stroking the cheroot burning between his teeth. Opposite them, Litz and Pisk and their men Hoss and Dee in unwashed plaids, dungarees, hobnail boots, scowls on their faces and curses on their tongues. Sure you don't need *some more* bohunks? said Dee, looking at his four against their six.

Molly was there with her own men, husband, ward, and father-in-law, all of them observing the show from a safe, excusable distance. If any unwanted passersby saw the Erwagens they might fairly assume they were happenstantial witnesses. The only unintentional guest in fact was Joe Fortes, who'd just finished his daily swim and was stomping out of the waves when he realized what was going on. Shimmering with a coat of saltwater, he said: I heard aboot no man game today.

Smith answered: *D. v. P.*

Rematch, cried Fortes, drying his neck with a towel. Man, I got to tell absol*ute*ly everbody aboot this.

Nuh-uh, said Smith, smacking Fortes's briny wet forearm and holding on—turning big Fortes right around with only this single quick move. This is a private competition, Smith said. You can stay and watch, but don't go complicating things.

No outsiders, no bets. Calabi and Yau were also present, having ducked out right after the parade and leaving their storefront closed up for the day to protect the secret from outsiders, Port Moodyites, New Westminsterites, Cowichans, Victorians. Calabi wasn't here as bookie, he and Yau were here to watch as bakers, honoured guests. While Calabi and Yau passed around pastries among the audience, Miguel Calderón and his portable Bar Rústico was also parked, along with his bellnecked goat, not far from the man game, providing libations (to Clough) as well as a cappella.

No grand ceremony accompanied the removal of the bandages on Pisk's feet. Nothing like the pomp set out for the arrival of a steam train or a new holiday. A moment of silence was all. Everyone stood around smoking and watched as Pisk sat on the ground and unwrapped the feet to reveal their toeless, purple mangled ends. Dark purple ropes stretched and wriggled over the feet and up his ankles, as if all the fattest veins were raised completely above the scarred flesh.

You can play on those blunts, eh? said Daggett, eyeing his opponent's impediment.

Good enough to stub out *you*, said Pisk.

Fine, said Daggett, ripping off his clothes. You're finally here Pisk, let this be the last time I see you. When I win here, you and Litz get oot a town for good. We don't see you around here again. Deal?

Without hesitation, Pisk said: Deal. So long as you're buck as me, the man game stays mine.

I'm getting buck as we speak, eh. What're you doing, spectating?

And if we win, you forfeit the Sunnyside, said Pisk, quickly undressing. Besides the fact we're moving back to town, that's always been our crew's bar, and we want it back.

True true, said Fortes.

Daggett tossed his evaginated socks on top of the pile of his clothes. Fine, he said, sneering. Shake on it.

I'll shake your hand when we start to play and no sooner.

Humph.

There was a calisthenic prelude. Even Pisk's stretches were intimidating. This was total flexibility on display. Daggett was doing one-handed jumping push-ups to prove he was just as ready. He did ten backflips and three splits. Then Pisk showed off his incredible muscle control. In a wavelike succession he flexed his calves on up to ears, not excluding the cremaster, dartos, rhomboids, mastoids, the entire lingual region. He quaked, rippled, and sprung to life in a finely tuned holistic gesture. Men on opposing teams assessed the information, and no one seemed sure what to think about these two giant men with unprecedented agility, intrepidness, and the kind of impoverished childhoods that make a man angry as fuck, ready to explode at the slightest provocation, and heavy with jealousy.

They shook hands, and backed off a few strides.

I'm here to prove something, said Daggett. You made a fool a me, now this is your turn.

After I beat you, every drop a booze I drink in this town'll be on your tab for the rest a my swallowing days—

Pisk came out animal style, with fingernails. He bared his teeth involuntarily and felt the saliva rush to the plate of his jaw and spool outward as he ran. It was only two, maybe three steps in all. Pisk kept his eyes down and would need to ask later if the roaring he heard was in his head or coming out his throat. His throat, he learned. He rounded Daggett's left and came behind on the right and saw the man try to compensate, twisting his lumbering torso trying to catch up with Pisk's great toeless sprint unhampered by the injuries—so it seemed—until Daggett swung out his elbow and Pisk cracked his jaw across it, a great rattan rope of spit jutting straight into the air as Pisk buckled to his knees. Immediately he stood back up, but then he realized there was no denying that Daggett had got him with a Bookend. Pisk lost the first point.

Keep wrecking his balance, eh, shouted Clough from the sidelines. Almost missed that point, and you should a had him *ea*sy.

Easy? said Pisk furiously. Makes no difference I got no toes.

Clough shook his fist at him. Then let's see you put some muscle behind that jaw a yours, or is all you got more spit?

The situation is the way I like it, said Pisk, admiring for a moment the ocean vista unobstructed by gamblers.

Daggett was unfazed through all the talk, keeping his eyes fixed to Pisk the whole time, but even with that degree of concentration, surely he allowed a little part of himself to relax after winning the first point.

Then to prove his mettle, Pisk began the first steps of a Litz, taking a comparatively slow swing so that Daggett would swoop under it and get in a few solid but unremarkable kicks in return, thinking he'd saved himself. In case it wasn't clear, Pisk did the same thing again: he took the first steps of a Litz, then let it drop. Daggett got frustrated and cursed Pisk's bloodline. Only now was Daggett concocting his retaliation, and was about to make the rookie predictable switch into a handstand, up and kicking with his feet, initiating a counter-move, but Pisk snuck up behind, jumped into the air, and choked Daggett in a classic Sausage Links {see *fig. 17.1*}. When Daggett fell to the ground, Pisk promptly went flying in with all his weight for a massive gutpunch that made another unusual sound, cracking like he'd really broken Daggett in half with his fist. It seemed he'd dented the ground beneath his opponent as well. His knucklemarks were there. Along with the cracking sound, when the fist rammed down into Daggett's stomach he burst out with the most foul tremulous screech, it came out of at least two of the man's orifices, like a deathrattle, and the force of the impact was so great that

---

FIGURE 17.1
Sausage Links, alternative sketch

among all the other hemorrhaging it even folded Daggett's eyelids up *{see fig. 17.2}*.

Oof, said all those present, averting their eyes only briefly, out of respect for gamesmanship. The only way to see if Daggett was okay meant looking again.

He was already on his feet. However brutal it looked, somehow it wasn't enough to keep the man down. He brushed his shoulders off and spat out half a lung and said: Pisk, you equals dead meat.

That jump-up sure bode trouble ahead for Pisk, said Joe Fortes.

Clough shook his head in admiration and said: If I ever stood up so fast from a slugger like that you know it's the devil.

Daggett made no comment on his recovery. He folded his eyelids back down and blinked thoroughly. After he was able to ungrit his teeth, he conceded the Point and Click, and the score was now tied one-one.

Let's fucking showtime, he demanded from Pisk.

From this moment on, Pisk decided he was after points. No more feints. No more exhibitions. He took no more chances. When the two men circled, waiting for opportunity, Daggett picked up a clod and hucked it to Pisk, who batted away a spray of dirt, anticipating the bully's plan by quickly sidestepping, then doubling Daggett over his fist when the man came in and took his best swing. Pisk played like that, with acrobatic precision, a slugger's focus, and brave enough to take a bullet. His actions were deadly fast. Pisk could deal Daggett a furious

FIGURE 17.2
The Point and Click, Calabi's early sketch

blow then catch him in his fall. Pisk won for knowing how to play without mercy, without murdering; for knowing how to give direction; for knowing how to make his opponent look like nothing more than a handkerchief in his fist; for knowing when to strangle when necessary and when to take a cut to land a decisive injury; for knowing when to slip away and when to come back hard. All Pisk's combined discipline, focus, and desire to win made Daggett look unprepared, or worse, unambitious. Pisk won five-two. By the end of seven points the men were both so haggard their flesh hung off them. Both knees on Daggett looked like freshly ground beef, oozing blood. Pisk had all sorts of abrasions on his back and chest, and many bruises. Their jaws gaped, mouth-breathers, exhausted.

Fortes cried: Sheer pandemonium.

Sammy threw his hat in the air and caught it again, put it back firmly on his head. No one has any patience anymore, *look*.

What Sammy said was true. Molly turned her attention away from her husband's warm neck and saw that no time was being lost before Litz stood forward, declared his intentions to emphasize Pisk's dominance, and paired up against Furry. The two men tore off, shook hands, and collided in a slow, dissident Greco-Roman. The pace was gruelling. Campbell could wait no longer: he took a few strides to the left of the game in progress and said he wasn't satisfied leaving in the shadow of Daggett's pure disgrace until he had his turn to gain back a little. Predictably, Hoss stepped forward to greet his rival. They started to undress. Campbell was kicking off his calicos and Hoss was shirtless when running down the sand embankment came a surprise in his Sunday best, and with a firm hand, he took Hoss by the shoulder and pulled him back a little and out of the fray; it was Sammy Erwagen.

Erwagen, said Campbell. 'The—, hey now, *you*?

That's right, me. Erwagen paid Campbell no more attention. He looked Hoss in the eye. Hoss was young and angry and never lost his appetite, and he was dented by a terrible childhood, but he understood this moment. He'd done the same thing himself. He understood not to argue, that they were now teammates. Hoss understood. To look Erwagen in the eye meant having to crane his neck way back, and, startled by the altitude, he could voice no argument contra the inventor's husband taking his place in line anyway. I'll take this round, Erwagen said, and proceeded towards Campbell. Hoss looked back to Molly for her reaction. He saw how she cheered her husband on, and felt heavier, more mule-like. Meanwhile Erwagen was working apart the shirt buttons and soon he was down to his creased slacks. For a young man, his frame was skeletal but it was not brittle. Smith's snowy complexion was at least pinked by his impeccable circulation. Erwagen's skin was pale like a bread mould. Some strength had returned though, that was most obvious in his toned shoulders and arms. But was he ready? No one, Campbell least of all, forgot to whom Erwagen was happily married. There was little time for Campbell to assess the risk. Sensing the opportunity for an easy win, Meier had already leaped forward to shake Hoss's hand and the two were to grunting, Moe Dee not far behind, taunting Boyd's lack of grooming. Soon enough everyone would be piled into the melee. It was already a riotous show before it infected Fortes at last, who threw off his towel and entered himself on behalf of Pisk and Litz to handle Smith. Every man was on his feet, matched up. Six weeks ago Sammy was an invalid. Today he was showing impressive bounce. What was his backstory, who was this Erwagen fellow? The bookkeeper was ready and so was the logger. They shook hands.

//

It was a simple motel bedframe without a headboard and no posts at the foot-end and with rivets and leaves, a pre-Ikea metal frame that required some assembly. With Minna's help I assembled this bed in my bedroom. I talked the whole time and I made her laugh. I had a joke for every screw and nut. We were friends. And it didn't take long to set up. Once the pieces fit, there was no keeping her. She had to go. She was *so* tired. It had been a long afternoon. We'd discovered a secret history. The bedframe was on castors. The last thing we did was roll the bed into a corner. I threw the boxspring on top, fitted the sheets on, puffed the pillows, and called it a day. At the apartment door, we embraced. It was a platonic embrace, full of love and friendship. I said goodbye and she said goodbye. I went and stood by the window and watched Minna unlock her ten speed, throw a leg over to the other pedal, and push away. She waved up to me goodbye. She knew I'd be there to watch her go. And I, from the window, waved back goodbye. Goodbye, Minna. Goodbye. I turned, and with that small-time sentimental goodbye still in my head, stared at my apartment and all its many shades of brown. Hardwood floors with dust. Beige curtains. Pine shelves. I wanted to listen to music but my roommate was watching a depressing movie, so I went to my room and sat on my new bed on top of the brown duvet. I lay down on the mattress for the first time, feeling its spring. I stared at the chalky stipple on the ceiling above me, stared with ambient fascination at the minor white topologies, thinking about the man game. Bedroom. Boredom. I was compelled to stand up. So I went and put on my shoes and locked the apartment door behind me, back downstairs and got into my Chrysler Dynasty and took off down the street. At first I wasn't sure if I was driving after Minna or somewhere else. Could I catch up to her, surprise her by following along beside her bicycle with my Dynasty, and with my spontaneity intact, amuse her some more, amuse her back into bed, amuse her into marrying me? As I drove I remembered Minna. I thought about her the whole drive that evening. What I really wanted was to drive and park my car in front of a completely different home, go and sit down in a whole new living room and ask what's for dinner. I drove for half an hour or more feeling delirious or bipolar as I made my way through Vancouver. I fought with the lights. It seemed I hit every red. The traffic was sludgy slow. By now the sun was gone and this being January, the air rapidly cooled down. The sky was a smoky purple. On my drive I passed through prickling rain in one mossy neighbourhood where an accident caused delays, and street repaving in another neighbourhood shrank traffic going both ways to one lane switching back and forth with the help of a po-liceman. Undeterred, I kept driving. I sought out the wild destructive core of things but at the very same time I was attracted to the rules. I wanted a set of principles like the stars that I could look up to and see, fear, and interpret. Stars were scarce in my world. I lived in a city surrounded by purple clouds. After I parked the Dynasty, instead of going all the way around to the backyard like we did this afternoon I just went up to the front door and knocked loudly. I was overwhelmed by a weird funny terror. I considered bolting. I rattled my carkeys in my pocket. Ken opened the door and while I tried to explain the reason I'd come back, he let me in without saying a word, and I said hello to Silas and Cedric who also came to meet me in the entrance, we all shook hands, and I followed them down the incline to the living room where they introduced me to her.